BEYOND THE PALE

A RAVENWOOD MYSTERY

SABRINA FLYNN

WWW.SABRINAFLYNN.COM

SABRINA FLYNN

BEYOND THE PALE

A RAVENWOOD MYSTERY

Published by Ink & Sea Publishing
www.sabrinaflynn.com

Book 8 of Ravenwood Mysteries.

ISBN 978-1-955207-01-0
eBook ISBN 978-1-955207-00-3

Book cover by MerryBookRound
www.MerryBookRound.com

ALSO BY SABRINA FLYNN

Ravenwood Mysteries

From the Ashes

A Bitter Draught

Record of Blood

Conspiracy of Silence

The Devil's Teeth

Uncharted Waters

Where Cowards Tread

Beyond the Pale

Legends of Fyrsta

Untold Tales

A Thread in the Tangle

King's Folly

The Broken God

Bedlam

Windwalker

www.sabrinaflynn.com

to the fallen

My every impulse bends to what is right - Homer

CRIME SCENE

"SUICIDE. *REALLY?*" LIAM TAFT STARED ACROSS A CORPSE AT A patrolman.

Officer Finley turned red and shrugged.

There was a perfect little hole between the dead man's eyes. No burn residue. Liam shifted the corpse's head to look for an exit wound. Blood matted the hair at the base of the skull.

"Was a gun found nearby?" Liam asked.

"No. This fellow was picked clean. He wasn't in nothin' but his long johns," Finley said.

"A robbery maybe?" Sam Batten asked. Where Liam Taft was middle-aged and tall with a physique his wife referred to as 'squeezable,' his partner Sam was half his age and size, and threw a mean left hook.

"That's what I said," Finley stood straighter, "but the coroner said otherwise."

Life was cheap in San Francisco. Even cheaper in Mission Bay, where the dead man had been discovered. "Though the body pickers down that way aren't so much the murdering kind. More like opportunists."

Liam squinted at the dead man's bruised and roughened knuckles. Surely he'd been a prize-fighter in life.

"I seen this fellow before, coming out of a boxing club around the warehouses. I went over there to ask after him. Close-lipped bunch. But I got it out of an old man that our corpse here had a fierce row with some other fellow a few weeks back. I asked to see his locker and I found this, so I told your lot."

Officer Finley held up a six-pointed bronze star with black lettering: *Pinkerton's U.S. Detective Agency*.

Liam took the bronze star and curled his fingers around it until the points dug into his skin. "I want to see where this dead fellow was found."

———

"FOUND HIM RIGHT HERE UNDER SOME GARBAGE," FINLEY SAID.

Liam frowned at the refuse-strewn alleyway. Not a pleasant place to meet your end. Sam signaled his agreement by turning his head to spit between his teeth. This was the type of neighborhood where that was acceptable.

Officer Finley glanced over his shoulder towards the gray light. Finley, a short, broad-shouldered man with a mushroomed ear, kept fondling his billy club like he enjoyed using it. And yet he seemed uneasy on his own beat.

"No wallet, no cash or coin, and stripped down to his long johns like every other unlucky soul I find around here."

"Happen much?" Liam asked.

Finley chuckled. "Every week."

"With a bullet between the eyes?" Liam asked.

Finley shrugged. "Not so much. Mostly beaten rotten. Some are drunk, though. Found a fellow face down in the creek last month with a knife in his back."

"All picked clean?"

Finley nodded. "Thieves are quick here."

Liam studied the star in his palm, tilting it this way and that in the silvery mist. "How do you know thieves aren't killing these folks?"

Finley tapped his head with his billy club. "I got the detective instincts. So do you know that dead fellow, then? He one of yours?"

There was hope in the patrolman's voice. If Liam claimed the man as one of his own, then it'd fall on the Pinkertons to investigate. That meant less work for the patrolman.

"We'll look into it," Liam said.

Finley gave his billy club a whirl, clearly pleased that he could wash his hands of the case. "Sorry about your operative. You need anything else?"

"Let us know if any of his gear turns up."

Finley snorted. "Probably scattered to every fence in the city by now."

"All the same."

Finley touched billy club to hat. "You watch yourselves 'round here."

"One more thing, Officer," Liam said. "Did you drag the body out? Or wait for the dead wagon?"

"I didn't touch him. Went straight away to the call box. It's a good walk, it is."

Liam shared a look with his partner, then thanked Finley for his help. After the officer left, Sam Batten spat again. "Lazy bastard."

Liam smoothed his drooping mustache in thought. "You reckon he got assigned to Mission Bay for his work ethic?"

Sam only shook his head in disgust as he studied the drag marks in the dirt. "Looks like he was shot, then dragged into the alleyway to be divested of his earthly belongings."

"Appears so," Liam said.

The two spread out to search the area, but thieves, police, and body haulers had trampled it.

"Not much here," Sam noted.

Liam followed the drag marks to the end of the alleyway where he spotted a dubious stain on the boardwalk. He crouched to rub a finger through the grime. Dried blood.

"Here we are," Sam said, drawing his Bowie. He used the tip to pry a bit of lead free from a wooden plank. "I wager it's a forty four."

Liam took the mushed bullet and eyed it, then tucked it away in a pocket. He turned to the street. It was more of a dust bowl lined with boardwalks than a street, and one that would fast become a mud pit in the rain.

"He *was* a big fellow, wasn't he?" Liam said aloud. Used to his partner's rhetorical questions, Sam didn't reply. "Scarred knuckles, built like a bull… I'd like to meet the man to get in a fight with a fellow that size."

Sam shrugged. "Size doesn't matter."

It was true, Liam knew. His partner Sam Batten was a boxer himself, the rangy kind. Having a boxer as a partner suited Liam; he needed young blood at his side. Liam had spent his own youth chasing hell, and now he was well past middle age and hell had caught up to him. He preferred desk work to fieldwork these days.

"You think this has to do with that other matter?" Sam asked.

The 'other matter' was a thorn in Liam Taft's side. "We'll find out soon enough."

The pair headed for a battered iron sign, hanging but too heavy to swing in the breeze: *The Den*.

Liam paused at the entrance. The Den was as dingy as one would expect in Mission Bay. The boxing rings were cobbled together from mooring lines and dirty mats—or in some cases smooth planks sprinkled with sawdust to soak up blood. Heavy bags, split and worn, dangled from rafters.

Two men sparred in the center ring, as an old man swept the floor, an endless task. The gym smelled of male sweat and rawness. Blood, too. Liam's wife would say it needed a woman's touch. Most places he visited needed a heap more women.

"You lookin' to get rid of that paunch, old man?" a wiry man called from where he was pummeling a bag. He had a straight nose, and the muscled physique of youth.

Just you wait, Liam thought. Time has a sense of humor.

Liam touched the brim of his Stetson. "I'm afraid you'd have your work cut out for you," he said, giving the fellow a smile.

"You're in the wrong place, mister."

"Usually am," Liam said. "Are you the owner of this gym?"

The young man slammed his taped fist into a punching bag, then stopped to regard him, the bag swinging lazily. "I like the sound of that. But, nah, I'm not fool enough to claim that." He nodded over to a corner where a bull of a man sat talking with two others. They all looked keen to pummel flesh.

Liam walked over to the men. "Gentlemen," he greeted.

They didn't return the greeting. No surprise. He was trespassing on their turf. "A member of your gym was killed down the street."

"You a lawman?" asked a man with blood on his shirt.

Liam lifted his coat, revealing a bronze shield with an "all-seeing eye" and the Pinkertons motto "We Never Sleep" below it. "Liam Taft. Pinkerton detective. This is my partner, Sam Batten."

Sam raised two fingers in greeting.

"Do you know the man who was killed? Big fellow. Scarred knuckles, mustache, crooked nose."

The others looked to a balding fellow with the jaw of an

ironclad. "Sure. That was Monty," he rumbled. "Montgomery Johnson. Look, we already answered Finley's questions. We don't know nothin'."

Liam took silent note of Ironclad's use of the officer's name. "Did Monty have enemies?" he asked.

The trio laughed.

"Monty is a salty sort," a blond fellow said.

"*Was*," Liam corrected.

The men sobered.

"You don't seem surprised."

They stared. Deadpan. "Rough streets," Bloody Shirt said.

"The body was moved, then plundered," Liam said.

"Rough streets," Ironclad repeated.

"How'd he die?" Blondie asked.

"A single bullet between the eyes." Liam hooked a thumb in his belt, and the trio's eyes were drawn to a row of ammunition. "About those enemies?"

"Easier to name his friends," Ironclad said.

"That would be helpful."

"Do we look like the helpful sort?" Bloody Shirt asked.

"No, but as of now, you're my only suspects."

This got their attention. Blondie and Bloody Shirt stood up to glare. Sam glared back.

"Thieves, addicts, and drunkards live around here like rats," Ironclad said. "It's why I started a gym. To give them something else."

"That's noble of you. Was Monty one of those fellows?"

"No, but he liked to gamble."

"He owe any of you money?"

Ironclad worked his jaw, but restrained himself. "Yeah, he did. But Monty owed money to rougher men than me. Gambling debts, for one. And sure, he was behind on his membership dues. But half this lot is. Why would I kill him? A dead man can't pay me back."

Blondie looked to his friends. "Who was that fellow he was always going on about? The one he beat to a pulp and rolled out the door?"

"Monty had a beef with just about everyone, including you," Ironclad said.

"Salty bastard he was," Blondie said fondly. "But no, I'm talking about that pompous ass fellow. Remember him? The one with the fancy walking stick? The one that came in and took a cheap shot with that stick of his."

"Andy Ryan, or something close," Bloody Shirt ventured.

A fellow at a nearby bag yelled out an answer. "Atticus Riot."

Blondie snapped his fingers. "That's the name. The two of them got into a rumble. Monty cleaned the arrogance right off his noble brow."

"And that fellow had a revolver too," Ironclad said. "Word is he's a gunfighter."

Liam rocked onto his toes and came down. "Now that's a place to start. Did any of you hear a gunshot a few days ago?"

Blondie chuckled. "Daily. I don't pay much mind to them in this part of town."

Or any part, Liam thought. He had to agree. Gunfire was commonplace in San Francisco. "Does this Monty have kin?"

The men gave an appearance of thought.

"Friends?" Liam asked.

"I seen him at Dusty's Place. A saloon down the way."

Liam handed over his card. "If you remember anything, I'd be obliged. Do you mind if I chat with some of your regulars?"

Ironclad shrugged. "I got nothing to hide."

Liam touched his brim and went to speak to the old man with the broom. Now that fellow was full of insightful information. And all roads led to Atticus Riot.

2

NO REST FOR THE WEARY

Wednesday, November 14, 1900

"ARE YOU POSITIVE SHE CAN HANDLE THIS ALONE?"

Isobel Amsel Riot glanced up from her book to the man across the cabin saloon. Atticus Riot, her husband of nearly two months. He had his face pressed to a porthole.

"Nervous, Riot?"

"You're the one holding your book upside down."

A hoarse voice shouted orders over the wind, then footsteps scrambled across the overhead deck. The cutter heeled and Isobel braced herself against a table that was bolted to the cabin deck while Riot steadied himself against the bulkhead. He was an odd shade of green.

"I'm merely conducting an experiment," she quipped.

"Which of us will crack first?"

Isobel sniffed. "No. Whether inverted reading will eventually become natural."

"You mean to say you're distracting yourself."

She gave him a sharp look, and his eyes danced in reply.

"Leonardo da Vinci wrote thousands of pages in mirrored script. With his left hand."

The cutter slammed back down into the ocean. With their bobbing world set aright, Riot stretched on the settee and placed a cushion under his head. "We could very well be inverted before the day is over."

"Jin will manage," she stated.

"I'm sure she will."

"Lotario has reinforced the *Pagan Lady*. If she does hit something..."

"Like the dock?"

"...then I'm sure the dock will be the one to suffer." At least she hoped.

"Just remember, I can't swim."

"I can't save Tobias, Jin, *and you*. You really must practice more."

Riot tapped his head. "Still recovering. Besides, the children are wearing cork vests. I'm in your hands."

Isobel snorted at his excuse, but it was half-hearted. Only weeks before he'd suffered a severe beating that edged him towards a grave. But the two weeks they'd spent strolling under redwoods and beside idle streams, then lounging on a sandy beach by the wild Pacific, had done wonders for his recovery.

The trip hadn't been devoid of excitement, but she expected no less from a man named Atticus Riot. And luckily children were resilient.

To her surprise, Isobel found she wasn't keen on returning to the city. It turned out she enjoyed indolence in the right company.

She studied him now. His beard needed a trim, his hair had curled, and the sun had bronzed his skin. In shirtsleeves and vest, with an open collar, he looked like some rakish Spaniard.

"I hadn't realized how dark you are," she noted.

Riot cracked open an eye. He had one bare foot braced against the table, making a lie of his calm façade, as the boat surged over a choppy San Francisco Bay. "I tan well."

So did she—the Azores blood ran thick in her veins—but not *that* well. Not for the first time, she mused over her husband's parentage. His mother was a crib whore, which led to an entire spectrum of possibilities.

Definitely some sort of Mediterranean descent, she decided.

"I try to stay out of the sun for that reason," he added, reading her line of thought.

"Ah." Any whisper of other than 'white' would close several doors for him. "A pity. The sun suits you."

Shouts sounded on the overhead deck, followed by a girlish scream, pounding feet, and a sudden turn of the cutter. Isobel glimpsed an alarming amount of wooden dock in her porthole. She braced herself for impact.

But the Pagan Lady only drifted sideways in the water to bump the dock before settling. Triumphant cries sounded on deck, followed by orders from a pint-sized acting captain. "And snap to it!" Sao Jin shouted.

Isobel took a deep, calming breath, and deliberately placed her book in its nook.

"Are we dead yet?" Riot murmured. He had his eyes closed.

"The day *is* young."

———

ISOBEL AND RIOT EMERGED ON DECK TO FIND THE CREW standing at attention. "Captain on deck," Jin announced.

The three children saluted. Jin stood proudly in the cockpit, Sarah beamed from the dock where she'd been securing the mooring lines, and Tobias vibrated with excitement, hopping on the cabin top.

"We did it!" the boy squealed.

"I can see that." Isobel looked down at Jin, returning the salute. "Excellent work, first mate."

"She is all yours, Captain Morgan."

Isobel surveyed the Lady. The sails were furled and the mooring lines were in place along with the cork bumpers to pad the cutter against the dock. All was in order.

"And I was so looking forward to rescuing you again," she whispered in Riot's ear.

He raised a suggestive brow at her. But then something shifted in his gaze, sending a frisson of alarm down her spine. One moment he was relaxed, and in the next blink he was lunging towards Sarah on the dock.

Riot grabbed Sarah's arm and yanked her into the cockpit as he drew his revolver left-handed.

Movement on another boat. A man with a rifle.

"Down!" Riot barked.

A policeman, Isobel realized as she pulled Tobias from the cabin top. He fell atop the girls, and the cockpit became a tangle of children and oaths.

"Atticus Riot! We have a warrant for your arrest! Drop your weapons, raise your hands, and step onto the dock."

Sarah froze, the blood draining from her face. Tobias made a gurgling sound, and Jin, who'd fought her way free, looked set to bolt.

"The three of you get down below," Riot said. The calm in his voice was so chilling that the children slithered down the hatch without argument.

As Isobel crouched next to Riot in the cockpit, she took stock of their situation. It wasn't just one lone officer waiting in ambush. A second officer with a rifle was positioned on a nearby vessel. And a group of men were walking down the dock towards their slip—a number of policemen in their company. She recognized a man in a bowler and dark suit as well as one of the uniformed officers: Inspector Geary and Sergeant O'Hare.

An inspector should've put her at ease. It didn't.

She'd encountered the inspector during a prior case that involved a message written in sand. Geary and Riot had a history. And she knew it wasn't good.

"Tell your men to stand down," Riot yelled back. "There are women and children aboard."

"If you behave civilly, so will we," Inspector Geary returned. His group had fanned out, positioning themselves behind various boats and crates for cover.

"What's going on?" Tobias's face appeared in the hatch, his eyes huge in the dark.

"Get back *down*," Isobel hissed, glancing at the mooring lines. Should they attempt to run? If Riot provided cover, she might be able to cut loose the lines and—

Before she could finish the thought, Riot holstered his revolver, and raised his hands.

"*Riot*."

He gave a shake of his head. They were cornered. There was no running. Before she could stop him, he hopped onto the dock, with his hands spread at his hips.

"Shall I dance now?" Riot asked.

"You're not amusing," Geary sneered. "Walk towards us nice and slow."

"Tell your men to take their rifles off my family and aim them at me. Unless you brought an army for two little girls?"

Geary gave a sharp gesture to the officers positioned on nearby boats. All rifles swung towards Riot.

"What's going on?" Sarah whispered from the hatch.

"Stay here," Isobel hissed. "If anything happens, untie the lines and let the Lady drift out to sea."

Before her daughters could argue, she climbed onto the dock to join her partner, who had stopped a good twenty feet from the men.

"…we aren't obligated to tell you." The snippet of conversation came from a man resembling a gargoyle. Everything about him sloped forward. Thick brows, heavy jowls, and a neck that rested on an expansive chest. Inspector Geary. He was looking smug after delivering that last statement.

Towering over the group was his giant uniformed shadow, Officer O'Hare. A strapping Irishman who was everything opposite of Geary. And then two men Isobel couldn't place. A bowlegged man with hooded eyes, a face etched with lines, and a drooping gray mustache; he looked like he'd come straight from a ranch. The lines beside his eyes crinkled as he touched the brim of his hat in greeting. The second stranger was a rough, wiry sort with longish brown hair, whiskers, and a bored look in his eyes.

"True, but it would be the polite thing to do after you trained rifles on my children." Riot's tone was conversational, despite being the target of several rifles. Geary certainly wasn't taking any chances.

"Show me the warrant," Isobel demanded.

"Well, if it isn't *Mrs*. Riot," Geary said. "Still wearing trousers, I see. That's grounds for arrest on indecency."

Isobel showed her teeth. "I'm within twenty feet of my boat, which is private property."

"You're here for me; leave my family out of this," Riot cut in.

Despite Isobel's orders, Sarah bolted onto the dock. Before she could stop the girl, Sarah threw herself between her father and the guns.

No, no, no…

The men froze. Even O'Hare.

Isobel thought her knees would give out.

"I won't let you kill my father!" Sarah shouted at the officers.

A tense moment—Riot afraid to make a move lest the men think he was reaching for a weapon, and the men afraid of shooting a child.

"Sarah, get behind me," Riot ordered. But Sarah wasn't having any of it.

The graying man cleared his throat. "That's noble of you, Miss. But we're not here to shoot your father." He gestured for the men to lower their guns, and after a stubborn moment the officers did so.

Riot slowly put his hands on Sarah's shoulders and forced her back. Isobel took a ragged breath and grabbed Sarah's arm, so she wouldn't run into the line of fire again.

"Put your hands on your head and turn around," Geary ordered.

Hatless, without a coat, Riot placed his hands on his head, and turned to face her. He looked so tired. Resigned, even. There was an apology in his eyes.

Both criminals and lawmen hunted him. Why couldn't the powers that be leave them in peace?

O'Hare stepped forward and wrenched Riot's arms behind his back to clamp handcuffs over his wrists. Each click of the cuffs made Sarah flinch like she'd been slapped.

"At least tell us what he's being charged with," Isobel pleaded.

"Are you acquainted with a Montgomery Johnson?" the graying man asked.

Riot twisted to look back at the man. "He was one of my agents."

"The word being '*was*'. Right up until you put a bullet between his eyes," Geary said with pleasure.

MURDER.

Isobel stood stunned while they loaded Riot into a patrol wagon. When the door clanged shut, Sarah tore out of Isobel's grip to pound on the wagon. It took two officers to peel Sarah away, and she kicked them both for their efforts.

As the wagon disappeared, Isobel climbed aboard the Lady, cursing up a storm. Tobias's jaw was unhinged, Sarah stomped aboard crying, and Jin clambered over from another vessel where a policeman had been stationed with a rifle. She had a knife in hand.

That gave Isobel pause. "Jin, were you planning on stabbing an officer?"

"Only if he started shooting."

Isobel considered her pint-sized daughter for a moment. Some sort of lecture was surely required, but she was at a loss. At least the girl had waited.

"Shooting someone sure sounds like the sort of thing Mr. A.J. would do," Tobias noted.

"You take that back, Tobias!" Sarah shouted.

"Well, it does…"

Isobel didn't wait to see if the pair came to blows. There was no time to comfort them. She disappeared below deck to don her 'proper clothing': a sensible blouse, tie, split riding skirt and matching coat.

Tobias was right. Montgomery Johnson, former detective for Ravenwood Agency, had betrayed Riot by hiring assassins to kill him. But the assassins had failed in their blundering attempt, and killed Mack McCormick.

When Riot went after Monty, he'd beaten Riot within an inch of his life and left him for dead. She'd certainly wanted to kill Monty herself, and news of his death caused her no grief. Quite the opposite.

"Did *Din Gau* shoot that man?"

Isobel looked up in surprise. Jin sat on the ladder, her question echoing Isobel's own thoughts. Din Gau. Rabid Dog. It was the hatchet men's nickname for Riot. A name born of fear and respect, and a good dose of hatred.

"Of course not. When did he have the chance?" Isobel hesitated over her own question. They *had* left Riot at the campsite for an entire day to go explore. And Jin knew it, too.

Sarah plopped down on a ladder rung. "They're going to hang him, aren't they?"

Before the waterworks could start again, Jin elbowed her sister in the shin. "Do not be so dramatic."

"They took him away in irons!" Sarah shouted.

"I didn't say anything!" Tobias yelled from the cabin top.

"Get down here, Tobias," Isobel ordered.

"You decent?"

"Yes."

The girls moved into the cabin to make way for Tobias, and Isobel placed a reassuring hand on Sarah's shoulder. She tried to look them all in the eye at once. Then told the harsh truth. "I don't know what's going to happen, but what I do know is that Inspector Geary and his partner dislike Riot a great deal. I need you three to help me. Can you do that?"

Three heads nodded as one.

"Good." She turned to a small captain's desk and started writing. "I need you to send a telegram to our attorney, Mr. Farnon. Then go straight home and tell Mr. Tim what happened. Clear?"

"Yes," they said as one.

Isobel handed Jin the note. "Then I need you three to gather all the newspapers that were published when we were at Willow Camp. I want to know what the press made of Monty's death."

"What will you do?" Jin asked.

"I'm going to find the only allies we have—Inspector Coleman and Sergeant Price." Before Geary and O'Hare could interrogate her husband in one of the City's famed 'sweatboxes.' But she left that part out. Honesty was well and good, but there were some things children did not need to know.

3

SCHEMES

"I NEED TO SPEAK WITH INSPECTOR COLEMAN," ISOBEL SAID TO the desk sergeant at the Hall of Justice.

The man glanced up at her, decided she wasn't a threat, and went back to filling out paperwork.

"It's important."

"Do you have an appointment, Miss?"

"I do not, but I have urgent information regarding a case," she lied.

"The inspector isn't in. But I can take down your information and pass him a message."

"When will he return?"

"The inspector doesn't leave his schedule with me."

"Is Sgt. Price in?"

"No."

Isobel shoved the door open as she left. Fresh air helped. She took deep, calming breaths of it. Her imagination was conjuring all sorts of horrors about Geary's interrogation methods.

The memory of Riot dumped in a gutter and covered in blood was all too stark in her mind. She swallowed down despair and focused on their current crisis. One problem at a time. Isobel spotted a small newsboy leaning against a column. He was as dirty as a dumpster and digging around in his nose.

"Well, if it isn't Bill Cody," she said.

"Heya, Miss Bonnie." He took his finger from his nose long enough to remove his cap, then slapped it back down with a puff of dirt. He'd gotten his name because he tended to charge the other cappers and snitches like a wild buffalo. "I'm your man if you need somethin'."

"Do you happen to know the present location of Inspector Coleman or Sgt. Price?"

Cody shrugged. "Bunch of bulls went to the Nymphia. I wager the Inspector's there. The Nymphia is old news, though. I'm here for the good stuff."

"You're a wise fellow." Knowing it would feed him for a week, she flipped him a silver dollar, and left.

"THEY'RE GONNA BEAT UP MR. A.J. AGAIN," TOBIAS SAID.

"They're police," Sarah said. "They wouldn't do that."

Tobias and Jin shared a look.

"Would they?" Sarah asked.

The three were hurrying from the docks to the closest Western Union office to do just as Isobel had instructed, like the good, helpful children they were.

Outside the telegraph office, Jin handed Sarah the note. "They will not kick *you* out."

Sarah quickly dispatched a telegram to Mr. Farnon. With all the trouble Atticus and Isobel got themselves into, their attorney was kept busy.

"How come we need to go home?" Tobias asked when she returned. He had his face pressed to the window. "Why don't we just *telephone* Mr. Tim?"

Sarah followed the boy's pointing finger to the telephone on an inside wall.

"That *is* a good point." Jin said.

"But Isobel told us to go home…"

"No, Miss Isobel told us to tell Mr. Tim. He might not be at home, he could be at Ravenwood Agency."

Jin nodded in agreement. "And then we must gather newspapers."

"At *home*," Sarah stressed.

Tobias shrugged. "We could just find them on the way."

"The way to where?" Sarah asked.

Jin and Tobias shared another look. "To the police station," they replied as one.

"Oh no," Sarah said.

"The police will not beat Atticus if we are there," Jin said.

Tobias gave a sage nod. "And you already disobeyed your parents when you got it in your mind to play a target. If you're gonna get a whoopin' might as well go all out first."

Sarah pressed palms to her swollen eyes. Could this day get any worse?

4

A WARM WELCOME

THE CAGE DOOR OPENED, AND O'HARE STOOD GRINNING IN the gray light. "You want to put up a struggle? 'Cause I can accommodate you."

"That's real thoughtful of you, O'Hare."

O'Hare slapped his billy club against the wagon to get Riot moving. The wagon wasn't tall enough to stand, so Riot stayed hunched over and shuffled forward with his arms locked behind his back.

He hopped down onto the street and was prodded with the billy club towards the 17th Street police station. It wasn't known for its hospitality.

Inspector Geary didn't so much as glance at Riot as he pushed open the door. But two men not in uniform watched him, standing apart from the police. The two from the dock. Riot had noted the tall graying man's bow-legged stride. It hinted at years spent in a saddle. The shorter, younger man was squinting from beneath his bowler and standing protectively beside his partner. Yes, Riot thought, definitely partners. U.S. Marshals or Pinkertons? He wasn't sure.

O'Hare paraded Riot past the lobby gate, down a hallway

lined with cells, and into a brick room with no windows. An electric light dangled brightly from the ceiling over a drain set into the center of the floor.

O'Hare pushed Riot to his knees, so another officer could hook his cuffs to a short chain attached to a rung on the stone floor.

"The city still hasn't given you the funds to remodel?" Riot asked, trying and failing to find a comfortable position. There wasn't one. But that was the point of this entire room.

"Always the funny one. We'll see how long that lasts." O'Hare bent down to rip off Riot's spectacles.

The door slammed, leaving Riot to contemplate the fate of his spectacles. He really should've left them on the boat.

5

THE NYMPHIA

A HORDE OF RELIGIOUS PICKETERS LAID SIEGE TO A THREE-story brick building on Pacific Street. Reporters mixed with preachers, and a line of police in front of the hotel's ornate gates kept the mob at bay.

Pacific Street was in chaos.

Newly opened the previous year, the Hotel Nymphia had been a simmering scandal in San Francisco from the moment of its conception. Isobel hadn't gotten around to seeing it. What with investigating her family's misfortune, being black-mailed into marrying a brute, her subsequent 'death' and miraculous rebirth, her divorce, remarriage, and adopting two daughters, there just hadn't been time.

Since she held no illusions of policemen ushering her through the gates, she turned the corner onto Stockton, and strolled past what looked like an abandoned building until she came to an alleyway.

She peeked around the corner.

Policemen stood at the back entrances and fire escapes. Steeling herself, Isobel marched up to the nearest officer. Or at least that was her intent. As soon as an officer spotted her, he rushed forward and made a grab for her arm.

She skipped out of his grasp, and he raised his billy club. "Trying to sneak around, eh?"

"Yes, actually."

"You won't run this time."

"You'll have to come get me, then."

The officer was handsome, youthful, and completely dim-witted. He rushed her, confident in his size. She stepped into his reaching hands, grabbed his wrist, and twisted with his body. The officer screamed as he dropped to his knees. She let go before the maneuver snapped his wrist and hurried to the door. He lunged to his feet.

The door was unlocked, so she slipped inside and turned the latch, as the officer thudded against the outside. Now to find Inspector Coleman.

The empty hallways were dingy and run-down, cheap carpet already showing its age in worn tracks. It smelled of mildew and cigarette smoke.

Lotario, her twin, had the highest standards for brothels. He would be appalled. He only worked out of the *Narcissus*, which equaled the Palace Hotel in extravagance.

Isobel followed her ears towards a commotion. She walked through a dirty kitchen, and pushed open a swinging door. About one hundred women, all naked save for garters, were corralled in a restaurant. They were shouting insults at the harried police officers, who were trying to quell the growing unrest.

An officer guarding the swinging door seized her arm. "Oi! Where'd you come from?"

"I need to speak with Detective Inspector Coleman."

The officer looked her up and down in confusion. She was dressed; the other ladies were not. "Why don't you just wait over there with the rest of the scarlet ladies."

"Splendid idea."

He shoved her into the crowd of disgruntled women. Isobel gave up trying to avoid brushing bare breasts, buttocks and thighs, and bullied her way to the front of the crowd. As the only clothed woman in the room, she attracted attention, puzzled glances and glares in equal measure.

"What's happening?" she asked a black-haired woman, who looked set to commit arson with her cigarette.

"Another raid. Usually they cart us away. But we've been stuck here for over an hour. Won't even let us get our clothes."

"You didn't even have time to grab a chemise?"

The woman eyed her up and down. "You haven't been here before, have you?"

"Charlotte Bonnie. Reporter. I snuck in the back."

"And I'm Anne Glory," she said dryly. "Women aren't allowed clothing in the Nymphia. We're required to be naked at all times."

It sounded like a crude joke, but it wasn't. Anne was serious, and the implications made Isobel's stomach churn. "Was everyone caught?" she asked.

Anne shook her head. "There's anywhere from a hundred to three hundred working girls at any given time."

Isobel tried to imagine that overflow of naked women streaming into the streets. Maybe they'd grabbed sheets first? "Do you have any idea why they're keeping you?"

"No. But the bulls are holding some johns across the way. They usually let the men off with a little slap to their dainty wrists."

Usually. But not today. Her mind leapt to the obvious conclusion.

Isobel slipped past the rest of the angry women until she found herself at the front of the group. Someone shoved her into the arms of a strapping officer with a billy club. "I have information about the murder," she said, quickly. "But I'll only talk to Inspector Coleman or Sgt. Price."

He frowned down at her. Then, like she'd given him a magic password, he shoved her into another officer's hands. "Claims she has information."

"Tell Inspector Coleman my name is Riot."

"Keep an eye on her," the first officer ordered his brother-in-arms, before he trotted up a stairway. She fluttered her lashes at the officer, then stood on her tiptoes to look into the room on the other side of the hotel lobby. Angry male voices rumbled from that direction. The men weren't behaving any better. She suspected they'd been helping themselves to the contents of the saloon.

Soon enough a familiar figure came pounding down the steps. He looked grave and disapproving, but then the bullish Sgt. Price generally looked like that. Although today his handlebar mustache was twitching.

He drew her off to the side. "What the blazes are you doing here, Mrs. Riot?"

"I need to speak to the Inspector."

"How'd you know about the murder?"

"Why else would you need a Detective Inspector to round up whores and johns, then detain them for so long?"

"Yes, but what the devil brought you *here*? This is no place for a proper lady."

"I usually turn up at improper places, Sgt. Price."

He couldn't argue with that. "What's happened now?"

"Riot's been charged with a murder he didn't commit. Inspector Geary and his goon O'Hare arrested him. They had a warrant."

The sergeant grunted. "Geary hates A.J.'s guts."

"Yes, I know, Riot being a 'pompous ass' and all. But given his recent brush with death, I don't think he'll survive whatever interrogation they have planned."

Sgt. Price muttered an oath. "O'Hare doesn't go easy on prisoners."

She must have swayed, because Price grabbed her arm. "I'll figure something out." Sgt. Price beckoned a pale man over. He wore a bowler and suit rather than a uniform, and his red hair curled from under his hat. "Doyle. Get down to the Mission station. Find Inspector Geary and tell him that Detective Inspector Coleman has you on guard duty for Atticus Riot."

"What's he in for now?" Doyle asked.

"Murder. Don't let Geary bully you. I don't want to find a blasted bruise on A.J. Clear?"

Doyle nodded, and left.

"Can you trust him?" Isobel asked.

"Doyle knows A.J."

Isobel felt like she could breathe for the first time in an hour. "Thank you, Sergeant," she said with feeling.

"You sure A.J. didn't do it?"

"Yes." At least the possibility was slim. "Now if you'll excuse me…"

Price tightened his grip, keeping her in place. "You need to stay clear of whatever mess he's fallen into."

"Riot's been accused of murder," she hissed. "I can't just stand idly by."

"If you go down to the station and make a fuss, Geary will toss you in jail, too. That won't do A.J. a jot of good."

She ground her teeth together. A dozen arguments and insults battled on the tip of her tongue, but he was right. Damn him.

"Look here, Mrs. Riot. The Inspector wanted me to escort you out, but… maybe you can help us."

"Tossing a bone to a yapping dog?"

"Something like that." Price flashed his teeth, then leaned in closer. "There's a dead man upstairs. We have close to two hundred suspects, and the murderer might have already slipped out. I don't want to be here till hell freezes over taking statements. Maybe you could speed things up as a…" He searched for a word.

"Consulting detective?" She liked the sound of that.

Price frowned down at her. "Don't go thinking you're some damn Sherlock Holmes."

"I'm far too short, sergeant."

"I'm going to regret this," he muttered.

6

INTERROGATION

BY THE TIME INSPECTOR GEARY RETURNED WITH HIS GOON, Riot's shoulders were cramping and his knees had gone numb.

"O'Hare, we're not savages. Get this prisoner a chair," Geary said, folding his hands behind his back. Given his resemblance to a gargoyle, Riot wondered if years of looking down at prisoners had shaped him, or had he started out like that naturally.

The two mysterious men walked in, too, stepping aside to observe.

O'Hare came back with a chair, then bent to unlock the chain from Riot's handcuffs. He kept the irons on, though.

Riot eyed the chair sideways, considering his options. He knew what Geary wanted—to watch him struggle to stand with pins and needles in his legs. The alternative was to stay on his knees. So Riot made himself a third option.

"Four men against one? Scared I'll bite, Inspector?"

A hand slapped the back of his head. "You can talk when you answer a question. Not before, Smart Ass," O'Hare growled.

"That's *Mr.* Smart Ass to you, O'Hare."

A billy club came down on his shoulder blades. Riot moved with the blow, lessening its effect, as he toppled to the stone. It still stung, but the fresh pain distracted from his cramping shoulders.

All things said and done, lying down was a relief. He shifted onto his side to wait.

"Pick him up, O'Hare."

The big officer wrenched him upright, but Riot's legs gave out and he fell onto the chair. Small victories, he thought.

Riot studied the graying man in the corner. As he watched Riot in return, the edge of his bushy mustache twitched upwards. A smile? Had the man realized Riot's manipulation of the officers? Riot doubted those squinting eyes missed much.

The graying man held a familiar revolver. Riot's own Smith and Wesson No. 3. The question was, who was in charge here?

"Aren't you going to introduce me to your friends?" Riot asked.

"You don't need to concern yourself with those two."

"Liam Taft. This is Sam Batten." Liam's voice was rough with gravel. He offered nothing more.

Geary thrust two fingers at Riot's eyes, then gestured back to his own. "I'm the one you need to worry about."

Riot shifted in his chair, trying to find a comfortable position with his arms behind his back. "I'm finding the knot in my shoulder too distracting to worry overly much."

"O'Hare will make you forget about that knot if you don't answer me, Riot. Where were you on November sixth?"

"What day was that?" Riot asked.

"The day you killed Monty in cold blood."

"I'd nearly forgotten you and Monty were friends." Riot wasn't watching Geary when he said it, he was watching Liam Taft for a reaction. But a quick, hard slap that rattled his head interrupted his observation.

Riot squeezed his eyes shut, grimacing.

"Answer the inspector," O'Hare warned.

"Let's see... today is a Wednesday," Riot said through clenched teeth. "What is it? The fourteenth?"

"Playing dumb won't work," Geary warned.

"I've been in Muir Woods and Willow Camp for the last week and a half. Do you think I usually dress like this?"

"Today is the fourteenth," Sam confirmed.

Riot nodded his thanks. "Let's see, we left for Muir Woods on the third. That was a Saturday. So... I suppose by the sixth we were at Willow Camp exploring the beach. Or hiking in the woods. I can't honestly remember."

"And I suppose you were with your mongrel 'family'?"

"I was."

"I'm sure they'll vouch for you," Geary said.

"Along with several people at Willow Camp, and likely some at the new inn up that way."

"Why, because you're so memorable?"

"Because my daughters and their friend were screeching and hanging off the gravity train. Then they got kicked out of the inn. I'm still not sure what they did. No one is talking."

"That may be, but that doesn't mean you were with them."

"It's easily verified."

"But you'd have plenty of time to take a ferry back, shoot your ex-agent, and pop on back over."

"What time was Monty killed?" Riot asked.

"You're not asking the questions here," Geary said. "And I'll not waste my time with your paid alibis. I'm sure that bullet between his eyes will match the one in your revolver."

"Considering how much you dislike me, I wouldn't be surprised, Inspector."

O'Hare slapped the side of Riot's head with his billy club. Riot's vision blurred, and when he'd refocused, Liam had shifted positions. He'd crossed his arms and turned his attention on the officers. But Liam was a hard one to read, especially without spectacles.

"Tell me about your fight with Monty," Geary ordered.

"Ask your goon to stop hitting me."

"O'Hare's just playing with you."

Riot squinted up at the looming gargoyle. "Monty beat me near to death. My head hasn't recovered. You hit me any harder and you'll have a dead man on your hands."

"So you had motive," Geary said. "Write that down. Revenge. And you knew where to find him. Opportunity." No one in the room wrote anything down. Riot doubted O'Hare could write. "Why'd you go visit Monty at his boxing club?"

"Same reason there's two Pinkerton operatives standing in the room." Riot's guess was confirmed when Geary hit him across the face. If he'd been wrong, and they *were* U.S. Marshals, Geary would've made sure Riot knew it. Geary did like to gloat. But Riot had wagered correctly, because U.S. Marshals would've been in charge.

Riot worked his jaw, tasting blood on his lip. "You seem more the vengeful type than me, Inspector."

"Always an arrogant ass, aren't you?"

"Funny, Monty said that same thing after he beat me up."

"Answer my question. Why'd you visit Montgomery Johnson?"

"There was an attack on Ravenwood Agency. A captured assassin told me that a man seen with the Pinkertons had hired them to kill me."

Sam Batten glanced at his partner, who only stared down at Riot in consideration.

"And based on that bit of information you surmised it was your agent?" Geary pressed.

"The man who hired the assassins fit Monty's description, and he wasn't at the agency during the attack. Monty had made himself scarce."

"Was there bad blood between you two?"

"You should know, Inspector. I wager the two of you talked about it."

Geary glared.

"Or was it him and O'Hare?"

O'Hare slapped the back of his head again. A wave of dizziness hit Riot full on, and his vision narrowed to a tunnel. His shoulders felt a long way off.

"He can't talk if he's *unconscious*," Liam said.

Geary snorted. "He's faking it."

"I don't think he is," said Liam. "Why don't you get this fellow some water and dim these lights."

"You're not in charge here," Geary said.

Liam raised his hands. "Just a suggestion, Inspector." His tone seemed to soothe Geary's ego. The inspector nodded to O'Hare, who reluctantly did as ordered.

Soon enough, the lights dimmed, and a tin cup of water hovered in front of him. It churned Riot's stomach.

"How badly were you beaten, Mr. Riot?" Liam asked.

"It laid me out for weeks."

"And yet you went camping," Geary said.

"Three weeks after the fact."

"After one of your agents was killed," Geary accused.

"In the attack on my agency. Yes. Mack McCormick."

"Then you confronted Monty. He got the better of you, and you went back and shot him. That's a little more than coincidence, considering your reputation."

"I was with my family. If I were you, Inspector, I'd be searching for the culprit who hired Monty to kill me."

"With the way you make friends, that'd be half the city."

Riot raised his head to look Geary in the eye. "You included?"

O'Hare raised his club to strike, but a knock on the door interrupted the blow.

The door opened, and a hesitant officer poked his head inside. "Sir, there's a—" the man didn't get to finish. A rough, edgy man bulled his way inside.

"Doyle, here. I'm to guard the prisoner." Doyle wore a cocked cap and had a scar along his chin. Pockmarked, with a face like leather, he was as tough as he looked. Riot nearly shuddered with relief. Without waiting for permission, Doyle took up a position at Riot's side, opposite O'Hare. The two men glared at each other, the tension thick enough to feel.

"On whose orders?" Geary demanded.

"Detective Inspector Coleman's."

Riot barely heard the words. They came from far away, every breath sending a sharp pain through his skull.

"Wait outside," Geary ordered.

"I'm not to leave his side, sir. Orders are orders. You'll have to take it up with the Inspector, sir."

Geary ground his teeth together. "And why does Coleman care about my prisoner?" He directed the question to Liam, who looked just as curious to know the answer.

It was Doyle who spoke. "A woman bullied her way into the Nymphia during a raid and made a nuisance of herself."

The Nymphia? Riot swallowed down surprise. He didn't have to ask who the woman was.

"Fine," Geary said. "Toss him in the yard till we compare those bullets."

7

CONSULTING DETECTIVE

SURPRISE RIPPLED THROUGH THE POLICEMEN AS SGT. PRICE LED Isobel to a third-story room. She ignored their puzzled stares, and when they looked to Price in question, he grumbled at them to mind their own damn business.

Although Isobel had entered through the back of the hotel where the corridors were dingy, the owners had attempted to spruce up the public hallways. Still, the Nymphia was showing signs of wear. Carpets needed beating, wallpaper was peeling, and the brass fixtures were smudged. And an unmistakable odor permeated the hallways—male sweat and lust battling with cheap perfume.

Doors stood open revealing disarray: a man's hat, a bare mattress, a discarded shoe. All signs the occupants had left in a hurry. Or tried to.

She eyed the narrow apertures at eye level in the doors, all with a coin-sized slot beside them.

A group of policemen conversed in front of one room. Sgt. Price slowed and put out a halting hand. "Wait here a moment, Mrs. Riot. I could get demoted for this." He steeled his shoulders and marched towards the group.

An officer on guard eyed her. But she was too fascinated by the setup of the doors to pay him any notice. The slits were peepholes, and a small locked box was affixed to the interior of each door. She tried to slide the peephole open, but it didn't budge. After further inspection, she fished around her satchel and slipped a dime into the slot. With a whir of gears, the face-plate slid aside.

Isobel arched a brow. Interesting. She was examining the locking mechanism when a throat cleared. "Mrs. Riot."

Isobel turned to the source of disapproval. Inspector Coleman was a studious-looking man with silver hair and a face lined by responsibility. Sgt. Price towered behind him, looking thoroughly chastised.

"Are all the doors fitted similarly?" she asked.

"Mrs. Riot, my sergeant was in error for bringing you into such a disreputable place. He'll escort you out now."

"It's a shame," she said, looking back to the door. "I could be of some help. Two wings, each with three floors, the first being reserved for dining and drinking, and the other two set up with these cubicles. Seventy-five rooms for each wing and floor. That's what... three hundred occupants? All streaming out during a police raid. Then you happen upon a corpse—a gentleman of some prominence. Otherwise, you'd have carted him away in a dead wagon some time ago. I imagine you have quite the number of interviews to conduct. Or did you just arrest the person who found the body?"

Isobel looked up at the last, and seeing that the blood had drained from the men's faces, she gave a tight smile.

"Told you, sir," Sgt. Price muttered under his breath.

Inspector Coleman ground his teeth together, but practicality overrode his gentlemanly sensibilities. "I'd be more comfortable if Mr. Riot were here..."

"He's not," she snapped. "I hope Sgt. Price informed you why I've come?"

"He did. But I'm afraid this matter is more pressing."

"Then let me have a look, and I'll speed up your investigation so you can help my husband."

"I'm not sure I can help him, Mrs. Riot."

"And I'm not sure I'll find anything here that you haven't already, but I'm willing to try." Isobel glanced at her fingernails. "And if I don't have something to occupy my mind with, I'll end up at the police station making a nuisance of myself."

Coleman considered her for a moment. "The crime scene is quite disturbing."

"I'm no fainting flower, Inspector."

"I've noticed." She could see the moment he came to a decision from the shift of his shoulders. "Do you swear to keep the details to yourself? This case requires discretion; we need to keep this out of the newspapers for as long as possible."

"With the exception of my partner, I do."

Inspector Coleman stepped aside and motioned for his men to clear the way. Price gave her a small smile. He looked eager to see what she would make of the scene.

Prepared for the worst, Isobel stepped into the cell-like room, and came face to face with something straight out of a gothic horror novel—a body lay contorted on the bed. Male, naked, and stiff with rigor mortis. The man's arms were raised, defying gravity, as if to block a blow. His legs, too, were frozen in the air, bent at an angle like he'd been sitting on a chair and fallen right off into death.

Isobel crossed the small room to peer at the man's face. Her throat constricted, but she quickly swallowed down rising bile. His face was most disturbing.

Focus on the details, she told herself.

Isobel wrapped a cool exterior around her beating heart, shoving emotion aside. But what she had done for years was becoming more difficult. Damn happiness.

The man's blue eyes were wide with horror. His face was

twisted, his mouth gaped in a frozen scream, and his throat bulged oddly. Scratches marred his neck and wrists, and bruises blossomed on his chest.

Isobel bent to examine his nails. Bloody and torn. It looked like he had engaged in a cat fight and lost.

She ventured a sniff. A faint odor of expensive cologne muted the scent of stale blood. His skin was cold to the touch, and he had an erection. She checked his neck. No marks of strangulation. But as she had learned during their last case, that form of murder didn't always leave an outward mark on the skin.

The man was in his twenties. Excellent musculature, but not that of a worker. Rather an athlete. Swimmer or rower, she decided from the development of his shoulders and the long leanness of him. He'd been handsome in life. Blond, blue-eyed, a square jaw without whiskers, and excellent teeth.

Isobel peered into his gaping mouth. "Do you have a battery light, Inspector?"

Riot always kept one on his person. As much as she detested its tendency to flicker, she had to admit the flashlights were useful. Price handed her one, and she thumbed it on, shining the light deep into the corpse's throat.

Isobel winced. Then flicked off the light and turned to the two men. "Have you decided on a cause of death?"

Coleman looked disappointed. "We're waiting on Coroner Weston's arrival to confirm cause of death."

"Yes, but surely you have your own theories." Isobel pressed.

Price glanced at the corpse. "With the way he's clawing like that… we think it's poison."

"May I?" She gestured at the corpse.

Coleman nodded, and both of them crowded around her as she carefully reached into the man's mouth. She doubted the two men, with their larger hands, could manage it. There was something white at the very back of the throat. She pinched it and pulled free a long length of cloth.

Isobel considered the twisted handkerchief. "I'd like to see Coroner Weston declare this one a suicide."

8
GOOD INTENTIONS

THREE CHILDREN SAT ACROSS THE STREET FROM A POLICE station, watching patrol wagons cart in prisoners. They struck an odd sight: a scarred little Chinese girl dressed as a boy, a small brown-skinned boy wearing a cocked fedora, and a white girl from Tennessee somewhere between hay and grass.

"Now what?" Sarah asked.

"We need to discover where bahba is being held," Jin said.

"Why is that important?" Sarah asked.

Jin eyed the brick building. "To break him out. I have dynamite."

"Whoa now!" Tobias waved frantic hands. "Stop being crazy, Jin."

The girl narrowed her eyes. "Why else would we come here?"

Sarah sighed. "We should've done as we were told."

"Say…" Tobias eyed the older girl. "They won't arrest a white girl."

Sarah gawked at him. "They will too."

"Not a lost one," Jin said.

"Or a hysterical one."

Sarah glared at the younger children. "Why do I listen to you two?"

Tobias rolled his eyes towards Jin. "Because otherwise she's liable to blow up a wall."

"Why are you carrying dynamite?" Sarah asked.

Jin raised a brow. "Does not everyone?"

"*No.*"

Jin worked loose a toggle on her quilted coat and reached underneath to flash the top of a fat round tube with a wick protruding from its top.

Tobias gawked. Sarah made a grab for it, but Jin was too quick. The girl skipped out of her reach. "You will give us away," Jin hissed.

"You didn't answer my question."

"Why would I not have a stick of dynamite?" Jin asked, puzzled.

Sarah's mouth worked, but no words came out.

"Where'd you get that?" Tobias asked.

"From those men in the woods. I found it in their things."

"What were you planning on doing with it?" Sarah asked.

Jin shrugged. "Light it."

"We could blow up a bucket or something with it," Tobias suggested.

Jin looked at the police station. "Or a brick wall."

Sarah closed her eyes and took a calming breath. She was tempted to tackle her adopted sister, but she'd likely lose that fight. In the end, she gave in. What harm was there in asking to see her father?

9

ROOM 136

"You've got darn good eyes, Mrs. Riot."

"Miss Amsel will do, Sergeant."

"We both thought it was some sort of poison. Strychnine, maybe. What do you make of his position?" Coleman asked.

"Poison *could* be involved," she acknowledged. And then realized she was holding a handkerchief possibly coated with something deadly in her bare hands. Too late now. In for a penny… She sniffed at it and recoiled. It reeked of bile and blood.

Isobel studied the silk handkerchief. This was no cheap, store-bought accessory, but finely woven silk with tight stitching along the edges, and a silver monogram: D.N. There were dark dots on the silk. Not blood, but nearly black. She handed the handkerchief over to Coleman, then considered the dead man.

Despite his state, he looked almost alive. Still fighting off his assailant in some frantic, clawing motion. What had caused his body to seize so rapidly?

Isobel tilted her head. Without asking, she pushed the body, rolling it onto its side. The corpse fell over easily, settling on the bed. On his side on the mattress, with his hands up near his face and his legs bent, the corpse now looked more peaceful than horrific. "Someone moved him after death." Isobel gestured at the corpse, "See this discoloration?"

"He died on his back," the inspector noted.

"Where he lay long enough for his blood to pool, but not long enough for rigor mortis to set in," she said.

Coleman was nodding in agreement. "And then someone rolled him onto his side to make it appear he was sleeping."

"What sort of time frame is that?" Price asked.

Coleman frowned at the bed. "An hour, possibly two. The police surgeon will know."

"He'll want a rectal temperature if you haven't already taken one, Sergeant," Isobel said.

Price took a step back. "That's not part of my job description. I think that's for consultants."

"I don't carry a thermometer."

"I'll make sure the coroner does it," Coleman cut in.

Price scratched at his chin. "So the murderer sat in the room for at least an hour before deciding to roll him over? That doesn't make sense."

"Maybe his conscience got the better of him," Coleman said.

"Or her," Isobel murmured.

"Then what? The murderer rolled him back onto his back *after* he got stiff?" Price looked dubious.

"Perhaps one of your men rolled him over?" she asked.

The officers shook their heads.

Isobel considered that bit of information. "Where is his clothing?"

"Not here," Price said. "I double-checked."

Coleman bent to study the man's back. "Look here. It seems he may have been laying on something long enough to leave an impression." A pale patch of rectangular flesh stood out against the mottled purple skin.

Isobel searched the stained bedding, but found nothing that would make a mark like that. She dropped to hands and knees to search under the bed with the flashlight. Bugs skittered across the floor as she slithered under the bed. "Aha!" She wrapped her prize in her own handkerchief, then scooted back out.

Triumphant, she unfolded the cloth to show the men her find. "I wager this is the source of the marks on the handkerchief and the impression on his back." It was a thick, flat pencil. Coming from a family of boatbuilders, Isobel recognized it as a carpenter's pencil commonly used by the working class to mark wood or even brick.

Price darkened like a storm cloud about to burst. "Apparently my officers need a reminder on how to search a room."

"I wouldn't be too hard on them, Sergeant," Isobel said demurely. "I was looking for it. It's easy to miss, wedged as it was."

Coleman's brows drew together. "How did you know to look for it?"

"The handkerchief was too far down his throat for a hand. And the marks on the cloth…" She held the tip closer to the light, wishing Riot was here with his magnifying glass. A small groove ran through the center of the lead.

"Then how'd the pencil end up under him?" Price asked.

"There was obviously a struggle. Blood under his nails, bruising, scratches…" Isobel turned to the bed, picturing the scene in her mind's eye. "But once the handkerchief was deep enough, our john here couldn't dislodge it. He might have sat up, clawing at his throat. The murderer dropped the pencil to restrain his arms, or simply tossed it on the bed and stood back to watch him suffocate. Then our john fell back, landing atop the pencil."

Her words conjured a grim scene. It was mirrored in the man's contorted face. She glanced at the peephole in the door.

No, not a scene. Almost a stage. Had someone paid a dime to watch the entire murder?

"If the pencil was there long enough to leave a mark on his back while the blood pooled, how did it end up on the floor?" Coleman asked.

"I don't know," she admitted. "But one thing is certain—someone hated this man a great deal."

Isobel took a slow turn around the room. Most brothel doors had a hidden lock, or so her twin claimed. Earlier, while waiting for the inspector, she'd fiddled with a door in the hallway. This brothel had an interesting setup. The doors could be locked, but not from the obvious latch. It was a false lock, so a john couldn't trap a prostitute inside.

The real latch was likely close to the bed, within reach... Isobel pulled on a hat hook, and the door clicked.

"There's a secret door too," Price said, nodding to another wall.

She'd hardly call it a secret. A crease in the wallpaper shouted out the passage.

The sergeant pushed it open, and Isobel stepped into a dimly lit corridor that connected to the backs of the rooms—a dark mirror to the public passages, with washrooms and a ready exit for anyone daring enough to risk the fire escapes. This back entrance was hastily numbered with red paint. Room 136.

Isobel stood in thought. The possibilities were endless. She needed to narrow things down. "So, are you going to tell me who this fellow is?" she asked, stepping back into the room.

Price glanced at his superior for permission. Coleman gave it. "One of my officers recognized him from his rowing club. We think this is Dominic Noble."

That certainly explained all the fuss. The Nobles were one of the most influential and wealthiest families in San Francisco. Dominic Noble was their only son, and heir to a fortune.

Isobel frowned down at his twisted remains. Anyone who'd even brushed the fringes of society knew that name. Isobel had met him at one of the endless society soirées she'd endured while investigating Alex Kingston. Tall and striking, Dominic Noble had had a trail of women falling over themselves to win his attentions. And he'd been courteous to them all.

But the dashing bachelor she remembered was barely recognizable in this twisted horror, curled on a filthy mattress.

What on earth would a man like Dominic Noble be doing in a run-down brothel like the Nymphia? There was the obvious, of course. But something felt wrong about this scene. It was too personal.

"Now, gentleman, what aren't you telling me?"

Price and Coleman exchanged glances.

"We have a suspect," Coleman said.

"Who?"

"We found a young man in the room during the raid. He *claims* he was locked in."

10

THE SUSPECT

THE YOUTH COULDN'T BE OVER FIFTEEN. HE WAS TRYING TO grow a mustache, but it looked more like a weed. As did the boy himself. A guard loomed over him, and he shifted uncomfortably, his wrists locked in iron behind his back.

Isobel followed Inspector Coleman and Sergeant Price into the room, then stepped to the side to observe. The boy's eyes darted from the towering men to her, puzzled by a woman's presence.

She was careful not to lean against the wall, or touch any surfaces. A brothel like this didn't have high standards of cleanliness, and she knew far too many details about her twin's occupation.

Price took out his notepad and Coleman folded his hands, looking down at the boy like judge, jury, and executioner. It didn't take five seconds for the boy to blurt out his life story.

"This is my first time here, I swear. I've never been in a cow-yard before. I didn't hurt that man," he said, his words slurred.

Coleman looked at Price, who cleared his throat. "State your name for the record."

"I didn't kill that fellow!" The last came out a squeak as his voice cracked. "I don't even know him."

Price remained poised with pencil and pad. "Name? And it best not be John Smith."

The boy looked confused for a moment. "No. I'm Jacob Dixon."

Price wrote it down. "Occupation?"

"I'm a sailor on the *Columbia*. My mates were showing me around town."

"First time in the city?" Price asked.

"Yes, sir." His gaze flickered to Isobel. "Why is she here?"

Coleman turned slightly, that same question flashing across his own eyes.

"You keep your eyes on the inspector and me," Price warned.

"Is she the whore that accused me of killing that fellow?"

Price cuffed Jacob on the side of the head, and Isobel flinched with the youth. Was Riot undergoing the same treatment, or worse? Instead of an open-handed slap, was he being pummeled with O'Hare's fists? The thought made her queasy.

"We found you in a room with a dead man. I'd say that's plenty incriminating," Price said.

"I was locked in there!"

"After you killed him or before?" Price asked.

"I swear I didn't kill him! I just… saw him all stiff like that and walked in to get a closer look."

"Was the door open or closed?" Isobel inquired.

"Why does she get to ask me questions?"

"Because I'm your best chance of escaping a noose."

"Mrs. Riot is a detective," Coleman explained.

Jacob started in surprise. His face changed expressions so rapidly that Isobel doubted the boy was capable of deception. His entire world had just been upended over the thought of a female detective. Never mind the Pinkertons had been employing women agents for decades.

"You're from Oregon, aren't you?" Isobel asked.

"How d'you know?"

Isobel gave a dismissive gesture. "You should pay attention to the men who can hang you."

"But I just walked into the room and there he was."

"Was the door open?" she asked again.

"No. I mean, yes. I think."

"You *think*?" Coleman pressed.

"I... it's a little blurry."

"How much did you have to drink with your friends?" Price asked.

Jacob turned an odd shade of green. "Not much. We went around to a few saloons before coming here. I needed some courage."

Isobel could smell the alcohol coming off him in waves.

"Did your friends get you to try anything else?" Price asked.

Jacob shook his head. Too quickly. His dilated pupils said otherwise. Jacob's obvious lies were not helping his case.

"I put my dime in the slot and looked through the peephole. When I saw that fellow and no one else, I tried the door and it just sort of... opened."

"Did you move him?" Coleman asked.

"No."

"You didn't roll him over?"

"He was on his back, naked, just lying there..." Jacob looked on the verge of being sick, so Isobel took a calculated step to the side.

"Why did you enter?" Coleman asked.

Jacob searched for an answer. "I thought it might be some act, like a circus freak show."

"You're lying, Jacob," Isobel said. "You touched him."

He turned red. "Fine, all right. He was covered with a blanket. I thought…" He looked helplessly at the two men. "I thought it might be a woman under there. I don't know."

Price cleared his throat behind a hand.

"That must've been quite a shock," Isobel said.

Jacob nodded.

"What happened after that?" she pressed.

"I stepped back, tripped, and hit my head."

Isobel studied her fingernails. The inspector and sergeant glowered, and Jacob shifted under their stares. "I want an attorney."

"Do you have the money for an attorney?"

Jacob hesitated.

"No, you don't," Isobel answered for him. "Besides, an attorney wouldn't be much use because you don't remember, do you?"

"I do. It's just… hazy."

"Hazy as in… you blacked out?"

"Look, I said I stumbled back and fell. When I came to the door was locked and then the whistles started blowing. I couldn't get out of the room."

Price scratched it all down in his notepad.

Jacob licked his lips, eyes darting from the pencil to the inspector. "It was poison or something? Wasn't it?"

"You tell me," Coleman said.

"I don't know. How else could he be like that? All stiff in that position."

"How long were you 'trapped' in the room?" Coleman asked.

Jacob shrugged. "I don't know. I don't have a pocket watch. But I was banging on the door for a good half an hour."

"What made you pause at *that* door?" Isobel asked.

Jacob turned a violent shade of red. "I was using up my coins, peeping and all. And… I don't know."

"So you were walking down the hallway, putting a dime into each slot? That's expensive."

"Well, no." Jacob's brows drew together with comical effect. She could see the boy thinking. "I thought someone came out of that room. He bumped me in the hallway. Seemed like he was in a hurry, so I thought maybe I could see what the whore was doing... you know, afterwards." He wouldn't meet her eyes when he said the last.

"Are you sure it was a man?" she asked.

"Of course it was a man. He was wearing a cap and coat."

"Large? Small? Hair color?"

"I don't know. I was out of it."

"Take off your shirt," Isobel ordered.

Jacob just stared at her.

"Do it," Price growled.

"I'm not taking off my shirt in front of her."

Isobel crossed her arms. "But you were going to pay a woman for sex?"

Jacob's blush spread down his throat as he stammered and made excuses. But when Sgt. Price stepped forward to loom, Jacob fell silent.

The boy removed his shirt, and Isobel moved closer to inspect his arms. Rough, calloused fingers, and wiry muscle. He was a sailor all right: But there were scratches on his palms and arms.

"From moving sacks," he said when she asked.

Inspector Coleman held up the carpenter's pencil. "Is this yours?"

Jacob looked confused. "No. I don't carry one."

Coleman pressed him further, but there was nothing more to glean from the youth, and he refused to give up the names of his friends. Finally, Coleman gestured Isobel out into the hallway while Price got the boy's particulars.

"What do you think?" Coleman asked.

"I think you have a scandal on your hands, Inspector."

Coleman frowned. "I meant regarding young Dixon."

"He's horrible at lying, and he's too inexperienced to know about dummy locks."

"That doesn't make him innocent," Coleman said.

"Or guilty," she pointed out.

"Found drunk in a locked room with a dead man? It certainly looks bad for him."

———

AN OFFICER STRODE QUICKLY UP THE HALLWAY AND SALUTED Coleman. "Inspector." He hesitated at the sight of Isobel. "Ma'am." Coleman didn't offer introductions. "We've finished taking names and statements of the residents and johns."

The thick notebook was full of names.

With every flip of a page, Coleman's mood darkened. Isobel leaned closer to read over his shoulder. "Amazing how many parents name their children John Smith and Alice Smith."

Coleman grunted.

"What will you do with the boy?" Isobel asked.

"I'll keep him until the police surgeon can confirm time of death and we can track his whereabouts. If our estimate of time of death is correct, and what Jacob says is true, he should have several alibis."

"And the family of the deceased?" she asked.

"I'll inform them. I'm sure the Nobles, along with the Chief of Police, will cry for a quick arrest."

"I wish you the best of luck, Inspector. Now if you'll excuse me, I need to go check on my husband."

"I'd like you to continue as a consultant for this case, Miss Amsel. If you can help narrow this list down…" He brandished the notepad. "I'd be much obliged."

Isobel was torn. Worry twisted her heart, but this murder offered an intriguing challenge.

"You can't help him, Miss Amsel," Coleman said. "And I'm not sure I can either. But one thing I'm certain of is you need to stay away from this or you risk tainting any investigation surrounding your husband."

"I can at least try."

"You'll get yourself *arrested*. I know Geary and his type."

Isobel suppressed a shudder. She'd barely tolerated her incarceration, and the thought of being caged again terrified her. But a risk she'd gladly take for Riot.

In the end, reason won over her heart. What could she do from a jail cell?

"Will I have free rein in this case, Inspector?"

He looked at her, hard. "You're a *consultant*; not a police inspector. You'll report to me. Understood?"

There were ways around that. "Understood."

Coleman offered his hand, but instead of shaking it, Isobel plucked the notepad from his other one. "Now…" She flipped through the pages, then thrust a finger at a name. "I want to talk with Anne Glory."

"Why?" Coleman asked, puzzled.

"Because she knows her trade."

11

THE BULLPEN

"How's your mother, Doyle?" Riot asked, as he was being led from a frying pan into a fire.

"Same as you—too stubborn to die."

"It's the smart ass in me."

Doyle chuckled and gave him a little shove for the benefit of the watching guards. "You caught yourself a lively one with that woman of yours."

"Bel is certainly unique."

"A looker, too. And what with you looking like a washed up piece of driftwood." Doyle gave a low whistle. "I may just rub your head for a bit o' luck."

"Best take the opportunity now."

A heavy iron door opened into a cage-like corral, where two armed guards stood on duty, watching the bullpen. Riot was pulled to a stop while Doyle unlocked his handcuffs. "I'll work on getting you into a private holding cell. Try not to get yourself killed in there, A.J."

"I'll need all my luck for that."

Doyle gave him a gentle prod with a billy club. "Luck might be better helped if you kept that mouth of yours shut."

"I've mellowed in my old age."

Doyle barked a laugh, then shoved him into the holding yard.

————————

THE PRISONERS WATCHED RIOT AS HE STUMBLED INTO THE barren courtyard. High brick walls topped with barbed wire surrounded the yard. Without his spectacles, everything beyond a five-foot bubble looked like runny watercolors. But he'd brought prisoners to this station before, so he knew there was a watchtower overhead with riflemen and a view into the bullpen and street outside.

The yard was a blur of shapes. Some dark, some light. By the voices, he could tell the groups apart. Cantonese spoken over to one side, Spanish on another, and English in the middle. Random blurry shapes were sprawled in the dirt. Those were likely drunks and addicts, who generally staggered around until they fell.

The bullpen wasn't the safest place for a detective. Something Geary was counting on. It sent two messages: You're not special, and I hope you die.

Fortunately, Riot didn't look much like a detective at the moment. Something Inspector Geary was too dense to notice.

Riot ran a hand over his overgrown beard, considering his options. A few bored whites were yelling insults at the Chinese, trying to provoke a reaction. But he couldn't tell if it was working or not. Faces were indistinct.

Riot started towards the whites, then veered, taking a leisurely stroll around the yard between the two groups, until the arguing quieted and he felt more eyes watching to see where he'd land.

Only he didn't land anywhere. Instead, he ignored the various groups and limped around the perimeter of the yard.

His head throbbed, sharp pains shot down his shoulders, and his knees ached from hours spent kneeling on a stone floor. So to distract himself, he mulled over his predicament.

Monty was dead. Murdered. No surprise there. In fact, he and Tim had expected retribution. Monty had failed in his attempt to kill Riot, and that made Monty a liability to whoever had hired him.

But why had Monty come short of killing Riot when he'd had the chance? A broken man lying dead in a gutter in Mission Bay would've been difficult to trace, but there'd been plenty of witnesses in the boxing club. So Monty had left it up to chance. A few more hours and Riot would've been dead.

Snippets of memory had returned to Riot during his convalescence at Willow Camp. *You ever stop to think I might have been trying to save your arrogant ass?* Monty had asked.

By nearly killing me, he thought grimly. Was there truth to Monty's claim? Riot didn't think so. Monty had hired thugs to dynamite the agency, because he didn't have the nerve to do it himself.

Now a bullet between the eyes—that was the mark of a professional. The thought made Riot stop in his tracks. Then he gave a grunt of realization and kept walking.

12

BEHIND THE CURTAIN

ANNE GLORY WAS LOOKING SLIGHTLY NERVOUS AS SHE SAT IN A room, smoking a cigarette. They'd brought her clothing, but the properness of the collar only seemed to heighten her beauty.

When Isobel walked in, some tension left, until Anne spotted the large sergeant on Isobel's heels.

Anne crushed her cigarette into an ashtray. "Charlotte Bonnie, wasn't it?" she asked.

Isobel presented her card. "Actually it's Isobel Amsel, with Ravenwood Agency."

Anne accepted the card with a sultry smile. "I'll be damned. We all followed your case. What you did took some guts."

"I was backed into a corner. I didn't have a choice." Isobel started to pull over a stool, but thought better of it when she saw the filmy layer on top.

"It's what we do when we're in that corner that matters. Am I in trouble?" Anne asked.

"I need someone to show me around this hotel."

"What's in it for me?" Anne asked.

Isobel nodded to Sergeant Price.

"If you help Miss Amsel, we'll waive your fine."

Anne's lips curved. "What's your angle? Looking to go undercover?"

Isobel smothered a flutter of unease. But she didn't quite stifle the small, shaky breath that escaped. Anne's question hit a little too close to home. Isobel *had* gone undercover after a fashion to marry a man blackmailing her. Alex Kingston. Her first husband. Not by choice. She'd thought she could handle the ruse. After all, women did that sort of thing all the time. They married for money or sold sex to men far more revolting than Alex. Her own twin had been doing it for years. But Isobel hadn't liked the person she'd become in that guise.

Lotario seemed to take pride in his trade, but it wasn't for everyone. She hadn't been able to endure it.

"I'm not cut out for your line of work," Isobel admitted. Something in her tone, maybe the sincerity in her voice, made Anne soften. But her eyes went hard the moment she glanced at Sergeant Price.

"If it's not the johns, it's the 'peace' officers. Men get you any way they can."

"Do we have a deal?" Isobel asked. She wasn't about to get on the topic of patriarchal society.

"Do I have your word that my fine will be cleared?" Anne asked, addressing Price.

"For harlotry. Yes. That's it, though."

Anne's eyes narrowed. "Something's happened, hasn't it?"

"It's not for you to know," Price grumbled.

Anne sat back. "It's murder, isn't it?"

"You know the police, Anne. They'll arrest whoever they find at the scene of the crime. I'm here to make sure that doesn't happen. But I need to know how this place operates. Do the residents pick their own rooms or are they assigned?"

"The manager assigns us. We come in the back way, pay

five dollars for rent, then stow our clothing and personals in a cubby that the manager locks. He doesn't want us girls walking around with clothes on, even in the back hallways, which really means he doesn't want us leaving without permission."

"Are you trapped here?"

"As long as we pay our rent and clear our tab, we're free to leave. I suppose there's some safety to it. Any woman wearing clothes stands out. This way we have to check in and out, so the manager knows who's working at any given time."

It was also a form of control.

"I thought you said you pay your rent beforehand?"

"We're supposed to. Some new girls don't have the cash for it up front, so he lets them work it off. If they're lucky, they can settle up in half a day, but not all of them know how to hustle."

"What room were you assigned to?"

"I'm a second-floor girl right off the stairway. Room ten."

"Is that a good room?"

"The first ten rooms are prime spots, because men usually still have money in their pockets. They haven't wasted it on peep shows or the saloon yet." She gave a laugh. "Even so, I've had johns pass out drunk while I was unbuttoning their trousers. I let them sleep it off and tell them they enjoyed my company."

"What about third-floor rooms?"

She wrinkled her nose. "No one wants those. They're not as nice and get the least amount of business. Most men don't make it that far. There are too many doors before that, so the girls have to leave their rooms to drum up business in the saloon, which means putting up with a heap of groping. All for free. The manager rents those out to negroes, orientals, and Mexicans. Men looking for some variety and spice go up to the third floor."

"Do you always get the same room?"

"I do. I'm popular." Anne gave her a wink. "I do this thing where—"

Sgt. Price cleared his throat, loudly. "Stay on subject, Miss Glory."

Isobel raised the edge of her lip. "You can tell me later." She slipped out her cigarette case and offered one to the woman.

"Now these aren't the cheap kind." Anne took two, tucked one between her breasts, and struck a match for the other. "Any road. I'm popular, so I get my pick. Some girls just give it a go for a week, and move on."

"Is that common?"

Anne wrinkled her nose. "The working conditions aren't great. Some don't make enough to pay their rent for the day. There's a lot of competition here. And some don't fancy the peep shows. It's one thing to wave your ass up in the air for one fellow, but to have a crowd of eyes watching… well, not all the girls can take the constant staring. It gets to you after a while. No privacy. No time to recover, or even clean up in private. If a man comes in while you're wiping yourself down from the last, you have to take him. There's no choice here."

Sounded like reason to murder a man.

"How long do the rooms rent out for?"

"Twenty-four hours. You can leave before, as long as your bill is settled. But most of the girls go till they drop. Then we take our earnings and live like queens for a week. I have a regular room at the Palace." Anne gave a shrug. "Whiskey gets you through a shift like that."

"Are there rooms that aren't occupied?"

"Sure," Anne took a long drag. "The peep hole stays open so men don't waste their coin on those. Too many complaints otherwise."

"Who keeps the dimes?"

"We do. But they cheat us. Most use slugs now." She made

a sound of disgust. "Some fellow down the street started selling fake coins. Twenty slugs for five cents. The bastard. Now there's a man I'd like to kill."

Sgt. Price cleared his throat. "I'll pretend I didn't hear that."

"Kind of you."

"What if a john gets rough?" Isobel asked.

Anne grimaced. "There's the watchmen. One out back behind the building, another in the manager's office. Then there's the rovers down in the saloon and poolroom to keep grubby hands away from us, and two watchmen on every floor, one for each wing. If you're lucky, you can throw the lock, and make it out into the hallway. Some times a watchman hears, and sometimes..." She paused to take a drag with a shaky hand. "Sometimes he's paid not to."

"Are there any men who regularly rough up women?"

Her twin never went anywhere without his bodyguard, Bruno. But then Paris, his working name, was the star of a burlesque show in a high-class parlor.

"The fellows ripe with cash are always the worst. They can't get away with the things they do to us at a high-end brothel, so they come here—the largest cow-yard in the world."

"Names?"

"There's a reason we call them johns."

"Do you know who rented room 136?"

A flicker of a lash. "There're upwards of three hundred girls in this hellhole. I don't bother with names on the upper floors, but you can ask the watchman. That's Becker's floor."

ISOBEL HAD THE BODYGUARD FOR THE THIRD FLOOR BROUGHT in. He hadn't fled with the others (or he'd been too slow) and didn't appear worried. As a watchman paid to keep the peace, she doubted he'd even be fined. He was just doing his job.

He was a sour smelling man, who had helped himself to a bottle of whiskey while being detained. Bruised knuckles, one black eye, and a cut lip.

"Had trouble on the third floor?" Isobel asked.

"Who are you?"

"Your judge and jury," Price said. He pushed the man onto a stool. The watchman bristled, but paused at the badge on Price's chest.

The men were of the same build. Both rough, but Price kept his whiskers orderly, and his uniform crisp.

"Your eye, Mr..."

"Becker. Earl Becker."

"Did you get in a fight?"

"Not a day goes by that I don't have to throw some drunk fellow out. Now what's a lady like you doing here?"

A 'lady like her' wanted to get as far away from this man as possible. Or knee him. He had the perpetual leer of a man who saw women as lustful possibilities.

"Questioning you, Mr. Becker. I thought that'd be obvious."

"But why?"

"Were there any disturbances in the past twenty-four hours?"

Becker considered the ceiling for a minute as he sucked on a tooth. "Sure, three fellows thought they'd get a deal if they all went in at once."

"And the woman in the room?"

"Some sort of Mexican or Apache, how the hell do I know? She ran out into the hallway screaming."

"And you..."

He stiffened. "I had some words with them. They went on their way. I don't like fellows roughing up the women. I got no use for that here. The whores give them what they want. Why the hell do these fellows have to put bruises on them too?"

Isobel found that the longer she stayed in this hotel, the sicker she was becoming. It was one thing to put a foot in the underworld, but quite another to spend any length of time in it as a woman.

"I don't know, Mr. Becker. But I do know that there is a dead man on your floor. On your watch."

Earl's eyes widened. She could feel Sgt. Price's disapproving eyes on the back of her skull, but there was nothing for it. She didn't have time to tiptoe around a murder investigation. Discretion was nice, but there was nothing like dangling the word murder in front of a suspect.

"What room?" Earl asked.

"One thirty-six."

He sat back.

"Do you know who was renting that room the last twenty-four hours?"

"Sure. It was a Japanese woman. There's only two in the cow-yard. That's how I remember."

"Do you remember the men who visited her?"

Earl barked out a laugh. "I'm not a log book. I remember which women are on my floor. I can't keep track of the men who come and go."

"Did anyone bother her on your shift?"

"No, no one." But that wasn't true. Isobel knew he was lying. He'd been too quick to shake his head.

Isobel looked to Sgt. Price. "Have one of your officers take him around to the detainees in the saloon to see if he can identify the woman."

An officer soon came to take Earl Becker away. "He knows something more," Isobel said.

Price shrugged. "Hard to tell. Most everyone is hiding

something here. I'll keep him overnight and let him stew till we can track down this woman and confirm his story."

"Let's check the lockers."

The manager was a thick, older woman wearing a faded silk dress and diamond teardrop earrings. She kept the keys to the lockers on a ring that could double as a bludgeon.

Mrs. Honeyford fumbled with her key ring as she searched through the keys. Eventually she located the right one, and opened the locker.

"Do you keep a logbook of who rents the rooms?"

"I don't ask no questions. I just let out the rooms and take the money."

"Do you give the residents duplicate keys?"

"All the keys are right here." The manager patted her key ring.

Isobel searched the clothing inside the opened locker. A ruffled white blouse, a plain gray skirt and matching coat. The shoes were dainty. Perhaps even smaller than Isobel's own feet. The personals were store bought, but the corset was strange. It had two buttoned flaps over the breast area.

Easy access, maybe?

Isobel sniffed at a stain on the fabric. Sour milk.

Ah. A nursing corset.

"Do you remember the woman who rented this room?"

Mrs. Honeyford shook her head. "My memory isn't what it used to be. And there's so many that come and go."

Isobel doubted that.

"Are there any nursing women in the saloon?" Isobel asked Sgt. Price when they were alone again.

"Why?"

"The locker had a nursing corset in it."

"Oh." He colored slightly. "I'll have the matron check."

"And if the clothes fit… Well, I've given you a place to start, sergeant. If you'll excuse me, I need to check on Riot."

He looked confused. "You're not going to follow up on this?"

"And comb San Francisco for a lactating woman with small feet and an infant?"

"A Japanese woman."

"So Mr. Becker claims," she said. "He may be tossing us an easy scapegoat. You know as well as I do how the courts treat suspects of oriental descent. Let alone a prostitute."

Price couldn't argue with that. "I'll read through the interviews. But she might not have a child."

"Why do you say that?"

Price turned brick red. "Some men pay for that sort of thing."

Isobel raised a brow in consideration. Then wondered if she was more naïve than she imagined. "Have someone bring the interviews by the agency when you're finished. I'll see if anything strikes me."

But he didn't leave right away. Sgt. Price insisted on escorting her out the gate. He wasn't about to let her walk unescorted through a brothel, and she found herself grateful for his chivalry. The place made her skin crawl.

"Had you heard about Monty's murder?"

Price shook his head. "Inspector Geary and O'Hare work the Mission Bay, and I don't recall seeing it in the newspapers, but I'm not the most diligent of readers. I don't much care to read about more crimes on my time off."

"Understandable."

"I'll see what I can dig up, though. Do you think it was the same people who attacked Ravenwood Agency?"

"Perhaps…" she hesitated, weighing how much she should share with Price. "We think Monty was the one who hired those men to attack the agency."

Price digested this. "Did Monty pan him out, too?"

She nodded. "Riot went to question Monty at his boxing

club. It ended badly. I think whoever hired Monty to kill Riot covered their tracks."

"A.J. told us the man who was hired to kill him was seen with the Pinkertons."

Isobel knew this, of course. Riot had told her what he'd shared with Coleman and Price.

"There were two men at the docks with Geary and O'Hare. They didn't introduce themselves, and they weren't wearing uniforms or badges."

"What'd they look like?"

She described both men.

"I don't recall any police inspectors who fit that description." Price frowned as he searched the street, but his thoughts were far away. "You say A.J. was with you the *whole* time you were in Willow Camp?"

"He was in no condition to go sailing off in the middle of the night to kill someone in the City."

"Have to admit," Price mused, scratching his chin. "Sounds like something he would do. All things considered."

"I would've noticed."

"Aye, but would you tell us?"

Isobel crossed her arms.

"Let's hope someone remembers him at Willow Camp besides you."

13

SIDEWAYS

"WHERE *IS* SHE?" TOBIAS ASKED.

Jin and Tobias sat on the curb, playing jacks across from the police station.

"Sarah is fine," she said, glancing at the sky.

San Francisco didn't abide by regular seasons. Half the time fog obscured the sun, so someone who wasn't familiar with the city had trouble telling time without a watch. But the city had its quirks, and longtime residents got by just fine.

The fog generally burned off by noon and the sun came out. Sometimes crisp and cold (it didn't matter if it was summer or winter) and sometimes hot and close. But around three o'clock the fog would roll in again, and the sky either turned a brilliant red or quickly darkened. Today it was getting cold and dark, which put the time somewhere around four o'clock.

"My ma is going to skin me."

"You say that every time." Jin adjusted her coat, feeling the reassuring stick of dynamite she'd wrapped in a newspaper. They'd done as instructed… after a fashion. Jin had picked through some old newspapers she'd found in a bin and read up on what happened with Montgomery Johnson. There was only a short three sentence blurb about his death. According to the newspaper, he'd been shot and robbed. That was all.

"*This* could be the time she finally does it. We need to do something," Tobias said.

"The police are probably giving Sarah tea and cookies, and letting her talk with bahba."

Tobias stood, dusting off his backside. "Probably." But he didn't sound convinced. Jin wasn't either.

"We'll just go… ask. Police can't arrest two kids for asking after their sister, can they?"

"Police can do whatever they like." Jin knew this for a fact. She'd seen too many policemen taking bribes from hatchet men and shoving runaway slave girls back into the hands of their captors.

"Maybe we should become policemen," he said, polishing an imaginary star on his breast as they crossed the street to the station.

———

"Was your father with you the entire time?"

The question was harsh. Demanding. But Sarah Byrne Riot did not cower, even though she'd rarely been so scared. Instead, she stared back at the officer, and repeated her demand. "I want to see my father," she said for the hundredth time.

Some hours ago, she'd entered the station and asked to speak with him. The desk officer left her waiting on a bench for a full hour until a man with thick brows and sloped shoulders came out. He was the same man from the docks.

"Were you with Atticus Riot these past two weeks?" the man asked.

"Yes, sir."

"Nice of you to come in and give a statement."

"That's not why I'm here," Sarah said.

The man smiled. An Inspector Geary, she'd later learned. "But I'm sure you want to, young miss. You might be able to clear your father's name."

"I just want to see him."

"Oh, so he wasn't with you the whole time? Is that why you won't give a statement?" Geary purred.

Sarah narrowed her eyes up at the man. "He was with me."

"Then there's no harm in giving your statement, now is there?"

A year before, Sarah trusted the police and would've given a statement. But she'd been a witness to murder. For her own safety, she'd gone into hiding, and then endured a tedious court trial. She'd learned a thing or two about the justice system.

"Not without an attorney," she said.

Geary nodded to one of his officers. "He'll show you the way."

But the big officer hadn't led her to Atticus. He'd taken her to a room with a table and chair and ordered her to wait. On his way out, he'd locked the door.

Sarah tried knocking, but no one answered, so she sat. And waited. Then waited some more. Until she had to pee so bad the corner looked inviting. Eventually that creepy policeman entered with his enormous shadow.

She couldn't even use the corner now. And they'd refused to let her use a toilet. The big policeman brandished a notepad and pencil and started hammering her with questions,

When did you leave?

What time?

What ferry?

Was Atticus Riot on the ferry?

The questions came, and the men loomed, until Sarah was close to tears.

They ignored her repeated request. Inspector Geary leaned forward to place his hands on the table. She could smell his breath. He'd eaten something with garlic.

"I'm going to ask you one more time." There was an obvious threat in his tone now. "Was your father with you the entire time?"

Sarah crossed her arms and glared back at him. "This is *illegal*, and you know it."

"So is obstructing a police investigation."

"I want to telephone my attorney. Now."

"Sure, Miss Riot. Whatever you wish."

Only the big officer didn't escort her to the telephone. He led her straight to a holding cell packed with other women.

The door clanged shut behind her. One woman ranted in a corner, another who was clearly drunk sang on a bench, and a dozen more stood staring vacantly at the floor.

"I don't suppose there's a toilet?" Sarah asked the sanest looking woman in the bunch.

The group parted, revealing a bucket in a corner. Considering the mess at its base, she wondered why they even bothered with a bucket at all.

THE FOG HAD ROLLED IN AND THE AIR HAD TURNED CRISP. IT cut straight to the bone, and it would only get colder over night. Riot didn't have a coat, or even a hat. At least he had a vest and his shoes.

No one had challenged him during his stroll around the yard, and now he sat with his back to a wall, trying to keep warm. One drunk stirred and stumbled off to urinate in a corner, while the group of excited white men started an impromptu prizefight that looked like colliding blurs to him.

Three drunk men snored on the ground, and a large, burly fellow had fought the others off for an entire bench to himself.

"Hey *hombre*, you got a light?" a man called.

Riot squinted. But he couldn't see much. Only a blur of white he thought was a Stetson on a head. Riot started to shake his head, but remembered he'd pocketed a matchbook he used to start fires at Willow Camp. Riot raised the matchbook between two fingers, and the man walked into view. His Levis showed the wear of a man who sat in a saddle most of the day.

"*Gracias*," he muttered, as Riot tossed him the matchbook.

The man struck a match and lit up with a sigh.

A loud crunch sounded from the vicinity of the prizefight and the group went wild. Riot reckoned someone had been knocked out. Whatever happened, the wild group turned their energy on the Chinese, shouting insults.

The cowboy muttered something in Spanish.

"Likely not a brain between them," Riot agreed.

The man looked down in surprise. "You speak Spanish like a gringo."

"I'm rusty," Riot said, climbing to his feet.

"What did they drag you in here for?"

"Murder."

The cowboy passed back the matchbook. "Is that why those orientals are looking at you sideways?"

"That's another affair."

"I'm Jorge."

"Most call me A.J."

Given the bounty on his head, it was best not to toss his name around, although it seemed several highbinders across the way had recognized him. Riot was almost glad he couldn't see anything.

Jorge didn't offer his hand.

"What about you?" Riot asked.

"Gambling," Jorge said, with a flick of ash. "I come to the city to enjoy myself a little, and where do I end up?"

"Can't you pay your fine and be done with it?"

"I'm not much of a gambler."

Riot chuckled.

The cage door with the police guards opened on the far side of the bullpen. The shouting prisoners turned their insults on the guards, as a small blur was shoved into the yard. Either a child or a very little person.

"*Pobre chico*," Jorge muttered, then spat. A little boy, then.

The blur charged the gate, spitting curses in Cantonese, until a guard prodded the prisoner back with a billy club.

Riot went still. He *knew* that voice. And he knew that was no boy. With a curse, he darted across the yard.

SAO JIN GLARED AT EVERYONE IN THE YARD. WHITE MEN wandered forward, snickering and jeering, while a group of Chinese men watched from across the way. She stood in a clearing, in a break between racial groups.

"He's full of spitfire, ain't he?" a man crooned. "Git over there, chink. Git with your kind." The man kicked at her, but she skipped to the side.

When he tried again, Jin screamed with fury and charged, latching onto his leg like a cat. He tried to shake her loose, but she punched upwards between his legs. The man dropped like a howling brick, and the yard burst with laughter.

Prisoners gathered around to watch the fight.

"What's this little chink think he is?" someone shouted.

Another bruiser rushed forward to teach the 'boy' a lesson,

but a hatchet man connected a kick to the man's jaw, sending him reeling backwards.

Then a dark-haired man rushed into the fray. Her *bahba*. Riot drove a fist into the first man's chest, knocking the wind out of him. A fist came flying, and he ducked under the blow, but an unidentified kick to the back of his knee dropped him.

All hell broke loose after that, and Jin was swallowed by a clash of prisoners.

RIOT WAS LOST IN A MOB OF SHOUTS, KICKING FEET, AND MEN slamming into each other. He stayed low, frantically searching for Jin in the chaos. There. A small form was crawling on all fours between the fighting prisoners' legs. Riot lunged after her, and the two broke free of the mob.

Riot scrambled to his feet to snatch the girl off her own. She screamed with rage, lashing out every which way and trying to claw out his eyes like a cat.

Riot fought off his frenzied daughter and tightened his hold. When he reached the far side of the yard, he dropped her to the ground.

She bounced up like a spring, ready to attack.

"*Jin*," he said, calmly.

She froze at the sound of his voice. Riot watched as blind rage cleared and she focused once again. Keeping an eye on the frenzied brawl, he crouched in front of her. Though she was on her feet, they were at eye level. His younger daughter was a pint-sized ball of fury of the likes he had never seen. He imagined Isobel had been much the same.

A dozen questions buzzed in his mind. He voiced the most important. "Are you hurt?"

Jin glared at the brawling men.

"You're *not* going back over there," he said.

Jin seethed, thrusting her finger towards the mob. "That man kicked me."

"Know when to back down."

"You have not learned that yet," she shot back.

He reached for her arm, but she jumped back, fear flashing across her eyes. Riot raised his hands. "I'm not going to hurt you," he said. Although he and Isobel had made progress, Jin was still skittish.

She relaxed a little and glanced at the fighting men. He held out a hand, and when she took it, he led her farther away from the brawl.

Riot glanced up at the guards. Their blurred shapes were leaning over a wooden railing, watching the fight. What did they care if prisoners killed each other?

"What on earth are you doing here?"

Jin reached inside her coat for a newspaper. "I brought you this. So you can escape."

Riot stared at the newspaper like it was a snake. A nagging worry itched at the back of his neck. He unrolled the newspaper, and stared at her 'gift.'

"Dynamite." Pride shone in her eyes.

Riot quickly folded the stick back into the paper. "That's mighty thoughtful of you, Jin. But I was wondering how you got in here."

"Sarah went into the station to check on you. She planned to cry and fuss, and maybe faint until they let her see you, but she never came back out."

"So you came to check on her?"

Jin dipped her head. "As soon as I asked about you and Sarah, the policeman told us we needed to give statements. I refused, so they threw me in here and charged me with disorderly conduct."

In her oversized cap, with her scarred face, and quilted coat, it was easy to mistake her for a boy. Her long braid just looked like a queue. "Didn't you tell them you were my daughter?"

"The policeman did not care that I was a girl. He said they only have one place for 'my kind.'"

A muscle in Riot's jaw twitched.

"I volunteered my knife, so they did not bother searching the rest of me."

A distinct sound of cracking bone came from the shouting mob, and a man screamed from the pack. The guards up top gave a whoop of encouragement.

Riot frowned at the brawl. Eventually the guards would step in with batons or rifles. Someone was sure to get killed, and he wasn't going to take chances with his daughter in the yard.

"Stay here."

"Why?"

"*Stay*," he ordered. Then caught Jorge's eye, who was leaning against a wall watching the fight. "Can you watch him?"

Jorge touched the brim of his hat.

As Riot walked around the perimeter of the yard, he took out a match to drag it along a brick. Fire flared, and he touched it to the wick hidden in a newspaper. He tucked the paper under his arm, then blocked the burning wick from prying eyes with his body until the time was right. When it was, he turned and tossed the stick into the mob.

Men screamed in panic, scattered, and leapt for cover. A split second later, the fog exploded with crackling bangs and a dazzling display of soaring lights. While everyone dropped to the ground, including the guards, Riot made his way back to Jin, who was gawking at the fireworks display.

He pulled her down, putting his back to the wall. After the echos of popping died, the guards shouted orders, and a stream of them finally rushed into the yard.

Jin narrowed her eyes. "Did you know it was a firecracker?"

"You didn't know?" Riot asked.

He could hear her teeth grinding. "Why would smugglers have firecrackers?"

"Do you really think I'd let you pinch a stick of dynamite?"

SHOTS WERE FIRED, AND A STREAM OF SHOUTING POLICEMEN poured into the yard. "On the ground! Hands on your heads!"

Everyone dropped.

Riot folded his hands behind his head, and nodded for Jin to do the same. She mirrored his pose, but glared at an approaching blur.

Doyle swam into view, a baton in hand that he slapped against his palm. "What did you start now, A.J.?"

"You know me," Riot said. "They put my daughter in here."

Doyle focused on Jin, who glared back. He gave a curse. "I thought she was a boy when I saw them tossing her in. Didn't know she was your kin."

"Can you get her out of here?"

"The guards wouldn't even let me in to break up the fight. I'm outnumbered here." Doyle glanced over his shoulder at a man groaning on the ground. "But I got to say, it's a *real* shame you both got injured in the fight."

The edge of Riot's lip quirked. "A real shame, isn't it, Jin?"

She stared, confused. Then it clicked. Jin fell over like a puppet without strings.

Soon enough, Riot was carrying a limp child in his arms, with Doyle pushing his way through the guards shouting about injuries. In the confusion, they let them through.

Doyle checked them into a holding cell, with an excuse of needing a physician. Then posted himself as a guard.

Jin lay on the cot, feigning injury, while Riot sat on the floor, reading the newspaper she'd brought him. Three brief sentences. That was all. Killed during a robbery.

Riot wasn't surprised.

"How long do I have to play dead?" Jin whispered in his ear.

"Until Bel brings an attorney."

"We wired Mr. Farnon."

"Then he should be along shortly," Riot murmured. A sudden thought occurred to him. "You said Tobias was with you?"

"Yes."

"What happened to him?"

"He is a traitor," Jin bit out with a snap of teeth.

"How so?"

"He offered to tell them everything."

"Everything?"

Jin gave a curt nod that made Riot shake with laughter.

"Why are you laughing?" she demanded.

"Have you ever tried to get a straight story from Tobias?"

"*Oh.*"

———————

"You say you went camping at Willow Creek?"

"I did. The Riots took me. Real nice of them, isn't it? Me not being their family and all, but we're great friends. And I saw the redwoods, and the ocean, and the railway car. And Mr. A.J. showed me how to pitch a tent and start a fire—"

"Mr. A.J.?" the policeman cut Tobias's narrative short. As soon as he and Jin had gone up to the front desk to ask about Sarah, a nice policeman came out and escorted Tobias to a room.

Tobias smiled at the nice man. They'd taken Jin off some-

where else. Something about a Chinese statement not matter-
ing. Then they handed him a paper bag full of candy and
asked about his trip. He was currently sucking away at a piece
of rock candy while he talked.

Tobias was talented like that.

"Sure, Mr. A.J. I guess you got him here. We came to see
him."

"Was he with you at Willow Camp?"

"I just said he taught me how to pitch a tent. You got any
more candy?"

The policeman glanced up from his notepad. "You have an
entire bag of candy."

"You ever been to the redwoods?" Tobias asked.

"What day did you leave?"

"I don't know. What day is today? I mean, does it matter
what the day is? It's always today, and tomorrow is tomorrow,
and yesterday is always the day before." Tobias popped
another piece of candy in his mouth as the policeman scribbled in his notebook.

Tobias leaned forward. "Whatcha writing? How d'you
become a policeman? Is there a school for it? Can you show
me around the station?"

The officer closed his eyes for a brief second. "Quiet," he
growled.

Tobias cocked his head. "I thought you wanted to get my
statement?"

"I do. But only answer my questions."

"I did. I don't know what day we left. Then you didn't
answer my question about what today is."

"Look, boy, you give me the runaround anymore and I'll
lock you up."

"You said I can't lie for this thing. I'd be lying if I told you
the day, wouldn't I? Cause I don't know."

"Today is Wednesday."

"Is it? Already? We left on a Saturday. I know that because it was the day before church. Only we don't go to church. My ma just has us sing the hymns then reads from the bible. Do you go to church?"

"Yes." The policeman caught himself, then narrowed his eyes. "You're not allowed to ask questions."

"You got something against your church?"

"Did you take a ferry?"

"We took Miss Isobel's cutter. She's teaching us how to sail. Jin is the first mate. I'm a crewman, and so is Sarah, and Mr. A.J. is the galley cook. You ever been sailing on the bay?"

"Was Mr. A.J. with you?"

"Well, we can't sail without a cook. You don't want to taste Miss Isobel's grub. Now, my ma, *she* can cook. Does your ma cook?"

The policeman's shoulders deflated, and Tobias White kept on talking.

14

BAIL

"YOU HAVE *NO* PROOF. IT'S ALL *CIRCUMSTANTIAL*," NATHAN Farnon insisted. Blond and balding, he wore a pince-nez that had a habit of falling off his nose. He adjusted the little glasses.

"The judge who issued the warrant disagreed with you," Inspector Geary argued. "I have numerous witnesses who state that Montgomery Johnson and Atticus Riot had words that ended in an all-out brawl. Riot got his ass handed to him." He paused to sneer at Isobel, who was standing off to the side as the men faced off over a counter in a waiting area full of people. Along with a reporter, whom she'd invited. Young Cameron Fry was busily scratching in his notepad with glee.

"And Riot told us himself that he believes Monty tried to kill him. That's motive!" Geary thrust his finger at the reporter, who also wrote that down.

Isobel was tired. Tired of the politics and the grudges and the justice department being more criminal than savior. Unless you were flush with cash, that is.

She kept a tight rein on her tongue, while she studied another man who was standing off to the side, observing the attorney versus inspector confrontation. He was the tall, graying man from the docks. With his squinting eyes and long drooping mustache, it was hard to read his expression.

"What judge issued the warrant?" Farnon asked. "My client was with his family at the time of death. He was seen on the Mount Tamalpais Railway."

"So *she* says. Her word is hardly trustworthy," Geary said.

"Mrs. Riot has the tickets," Farnon retorted.

"He could've hiked back and taken a ferry."

"So what you're saying, Inspector, is you arrested a man on the word of a few ruffians at a boxing club," Isobel said.

"We have more proof."

"Have you verified my husband's whereabouts and alibis on the third of November?" she asked.

Geary looked down his nose at her. "Monty was killed on the *sixth*."

Last Tuesday. She noted Geary's use of 'Monty' instead of 'victim' or Mr. Johnson.

"I'm sure the *reporters* of this fine city will verify Riot's whereabouts quicker than your detectives, Inspector." She paused to make sure Mr. Fry had caught her hint. "Now I'd like to speak with my husband."

"That's not allowed. I can hold him for four days while we look into this matter."

Isobel ground her teeth together. She wanted to strangle Inspector Geary and his sneer. But before thought gave way to action, a strong hand wrapped around her arm.

"Cool it, girl," a familiar voice whispered. She turned in surprise. It was Tim, his bald head gleaming under the lights and his white beard as bushy as ever. He flashed the inspector his gold teeth, making her think of a maniacal leprechaun.

Since Tim was here, it meant the children were safe at home. At least there was that, she thought.

Farnon led them off to the side. "They can't legally deny access to an attorney. I'll see that Mr. Riot is comfortable."

"You haven't spoken with him yet?" Isobel asked.

Farnon glanced at the officers. "No, they claimed there was a disturbance in the yard."

A lump formed in her throat.

"Mrs. Riot, as your attorney, I urge you to stay out of this. You *can't* investigate this matter. Do not interfere."

"I can't just stand by," she snapped.

"If you don't, then you risk doing more harm than good. The inspector is right. Legally, they can hold him up to four days when there's a suspicion of murder."

"I know the law, Mr. Farnon."

The man adjusted his pince-nez, unfazed and well used to her sharp tongue. He had seen her at her lowest, during her own court case and incarceration.

She took a breath. "I apologize."

"I know. You're worried. It's understandable. But if this goes to trial, any evidence you uncover to support his innocence will be tainted. The prosecution will accuse you of tampering with evidence and concocting alibis."

Farnon focused on Tim, who had his hands in his pockets and was rocking back and forth on his feet. "And that goes for you too, Mr. Tim."

"I have complete faith in the powers that be."

The old man looked far too innocent. Isobel wondered what he was planning.

"I can pass on a message," Farnon said.

"Tell him…" Isobel hesitated. "Tell him we'll manage."

A throat cleared, and the three turned back to Inspector Geary, who was looking as smug as ever. "There's another matter."

Ice trickled down her spine. "Yes?"

"Are you the mother of…" Geary held up a sheet of paper, and read. "… Sarah Byrne Riot and Sao Jin Riot?"

Cameron's head whipped up.

Isobel stepped back to the counter. "What has happened?"

"Miss Sarah has been charged with obstructing a police investigation. She refused to give a statement. And your Chinese child threatened us with violence."

"Where are my daughters?" Isobel asked through clenched teeth.

"The bullpen," Geary replied.

It was Farnon who snapped first. "You threw children into a *bullpen!*"

"A criminal is a criminal, Mr. Farnon. You should know that. But I'm a lenient man, so I'll drop the charges as long as you pay a small fine."

Isobel stared daggers at the man. She saw what he was doing. Refuse, and Jin and Sarah would wait for trial in a jail cell. Pay the trumped up fine, and they'd be released today.

Now it was Farnon who looked set on strangling the inspector.

"What about Tobias White?" she asked.

"The negro boy?" Geary asked. "He's giving us a statement."

"Without an attorney present?" Farnon asked.

"He volunteered. Very helpful boy."

Tim gave a wheezing laugh.

At any other time, Isobel might have found it amusing, but not with Riot in jail for murder.

Isobel checked her billfold. "I'll pay you two dollars, Inspector."

Geary snorted. "Twenty. A piece."

"Two dollars or I'll have the press hounding your every step. I do wonder what the good reporters of this city would uncover. You know how diligent they are."

Geary crossed his arms. "Are you threatening me, Mrs. Riot?"

"Do you have something to hide?"

Farnon hastily stepped forward, taking out his own bank-book. "I believe my client is short on cash and is only trying to get her children out of a holding cell, Inspector. I'll cover their fines."

Isobel swallowed her pride as Farnon paid. Not long after two sober girls were escorted into the lobby along with one cheerful little boy with sticky fingers.

THE MOMENT THEY STEPPED FROM THE STATION, TIM LIT HIS pipe, and Isobel took a deep breath, savoring the earthy smell of pipe smoke. She found it comforting.

Cameron Fry came bounding out after. Lanky, with a shock of blond hair and a sunburn on his freckled face, he reminded her of a large puppy who hadn't yet gotten used to his long legs.

"Are you all right, Miss Sarah?" the boy asked.

Instead of blushing, Sarah directed a glare at the police station. "Those brutes kept me in a locked room and were trying to force me to give a statement about my own father. I told them I wouldn't without an attorney. Then they stuffed me in the women's bullpen."

Isobel bit her tongue. She'd ordered them home.

Tim wasn't so diplomatic. "I can't imagine Miss Bel here telling you to take a stroll down to the station." The old man patted Sarah's shoulder. "Looks like you three learned your-selves a lesson. I'll get us a cab."

Tim took off down the street, and Cameron scribbled in his notepad.

Sarah gawked. "Cameron Fry, I told you not to write anything more about me."

Cameron looked up, innocence painted on his face. "But Miss Sarah, the world has to know about those brutes.

Besides, it will help your father when I go sniffing around Sausalito."

"So you picked up on my hint?" Isobel asked.

"Yes, ma'am," Cameron said, voice cracking. "I'll spread the word, and there'll be a race to verify Mr. Riot's whereabouts."

"I appreciate it, Mr. Fry." Cameron Fry had a mind on him, and the youth had once told Riot that persistence was his middle name.

Cameron raised his cap, gave Sarah a little bow, and made to strike off down the street, but not before he nearly ran into a station pillar.

"That boy," Sarah said with a shake of her head, but her gaze lingered on his back. At least Sarah had stopped making doe eyes at Lotario.

"If you kiss that gross boy you will get pregnant, and the doctor will cut the baby from your belly," Jin said matter-of-fact.

Sarah blushed, and Tobias's mouth fell open. He lost a piece of candy that rolled right out and shattered on the ground.

"*Jin*," Isobel warned. "All three of you are on thin ice right now."

Jin looked down at her feet, puzzled. Having spent most of her life as a house slave, then in a brothel, the finer points of social interactions were lost on the scarred girl.

"Thin ice means you're in trouble," Tobias explained, popping another hard candy into his mouth.

"And you aren't?" Sarah asked.

"Where did you get candy?" Jin demanded.

Tobias hugged a paper bag to his chest. "A policeman gave it to me."

Both girls gawked.

Isobel rubbed at her temple. She should be ecstatic that

Inspector Coleman had asked her to consult on a murder case. Instead, she was worried sick and on the verge of screaming at three children.

A cab pulled up to the curb and Tim hopped down from beside the driver to open the door. "Appreciate it, Big Jim. I'll ride inside for now."

'Big Jim' wasn't much larger than Tim, who was shorter than Isobel. As the children continued their squabbling, she pushed them into the cab, then paused on the step.

"Did you know Monty was murdered?" she asked Tim.

"I did," he said with a puff of smoke.

"What did the papers make of it?"

"They didn't make nothing of it," Tim said. "Reported it as a robbery."

She frowned at this. "The papers didn't tie his murder back to the agency?"

Tim shook his head.

"That means there's money involved here."

"It also narrows down A.J.'s list of enemies."

Alex Kingston being the foremost. But she had no proof, and she wouldn't jump to conclusions. "Have you made any progress on finding out who hired Monty?"

Tim showed her his gold teeth. "I learned Monty was hanging around the Oakland racetrack an awful lot. He racked up quite the debt."

"To whom?"

"Anyone who would loan him cash."

Isobel tapped a finger on the cab door.

"I'm becoming a regular there," Tim confided. "I'm sure I'll hear something soon."

Tim had a way of weaseling into social circles. She'd first thought he left things up to chance, but that wasn't the case. There was a method to the way he worked. A cunning one.

"Isobel, I have to *pee*," Sarah hissed.

Jin pointed to an alleyway. "You could go there."

Before the girls started arguing again, Isobel climbed in and Tim followed. The cab was soon rocking over cobblestones towards Ravenwood Manor.

"Now whose idea was this?" she asked.

The three children were stuffed together on one cab seat. Jin stared back in defiance, Tobias was sucking on hard candy, and Sarah was fidgeting with a handkerchief.

Isobel drilled her gaze into the weakest link. Sarah. But the girl didn't crack. All three kept quiet. She sat back, impressed. "I'm happy to see that you three aren't turning on each other. There's nothing I hate more than a snitch."

Sarah looked up, shocked. "I don't think you're supposed to encourage us, Isobel."

Isobel raised a shoulder. "You were trying to help Riot, weren't you? How could I possibly be upset? It was a good plan, whoever came up with it."

Tobias perked up. "I did!"

Jin closed her eyes, putting a hand to her forehead.

It took Tobias a full ten seconds to realize what he'd just done.

"Well, at least I know who the ringleader of this trio is," she said, leveling her gaze on the boy.

"Jin was gonna dynamite the station," Tobias muttered.

"I'm relieved you came up with an alternate plan, Tobias," she said dryly.

Tim scratched at his beard. "Did you see A.J.?"

"I did," Jin said.

Isobel leaned forward. "How is he?"

"He is well."

There was something about the way Jin said the last that raised Isobel's hackles. "What aren't you telling me?"

Jin thought a moment, her list likely a long one. "They put me in the men's yard."

Isobel nearly choked. "*What*?"

"The policeman said there were no segregated cells for Chinese women, so I might as well be with 'my kind.'"

Sarah gawked. "They put you in with the men?"

Jin shrugged. "I was able to get bahba into a safer cell."

"How d'you manage that?" Tim asked around his pipe.

"I started a fight. Then Atticus threw my dynamite into the mass of brawling men, and I pretended to be injured. Officer Doyle had him carry me out into a private cell."

"Dynamite?" Isobel asked.

Jin deflated. "It turned out to be a firecracker."

Isobel tried not to think of everything that could've happened, instead she focused on Tobias. "And what did you tell the police?"

Tobias popped another piece of candy into his mouth. "Everything."

15

WARRANT

A POUNDING KNOCK SHOOK ISOBEL FROM A RESTLESS SLEEP. She fought with the bed sheets to sit up, casting about in confusion. She was facing a wall and her pillows were at her feet. The bed was empty. Confusion gave way to reality—Riot was gone.

The next pounding knock shook sense back into her. It was coming from downstairs. "Police! Open the door!"

What the hell?

Isobel flew from the bed, snatched robe and revolver, and stepped out of her room into the hallway. She leaned over the railing to see a flood of nervous lodgers gathering at the entryway—some were already dressed and on their way to work, others still in robes.

Sarah came out of her room, looking perplexed, and Jin poked her head over the railing a floor above. "There is a large group of policemen and detectives surrounding the house," the girl shouted down. "One has a sledgehammer."

Isobel let out a curse that made Sarah's eyes bulge. By the time Isobel joined the other lodgers, they were parting ways for the landlady, Miss Lily. Unlike Isobel, she was an early riser, and she was impeccably dressed in high collar and crisp skirts, with her black hair pulled into a neat bun.

The two women shared a look. For a moment, Isobel thought the usually calm landlady would bolt, but Miss Lily gave a curt nod and steeled her shoulders. Isobel cinched her robe and pulled open the door.

Inspector Geary nearly knocked her in the face with his raised fist.

"Inspector," Isobel purred. "What a pleasant surprise. So nice of you to come in person." She shifted to look around his girth. "I see you brought guests."

As Jin had reported, several officers and non-uniformed men were present. She noted the graying bow-legged man from the day before. He raised his hat to her.

"We have a warrant to search your home."

Isobel held out her hand. Geary fished around his pockets and produced said warrant, signed by a Judge Carroll Cook.

"I hope you're familiar with the fourth amendment, Inspector. A search must be conducted in a *reasonable manner*."

"Step aside," Geary ordered.

The inspector tried to push past her, but she held her ground. "The warrant is for the property of Atticus Riot. This is Ravenwood estate."

"He's the estate holder."

"It's a boardinghouse, Inspector. Residents rent rooms here. Their rooms are private property, and you don't have a warrant for every lodger here. By law you can search common areas, along with my husband's rooms. No more."

"Only someone who's hiding something would pull that one."

"I don't want your men stomping through our lodgers' rooms making a nuisance of themselves."

"We'll search where we like."

He pushed her aside, and she called to his back. "Yes, but if you find something that isn't in Riot's rooms, then it won't hold up in court."

Geary swung to face her. "Watch your mouth or I'll arrest you for obstruction of justice."

"I don't think you know the meaning of that word." Her voice dripped venom, and the closest man to her hastily ducked his head and hurried past.

Tim appeared from around the lane. He was puffing away on a pipe, chatting up a policeman, but he had an eye on her in the doorway. "Some of you fellows can search the stables," he called.

Geary jerked his head, and a few officers peeled away. "I want all the residents corralled into the backyard. That clear?"

Isobel led the way up to her and Riot's room, and stood by watching as the police overturned their belongings like a bunch of hoodlums. They rifled through books and tossed them on the floor, flipped over the mattress and slit it open to pull out the stuffing, and threw the contents of their wardrobes on the floor.

A pair of arms came around her waist, and for the first time, she noticed her daughters. Sarah was hugging her. "I can barely watch."

Jin looked set to commit murder.

"You both head to the yard." Isobel tried to peel the girl off, but Sarah was glued on tight, and Jin had a stubborn tilt to her chin, with her hand in a pocket.

Oh hell.

Isobel touched Jin's arm. "Whatever you're planning, *don't do it*," she warned.

The girl ground her teeth together.

The police took a rifle from Riot's wardrobe, along with a box of ammunition and the box that held the revolver Jin had used to shoot a hatchet man.

Footsteps pounded all over the house, as the police turned over every inch of Ravenwood Manor. Isobel felt helpless. There was nothing she could do to stop it, except telephone Farnon. Again. The attorney would retire early at this rate. But she doubted even he could do anything about a signed warrant.

"Come on. Let's wait outside."

A policeman pushed open Sarah's door, and the girl darted into the room with a cry of protest. "Get your dirty hands off my sketchpad!"

Isobel hurried over in time to see Sarah trying to grab her sketchpad from the officer's hands.

"Let him look through it," Isobel said.

The officer flipped through the pages, upended it, and gave it a shake, then handed it over.

Before one of her daughters attacked an officer, Isobel ushered them downstairs, where they joined the other lodgers congregating in the yard. The group was staring sullenly at the house, listening to the rampage.

"Of all the indecencies!" Mrs. Clarke said.

"I'm giving my notice immediately," Mr. Dougal said to Miss Lily. "I expect a full refund of any damages incurred."

Isobel tried not to roll her eyes.

Mr. Hughes fidgeted, looking from one officer to the next, and on the verge of bolting.

"This is hardly Mrs. White's fault," Amelia Lane said, keeping a firm hand on her son. "You heard Mrs. Riot, the police aren't allowed to search our rooms."

"American police officers are brutes," Mr. Knight drawled.

A wiry man who Isobel took to be the graying man's partner, was walking around the group, eyeing them. His gaze lingered on the White family. Only Grimm wasn't here. Isobel was careful not to glance at the stable in case he was hiding there.

Miss Lily stood with protective arms around Maddie and Tobias. Standing stiffly, ashen, she closed her eyes briefly, in what must've been a silent prayer.

Miss Dupree interrupted the wiry man's scrutiny. "How long will this take?" Her question, or more likely the woman, distracted the man. Annie Dupree had a voice that seemed to bypass a man's ears and go straight between his legs. The ex-governess turned prostitute, and now their children's schoolteacher, wasn't dressed. She lived a more nocturnal life, and her thin robe barely concealed a shapely body.

The woman fascinated Isobel. She also didn't trust her.

"As long as it takes, ma'am."

Miss Dupree sidled up closer to the wiry man, who licked his lips, and shifted. "I didn't get your name," she purred, fingering the lapel of his coat.

"Sam Batten."

The rest of the conversation fell away when a graveled voice spoke at her side. "I'm sure this is distressing to you, Mrs. Riot."

Isobel looked up, surprised to find the tall graying man with the handlebar mustache standing beside her. His Stetson was pulled low on his head.

She arched a brow. "You think?"

"It is, no doubt."

"And you are?"

"Liam Taft. Pinkerton operative."

Liam extended a hand, but she didn't shake it. "And why are you here, Mr. Taft?"

"We're investigating a murder."

"The papers said it was a robbery."

"We think otherwise."

"We, as in the San Francisco Police department, or the Pinkertons?"

"My agency is still gathering evidence. Inspector Geary thinks he's found his man."

It could be a trap. Play friendly, get her talking, and see if she slips up. Pinkerton operatives were skilled interrogators. But for once Isobel had absolutely nothing to hide.

She turned back to the house. "My only worry is that the inspector will plant evidence."

Liam smoothed his mustache in consideration.

"Geary doesn't care for my husband."

"I noticed," Liam admitted. "Why is that?"

Isobel pondered the question. "Riot doesn't take bribes."

"Our operatives don't either."

She snorted. "No, but they take money to kill men."

"Why do you say that?"

"Monty hired on with your agency. Then he hired some lowlifes to blow up our agency. He used to work for us."

"So I've heard. Any idea why he left?"

"He didn't much care for women detectives. I take it your branch here has none."

"So your feminine presence drove Monty to put a hit out on his old boss?"

Isobel lifted a shoulder. "I'm told I have that effect. Now why are you really here, Mr. Taft? I've heard your operatives aren't daft. The police have had Riot in custody for nearly twenty-four hours. Time enough to confirm his whereabouts."

"We're not the police. Only assisting them."

She met the man's gaze. Was this the Pinkerton that the bartender at the Morgue had seen with Monty? The agency worked as railroad police. The railways were owned by powerful men who'd kept Alex Kingston, her ex-husband, as their attorney on retainer.

Isobel took a risk and dove in headfirst. "I'd like to see where Monty was killed, Mr. Taft."

"Why is that?"

"Monty hired some men to kill my husband. We think he was acting as a middleman. I suspect whoever hired Monty killed him to muddy the trail. If we find out who wants Riot dead, we'll find your operative's assassin."

A crinkling of Liam's sun worn skin made his eyes nearly disappear. It wasn't a smile. "I'll see what I can do."

16

A NOSE FOR NEWS

CAMERON FRY DISEMBARKED AT THE SAUSALITO FERRY terminal with Mrs. Riot's words echoing between his ears.

"I'm sure the reporters of this fine city will verify his whereabouts quicker than your detectives, Inspector."

He felt like a knight-errant serving a king. Or maybe a queen. Trying to win the hand of the princess. Maybe he'd read too many stories. But wasn't that what Mr. Darcy did to win over Miss Bennett? Gads, that book Mr. Riot had made him read... He'd read it again since.

And just like Miss Bennett had glared daggers at Mr. Darcy, so did Miss Sarah. Surely that was a good sign? Either way, getting an exclusive from that family was good as gold. And he owed it to Mr. Riot.

Miss Sarah had noticed him. That soft, drawling voice of hers made his stomach twist into knots. He felt like he was floating. And her despair cut right to his heart. Miss Sarah's adopted father was in danger. Cameron had to do something.

And if he could prove Mr. Riot's innocence, then maybe he'd win Sarah's adoration.

Not to mention the exclusive would make him a tidy sum.

His editor had steered him right. *A man is only as good as his word* and *Never sacrifice integrity for a story.* The advice wasn't something one heard often in the reporting business, but Cameron Fry had taken it to heart.

Cameron stopped to check his watch. The ride had taken fifty minutes, but the Riot family hadn't taken a ferry. They'd sailed across the bay. He'd have to check the tide charts and weather, to find the likeliest time of departure.

Cameron surveyed the area. So where would they have docked with a private sailboat?

It didn't take long to figure that out. Richardson's Bay was full of pleasure yachts, fishing boats, and houseboats. It took Cameron all of two hours to locate a dockmaster who verified the *Pagan Lady* had moored in the bay.

"I remember it. A fine cutter, it is. It was me they paid to keep an eye on it. 'Course I did, it being docked right over there next to my boat."

His boat was a square barge that looked like someone had stuck a house on top.

"Did the cutter remain docked the entire time?"

"Yes. For over a week. It didn't move."

Cameron took down the man's name.

"What's all this about?"

"It's for a story."

"'Bout who?"

"The Riots. Atticus Riot was accused of a crime. I'm trying to prove his innocence." Cameron knew the Riot family was popular with residents of the city. Most of them, anyway. San Francisco loved a good rebel.

The dockmaster snorted. "You mean the Amsels."

"Ah, no. The Riots."

The man shook his head. "That girl is an Amsel. Don't matter who she married. Always will be from our bay."

"Yes, sir."

"She's trouble, too." He gave a fond chuckle.

"Do you know where the family headed after they moored?"

The man glared with his remaining eye. "Are you *sure* you're looking to prove her husband innocent?"

"Yes."

"'Cause if you're lying to me…"

"I'm not, sir. I love their daughter," he blurted out that last without thinking, and then stammered, feeling his cheeks heat.

The old man chuckled, then slowly shuffled back to his houseboat, muttering under his breath. Cameron thought that would be the end of it, but the old man yelled out of his cabin. "Stay put, young fellow."

Cameron waited, listening to the lap of water, and wondering if he could still make it to Willow Camp that day.

The man soon emerged with a newspaper, which he slapped against Cameron's chest. *The Sausalito News.* "That's where they were. Don't know how they'd be getting back to the city when they done all this."

Cameron took the paper, read the headlines, and gaped.

THE FIVE MEN IN THE CELL WERE AS SOUR AS COULD BE. THEY were a rough sort, but then robbers usually were, weren't they?

"So you watched the family for some days before deciding to rob them?" Cameron asked through the bars.

"No, we didn't try and rob them. That's what *they* claim."

"Right, well. Before the children caught you…"

"It wasn't no children who seen us. It was that gunslinger fellow." All five members of the gang nodded as one.

"And the woman?" Cameron tossed in for good measure.

"No woman caught us, either."

"Right." Cameron scribbled in his notepad. "Look here.

I'm writing a story on the unscrupulous nature of that family. They're a menace to proper society. If I'm able to tell the truth on just how improper they are..." Cameron lifted his shoulders. "It may look bad for the lot of them and make you lot look like saints."

Making this lot look like saints would take the devil himself, Cameron thought.

The gang pondered this. Cameron could see the light getting brighter in their eyes. Most criminals wanted their time in the spotlight, and Cameron wagered these men were no different. They didn't strike Cameron as the calculating kind, either. Those kinds were all holed up on Nob Hill.

"Come on, you lot," the sheriff said. "You were caught red-handed with stolen and illegal goods. A 'not guilty' plea won't help your case."

"Is that family famous or something?" one thug asked.

"Very," Cameron assured.

The men grumbled, scratched their chins, and exchanged darting glances until a fellow with a missing ear shrugged.

"We first saw them walking through the big trees."

"What day was that?" Cameron asked.

The men glanced at each other in thought. "I guess that would be about Sunday we first saw them."

"The fourth," the sheriff supplied.

"Can you describe the family?"

"A Chinese boy, a young lady, and a negro boy. Then some woman in trousers dressed for rough living. And a black-haired fellow that had a little pack. He looked like he was having a hard time of it. So we thought they was easy pickins."

"The man. Can you describe him?"

One-ear shrugged again. "Mostly black beard. A bit gray. Looked... winded. Bruises on his face. Not our doing."

"He had spectacles, and a white streak in his hair." A

hulking fellow traced a line along his temple. "We was all laughing 'cause his woman had the bigger pack."

The memory produced another round of laughter, but then they all sobered when they remembered what happened next.

"So you jumped them right then and there?" Cameron asked.

"Nah," One-ear said. "They was camping in the woods. Then walking a bit towards Willow Camp, taking their time on account of the black-haired fellow. So we decided to waylay them at a spot on the trail."

"What day was that?"

"Tuesday, maybe," One-ear offered.

"Are you sure?"

"Unless the days changed on us," Hulk said.

"And the black-haired man... he was with them?"

"Don't say no more," a hairy fellow warned.

One-ear ignored him, rubbing a shoulder. "Well, that fellow shot me."

In fact the entire gang looked worse for wear.

"Look," Cameron said. "There's no shame in it. That fellow is a famous gunfighter. How were you to know?"

Hairy perked up. "Really?"

"Someone might feature you in a dime novel."

But no one budged. The gang pressed their lips together, unwilling to say anything regarding their capture.

It was the sheriff who answered. "After the Riots fought this lot off, Mrs. Riot and her daughter came and got me. Then me and Mr. Riot tracked them back to their hideout." The sheriff smiled. "Turns out these fellows were causing trouble at Willow Camp."

"What day was that?"

The sheriff consulted a notepad. "The sixth of November."

Cameron scribbled the last. "Would you be willing to testify to the fact you saw Mr. Riot in the woods on that day?" he asked the sheriff.

"Why wouldn't I? He's a cool hand, I'll say that. Saved me a heap of trouble."

Cameron couldn't stop the grin spreading over his face. This would make a laughing stock out of the police department.

Inspector Geary hadn't even tried to verify Mr. Riot's whereabouts. He just arrested him. But his grin soon faded— Cameron knew enough about San Francisco to sense when strings were being pulled.

17

REFLECTIONS

ONE POSITIVE THING ABOUT JAIL TIME WAS IT AFFORDED REST. And contemplation. Riot would've preferred a book. But truth be told, his head was thankful for the lack of stimulation. So he lay on his bunk, toying with his overgrown beard and staring at the ceiling.

He would've liked a proper trim and bath before being tossed in a cell. But such was life.

At least Geary had released Jin and Sarah. Mr. Farnon had assured him of that, and so far Riot remained in a private cell. He likely had Inspector Coleman to thank for that, along with a steady rotation of loyal guards.

All things considered, his situation wasn't that bad. Now he just needed to figure out who wanted him dead.

The squeal of a cell door startled him awake. He must've dozed off again. Riot sat up to find Liam Taft standing inside the cell. Doyle was no longer in the hallway.

"Your bodyguard is still outside," Liam said. "I've just asked him to give us some privacy to talk."

"I'd offer a chair…" Riot gestured at the sparse cell: a hard bunk, brick walls, a small barred window, and a steel toilet that probably started life as a bucket.

Liam didn't close the cell door. Maybe he was hoping Riot would make a run for it. Liam reached into his breast pocket and pulled out a pair of spectacles. "They're a little bent," he said, tossing them over.

"Thank you," Riot said with feeling. He quickly threaded the wire over his ears, and the world sharpened once again. It was currently a dingy world. "I see you got the role of the nice detective."

Liam chuckled, and reached under his coat for a tobacco pouch, then went about rolling a cigarette. "I don't play nice."

The man was unhurried in his movements, with no inclination to fill the silence. He offered the cigarette to Riot, who shook his head. Liam scratched a match across the brick, and cupped his hand to light the end. "I hoped we might talk," he murmured.

Riot spread his hands. "I find myself with little else to do."

"You don't seem worried."

"I have the utmost faith in the justice system."

"Do you?"

"Don't you?" Riot asked.

"I suppose I should. I'd be in the wrong business otherwise."

"Or the right business," Riot said.

Liam narrowed his eyes, the cigarette hanging from his cracked lips. "Who do you think killed Montgomery Johnson?"

"Whoever wants me dead."

"Could this person be targeting your agents, too?"

"Maybe," Riot acknowledged.

"Could your wife be in danger?"

"She likely is."

"And that doesn't concern you?"

Riot held the man's eyes with his own. "It concerns me."

"You mentioned Monty tried to kill you."

"He paid a group of men to attack the agency. They tossed dynamite in through the windows."

"You have proof?"

"He didn't deny it when I confronted him at The Den."

"Was that right before you shot him?"

"That was right before he beat me to a pulp."

"The fellow at the club said you took a cheap shot with a gentleman's stick."

A pang of regret clutched his heart. Riot had lost control. He'd given in to impulse and nearly gotten himself killed. Only that wasn't quite true. He'd lost control, but regained it before pummeling Monty into unconsciousness. And that act of restraint had cost him the fight. "We weren't sparring," Riot said simply.

"And yet he didn't kill you."

"No, he left me for dead in a gutter. The only reason I'm still here is because my wife found me in time."

"Remarkable woman. I'm married too. And I can tell you right now, I'd shoot any man who threatened my wife," Liam admitted.

It was true, Riot knew, from looking into his eyes. But it was an odd thing to admit. Unless, of course, one was playing nice to get a confession.

"Monty was only a middleman," Riot said. "I want the name of the man who hired him, and now that Monty is dead, I'll have a harder time finding it."

Liam flicked ash out the bars. "Especially from a cell."

"Even harder if I hang."

"So let me get this straight. Your ex-agent was seen with a Pinkerton—"

"He hadn't quit yet," Riot clarified. "Were you that man?"

"I'm a Pinkerton," Liam said. "And I can't tell you all the men I've been seen with. Can you?"

He had a point.

"Did Monty tell you he joined up with the Pinkertons?"

"He didn't deny it," Riot said.

"You used to be a Pinkerton operative."

"On occasion."

"Why'd you quit?"

"I'm sure you have an entire file on me and Ravenwood."

"Your partner."

Riot nodded. The words stung, but he resisted the urge to correct the man: former partner. That would open up a line of questioning he wasn't keen on reliving. Was that what this was about? Riot's wrongful vengeance for Ravenwood's murder? Now, those men he *had* gunned down.

"You don't have a deck of cards by chance?" Riot asked.

"Cards?"

"I wasn't allowed to pack a bag."

"That's right, you're a gambler."

"Was."

"Getting twitchy?" Liam asked.

"Shuffling helps me think," Riot said.

Liam called back to his partner, who brought a tattered deck from a guard room. The cards were a ruin but they'd do. He started shuffling, acquainting himself with this new deck.

"Ravenwood and I quit," Riot said without prompt, "because we didn't like the direction the Pinkertons were headed. When you cast your lot with rich and powerful men, it's easy to lose sight of your own morals. I still can't stomach strikebreaking."

"A lot of those miners, like the Molly Maguires, turned to violence," Liam said.

The cards flew in Riot's hands, steady and rhythmic, a blur of motion that soothed his mind. "When you corner a man and his family, all he has left is violence. Treat a man fairly and he won't bite back."

Smoke wafted from Liam's forgotten cigarette, a trail of ash fluttering to the floor. "Is that how you see it?"

"I saw it as men trying to feed their families," Riot said. "The mine owners targeted the unions, cut workers' wages, forced them to work longer hours, added another day, and made them pay for hovels with walls so thin ink froze in winter. Rich men squeezed those miners till they cracked—all to fill their overstuffed pockets."

Liam flicked ash away and took a long drag. "Not everyone sees it that way."

"Do you?"

"What I think doesn't matter," Liam said. "Is that the only reason you left?"

Riot turned over a card—the ace of diamonds. "You know what happened, Mr. Taft."

"I prefer firsthand reports to secondhand."

Riot shuffled for a time, then squared his deck. "I reported operatives who were taking bribes and extorting businesses. Only the superintendent didn't believe me."

"The report said you had no proof."

"I had my ears. Ravenwood had his instincts. I wrote a report. It wasn't looked on favorably. Those men remained; we left."

"But they were eventually fired after a *proper* investigation."

Riot ran a finger over the edges of the deck, then smiled at its secret.

"What is it?" Liam asked.

"There's a cheat in the guardroom. It's a marked deck." To demonstrate, Riot pulled out the ace of spades from the stack.

"I don't think that's what you were smiling about."

"Ravenwood once called the Pinkerton agency a 'ponderous one-eyed giant prone to tripping over its own feet.' Or something to that effect. The cogs of investigation moved too slowly for his liking."

"And yours."

Riot didn't deny it.

"I read Ravenwood's file," Liam admitted. "It said he was intolerably arrogant, prone to wild leaps of deduction, impatient, and impossible to handle."

"All of that was true."

"You're not going to ask what your file said?"

"I know what my file says."

"Humor me."

"A wild card. Unrestrained, brash, rebellious to authority. Does not follow orders, resistant to procedure, and… what am I missing?"

Liam smiled around his cigarette. "Excellent in a gunfight. Expert tracker. Remarkable memory. Ambidextrous—I had to look that word up. And you had a reputation."

"Most men do."

"I quote: 'If it's dead or alive, Atticus Riot will bring a suspect back dead.'"

"Most men put up a fight when cornered."

"According to your file, you cornered quite a few criminals. The official count in the few years you worked for Pinkertons was close to twenty men."

Riot didn't say anything. He wagered the count was much higher.

"Does that trouble your conscience?" Liam asked.

"I don't much care for bullies. Of any sort."

"Have you ever wondered if you're the bully?" It was said in a reflective tone, as if Liam was asking himself that question.

"Not while I was with Ravenwood Agency."

"Things changed when Allan Pinkerton died," Liam admitted.

"Things changed when his detective agency was on the verge of bankruptcy," Riot corrected. "Allan Pinkerton needed money, so he cozied up to railroad barons and mining magnates."

"I hear your agency is in the same situation."

There was no denying it. "What's this really about, Mr. Taft?"

"Just thought I'd chat. It can get tedious in here."

Liam left, and Riot sat and shuffled and thought. He had little else to do.

18

THE TROUBLE WITH TWINS

ISOBEL STOPPED ABRUPTLY AND STARED, EQUAL PARTS APPALLED and impressed. The last time she'd seen the office, nearly a month ago, the brick had been scorched by dynamite and the windows boarded up. The door hadn't even been functioning.

Now the door was repaired, painted black with gold accents, and the brick whitewashed. It looked like someone had transplanted a residence from Belgravia to the Barbary Coast. The building was an oddity on the otherwise dingy street.

Lotario usually had a better sense of aesthetics. She paused at that thought. Well, maybe not. He leaned towards the flamboyant.

The glass windows were tinted and gleaming, with gold letters swirling across the front: Ravenwood Detective Agency.

How much had this cost her twin?

"Dear God," she said to the man at her side.

Tim chuckled. "If A.J. survives jail, his heart will surely stop when he sees this."

"Did you approve?" she asked in shock.

Tim gave a puff of his pipe. "I sold my share. It's none of my business anymore."

"How much did you sell it for?"

"A dollar."

"You're either insane or brilliant. I suppose time will tell."

"Don't have much faith in your twin?"

"Oh, I have faith. It's just that Ari has a short attention span and is prone to extravagance." She gestured at the opulent building.

A bell jingled as Isobel stepped into a transformed entryway. Sleek wood paneling, papered walls, electric lights, and leather armchairs. For a moment, she feared Lotario had turned the office into a brothel. Or perhaps a gambling den, she thought, eyeing the reinforced doors branching off the small lobby.

Men and women sat in chairs. All colors and shapes, and varying degrees of grooming.

A chipper girl smiled from behind a bank-style counter. "Good afternoon, Mr. Tim. Mrs. Riot. May I take your hat and coat?"

Isobel stared at her. The girl couldn't be over sixteen. "It's Miss Amsel. Have we met?" Isobel asked.

The girl thrust her hand over the counter. "Daisy Reed. And we have not, but you look enough like Mr. Amsel that I put two and two together."

Hammering was coming from the top floor and all sides. What else was Lotario building?

"He's reinforcing the walls with plated iron," Tim whispered. "Some doors, too."

Lotario certainly wasn't taking any chances.

"Are all these people here to hire us for cases?" Isobel asked.

"No, ma'am. They're interviewing for positions."

Isobel swallowed down her worry. "Where is my twin?"

"He's interviewing an applicant now." One look at Isobel's

face, and Daisy swallowed and gestured to a side door. "The last door down the hallway, Miss Amsel."

Isobel walked through the door into an unfinished hallway that was lined with more doors. The saloon was unrecognizable. Had the old agency been large enough for all this? Isobel poked her head through one of the doors into what appeared to be an interviewing room. Comfortable chairs (velvet, good God) and a small tea table.

A telephone rang from the depths of the office. Isobel located the source in a room with no door. Several desks and a wall of filing cabinets sat in the room, along with Matthew Smith, who was hunched over a desk writing a report.

The man who answered the telephone had his boots on a desk and sported a curling mustache. He spoke with a British accent mixed with a hint of Caribbean and wore a white summer suit that complimented his light brown skin.

Matthew quickly shot to his feet. "Mrs… Miss Isobel."

"What do you think of all this?"

"I welcome the help." It was true. Matthew looked run ragged. After Riot's fight with Monty and the Ella Spencer case, she and Riot had left to recover without a thought for the agency. "How is Mr. Riot?" he asked.

"Hopefully he's getting plenty of rest."

Isobel left Tim with Matthew to confront her twin. She found him in the door at the end of the hallway. Lotario Amsel was dressed like a businessman. But he couldn't resist a little flair. His tie and handkerchief were a startling electric blue that contrasted with his somber suit. His blondish hair was slicked back, and he sported a pair of pince-nez perched primly on his nose.

A short, weasel-like man stood with a cap in hand. He was staring at a garish woman wrapped in scarves, who appeared to think she was on some sort of display pedestal. A rat was perched on her shoulder.

"Well, if it isn't the diva herself. Gone and run off again 'ave you," Miss Lucky Off snickered.

"I'm back to torment you, crone."

The woman cackled and flipped her grey hair.

"And interrupt our interview," Lotario said.

"Don't mind me." Isobel dragged a chair beside the desk and sat to study the weasel-like man.

Lotario leaned over to stage whisper in her ear. "He's applying to be a detective."

Isobel bit back a comment. The hiring should be left up to Riot, not her twin. But now wasn't the time to argue, and that was precisely the reason he'd chosen to tell her now. She'd give him hell as soon as everyone left.

"Excuse the interruption, Mr. Thatcher. Proceed." Lotario waved a languid hand.

"Yes, sir." Thatcher turned his cap over in his hands as he studied Miss Off, who acted like she was modeling the latest Parisian fashion instead of a plethora of scarves and frills. Isobel thought the woman must be aiming for a gypsy fortuneteller at a traveling circus.

"I'd put her age at... seventy."

Miss Off glared.

"And at about five feet four inches. Maybe a weight of two hundred pounds."

"You're a *bastard*, that's what you are. Blind as a bat, too," Miss Off seethed.

"Profession..." Thatcher hesitated at this. "Spiritualist. Heavy into drink. Probably gin. And smokes like a train engine."

Miss Off crossed her arms, which exposed an alarming amount of cleavage.

"Anything else?" Lotario asked.

"She's disagreeable."

"Thank you. That will be all for now. Make sure you leave

your contact information with Miss Reed." Lotario gave the man a dismissive wave. "Miss Off will escort you out."

"Oh, I'll lead him right to hell, I will. Saying such things about me." Miss Off grabbed the man's arm and started a proper tongue lashing as they left down the hallway.

Isobel shut the door on her tirade, and Lotario picked up a receiver. "Daisy, please hold the next interview."

Isobel raised a brow. "An interoffice telephone?"

Lotario leaned back, massaging his temples. "Not you too, Bel. I've been inundated with people stating the painfully obvious all morning."

"I wasn't stating the obvious; I was making a subtle jab at your innate laziness."

He looked pleased by her insult. She perched on the side of the desk to better look down at her twin.

"Yelling down a hallway is so unprofessional—" He stopped at the look in her eyes, the edge of his lip twitching upwards. "I feel a storm coming."

"You haven't run any of this by Riot," she bit out.

"I'm part owner."

"Thirty percent."

"Actually, Tim put you in debt. I paid off the agency's debt, so until Atticus pays me back... I own it. I'm your boss, Bel. And I don't have to put up with your disapproval."

"It's not *just* that. You're stretching yourself financially, Ari. How can you afford to hire all these people?"

Lotario clucked his tongue. "You have no sense for business, and Atticus has even less. One must spend money to make money. It's the most basic rule of business. Atticus and Tim treated this agency like an afterthought and a lending bank. It's a small wonder Monty didn't try to kill him sooner. Atticus was hemorrhaging funds."

"And you aren't?"

"I'm *investing*."

"You've taken over Riot's business. This is his life."

"*You* are his life."

Isobel faltered. She couldn't argue with that, and her twin knew it. "Yes, but he'll want to interview any new agents himself."

"Atticus hired someone who tried to *kill* him," Lotario pointed out.

"Ravenwood hired Monty."

"And Atticus kept him on, even after the man constantly insulted you. I will have none of that."

"I would've been furious if he'd fired Monty because of me."

"Yes, well. Now I've taken that little issue out of both your hands." Lotario spread his own hands. "I can't wait for his leisure, Bel. Atticus shouldn't have gotten himself beaten to a pulp and charged with murder."

"That is unfair."

Lotario mirrored the look on her face. "Do you have any issues with the people I've hired?"

She was on the verge of saying Miss Off, but caught herself. Riot had hired the crazed woman.

"I don't know any of them, but that receptionist you have in the waiting room looks like she's sixteen. We deal with rough sorts, Ari. I certainly wouldn't allow Sarah to work here."

"What about Jin?"

"No," she blurted. Jin would likely stab someone on her first day, but Isobel kept that part to herself.

"I'm disappointed in you."

"Why?" she asked suspiciously.

"Daisy is our age."

"I don't think so."

"All right, perhaps a few years younger," he admitted. "She was the resident virgin at a brothel, and she's looking to start a new life. If you think she can't handle herself around rough men, you're sorely mistaken."

"Are all your hires ex-prostitutes?"

"If you're referring to Garrett... no. But he could sell a flask of paraffin to a man in a burning house. *Never* buy anything from him."

"Riot likes to know the people he works with."

"Like Monty?" He batted his lashes. But when she only gave him a blank look in return, he explained. "Prostitutes are observant by nature. We have to be to survive. And I'm only hiring people I trust. I would think you'd have more faith in me."

"I do, Ari. It's only this is Riot's agency, and he has no say in how it's being run."

Lotario steepled his fingers to study her over their tips. "Why do you insist on calling Atticus by his surname? It's so... stuffy."

"Are you familiar with the definition of riot when it pertains to 'a riot of color'?"

"Yes. A *impressively large or varied display of something*," Lotario recited.

Isobel glanced at her fingernails.

"Must you gloat, sister dear?"

"I know how it irritates you."

Lotario leaned forward and took her hands in his. "Don't worry about the money. I have my accountant helping, too. She used to run a profitable brothel. And the press that you and Atticus generate has tripled our caseload."

"With only Tim and Matt to handle the cases? No wonder Matt looks exhausted."

Lotario got an impish look in his eyes. She knew that was never a good thing. "And me."

"You've been investigating cases?"

Lotario inclined his chin towards a stack of files. "All solved."

She eyed the caseload. "Impossible."

"Have you ever heard of an armchair detective?"

"You solved them all. From here?"

Lotario smiled like a cat. "It's been quite diverting."

Isobel shot to her feet. "You can't solve crimes from an *office*, Ari. What if your deductions are wrong?"

"They're not," he challenged.

A small growl rose from the back of her throat.

"You and I have played at it often enough," he purred. "I'm only putting my talents to practical use. Besides, Matthew tells me you did the same on one of his cases. He's delicious, by the way. Do you think he prefers men?"

Isobel would not be diverted. "Yes, but then Matt confirmed my deductions."

"Was that a yes to my question?"

"*No*."

"No, he doesn't?"

"Ari," she warned.

"You're never any fun anymore."

"My husband is in jail."

"He's being held on suspicion. It's probably the best place for him. And don't worry, I'm having Matt confirm my deductions. While he's not the brightest, he is sweet. And handsome in a footballer sort of way."

Her hackles lowered, somewhat. "How are the interviews going?"

"Horrid. Most wouldn't spot a wolf disguised as a sheep in their own bedroom."

"I may have some names."

"Do write them down."

"I will, and then I need to borrow Matt."

"Atticus hasn't been in jail for two days yet, and you're already casting your net for another catch?"

"I'm liable to hit you, Ari."

"Oh, but I make such a racket."

"And you'll sulk for a month."

"Or I'll just decorate the agency like a bordello."

"It's nearly there."

Lotario pretended to gape. "How could you possibly guess my backup plan if the detective agency should fail?"

She glared. Mainly because she wasn't entirely sure her twin was joking. "At least this would be a high-class brothel. I was at the *Nymphia* on Wednesday."

Lotario grimaced. "Appalling. The ladies are treated like cattle, and the decor is a disaster."

Isobel wasn't entirely sure which was worse in her twin's mind.

He narrowed his eyes "Your husband was arrested on suspicion of murder and you went to a cow-yard? Are you feeling well? Aside from irritable."

"The police came to the house with a warrant yesterday. I don't want to think about the state of our rooms."

"Did they find anything?"

"They took every firearm in the house and left a disaster."

"Farnon telephoned me," Lotario said with a sigh. "*And* he's reporting to mother."

"And to you, apparently," she said.

"He told me you aren't to go near the investigation."

"Yes, I know. Farnon made sure to keep me occupied with legal matters after the raid. What else am I supposed to do?"

"Clean your room?" he quipped. "Where are you taking my sweet detective?"

"I'm headed to the city morgue. I need to ask Sims if he's found out anything about Monty."

"We just went over this—you're supposed to stay away from the investigation."

"Asking Sims about a body is not interfering."

"Why did you go to the Nymphia?"

"You're trying to distract me."

"I'm trying to keep my nosy twin away from an investigation that could put my delicious brother-in-law in a hangman's noose."

Isobel felt sick at the thought.

Lotario placed a hand over hers. "There are other fish in the sea. If it comes to that."

She shot him a glare, but let herself be distracted.

"I played consulting detective to the police for an afternoon. A man was found dead in the Nymphia during a raid."

"*Do tell.*"

Before she could start, one of the telephones on the desk rang. The interoffice one. Lotario picked it up. "Yes?"

Isobel rolled her eyes. She preferred Miss Off's crass 'Ahoy there!'

Lotario's brows shot up. "I *see*. Escort the lady to the interview room. Miss Amsel will be there momentarily."

"*I will?*" Isobel asked when he clicked the lever.

"You've been requested."

"Someone likely lost their dog," she snapped.

Lotario waggled his brows. "But did it bark in the night?"

"I'm not being dragged into another case while Riot is in jail for murder." Isobel started gathering her things.

"A pity." Lotario rested his chin on a hand. "A mysterious woman draped in a mourning veil has asked to speak with you. She claims you came highly recommended by an Inspector Coleman."

Isobel paused, her mind racing with possibilities. Damn her curiosity.

19

WOMAN IN BLACK

ANNOYED WITH HERSELF, ISOBEL STALKED DOWN THE HALLWAY and into the interview room without ceremony. It was just as Lotario had said. A figure draped in mourning black stood in the room, ignoring the chair as well as the tea and cakes. Slim hands worried at a white silk handkerchief.

White, pristine, with a familiar black border.

Isobel stepped to the side to let Lotario enter. The sight of her twin caught the woman's attention. "*Lotario?*" she asked in surprise.

Lotario paused, his hand still on the doorknob. He hadn't counted on someone knowing his name. When the woman lifted her veil, he paled.

"Katherine," he said, closing the door with a click.

A large, black hat perched on her Gibson Girl-styled hair. She had golden brown hair, green eyes, and ivory skin. Her pigeon silhouette was in high fashion: bosom pushed out, back arched—molded by the popular corsets that forced the body into that shape. Her fur-trimmed dress wasn't store-bought, nor was anything on her person, including a large diamond brooch.

"What on earth are you doing here, Lotario? I hardly recognized you."

Lotario gave a flippant gesture. "I like to dabble here and there. Gentleman detectives are all the rage in London."

"I see." She put a hand to her breast. "I find this oddly reassuring. And you must be Mrs. Riot."

"Miss Amsel will do."

Katherine looked at the twins. They were dressed differently enough that their resemblance was not quite so striking. Lotario had his platform boots on as well (he did like to be tall) so they seemed more brother and sister than near-identical twins. The two didn't like people to know how much alike they were in appearance.

Lotario stepped forward to take her hands. "What has happened, Katherine?" he asked.

Katherine gave a weak smile, then looked to Isobel. "Your brother knows… *knew* my Donny—" She lost her composure then, and Isobel quickly shoved the woman into a chair before she could faint.

Isobel glanced at her twin in question. But all the blood had drained from his face. She shoved him into a chair, too. "What do you mean, knew?" Lotario whispered.

"You haven't heard?"

Lotario had a white-knuckled grip on the armrests.

"Of course you haven't. I don't think the Fuzzy Bunch knows yet." Katherine met Lotario's gaze. "Donny is dead."

"*How?*"

Isobel could feel the single word tearing from her heart as if her twin's shock were her own.

"I was told he died in bed, at home. His father found him Wednesday morning."

Isobel glanced at Lotario. His face was austere, but his hands trembled. "I'm getting half a story here, Miss Hayes. What was Donny's name? And what was he to you?"

"Oh," she said, dabbing at her eyes. "I thought the entire city knew."

"I've been... occupied."

"Donny and I were engaged to be married. I was to be Dominic Noble's wife."

Isobel arched a brow. Something was very wrong here. But after the inspector's warning about secrecy, she was careful not to give anything away. "And Inspector Coleman recommended *me* to you?" Isobel asked.

"Yes."

"You say Dominic died at home?" Isobel knew very well he had not, but she wasn't sure how much Miss Hayes knew, nor why the deceased's fiancée was being kept in the dark. "If so, why do you require my services?"

Katherine glanced at Lotario. "This mustn't leave the room. I don't want rumors circulating at the clubs."

"It won't," Lotario assured.

"You were one of his dearest friends. I... Something isn't right about the circumstance of his death. The family's physician claims his heart gave out. But his father won't let me see his body, and has dismissed the police. I went to the Detective Inspector myself and he directed me to you."

Ah, Isobel thought. The Noble family was one of the richest and most powerful families in San Francisco, which meant they had the Chief of Police in their pocket. That also meant Inspector Coleman's hands were tied and he was not happy about it.

"I want to know the truth, Miss Amsel," she implored. "I think... I think his father may have killed him."

Isobel found herself in a precarious situation. On one hand, she'd sworn discretion to Inspector Coleman. On the other hand, he'd sent Katherine to her.

Was he also sending a message?

She glanced at her twin. His face was pale, his lips a tight line. He was silent, which wasn't like him at all. Dominic Noble meant something to him. But what? Until she got the full story, she decided to tread carefully.

She wasn't about to tell Miss Hayes that her fiancée had been found in a brothel, naked and with a handkerchief stuffed down his throat. Not yet, at any rate.

"Why do you suspect his father?" Isobel asked.

"The family didn't know of Donny's death until an inspector called at their home asking to speak with Ian Noble. I found out from Helen, his youngest sister, that Dominic hadn't come home that night. He was never *in* his bed at all. Why else would Ian Noble lie to me about where his son died?"

Isobel knew precisely why the man would lie—to keep the family out of a scandal. "Did Dominic quarrel with his father?"

Katherine leveled a cool gaze on her. "You don't know Ian Noble."

"Enlighten me."

"He's a brute of a man. Always bellowing, always angry, and always finding fault in others. Especially his son."

"So Dominic and his father didn't get along?"

"Not at all. Dominic couldn't stand the man."

"Did Ian Noble approve of your marriage?"

Katherine's shoulders sagged. "Yes," she said faintly. "But only because I come with a great deal of money."

"What does your family do?"

"My father is from old money, but he also deals in antiquities. It's a hobby of his."

"Perhaps Dominic was in his room at the Palace?" Lotario suggested.

Katherine shook her head. "I asked at the Palace. He wasn't there, and I know they'd tell me."

"Did Dominic seem different to you before his death?"

Both Katherine and Lotario flinched at the word death.

"He seemed... distracted."

"About what?"

"He mentioned a fight with his father. An argument."

"Over what?"

"I don't know. He wouldn't say. I got the sense it was a... private matter between gentlemen."

Isobel shot to her feet. Lotario's involvement was distracting her. "I must warn you, Miss Hayes, you may not like what I uncover."

"At least it will be the truth."

"The truth can be painful."

Katherine stood, gathering her things. "I'm already in pain, Miss Amsel. Will you take my case?"

Isobel hesitated, glancing at her twin, who had risen as Miss Hayes stood. He was as stiff as a stone statue. "I'll contact you tomorrow."

"Money is no matter. I know I'm not imagining things. Something is *wrong* here," Katherine said, gripping Lotario's arm. "Surely you agree? Donny was as fit as a fiddle. How could his heart possibly 'give out'?"

"We'll do everything in our power," Lotario said, squeezing her hand. "I swear."

As soon as Miss Hayes left, Lotario headed for his office, where she found him pouring a shot of whiskey. He glanced at her, downed it, and poured another as she closed the door.

"The murdered man at the Nymphia… it was Dominic, wasn't it?"

"How did you know?"

He shuddered. "You didn't ask near enough questions for an interview, Bel. I could tell you already knew more than she did." He turned his back on her to brace against a sideboard, downing another shot.

Isobel poured herself a whiskey. "Were you two close?"

"Tell me what you found."

"It's not pretty, Ari."

Lotario's eyes burned with tears. "The truth never is."

There was more here than just friendship. But she loved Lotario, so she didn't hold back. She gave him facts. Cold. Hard. Cruel.

By the time she was finished, he was sitting in his chair in a daze, a whiskey bottle cradled in his arm. "You can't investigate this," he whispered.

"Why?" she demanded.

"Because Dominic loved his family. He wouldn't want to cause a scandal. This will taint his sisters' reputations."

"And let a murderer escape?" she asked in shock.

"There's more at stake."

"Tell me."

Lotario focused on her. "Dominic was a *close* friend of mine."

There was no mistaking the way he said 'close.' But she said it out loud, anyway. "A lover?"

"A client first, but then… yes. It's complicated. He meant a great deal to me. He was a *good* man."

Isobel perched on the edge of the desk. This revelation raised even more questions. "Why would he be in a cow-yard like the Nymphia?"

"I don't know," Lotario admitted. "But if you look into this… you could expose more than his killer."

"Meaning?" she asked.

Lotario started gathering his things. "Meaning the deeper you dig, the more people you risk exposing."

He gave her a pointed look. Her investigation into Duncan August earlier that year had endangered Lucie de Winter, one of her twin's personas.

"I'll be discreet, Ari."

"It won't bring Dom back."

"You don't care about justice?"

"Justice?" he asked with a twist of his lips. "The same justice system that sends men like me to prison for loving someone? We live in the shadows, Bel. And if we're truly lucky, we die there."

Isobel reached for her twin, but he pulled away. "Can you ask Tim to take over for me? I need to… I need to be alone."

Isobel didn't want to leave Lotario alone, but cornering her twin would only aggravate him. She tried to put herself in his place as she exited the office. It seemed no one wanted Dominic Noble's murder investigated save for his fiancée. Did Katherine know of her soon-to-be husband's other life?

Had Dominic's father known?

The horror on Dominic Noble's face. The blood under his nails. The handkerchief forced down his throat with a carpenter's pencil. It kept flashing behind her eyes, gnawing at her.

How could she ignore a silent plea from the dead?

Isobel stopped in the room of desks. Where were she and Riot supposed to work?

"Your office isn't finished yet," Matthew said, standing up.

"You'll have your own to share with Mr. Riot, or so Mr. Amsel says."

"Oh."

Matthew drifted closer. "Is Mr. Riot all right? The 17th Station isn't known for its… progressiveness."

"Inspector Coleman bullied his own guards in there," she confided.

Matthew blew out a breath that puffed up his cheeks. "No small feat."

Garrett had an ear cocked their way as he lounged at his desk, so Isobel moved off to the side. "Does it put Coleman in danger?"

"There's just as many bullies inside as out." Police politics had made Matthew so angry that he left the force. "I can ask around to some of my old friends. See if they've heard anything."

"I'd appreciate that."

"What else can I do?"

"Do you know where Monty lived?"

Matthew shook his head. "I think he moved around from one hotel to the next. He didn't like me much."

"Nor me."

"I'm not sorry he's gone."

"No…"

Matthew leaned in and lowered his voice. "*Did* Mr. Riot shoot him?"

"Why does everyone keep asking that?"

Matthew made a face that said *seems like something he'd do.*

Good God, even Riot's friends thought him guilty. Small wonder Inspector Geary had hauled him in as a suspect.

She caught Tim's eye, who was conversing with Miss Off. The old man came over, and Miss Off took that as invitation to follow.

"New case?" Tim asked.

"Something like that. Can you take over interviewing?"

"What happened to Lotario?"

"He's not feeling well."

Miss Off snorted.

"What are you gonna do?" Tim asked.

"I'm taking Matt to the morgue."

"You are?" Matthew asked.

"If you can spare the time," she said.

Matthew eyed her suspiciously.

"Of course he can spare it," Tim said. "You need a bodyguard."

"Them bodies explodes," Miss Off said with a little cackle.

Matthew turned green.

"It will build character," Tim agreed.

Isobel didn't need a bodyguard; she just didn't feel like being alone with Mr. Sims. Not because the body hauler was threatening, but it helped to have a buffer. Sims tended to talk. A lot. And he had no concept of personal space.

Matthew grabbed his hat and coat, and they started to leave the office. But someone caught her eye in the waiting room of hopeful detectives—a tall, striking youth between hay and grass stood slouched in the corner. His cap was pulled low and his fine hands were thrust in his pockets.

For as tall as Grimm White was, he could make himself near to invisible.

The sight of him stopped her, and Matthew nearly ran her over. Perhaps there was a way to keep her twin from drinking himself into oblivion. For a few hours, at any rate.

"Mr. White," Isobel said. At her sharp call, the young man looked up. Not in surprise, but resignation. Of course he had noticed her. Very little escaped Grimm. "Won't you come in?"

"Hey! I was next." A red-faced fellow sprang from his spot on the wall.

"Then it won't harm you to wait a little longer," Isobel replied.

"You don't get to decide who's next. I got here first, and I'm not waiting for no negro."

Isobel turned to Daisy Reed, who was eyeing Grimm with interest. "Miss Reed, would you inform this gentleman that his application has been rejected, and kindly have him leave my agency."

"Of course, Mrs. Riot."

The fellow was left fuming and grasping for some sort of argument, but then Matthew crossed his arms and put on his policeman face. He did have his uses.

Isobel led Grimm to a room where Tim and Miss Off were set to conduct the next interview. She motioned them all to follow, then pushed open the door to her twin's office. He was putting on a hat.

Lotario glanced her way, his eyes tired.

"I have one more interview for you," she said.

"I'm not in the mood—" He cut off when he saw Grimm slouching behind her.

"I think you'll want to interview this gentleman."

Grimm entered, followed by Tim and Miss Off.

"Ten minutes with her and you're lookin' near to death's door," Miss Off muttered.

Lotario ignored the woman and set his hat on the desk. "Grimm, isn't it?" he asked.

"I've come to interview for the detective position, sir," Grimm said.

Tim leaned against a wall, crossing his arms.

"Does your mother know you're here?" Isobel asked.

Grimm had removed his cap, and now held it in his hands. He shook his head. At least he was honest.

"I'm not sure we should cross your mother, Grimm," she said.

Miss Lily had given permission after a fashion. For occasional work (as long as it wasn't dangerous) and driving the carriage. But that was limited.

The young man took a deep breath. She thought that would be the end of it, but he surprised them all. "I'm my own man, or trying to be." Grimm's voice was unused, forgotten, but it was firm.

Tim slapped his hands together and gave a little whoop. "You're hired, boy."

Grimm dipped his head. "I don't want special consideration, Mr. Tim. I just want a chance like everyone else."

"You'll have it," Lotario said.

"What's she so 'fraid of? His ma keen on shootin'?" Miss Off asked.

"His mother is a friend of mine," Isobel explained. "It feels like I'm going behind her back." Why was she explaining anything to Miss Off?

"Nothin' worse than a boy shackled to his ma's apron."

Tim nodded in agreement. "Let's see how he does. No harm in that, is there?"

That was just it. Isobel didn't know if there was harm in it, or not. What she did know was that the White family was hiding something. But as she'd hoped, Lotario had perked up with interest. He was as curious as she.

"Miss Lily will probably ban you from the kitchen, Tim," Isobel said.

"I'm the one hiring," Lotario said. "I'll take responsibility." He gestured to Miss Off, who resumed her Aphrodite pose. "What can you tell me about this woman?"

Grimm studied the woman in silence. He wasn't rushed, he wasn't fidgety or dismissive. He just watched her. Even Miss Off took note of his stillness and grew self-conscious under his scrutiny.

"Is he daft in the head?" Miss Off finally asked.

"Aren't we all?" Tim asked around the stem of his pipe.

Miss Off thrust her chin at Isobel. "Her maybe; not me." Then she cooed at the rat on her shoulder, making kissy noises.

Grimm finally nodded to Lotario, who waited for an answer. When none came, Lotario pushed forward pen and paper. "Would you prefer to write your answer?"

Grimm sat, took up the pen, and began scratching out his observations. When he finished, he slid the paper over, replaced the pen, and left without a word.

Isobel had spent enough time in the young man's presence to know he was easily spooked when he was the focus of attention.

"He's a strange one," Miss Off noted.

Lotario picked up the piece of paper, and Isobel leaned over his shoulder to read.

"What'd he say 'bout me?" Miss Off demanded.

Grimm's assessment generally described Miss Off: height, weight, hair and eye color, estimated age, skin color, and notable birthmarks. All accurate as far as she knew. But it was his summary that caught her eye.

She's lived a hard life. More intelligent than she seems. Her frivolity is an act to hide pain. Former drinker.

Cause: grief, maybe; to forget, possibly. Pretends to be addled as a defense. Has a pet rat that she dotes on.

Conclusion: Lost a child or husband. Possibly a former prostitute. A kindhearted woman who shouldn't be dismissed based on outward appearance.'

Lotario laced his fingers in thought. "What an oddly beautiful mind," he murmured.

Miss Lily wasn't going to be pleased.

20

WHAT THE DEAD SAY

"Mrs. Riot!"

"Hello, Mr. Sims."

Mr. Sims was a large man in girth and height. His apron was stained with blood today, and his cuffs rolled up to his elbows. He chuckled endlessly, talked to dead bodies, and tended to laugh at the oddest times.

"Or is it Miss Amsel? Or Miss Bonnie?" He shook his head, wisps of his remaining hair catching the light.

"Miss Amsel, will do."

"And where is your better half?"

"In a jail cell."

"Hmm, and what does that say about the half that's not?" He laughed at his own joke as he stabbed a bloated body with a metal tube. A hiss of foul smelling air escaped.

Matthew turned his head. He'd already pressed a handkerchief to nose and mouth.

Sims beamed as he lit a match. "We have a fainter!" He balanced on one leg, and hooked his foot around a nearby stool, then gave it a push towards Matthew. "Best to sit. Never ends well falling face first into one of my friends. Sometimes they're squishy."

Sims gave the hissing cadaver a fond pat, then lit the air. A blue flame roared from the tube.

Isobel pushed Matthew down onto the stool. Though as tall as he was, it was more like hoisting a mainsail.

Sims' mannerisms suggested a man better suited to an asylum, or one regularly inhaling laughing gas. Both might be true, for all she knew. But who was she to judge sanity? One fact was inescapable, though: Sims had an eye for detail.

"I'm not a fainter," Matthew said, sweat beading on his brow.

"This is Matthew Smith. He's one of our... veteran agents."

"I thought maybe he was your brother."

Isobel eyed the blond, blue-eyed, strapping man. "He could certainly pass for one of them. At least half the family."

Sims squinted in thought. "What does the other half look like?"

"Brooding thunder storms."

Sims made a pleased sound. "It is most curious, isn't it?" His question was directed to a corpse on a slab. "We're all blood and bone and meat ropes on the insides, but we're decorated so differently. Just like little cakes with different frosting."

Matthew turned green and hurried out the morgue to retch. So much for Matthew as her buffer.

"I suppose you've come to see my friends."

"Yes, two actually."

Sims rubbed his hands together. "*Two*? My, you've been busy, Miss Amsel."

"Something like that," Isobel said. "The first was killed with a handkerchief."

"The Sleeper." And then he started shaking his head. "I'm sorry, no. He makes a lovely corpse, but I can't show you."

"Why not?"

"They took him away already."

"*They*?"

"Barston and Barston. Undertakers."

"After the postmortem?" Isobel asked.

Sims shook his head. "The family didn't want one."

"Did the police surgeon at least check for poison or alcohol?"

Sims covered a corpse's ears and glanced around to make sure no one else was eaves-dropping. Isobel wasn't overly worried about the other corpses. "I may have... acquired a sample from Barston and Barston."

"Friends of yours?"

"They buried you."

Isobel blinked at the comment, and Sims chortled with mirth. It took a few seconds for her to get the joke. The undertakers had buried a woman who bore an unfortunate resemblance to her—a prostitute named Marabelle was murdered, then buried in a mausoleum marked for Isobel Kingston. So far Alex had left the grave untouched. Maybe he was hopeful Isobel would end up there after all. Or he was planning to put her there.

Sims' eyes twinkled with amusement. "We were curious."

"Whether poison was involved?" she asked.

"No, no. Well..." He tapped his lips in thought. "Yes. Mostly how a handkerchief could be stuffed down the throat of such a fit young man."

"Was he drunk?"

"Alcohol and laudanum."

"Enough to incapacitate him?"

Sims shook his head. "You saw the bruises and scratches, the torn nails?"

"He wasn't drugged enough that he couldn't fight."

Sims beamed, pleased she had made the connection.

"There were signs he was sodomized, too." It was said so bluntly, with his beaming face, that it took a moment for Isobel's mind to catch up.

"Did he die in the act?"

"Barston and Barston believe so."

"But you don't?"

"Our Sleeper is very secretive, but there was no blood. I think the tears may be old, or possibly happened after he died."

Isobel grimaced at the thought. After he was dead. How long had the man lay there? Had someone stripped him after the fact? He'd obviously been moved, and more than once.

"He was moved," Sims echoed her thoughts. Then waited for her to divulge more information. But Isobel disappointed him.

"Thank you, Mr. Sims. Was the police surgeon able to estimate time of death?"

"Tuesday night, early Wednesday. Somewhere just after midnight, I think."

Meaning Dominic Noble lay in a lowbrow brothel for an entire night. Dead.

"When do you think he was moved into that sleeping position?"

"Two hours after death, maybe." Sims seemed to hum under his breath. "We had a peek inside his throat. Bleeding, tearing, bruising. The Sleeper had a terrible death. I'm afraid he'll never rest easy."

"I'm working on that," she confided.

"But the police…"

Isobel put a finger to her lips. "I'm not the police. Not a word, Mr. Sims."

Startled, he glanced down at the bloated corpse spewing blue flame. "But I tell them everything."

"Are they good at keeping secrets?"

"Very," Sims said.

"Then I'm sure that will be all right."

Matthew returned with a muttered apology. It was probably best he had missed the details of Dominic Noble's death.

"Some find death disturbing," Sims noted.

"It's part of life," Matthew said grimly.

Sims hummed to himself as he looked around the room at his charges. "If only we slept so soundly in life."

Isobel didn't have a reply for that. She didn't think she wanted to stray down that line of thinking. "The corpse with a bullet in his head."

"I have a few of those, but you'd be wanting to see your ex-agent. He's had quite the number of visitors."

"Who?"

"Most recently, a rude inspector and his lug of a shadow. No respect at all for my friends," Sims muttered to himself as he led them towards a back room.

"Anyone else?"

"Two quiet men. One graying. Rough as leather. And a shorter man who didn't enjoy being here. Why, I can't fathom. They came with a patrolman first, then returned with the rude inspector."

"Pinkerton operatives," she said.

"Oh, were they? How strange. And Tim! Always nice to visit with Tim."

Sims and Tim had met at her and Riot's wedding. The pair made quite the contrast. One large and slow, the other short and wiry. One cackling and the other humming.

"It was strange being at your wedding, you know. Not many people invite me places," Sims confided. "But Tim is as easy to talk with as my friends here."

"Tim would likely say it's because he has one foot in the grave," Isobel quipped.

Sims laughed as he swept back a sheet to reveal a gray

corpse. Monty. He looked… peaceful in death. All the lines of anger and cynicism smoothed by the hole in his forehead.

Sims tapped the bullet hole. "No secrets here. You can't tell from looking, but if you feel around, you'll find the skull is shattered. Turned his brains to mush, and barely made it out the back."

Isobel glanced at Matthew to see his reaction. He'd worked with Monty for over a year, and she noted something close to regret in his eyes.

Isobel turned Monty's head to the side. She found she had no remorse for the ex-agent. Not after the brutal beating he'd given Riot. Not after dragging her husband, bleeding and broken, to a gutter and leaving him to die. And not after Mack's death. This was simply justice served.

"Miss Amsel? Is everything all right?" Sims asked.

"Of course."

He gave a nervous chuckle. "You look set to kill him again."

She ignored his observation. "No matter how obvious a death, you always tease more secrets from the dead. What else can you tell me about Monty?"

Sims blushed at her compliment. "I wouldn't call it a secret. It's obvious. He was shot in the head while he was smoking."

"How do you know he was smoking?"

Sims picked up a stained hand. "Faint traces of ash in his mouth. He fell back, then was dragged shortly after into a dirty place. Postmortem bruising along with old bruises." Sims tapped each bruise. "Handled roughly. Since he came in wearing long johns, I'd say he was robbed. Except…"

Isobel waited as Sims patted down his person, before turning to a work table. He plucked up a scalpel handle and put it to the hole, then angled it just so.

"Here is the angle of the shot."

"He was on his knees?" Matthew asked.

Sims shook his head. "No, at close range a forty-four caliber would've made a mess of the front of his head."

Isobel's heart sank. Riot used a forty-four caliber cartridge. But that caliber was the most common type thanks to Mr. Winchester. Interchangeable ammunition for both rifle and revolver were popular.

"Just as well," Sims said. "Monty here likes his skull. He's glad that it didn't ruin his mustache."

Matthew's eyes widened as he stared over the handkerchief still pressed to his nose.

"So he was shot from above, and likely at a distance," Isobel mused aloud. "Do you still have the bullet?"

"The inspector took it."

"Can I see his clothes?"

"There's not much."

Sims took her to a wall of cubbies to retrieve a sack of Monty's possessions. The only thing in there was a union suit, stained with fluids from death. "As you can see, he was robbed."

"Did the Pinkerton operatives say they found anything else at the scene of the crime when they came to identify him?"

Sims frowned in thought. "Monty didn't know them."

Isobel looked up sharply. "Are you sure?"

"Positive. The patrolman who found Monty brought the operatives in to identify him, but they didn't recognize him. They only looked."

"Are you sure?"

"They didn't sign the papers. Mr. Tim did."

21

PINKERTONS

IT WAS LATE. ISOBEL WAS TIRED AND WORRIED. AND FUMING. Her husband was in jail for a murder he didn't commit, her home had been ransacked, and her hands were tied to investigate any of it.

She'd had enough.

"Are you sure about this?" Matthew asked.

"No."

"I don't think this is a good idea, Isobel."

"Probably not," Isobel said, as she shot up the last staircase of an office building. Matthew was close on her heels. "You don't have to come inside."

Matthew winced as she shoved open the door to Pinkertons Detective Agency. There were two women sitting behind desks, multiple telephones, file cabinets, and a clerk standing at a waist-high counter. A wall of frosted glass divided the offices.

"I need to speak with Liam Taft. Now," she said to the clerk.

His eyes darted to the side. "Do you have an appointment?"

Isobel didn't wait. Before anyone could stop her, she

rounded the counter and pushed open a frosted glass door. Liam Taft sat at a desk in the back of the office. When he saw who'd charged in, he holstered a revolver back on his hip.

She planted her palms on his desk. "Monty *wasn't* a Pinkerton, was he?" she hissed.

His eyes darted to the other agents in the room, then nodded towards a side door. She took his hint. As soon as they entered a small interview room, she rounded on him.

"Mrs. Riot," he greeted.

"I'm not here for pleasantries, Taft. Answer my question."

"You seem to already know the answer."

"I'm asking you."

"Why are you so certain of that, Mrs. Riot?"

"You didn't identify Monty in the morgue."

"I don't know everyone in the office."

Isobel gave a pointed look towards the door. "That's an awfully small memory you have for a detective."

"I remember what's important."

"And what is important, Mr. Taft?"

"Law."

"Law *or* justice?" she asked.

"Justice is subjective."

Isobel gave a small smile. "Good answer."

"I didn't know this was a test."

"Everything is a test," she said. "Why are you targeting my husband?"

"I'm not. The trail led to your husband. Inspector Geary had enough probable cause to issue an arrest warrant."

"And you?"

"Time will tell, along with some proper detective work."

"Ravenwood Agency isn't in the business of arresting someone without proof."

"Neither is my agency."

Isobel considered the man. "You were already investigating Monty, weren't you?"

"We take the integrity of our agency seriously."

"So Monty *was* claiming to be an operative?"

Liam smoothed his drooping mustache. "According to Ravenwood Agency."

"We didn't start that rumor. The proprietor of the Morgue said Monty was seen with a Pinkerton operative. And Monty..." she stopped there. Based on clues, Riot had deduced Monty left Ravenwood Agency to take up with the Pinkertons. So Riot had tossed that theory out like bait, and Monty had answered. After a fashion.

Over the course of Riot's recovery, his memory had slowly returned. What had Monty said? That 'a man can move up there.' And that he 'needed the money without the hassle of writing reports.'

But Monty had worked with Riot for years. He knew Riot's methods, and baiting a suspect to reveal the truth was a common enough tactic. One Liam Taft had just used on her.

"Monty what?" Liam asked.

"Does your agency still require agents to write reports?"

Liam's eyes narrowed. He had such a pronounced squint that it was a wonder he could still see. "Yeah," he said, that single word dripping with distaste. "Ask Sam. He'll tell you how much I love reports."

"What's really going on here, Mr. Taft?"

"I'm investigating a murder."

"A robbery, according to the newspapers. Hardly worthy of the Pinkertons."

Liam spread his hands. "I get paid hourly, ma'am."

"Who's paying you?" Isobel asked.

"Do you ever back down, Mrs. Riot?"

She met his gaze in challenge. "No."

Liam shifted, and to her surprise he slipped two fingers into a vest pocket and brought out a badge. She took the six-pointed star from his hand. "Are you trying to recruit me?"

"Are you for hire?" he asked.

"I'm flattered," she said dryly. She glanced at the badge pinned to his vest. His was shield-shaped, while the one in her hand was star-shaped. Both had the same words emblazoned on the metal. "Is this a badge for a new branch?"

Liam shook his head. "The patrolman found it in Monty's locker at the boxing club, so he contacted us."

Isobel frowned in thought. "It's a fake."

A crinkling of his eyes confirmed it. What had Montgomery Johnson been up to? Aside from trying to kill Riot.

She handed the badge back. "I think we're on the same trail, Mr. Taft."

"And what trail would that be?"

"The one that leads to a killer."

22

THE ART OF DEDUCTION

THE LAST TIME ISOBEL WAS IN MISSION BAY IT HAD BEEN DARK and she feared for Riot's life. She'd found him face down in a gutter, covered in his own blood, and close to death. She shuddered at the memory.

Riot is alive, she told herself. He's under guard, with an honest police officer. What better place for a restless man recovering from a head injury?

Riot was infinitely capable, confident and cunning, and had survived more gunfights than he likely remembered. But that night had shaken her. She'd nearly lost him.

The carriage stopped, and Tim paid their fare while she studied the run-down street.

"This is no place for a lady, sir," the cab driver called down to Tim. "A dangerous place even for you."

Tim cackled. "I'm as curly as they come, son. But thanks for the warning."

The driver tipped his cap, then clucked his horse forward, eager to leave.

"I suppose we do look like prey," Isobel noted.

"*God made man, but Sam Colt made them equal,*" Tim quoted.

"And women."

She spotted Liam Taft and Sam Batten down the street, along with two others. Isobel ground her teeth together. Inspector Geary had come with the patrolman who'd found Monty. An Officer Finley. At least Geary had left his lug of a sergeant behind.

As she and Tim approached, the Pinkerton operatives touched the brims of their hats. But Geary offered no such greeting. He kept his hands firmly on his lapels, and had a smug expression plastered on his face. "You're wasting my time, Mrs. Riot."

"I didn't ask you to come, Inspector," she shot back.

"And let you tamper with evidence?"

"Did your men leave behind evidence?" she asked, fluttering her lashes.

Geary scowled.

And she looked to the patrolman. "Show me where Monty was found."

Finley led the way. He looked like the sort who didn't like to walk much. Isobel thought he was more the watching type. From a bench.

They made quite the crowd as they stopped in front of a rubbish-strewn alley. "I'll be watching you closely. Don't touch anything without running it by me first," Geary said.

Isobel gestured toward the alleyway. "Your men trampled anything of value, Inspector."

"Not to the discerning eyes of a professional," Geary said.

Liam gave a little cough, blowing out his mustache.

"What attracted you to the body?" Isobel asked Finley.

Geary chuckled at her question. "Never smelled a body, Mrs. Riot? It'll curl your toes."

Isobel ignored the comment. She was on the hunt and wasn't about to be distracted by men offering advice.

"He was covered by the garbage here, ma'am," Finley said.

"I heard a catfight, so I stopped to watch. Only I seen the vermin swarming on the pile. Along with gulls. And a pair of feet poking out."

Isobel glanced down the street towards The Den, then studied the boardwalk. Geary started to step inside the alleyway, but she held out an arm. "Please. Don't."

"I don't have the patience for you to play at being some sort of dime novel detective."

"Humor me. Then you can tell your friends at the station about how I made a fool of myself."

Inspector Geary grumbled. Never mind that she and Riot had solved the murder of a man in a bathtub that Geary had proclaimed a suicide.

She blocked out the watching men to study the ground. Too many boots had passed. But there was a distinct scuff in the dirt.

"Did the dead wagon carry him out on a stretcher?" she asked.

"Of course they did," Geary said with a snort.

Liam moved beside her, while Tim kept an eye on Geary.

"Are you a tracker, Mrs. Riot?" Liam asked.

"I'm learning. Are you?"

"Batten is."

"What does he make of this?"

"I'm more curious what you make of it."

"Monty was dragged into the alley. After death. And someone buried him under a pile of rubbish." She shot to her feet, and searched the boardwalk until she found a faint stain on the boards. "He was shot here."

"Yes," Liam confirmed. She looked up, annoyed that the Pinkerton operative got there first. "Go on, Mrs. Riot. I don't mind another pair of eyes."

Her gaze fixed on a notch in a wood wall, low to the ground. "Did you find more than one bullet?"

Liam shook his head. "Sam went over it."

"And my men," Geary said.

"One shot," she murmured, then eyed the men. "Inspector Geary, you're about Monty's height. Would you stand over here."

He glowered.

"It's not like being tall is an insult, your highness," Tim grunted.

Geary shot him a glare, but moved into place.

"Does anyone have a pen or pencil?" She grimaced inwardly at the word pencil. She hadn't forgotten about Dominic Noble, but the dead could wait; the living, especially her husband, could not.

Sam Batten produced one, and she stood on her tippy-toes to jab one end against Geary's forehead.

"Oy, now!"

"For God's sake, I'm harmless," she bit out.

Geary stepped back into position, and she reproduced the angle of the shot that Sims had shown her, then turned Geary so his back aligned with the notch in the wood. Isobel craned her neck around to search the buildings. A window in a second story warehouse across the street caught her eye.

Without a word, Isobel took off in that direction. She didn't care if the others followed. The warehouse door was hanging on a hinge. She stopped to fiddle with it for a second, then climbed a rickety staircase that was ripe with rot. She paused at a window with a cracked pane, then snatched up a loose board to mime the shot.

Footsteps filed in, the floorboards straining under the added weight. "Tim, could you make this shot?" she asked without looking around.

Tim stepped forward to eye the distance. "I reckon I could. Only about forty yards or so."

Isobel looked at Liam, who had a thoughtful look in his eyes. "Could you make this shot?"

"A good many could."

She nodded, satisfied. "I'd like you to note the distance, Inspector Geary."

"Why?" he asked.

"You've arrested a myopic gunfighter who favors a revolver. Have you ever tried to aim a rifle while wearing spectacles?" Geary frowned at her. He likely didn't know what myopic meant, so she clarified. "Riot is nearsighted. Even *with* his spectacles, everything is a blur at this distance. There's a reason he carries a revolver."

"Nothing says the shot was taken from here."

"Except the path of the bullet through Monty's skull."

"Could *you* make this shot?" Geary asked.

"I could."

"Maybe I should be arresting you."

"Your accusations tread farther onto thin ice every second," she said, while searching the floor for a casing. "Did your men search this warehouse?"

The Pinkertons shook their heads, while Geary puffed up his chest. "I think I've humored you enough."

But she was already walking back across the warehouse to the stairwell. She stopped at a back window that looked out onto Mission Creek, then casually tossed her fake rifle out of the window, noting where it splashed in the creek. She picked her way down the stairwell, vaguely aware of a grunt behind her as someone nearly fell through a rotted plank.

Isobel stopped at the bank's edge, and there she finally hesitated. There was nothing for it. "Did your men check the creek, Inspector?" she yelled, a note of hope in her voice.

Inspector Geary was busy cursing at nearly falling through another rotten plank.

"Mr. Taft?" she asked as the Pinkerton arrived.

"No, we questioned everyone at The Den."

"Inspector?"

"Are you volunteering?" he shouted.

Isobel clenched her jaw and started unlacing her boots.

"You really going in that, girl?" Tim asked at her side. He was eyeing her with skepticism. "I'm sure we could bully Geary into having a police crew dredge the creek with hooks."

"Riot has already spent three days in a cell with a brutish police force, and he's missing his daughter's thirteenth birthday today. I don't want to wait for Geary's leisure."

Tim frowned, scuffing a boot against the ground. Sarah had woken up forlorn on her birthday. She'd refused to open her gifts, and asked Miss Lily to hold off on any cake until her father was released. It made Isobel want to brain Inspector Geary with his sergeant's billy club.

"I'll go, then," Tim offered.

Isobel snorted. "And let you take all the glory?" Before she changed her mind, Isobel shrugged off spare clothing, and slipped down the garbage strewn bank into filthy water. She tried not to inhale, or use her nose, or think overly long on whether the water was muddy or a cesspit. Thankfully, it wasn't deep, and her split riding skirt was lightweight enough that it didn't bog her down.

She waded to the spot where her makeshift 'rifle' had landed. Her foot touched something sharp, and she regretted removing her boots as her stockings snagged on a bit of glass. Dying of an infection was the last thing she needed, but she couldn't feel for a weapon with her boots on.

Isobel gingerly prodded the muddy creek floor until she felt what she was looking for. Taking a breath, she dipped beneath the sludge and pulled her prize from the mud, surfacing with a Winchester rifle in hand.

"I believe you'll find this matches the bullet in Monty's head," she said.

Tim offered a hand, his eyes glinting with pride. "Wouldn't want you hunting my tail, girl," he said as he pulled her up the bank. She stumbled, nearly falling from the weight of muck clinging to her.

Sam Batten quickly looked away. Finley stood there and leered at her breasts. She had a sport's bodice under her wet blouse, but apparently even the sight of a bodice got the man's imagination going.

"Well done, Mrs. Riot," Liam said, impressed. He took the rifle from her hand in exchange for her coat, then began to check it over. "Winchester 1873. Most common rifle there is. The serial numbers are scratched out." He pulled the lever, and a casing popped out onto the ground. Liam shook out his plaid handkerchief to pick it up.

"How could you possibly know the shooter tossed his rifle in the creek?" Geary asked.

"It's called deductive reasoning. Try it some time, Inspector, before you arrest an innocent man again. Now if you'll excuse me, gentlemen, I need a bath."

23

RIDDLES AND WARNINGS

Of course day four of Riot's incarceration *would* fall on a Sunday, Isobel thought as she dressed for the day. As a rule, she disliked Sundays, equating them with church and leisure. Both of which she found tedious.

Sundays before she met Riot, at any rate. She glanced at the empty bed in the mirror as she battled with her hair. It was too long to leave down, and too short to put up. So it was a wild, wispy mess of curling blonde hair that made her look like some fae creature.

A knock sounded at the door, the knock telling her precisely who it was. "Come in, Sarah."

She eyed Jin and Sarah in the mirror as they entered. Yesterday Sarah had wandered the house looking forlorn and tragic, but she looked better today. Jin was practically chipper as she ran across the room brandishing a newspaper.

"Did you see this article?" The girl thrust it up under Isobel's nose.

"I could kiss Cameron," Sarah said.

Isobel abandoned her hair for the paper, giving Sarah a sharp look in the mirror. "And Riot will shoot him."

Jin snickered.

"You'll want to kiss him too, after you read what he wrote."

Sarah was looking more and more like a young woman every day. Why in the world did girls mature faster than boys? Should she have some sort of talk with the girl?

"Stare at the words, not Sarah," Jin ordered, jabbing a finger at the small print.

Isobel dutifully read.

Police Arrest Detective On Whim

Atticus Riot, famed detective of Ravenwood Agency, was arrested on suspicion of the murder of Montgomery Johnson, a former agent and friend. The two men got in a row at The Den some weeks ago. Monty, a skilled pugilist, beat Mr. Riot near to death, then dumped him dying in an alleyway.

Mr. Riot was bed-bound for some weeks afterwards, while Monty went about his business, until the former agent was found dead and robbed near The Den. He was shot by a single bullet to the head.

Police detectives and Pinkerton agents arrested Mr. Riot as he was returning from a holiday with his family. Without weapon, motive, or proof, Inspector Geary of the SFPD handcuffed the detective and led him away in front of his family based solely on the fact that Monty had nearly beaten his former employer to death.

On the third of November, to further Atticus Riot's recovery, the Riot family left San Francisco to convalesce in Willow Camp.

Not only were there multiple witnesses who saw and spoke with Mr. Riot and his family on November sixth, the day of the murder, the local Sheriff swears to the fact that Atticus Riot helped him apprehend a criminal gang operating in the woods.

It leaves the question of how a SFPD detective and Pinkertons could arrest an innocent man based on nothing more than a whim, without the merest effort of investigation. Given the recent attack on

*Ravenwood Agency, the question begs answering: Do Atticus Riot and
his agency have a target on their back?*

*Sheriff Blake plans to head to the city straightaway to vouch for
Atticus Riot and clear his name.*

Sarah was right. Isobel could kiss Cameron Fry. Inspector
Geary wouldn't be happy with the article at all. But that's what
he got for having a shoddy work ethic. She handed the newspaper back. "What are you two doing today?"

"We're headed—" Jin elbowed Sarah in the ribs. "Uhm.
We're walking. Around."

Jin looked at the ceiling.

"Do *not* go to the 17th Street police station." One look at
Jin, and Isobel clarified. "Do not go across the street. Around
the block, or in front of it, nor to the side buildings."

Jin gave a little growl.

"But what if Atticus is released, and he comes out all
alone?" Sarah asked. "That just wouldn't be right."

"It's Sunday, Sarah. I doubt he'll be released today."

The girl deflated. "I guess I'll go to church. Alone."

"My mother will probably be at St. Francis," Isobel said.

"I'm not catholic."

Isobel bit back a comment. She might have her own strong
feelings about religion but she wouldn't belittle Sarah's beliefs.
"When Riot is released, he'll help you find a church."

Jin crossed her arms. "Coward."

"What?"

"You are volunteering bahba so you do not have to take
her."

"He'll be happy to spend time with Sarah. Would you
rather go?"

"I will take Sarah to meet Tan Ling and Sammy."

Isobel didn't know how she felt about Jin building a friendship with the ex-hatchet man who worked with the men who

had killed her parents, but… Well, there it was. "I thought Riot said you couldn't go for a visit without him?"

"He said not to go *alone*."

Isobel scrutinized the girl. Jin stared back, unblinking. "We can roam the city instead," Jin finally suggested.

That was a worse idea. "Fine, you can go visit Tan Ling, but stick to the main streets. No alleyways." Chinatown would be full of tourists today. It should be safe enough as long as the two didn't go around announcing they were Din Gau's children.

Jin started to pull Sarah away.

"*Wait*," Isobel ordered.

"Yes?" Jin asked.

"You didn't agree to my terms."

"We will stay out of alleyways," Jin said.

"And no stabbing people."

Jin muttered under her breath. The eleven-year-old was entirely too quick with her blade. "Fine, we will let bad men take us instead."

"You know what I mean," Isobel said.

Jin stuck out her tongue.

"Where are you headed?" Sarah asked.

"A social call."

The girls stared with nearly identical raised brows as Isobel pinned on a hat.

"Don't look at me like that."

Jin crossed her arms. "You never make social calls."

They had a point. Perhaps if she took the girls it would look more like a social call than an investigation. "Would you two like to come with me?"

Of course they would. Isobel finished dressing and turned to grab her satchel. Jin was squinting at a missive she'd picked up from a stack of books.

"Whose hands are tied?" the girl asked. "And how can they send a telegram if they are being held captive?"

Sarah moved over to read the missive. "I think it's a figure of speech?"

Isobel snatched the missive from her daughters. "It's a reply from an inspector."

"Does this have to do with bahba?" Jin asked.

"No." After interviewing Katherine Hayes, Isobel had wired Inspector Coleman with a cryptic question: *Really?*

His response: *My hands are tied.* It confirmed her suspicions. "It's not polite to read other people's telegrams," she said, stuffing the missive in her satchel.

"You do it all the time," Jin accused.

"At least I do so in *secret.*"

As Isobel ushered the two out of her room (which was still in complete disarray) Sarah rolled her eyes. "You are definitely a bad influence on us."

"Think of me as a shining example of what *not* to do."

Jin snorted.

Isobel left the girls in the kitchen while she sought out one of the lodgers at Ravenwood Manor. She found Annie Dupree in the greenhouse, sitting at her favorite dining spot. She read alone at a little garden table.

Isobel was never one for pleasantries. "Do you know Dominic Noble and Katherine Hayes?" Then she paused a moment, taking in Annie's perfectly styled hair and prim tea gown. "And do you have a lady's maid hidden in that room of yours?"

Annie lowered her newspaper. "Which question would you like answered first, Miss Amsel?"

"Good God, we live under the same roof. Call me Isobel." She sat down without invitation and watched Annie take a dainty sip of tea. She tried not to think about Riot's prior dealings with the auburn beauty. It was fortunate Isobel wasn't the jealous type or Annie Dupree would be out of house and home.

"Would you like some tea?" Annie asked.

"No, and I'd like my second question answered first."

"Is there a reason why you're inquiring about a lady's maid?"

"I'm thinking of rejoining society."

Annie studied her a moment. "A dangerous undertaking."

"Without a doubt."

"A case?" Annie asked.

Annie Dupree was very perceptive. Along with being a prostitute, she was also their children's teacher. And probably a spy for Riot's half sister. Annie had her uses, though. The woman took Jin's rages, insults, and shocking comments all in stride while keeping the girl engaged and curious. No small task.

"Why else would I wade into a sea of lace and shallow minds?" Isobel asked.

"Will it be so easy for you?"

"What do you mean?"

"You have a reputation. San Francisco might be forgiving, but society ladies are not."

"I don't plan on being recognized."

"Aah." Annie took another sip of tea. "I do my own hair. And I don't know Katherine Hayes."

"But you know Dominic Noble?"

"I cannot say."

"A client?" Isobel asked.

"You sound surprised."

"He was engaged."

"I heard he died in his sleep. Surprising and tragic. But for you to be involved…" Annie leaned forward. "What really happened?"

"Professional discretion. Same as you."

"Unlikely the same."

"Along the same lines," Isobel said.

Annie frowned into her tea. "Ian Noble, his father, is a brute. I imagine his son followed in his footsteps."

"But you don't know for certain?"

"I met Dominic Noble at a party once. Attractive man. But I don't think I left much impression on him."

"Why do you say his father is a brute? In what regard?"

"Social. Business. He knows what he wants, and he takes it."

"Women, too?"

"I don't have firsthand experience," Annie admitted. "I'm more selective with my clientele, and I don't ignore whispers. Ian Noble made his fortune in mining. From what I hear, he dotes on his daughters and is protective of them. The eldest is engaged to an Englishman in New York. The Nobles are rich, but they're new money. They don't fit into New York society, and most especially British society."

"So Ian Noble is marrying off his daughter for the title, and the titled gentleman is eyeing their money."

"That's a cold interpretation," Annie noted.

Isobel arched a brow. "Is there another?"

"Love, perhaps?" Annie's voice was light and wistful. She was also an excellent actress.

"I find that the transactional nature of high society shares alarming similarities with prostitution."

"One could say all relationships are transactional."

"True."

"Even your own." It was nearly a purr.

The edge of Isobel's lip quirked. "Hmm," was all she said. Some secrets were too delicious to share. "What did Dominic Noble and Katherine Hayes stand to gain from one another?"

Annie studied her from beneath long lashes. "Katherine

Hayes is considered a spinster and Dominic was a confirmed bachelor."

The words were heavy with suggestion. Isobel absently fiddled with a teaspoon, possibilities spinning in her mind. The only picture she had of Dominic Noble was his naked corpse frozen in terror. It was hard to think of him as an aggressor, given the method of murder.

But there was Jacob Dixon to consider. Had Dominic gone there for a liaison with a man *or* a woman? Had he shared his father's brutish nature? Lotario was fond of him, but that didn't mean Dominic would have treated women in a lowbrow brothel the same as he had her twin.

"How is Mr. Riot?"

Isobel stopped tapping the teaspoon against the table. "Unless Inspector Geary is utterly corrupt, I suspect he'll be released tomorrow. At least I hope."

"I find it curious that the Pinkertons are involved."

Isobel's eyes narrowed. "Have you heard something?"

"I'm not a gossipmonger."

"Sam Batten seemed taken with you during the police raid."

Annie's lips curved. "Do your questions about Dominic Noble have anything to do with the Nymphia raid?"

Isobel returned the smile, then stood. "Enjoy your brunch." She started to leave, but stopped at the call of her name. "Yes?"

"The Pinkertons are not all they seem in San Francisco," Annie said carefully.

"I don't like riddles," Isobel said. Though she did, in fact, love riddles.

"It's not a riddle; it's a warning."

24

RAG AND BONE

IT WAS SUNDAY. THE DAY *AFTER* SARAH'S THIRTEENTH BIRTHDAY. The thought stung as Riot lay on his cot, eyes on the stone ceiling, idly shuffling a worn deck on his stomach. At least he had the cell to himself. Along with his demons.

There were plenty of those. He'd been sifting through the past decades, cataloging his numerous enemies. And that was only the ones he knew about. Every action has consequence, even the smallest ones.

His thoughts kept returning to Liam Taft, and their conversation. Why had the agent been interested in his days as a Pinkerton? And specifically about why he and Ravenwood left the agency.

Twenty years ago the Pinkerton Detective Agency hadn't had an office in San Francisco, so Ravenwood took the occasional case as a consultant, which led to Riot's recruitment as a tracker.

Then there was that business with Jim Hagen. Nothing dramatic. Just a detective who was more criminal than lawman. It was unfortunately commonplace. A badge gave men power. And power corrupted. Though he suspected power was more akin to water on a seed that had already been planted.

Footsteps sounded down the hallway and a guard stopped in front of his cell. "Time to go."

"On a Sunday?" Riot asked, climbing to his feet.

"Inspector Geary doesn't want you in here a minute longer."

The back of Riot's neck prickled. This guard was a regular at the station, not one of Inspector Coleman's officers. "Come on, then."

Riot didn't have a coat, or anything to gather, so he squared his deck and walked out. "I believe this is yours."

The guard frowned at the deck. "No, that's Blue's deck."

"It's marked."

The guard turned red. "That *bastard*," he swore.

Riot placed the deck in the guard's hand. "Blisters on the back of the aces. You could turn it around on him for at least one game."

The guard ran a rough thumb over the back of a card. "Suppose I could. Thanks."

Given the cracked skin on the guard's hands, Riot doubted he could feel the pinprick indentations. "Will my revolver be returned?"

"Whatever you came in with."

The guard ushered Riot through another cage door, to where two other guards lounged at a table. The guard tossed down the tattered deck, then pushed a newspaper into Riot's hands. "That's why you're being released."

The other two guards glared. "What's that about, Oakes?"

"Shut it."

As Oakes led the way through yet another door, Riot read the front page headline. Cameron Fry had a way with words, and Riot recognized the youth's style. He'd gone straight at the police station and dealt them a hard blow.

The office was subdued as Riot signed his release papers. He passed through a waist-high barrier into the lobby, and the desk officer handed over his holster and revolver. Riot checked the chambers. They were empty and his leather holster had been plucked clean of ammunition.

"Used them all up testing ballistics," the officer explained.

"Of course," Riot said. "Can I make a telephone call?"

"No."

Released from jail on a Sunday with no ammunition. Riot didn't like the feel of this at all. Was he being paranoid? Yes. But he was also alive because he was cautious. The two went hand in hand.

Oakes hesitated at the desk. "I'm taking a smoke break," he announced, then walked out the front door.

There was no point buckling on his shoulder holster, so Riot walked outside a free man with his gear in hand.

Oakes stood off to the side, as Riot squinted into sunlight. The fog had burned away, but the air had a bite.

"I owe you," Oakes said, raising a hand towards his holster.

Riot was on the verge of leaping at the guard, but instead of reaching for his gun, Oakes plucked out some cartridges.

"Don't tell no one." Oakes dropped six cartridges into Riot's palm. "For the tip about Blue's deck."

"I appreciate it."

"We're even," Oakes grunted. He disappeared back inside without taking a smoke break.

Splendid, even the police suspected an ambush.

Using a column as cover, Riot watched the street as he loaded his revolver. Then he slung the holster on and buckled it. The weight was reassuring.

Instead of striking off, he lingered near the station's turret tower, searching the windows and doorways across the wide street. No hat, no coat, no billfold. At least he'd put on his boots before being arrested.

He headed down Valencia Street. It was lined with homes and businesses squashed shoulder to shoulder. Church bells rang out the noon hour, and he began to relax. Since it was Sunday offices were closed, and families were at church, inside homes, or out in parks.

The barren street was normal, he told himself. So why was he uneasy? Riot had learned to trust that prickling sensation climbing up his spine. The dead were the ones who ignored it.

He ducked down the first lane he came across, and cut behind a paint supply store to hop over a fence. Then hurried through a tiny backyard garden and climbed a trellis with a yapping dog at his heels. Riot landed on the other side. A rattle of wheels and the ringing of a bell spurred him onwards. He spotted the rag-and-bone man plodding in the middle of a street lined with homes.

Riot searched corners and windows for an ambush, as he unbuckled his holster, removed his vest, and slung the holster back on. With vest in hand, he flagged down the rag-and-bone man.

"I need a hat and coat. What will you trade for this?"

The man examined the fine wool. It wasn't one of Riot's silk gray and black vests, but it wasn't store bought either.

The man glanced at him. "I got nothin' but rags. Ain't a hole in this."

Riot held the man's eyes for a tick. "I'll take whatever you have. Otherwise, it's likely to have a hole in it soon."

The fellow eyed his shoulder holster, then turned and rifled through his tottering wagon. He came out with a battered cloth cap covered in brick dust and a moth-eaten coat.

"That will do." Riot exchanged vest for rags. "Can you throw in a cigarette?"

The man handed one over. "Need a light?"

Riot held up a matchbook, then popped the unlit cigarette between his lips and struck off down the street. As he turned a corner, he noted the man exchanging his own vest for the new trade.

With a small smile, Riot flipped up his collar, adjusted the cap low, and strode back onto Valencia Street smelling of moths and whiskey.

25

THE UNKNOWN

MONEY WAS ALWAYS A MOTIVE, BUT ISOBEL HADN'T EXPECTED this much of it. Jin stopped at the gate to gawk, and Sarah frowned, eyeing Isobel's no-frills coat, split-skirt, and practical boots. "Are you sure we can call here? I'm not dressed in my Sunday best."

Isobel flicked her cuffs. "We're working, Sarah. Not visiting."

"Didn't you invite us along to make it look like a social call?"

Jin stirred. "I do not think you have friends here."

"My ex-husband's mansion is just down the street," Isobel said, pushing open the gate. "And it's even bigger."

It was true. While Katherine Hayes's estate was large, it wasn't one of the mansions that hogged an entire block. It was more along the lines of Ravenwood Manor, only well-maintained and with a gated wall around its grounds.

When no sound of footsteps followed, she stopped and turned to find her daughters looking hesitant. "Are you two coming?"

The girls hurried to catch up.

"Never be intimidated by wealth. It's only decoration. Rich or poor, everyone needs a privy," Isobel said as they walked.

Despite altering her words for their young sensibilities, Jin blurted out, "You mean everyone shits."

"Jin!" Sarah said.

"It is true."

"You can't use bad language."

"I just did."

Sarah spluttered. "Isobel, aren't you going to say something?"

"I'm hardly qualified to lecture Jin on language," Isobel muttered. "And I loathe hypocrisy. Now then, be on your best behavior." She arched a pointed brow at Jin. "Pretend you're Sarah."

Jin wrinkled her nose.

"And no eavesdropping."

"You have no faith in us," Jin said.

"Oh, I have faith in you," she said. "Just not to behave."

"There's a mourning crape, Isobel. Are you sure we should be calling?" Sarah asked as they walked up the stairs.

A black bow was tied to the knocker with a white ribbon.

"Clearly someone was murdered. Why else would Isobel come here?" Jin asked.

"I do have friends," Isobel defended.

Jin snorted, as she stood on her tippy-toes to bang the knocker against its plate. She seemed intent on rousing the entire street.

The door opened, and a man frowned at them. Around thirty, with a square jaw and a thin mustache. His queue nearly brushed the floor, and he wore the traditional *changshan*—a silk robe-like tunic usually worn by officials.

"Miss Hayes is expecting us," Isobel said, offering her personal calling card.

He took the card, then glanced from Sarah to Jin, his dark

gaze taking in her features, along with the oversized cap and boy's suit she favored.

"My daughters. Sarah and Jin."

A twitch of his brow betrayed surprise. "Mr. Chang," he introduced. "I'll inform Miss Hayes of your arrival. You may wait in the parlour, Mrs. Riot." He bowed them inside with a sweep of an arm.

"Is that a *mummy*?" Sarah asked, staring at a preserved corpse in a glass case. It was an odd thing to have in an entry hall.

"Yes, Miss Riot," Chang said.

"From Egypt?" Sarah asked.

Isobel suppressed a sigh. She supposed it was possible that the Hayeses embalmed as a pastime.

"Mr. Hayes is a great collector of antiquities." He showed them into a second parlour. "If you'll wait here."

"Will we be meeting Mr. and Mrs. Hayes?" Isobel asked.

"Mrs. Hayes passed away some time ago. Mr. Hayes is currently away on business."

Isobel nodded, and Chang left, queue and robes flirting with the carpets.

Her daughters waited exactly thirty seconds before rushing to the door. Jin slipped through to gawk at the mummy, and after a backward glance to Isobel (who lifted a shoulder in answer), Sarah followed.

Isobel breathed in the scent of wealth. It had a distinct smell of polish, beeswax, oils and fresh flowers, with a gleam to everything that required an army of servants. But whereas her ex-husband, Alex, preferred austere gilt and vast masculine spaces, it seemed the Hayes were the extravagant collector types.

Unlike the entry hall, a woman's touch was noticeable in the parlour. If not Miss Katherine Hayes, then a leftover from her mother, perhaps. Isobel paused at a charcoal sketch of sailboats at sea. Faint pencil marks flowed under the charcoal where the artist had sketched out the landscape before applying color.

Soon enough Sarah and Jin darted back inside, and were standing innocently by the settee when the first sound of clicking heels reached the room.

Katherine hadn't kept them waiting long. She hurried into the parlour, then stared in bewilderment at the children. Pale, with shadowed eyes, she had the look of a person who'd just lost something dear.

Thankfully, there were no brimming tears in the woman's eyes. Isobel was not up to the task of comforting a distraught woman. That was Riot's specialty.

"I brought my daughters so it would look like a social call instead of business," Isobel explained. "Can they wait somewhere while we speak?"

"I didn't think you'd come," Katherine said. "And yes…" She gave a sad smile at the children, then poked her head into the hallway. "Will you show the children around the house, Mr. Chang?"

"Of course, Miss Hayes."

Sarah hesitated before leaving. "I'm sorry for your loss, ma'am."

Katherine's eyes brimmed with tears, and Sarah gave her hand a squeeze, before darting after her sister.

Mr. Chang paused in the doorway, concern plain on his face. "Do you require tea?" he asked softly.

"No, thank you," she said, dabbing at her eyes.

When Mr. Chang closed the doors, Isobel nodded towards the sketch. "Who is the artist?"

Katherine colored. "I am. My mother insisted on hanging it there. I'm afraid only a mother would love it. After she passed, I could hardly change this room. Won't you sit, Miss Amsel?"

"I think it better if you do."

"Have you discovered something about Donny's death?"

Isobel clenched her jaw. She'd debated this part. To tell or not to tell? But she'd been hired to find the truth, not to sweep a veil over the woman. And she'd taken Inspector Coleman's cryptic reply to her telegram as permission.

"Has it occurred to you that the details of your fiancé's death are being kept private for a reason?" Isobel asked.

Katherine frowned. "I was to be his wife. Wouldn't you want to know the truth?"

"No matter how unpleasant?"

Katherine sank into a chair and stared into the cold hearth for a time. The mantel clock ticked into silence. Then Katherine straightened, squaring her shoulders. "I must know. No matter how unpleasant."

"Very well," Isobel said, with a dip of her chin. "During a police raid on the Hotel Nymphia…" she paused to let that sink in first, gauging the woman's reaction. Katherine blinked rapidly. "A dead man was discovered in one of the upper-story rooms. A policeman recognized him as Dominic Noble."

Katherine was shaking her head. "That's impossible."

"Unless he had a twin that died on the same day, I assure you it is not."

"How did he die?" she asked, her voice a thin waver.

"Suffocation," Isobel said bluntly. "With a handkerchief." She left out that it had been stuffed down his throat with a carpenter pencil and he had been found naked. No use leaving the woman with a horrendous last image of her fiancé's face.

Katherine stared numbly at nothing. "That's impossible," she whispered again. "Donny… he wouldn't."

"How can you be certain?"

Katherine focused on her. Horror, confusion, shock. "His parents… his mother. She's one of the founders of the Knights of Chastity."

Isobel nearly laughed. Yes, no son had ever visited a brothel without his mother's approval. She bit back the sarcastic remark, and sat down. "Knights of Chastity?" she asked instead.

"A group of people opposed to vice. They've fought the Nymphia since its conception. Early on Mrs. Noble learned the owners intended to call it the Nymphomania, and marshaled the city priests and influencers to close it down."

Isobel had heard that. The hotel was supposed to be a home for women afflicted with that condition, but city planners quickly shot the name down, so the owners changed it to something more acceptable.

"Miss Hayes, can you think of any reason why Dominic would enter such a place?"

Katherine blushed. "I know what you're thinking. That Donny is a man, and men must satisfy desires that come naturally to them. But I assure you Donny wasn't that sort of man."

That had not been what Isobel was thinking.

"A woman knows," Katherine said firmly.

Isobel changed tack. "What can you tell me about Dominic's activities during the days leading up to his death?"

"You mean his *murder*."

Isobel inclined her head.

"Donny was busy that week. I saw him only once. We met at the Palace for dinner."

"And what day was that?"

"That would have been Sunday."

"Did he seem troubled at all?" Isobel asked.

"He was troubled by the argument he'd had with his father. But when I asked after the details, he waved the matter away. Clashing with his father was a common enough occurrence that I didn't press him. But he did seem… distracted. I could tell something was weighing on him."

"Why didn't they get along?"

"Donny didn't approve of his father's business ethics. And Mr. Noble... well, he has a temper."

"Did his father threaten him directly?"

"All the time. Before Donny met me, Ian threatened to take away his inheritance if he didn't marry. He called him lazy and useless. The two couldn't have been more opposite."

"Why do you think his father killed him?"

Katherine sighed. "I thought because they argued—because Mr. Noble is a frightening man and the family lied to me. But I see now..." She paused to swallow, looking suddenly ill. "I see why that might not be the case."

Isobel watched as the woman twisted a handkerchief in her hands. Katherine suddenly stopped, staring down at the bit of cloth in growing horror. "Surely the police are looking for the man who murdered him?"

"It may not be a man."

"It couldn't be a woman."

"He was in a brothel, Miss Hayes."

Katherine's lip formed a sharp line. "Must you keep reminding me?"

"It's a fact. I can't change it. And that fact, I'm afraid, will eventually leak out to the public if this investigation continues."

"I've hired you for your discretion."

"And you have it," Isobel said. "But murderers are publicly prosecuted. A trial will put Dominic, you, and his family in the public's brutal eye. Every facet of his life will be laid open. Including private matters. I know. I went through it myself."

"Are you asking me to drop this?"

"You hired me to discover what happened to your fiancé. I've done that. The question is, do you wish me to continue my investigation?"

Katherine shuddered slightly, then stood and braced herself on the mantel for support.

Isobel wished Riot were there—not because she felt inadequate, but because Riot was so much better at this than she was. He had an uncanny way of reading people. Something she often failed at. Riot would surely let the silence remain, but Isobel broke it.

"Dominic was clearly murdered, Miss Hayes. But as to his father's involvement… it's plausible Ian is simply trying to prevent a scandal to protect his son's name. Ian Noble is rich and therefore influential. It's in his power to shut down a police investigation."

Katherine spun on her. "And allow a murderer to *escape justice*?" she hissed. "Isn't it also possible that his father doesn't want the murder investigated to hide his own sins?"

Isobel cocked her head at the plural use of the word. "What sins are those?" she asked.

"It's your job to discover that!" Grief could take many forms, but Isobel wasn't sure whether this was a glimpse into Katherine's true temperament or that churning sea of despair.

Isobel kept her voice even. "Did Dominic use laudanum?"

"Why do you ask?"

"It was found in his stomach."

"He pinched a nerve in his shoulder during a race."

"A race?"

"Rowing. He's a member of the Triton Rowing Club. A doctor prescribed laudanum to help with the pain."

"Can you think of any reason Dominic would go to the Nymphia?"

Katherine looked at a loss. "I can't fathom one. Donny was devoted to me."

"And yet he only met you for dinner once in a week's time."

"He's a busy man."

"Did he work with his father?"

Katherine hesitated. "No… not really. He held a position in his father's company, but in name only."

"And yet he was busy?"

"Donny was involved in clubs and parties. It's easier to name a club he didn't belong to, and… Why are you interrogating me?"

"I'm investigating, Miss Hayes. It's never pleasant." Isobel adjusted her cuffs, and stood. "Do you wish me to continue, or not?"

Katherine closed her eyes, pressing the handkerchief to her lips. "What is worse," she whispered. "A brutal truth or a pleasant lie?"

Isobel hesitated. Professionalism told her to be quiet. Her own twin didn't want the murder investigated. It would be messy—dangerous even, considering the money that was involved. But justice had a way of raging from the grave. She felt its pull.

"The unknown can cripple a person for life," Isobel finally said into the silence. "If it were me, I would *need* to know. You'll never make peace otherwise."

26

HEAVENLY GODS

SAO JIN STARED UP AT HER ADOPTIVE MOTHER AS THEY WALKED. Or rather, as Sarah talked and Isobel drifted. That was really the only word for it. Isobel was drifting down the sidewalk.

"It's like a museum in there," Sarah was saying. "Tiger skins and jade statues and little Egyptian figurines. And the most beautiful beaded necklace. Mr. Chang said that Mr. Hayes is rarely ever home. The Hayes own a shipping business and so the family can hop on a ship whenever they wish." Sarah gave a wistful sigh. "I'd love to sketch the pyramids. And parrots. Have you ever seen a parrot?"

"Parrots do not live in Egypt," Jin pointed out.

"If I went to Egypt, I'd travel on to other places. Don't you want to travel?" Sarah asked.

Jin glowered. "I do not think government officials would let me back into America if I left. Adoption paper or not."

"Mr. Chang travels. He said so. With Mr. Hayes. He's been all over, too."

"True," Jin said. "But I do not think he is actually a butler."

"He opened the door for us."

Jin sighed at her sister.

Isobel stopped suddenly, eyes focusing like daggers on the girl. "Why do you say that?"

"He did not offer us tea. That is an insult. Why would a butler insult guests of a woman who wishes us to be there?"

"Is that the only reason?"

Jin's brows scrunched together. "No… many little things. He carried himself as an equal."

"Servants aren't inferior," Sarah pointed out. "They're just employed. Mr. Hop argues with *avó* and drinks with *vovô* all the time."

"There was tea in the study. At the big desk. Would Mr. Hop sit at *vovô's* desk and drink tea?"

"Are you sure it wasn't Miss Hayes's desk?" Sarah asked.

"We saw her little writing desk in the sunroom."

Isobel began walking again, her thoughts on Jin's observations. The lines between servant and family had blurred long ago between Isobel's family and their long-time butler—her father and Hop were more akin to brothers who worked together. But even as close as they were, she could not imagine Hop sitting at her father's desk to drink tea. A desk was as personal as a bed in some ways.

She tucked the information aside for later. It was too early in the investigation to form theories.

In the end, Katherine Hayes wanted justice. She wanted the truth. But a part of Isobel worried she'd overstepped her professional bounds and nudged the woman towards a choice she'd regret.

Again, she ached to talk with Riot. For the pleasure of his company and his insights. With Riot a suspect in Monty's murder and an unknown assassin on the loose, adding this investigation would split her time and attention. She should've kept her mouth shut.

"Where are we going?" Sarah asked, intruding on her thoughts.

The street came into focus for the first time since leaving Miss Hayes's home, and Isobel cursed. She was in Nob Hill, on the gated corner of her ex-husband's mansion.

Isobel quickened her pace, forcing the girls to a near run to catch up. She hurried past Alex's home, eyeing the grounds and windows with a simmering rage. She wanted to confront her ex-husband, but had no proof whatsoever that he'd hired someone to kill Riot.

Wouldn't he direct his anger at her instead? Or would that come later?

Once her heart slowed down to a normal pace, she answered Sarah's question. "The agency."

"Why?" Jin asked.

"I have reports to write," she lied.

Jin wrinkled her nose. "We will go to Chinatown." And as Isobel was about to remind them of everything they weren't supposed to do, Jin recited, "We will not go to, around, or across the street from the 17th Station. We will not go down alleyways, and I will not stab people unless we are in danger."

Isobel glanced at Sarah, who nodded. She was sure there was a loophole in there somewhere, but she didn't have the energy to delve into tedious detail. The girls would do what they would do.

Still, she added one more thing. "I want you home before the street lamps are lit."

Isobel ignored Jin's eye roll, and the three parted ways. God, she was starting to sound like her mother.

Ravenwood Agency was closed, but Miss Off was there to answer the telephone. Isobel cut off the woman's ritual of insults. "Is Lotario here?"

"Look for your damn self. I'm not your maid."

Isobel was already walking towards the back office. The

door was locked, and after she employed her lock picks, she saw it was empty.

"There's keys, you know."

"I need the practice."

Miss Off harrumphed, then waved a slip of paper at her. "Some dirty rotten scamp banged on me door. Said it was important you get this. Made me pay him. I'm adding that to my wages."

Isobel snatched the folded slip of paper, and her heart skipped a beat when she read it.

LATE FOR THE MAGPIE

Isobel grinned with relief. It was Riot's neat handwriting, and she understood the cryptic message immediately. A heavy weight fell from her shoulders.

"I can't make no sense of it. That brat better not have conned me," Miss Off muttered.

"He didn't. Thank you, Miss Off." She tucked the message away, and went off to find her twin.

———

SUNDAY MORNINGS WERE FOR CHURCH, BUT THE AFTERNOON was for pleasure. All that talk of sin got the mind thinking, and the Barbary Coast was the place to go, waiting with arms wide open.

Isobel had swapped her skirts for shirt and trousers, and now walked with her hands in her pockets, taking in the sights. Women called from their windows and doorways, boys shoved pasteboard cards and bawdy pamphlets in her face trying to lure her in as a customer.

Keeping in character, she took a few and surveyed them as she walked. Isobel certainly hoped Lotario wouldn't start advertising Ravenwood Agency in the same manner. Surely he had more class than that?

She wound her way through a maze of narrow lanes until she came to an alleyway, then cursed under her breath and kept walking. A working girl was entertaining a client against the wall, right in front of the secret entrance (or rather escape door) of the *Narcissist*.

She could wait for the pair to finish, but the noises coming from the filthy alley made her wonder if a pig was involved. Isobel went around to the front entrance—a dark door set in a recessed archway.

She pulled the bell and a peephole slid to the side, revealing a pair of eyes. They looked unimpressed until the gaze settled on her face. The eyes widened in surprise.

"Don't ask," she drawled, mimicking Lotario's voice and mannerisms. "Just open the door."

The eyes hesitated—only a moment—before the door opened.

Isobel stepped inside a marbled foyer with a mural of muscular young men, sans clothing, competing in ancient Olympian games. She appreciated the historical accuracy.

The chiseled watchman stared down at her in puzzlement. "I thought you were getting ready for a show, Paris?"

Isobel plucked an Apollo mask from a table, and exchanged it for her cap. "I'll be late if I explain." She waved a flippant hand and started for the black velvet curtains, slipped past twin David statues, and into what appeared to be a festival to Dionysus. Some masked men wore togas. But not many.

Isobel tried not to brush against anyone as she wove her way through the celebrants, until she finally pushed through a side door and past a bodyguard in Spartan armor, wearing what looked like a real sword.

Isobel lifted up her mask. "I need to get to my dressing room," she said breathlessly.

The guard didn't ask questions. Without makeup, she and Lotario were near to identical, but there were subtle differences when compared side by side. The Spartan opened the door, and she slipped into a backstage dressing room.

Isobel had toured the brothel only in theory, as she'd made Lotario describe the interior of the *Narcissist*. So she was relieved to find the layout hadn't changed when she opened the door to his private dressing room.

Bruno, his hulking bodyguard, was helping him lace a glittering bodice. His skin was oiled, his eyes were lavishly painted, and his hair was a wig of flowing blond hair. The rest of his costume was... sparse. Isobel kept her eyes above his waist.

"What on earth are you doing *here*?" her twin hissed.

"I came to check on you."

"I'm working."

"Yes, I see that. Ari—"

"I'm fine. I have a show to put on."

"Then I'll wait and we can talk afterwards."

"I'll be entertaining the highest bidder."

Isobel looked at Bruno. "Is he fine?"

Bruno shook his head.

"Traitor," Lotario said.

"But Paris does have a show," Bruno pointed out. "And Hera won't be pleased if you agitate him before a performance."

"Oh, we wouldn't want that," Isobel said dryly.

Bruno frowned. "Careful what you say."

"She's my *twin*, Bruno."

"I know. That's why I'm warning her. I don't want you hurt if she gets herself into trouble."

"How much time do I have?" Lotario asked.

Bruno started to check his pocket watch, but Isobel stopped him. "I won't keep you. But I want you to know I spoke with her again. I told her the truth. She wants me to continue."

"Is this about Dom?" Bruno asked.

Isobel raised a brow at her twin. "You *told* him?"

"Bruno is my other twin."

She glanced at the pair—one a giant with dark brown skin and bulging muscles, the other as pale as alabaster with a dancer's lithe physique. "Are you identical?"

Bruno rumbled a laugh.

Lotario wasn't amused. "Bel, I've said my piece. God knows I can't stop you once you get something in your head…"

A knock interrupted his tirade, and the door opened, revealing the face of the Spartan from outside. Based on his musculature, he was clearly a man who tossed weights around all day. Isobel wondered if he could use that sword at his hip, or was the man just decoration.

"Hera would like to see you," the man said. Given his size, he had a startlingly soft voice.

"Now?" Lotario asked. "I have a show in—"

"No. *You.*" The Spartan pointed a finger at Isobel.

A breath swept past Lotario's lips. "The audience can wait. I'm the star of the show…"

The Spartan shook his head.

"Just remember, Bruno, I'm not the one who agitated him. This fellow did." Isobel placed a careful kiss on her twin's cheek and whispered in his ear. "If Hera is the family you say she is, then everything will be fine. Correct?"

She felt the tension in his body, the flicker of a long lash, and then he gave her a dazzling smile. "Of course."

"Enjoy your… festivities. Oh, and Riot was released."

"At least he'll be around to drag you out of trouble."

The words were light, but Isobel shared a more serious look with her twin, then donned her mask and left. She followed the Spartan through a maze of laughter, music, and gauzy curtains into a sitting room that bore no signs of a pagan festival, save for the woman standing in the room: petal-soft pink skin, full lips, and black hair piled high and bound in a golden serpent tiara. Flowing white linen trimmed with gold was draped around her sensuous body. It managed somehow to be more revealing than the Spartan's spartan armor.

"Remove your mask," the Spartan ordered.

Isobel did so.

Hera gestured for the guard to leave, and when he was gone the women studied one another in silence. It was Hera who broke the standoff. She slowly sauntered around Isobel, who slightly turned with the woman.

"You are near mirrors of each other," Hera finally said. "*Both of lovely shape like none of the heavenly gods.*" Her voice startled Isobel, a sultry baritone that contrasted with tumbling hair and full lips.

"I'm afraid my Greek mythos is rusty." It took Isobel a moment to place the source. "Apollo and Artemis, isn't it? Twin brother and sister, born to Zeus?"

Hera's lips curved as she sank into a chair, then gestured Isobel to do the same. "The *Theogony*, an epic poem by Hesiod."

"I believe Hera was infuriated by the twins."

"With her husband. Though stories are conflicting. Hesiod places Zeus and Hera's marriage after the twins' birth. What do you think of the Greek epics?"

Isobel swallowed down a well of impatience. She disliked games and idle chat. But then nothing about Hera struck her as idle or amusing. Dangerous, yes. Something about the woman raised her hackles.

Perhaps the name she had chosen for herself? Hera. Queen of Gods, sister and wife to Zeus—after he tricked and raped her. Vengeful. Jealous. Goddess of Women. Only this Hera had the underpinnings of a male. Or was Isobel looking too closely at a name?

Lotario often switched personas. She took his transformations as part of him. Whether male or female, Lotario was still her twin. It didn't change the person within.

Layers of masks, of identities, and a name that spoke of pain. Who really was this person Hera? That was the crux of her distrust. Isobel knew nothing about this figure, except that she had power over her twin. And Isobel didn't know its source.

"I think they were written by people with too much time on their hands, who wanted an excuse to have orgies. What do you want, Hera?"

Hera smiled, but it wasn't charming; it made Isobel itch for a knife. "Paris would never be so blunt."

"I'm not my twin."

"I see that. Near opposites, like a mirror's reflection. Except, of course, your shared interest with investigation. I was surprised when he came to me with his business proposal."

Isobel stopped herself from grinding her teeth.

"I can't say I'm pleased with this little detective venture of his."

"You make it sound like he needs your permission to work at Ravenwood Agency."

"I think his talents are better suited elsewhere."

"And where is that?"

"With me."

"I disagree."

"We both care for him, Miss Amsel. I can see that. We simply disagree on what's best for him."

"*Care* isn't the word I'd use. What do you want from me?"

"I'd like you to drop your investigation into Dominic Noble's death."

Isobel stifled her surprise. Had Lotario told Hera about the murder, too? No, he wouldn't, would he? She didn't know that answer, so she decided to play dumb.

"There's nothing much to it. Dominic died in his sleep."

"I can tell you value directness, Miss Amsel, so I'll skip the wordplay. Dominic was murdered in the Nymphia. You were there, on the crime scene, and you consulted with the police."

"How do you know?"

Hera gestured towards the door as if presenting the room on a platter. "There are worlds within worlds, and ours is a small, shadowed one."

More likely Hera had connections with someone in the police department—the same someone who took bribes to turn a blind eye to her brothel.

"I was hired to find his murderer," Isobel said. "Who better to investigate than someone who understands the delicacy of the situation?"

"I don't think you truly understand delicacy, Miss Amsel."

"Where my twin is concerned, I do."

"You nearly exposed Lucie during the August Duncan affair."

"My twin was *abducted*. And *we* took care of it."

"So you think," Hera said. "Do you know the lengths I went through to keep that scandal from the public eye?"

Isobel raised a brow. "Likely the same lengths you take to operate your brothel."

Hera gave a small smile. "You've been warned, Miss Amsel. Paris is special to me, but I have more than your twin to protect."

"Is that a threat?"

"No. A warning. There are limits to my influence. I won't always be able to protect him from your blundering."

Isobel bristled. "And what of Dominic Noble? Doesn't his life demand justice?"

"Justice is not blind. And where people like me are concerned, we are the fodder that burns."

"People like you aren't fodder, Hera. You're the ones with torches. Money is power, and you have a great deal of it."

"What makes you say that?"

"Forbidden fruit doesn't come cheap."

Hera rose to her feet like a queen over court. "I'll ask you to leave now. It was… intriguing to finally meet you. I can only hope you'll heed my advice."

"Or what?"

"If your investigation shines a light on my world, you will discover why I call myself Hera. Tread softly, Miss Amsel."

27

TIME AND TRINKETS

LATE FOR THE MAGPIE. TO ANYONE ELSE THE CRYPTIC MESSAGE would have meant nothing at all, but it told Isobel several things: Riot was free, but had not gone home. He was being cautious. The word 'late' had to do with time. And magpies, though debatable, were attracted to shiny baubles. Time and trinkets. That pointed to a certain landlady named Mrs. Beeton, who ran the Sapphire House where Isobel kept rooms.

A simple but effective cipher.

Isobel wanted to rush straight to Sapphire House, but Riot's caution gave her pause. So instead she transferred from cable car to cable car, until she was certain no one was following her. And as an added precaution she circled around to the back of the boardinghouse to climb a drainpipe.

The window to her rooms was closed when she came balancing along a ledge. She tested it, found it unlocked, and pushed it up to slip through. A single gas lamp burned in the dim, casting its light on an array of trunks, clothing racks, and a bed that had been shoved into a corner.

With its central location, Sapphire House made a convenient place to store disguises, so it was more storage room than living space right then.

A shift of movement in a corner of the room caught her breath. The click of a revolver, and a quick holstering of the weapon. She turned to the shadowed corner, where a man rose from an armchair, a glint of silver around his eyes.

Isobel was pulled toward the man—by that unseen, electrifying current that seemed to zip over her skin every time he entered a room.

With a laugh of pure joy, she rushed into his arms. Riot buried his fingers in her hair and kissed her temple, his beard tickling her face. He took a deep breath, and she felt his sigh.

Isobel pulled back to inspect her husband. He was worn around the edges, his eyes shadowed, but he was clean, smelling of sandalwood and myrrh, and fresh soap. She ran fingers through his trim beard. "And here I was worried about you."

"After four days in lockup, there is nothing so satisfying as a trip to the barber, a good meal, and a hot bath."

She glanced at the half-eaten sandwich on a plate near a bottle of whiskey. "I come second to a sandwich?"

"Not the sandwich; maybe to the whiskey, though."

"That *is* excellent whiskey," she said, running her hands up his bare forearms. His shirt was clean, collar open, and sleeves rolled up to the elbows. He'd obviously found the trunk of clothes she kept for him, along with her medicinal beverages.

"I also found your coin purse," he said, seeming to read her thoughts. "I stole from it to pay for a barber and a meal."

Isobel clucked her tongue. "Rogue."

"At least I'm an honest one."

"And a charming one."

"So you claim." Fingers brushed her neck, and her skin came alive. Pounding hearts, her own and his, a soft exhale, and she met his lips. The intensity shocked her. Both of them. A moment turned into two, and a caress turned into more.

SOMETIME LATER, RIOT JERKED AWAKE. HE FLUNG OUT HIS arm, fingers wrapping around a pistol grip, but he stopped himself from fully drawing. Instead, he listened as he searched the dark room.

Nothing moved, except the shadows cast by a glowing hearth. His skin smelt of her. Their mingled sweat cool on his body. He relaxed at the sound of water splashing in the bathroom, and his head fell back onto a pillow.

He was spent—drained of strength. Small wonder, he thought, considering Isobel's passion. It was more akin to a wildfire. There was nothing halfway about the woman.

After a time he sat up, found his spectacles nearby, and threaded them over his ears to look towards the window. Night had fallen. A thermos, a bowl of fruit, and a package wrapped in paper sat on top of a trunk. How long had he slept?

Riot pulled on a pair of drawers, and padded over to the window. Standing to one side, he shifted the curtain open with two fingers to search the narrow lane below. Nothing moved.

The bathroom door opened, and Isobel emerged from a cloud of steam. She was naked and glistening, and he stirred with desire. He clearly wasn't as tired as he'd first thought.

"I forgot my robe." Isobel gave him a knowing smile as she reached for the garment, but only loosely tied it, leaving a tantalizing expanse of throat and shoulder exposed. "You seemed worn out, so I didn't wake you."

"Sleep was scarce in jail. I'm getting too old for cell bunks."

"Is anyone ever young enough for a bunk?" she asked, pulling over a dressing stool to sit by their makeshift trunk table.

"I don't remember them being quite so hard."

"You were just missing *our* bed."

"You could tell?"

"A little," she said, as she nudged the paper package and thermos towards him. "I got you a proper meal. And tea. Though I'll be having whiskey."

Riot unwrapped the paper to find a warm meat pie. His mouth started watering.

"I also telephoned our daughters. No gunshots, stabbings, or explosions. I told them we'd be out for the night. I didn't want them overreacting. They always think we're in mortal danger..." Isobel trailed off at the look in his eyes.

"Thank you, Bel."

The edge of her lip quirked. "I do occasionally perform *some* domestic duties."

He took a bite, considering. "I'm not sure barging into the Nymphia during a police raid would commonly count as a domestic duty."

"How did you—" She caught herself. "Ah, you spoke with Liam Taft, didn't you?"

"It was more of a casual interrogation."

Her eyes flashed like steel in the fire's light. "Was he rough with you?"

"O'Hare was certainly keen on a proper interrogation. But thanks to your quick thinking, reinforcements arrived. Doyle was a godsend."

Isobel studied his face. Although shadowed, his eyes were free of pain, and showed no signs of suffering a headache.

He gave her a half smile. "You're worrying, Bel."

"Not as much now. Was Taft in charge?"

"I wouldn't say he was in charge. The Pinkertons and police have a long history. He was there because an operative was gunned down. It's standard proced—" Riot cut off when Isobel gave a shake of her head. "What is it?"

"Monty wasn't a Pinkerton."

Riot frowned. "But he said…" he trailed off in realization. Riot half wished Ravenwood were there to tell him what a fool he was. Monty had played him.

"Don't be so hard on yourself," Isobel said. "You were *half* right."

"He was either a Pinkerton or he wasn't."

Isobel poured herself a tumbler of whiskey. "Try again."

Riot chewed in thought, but was distracted by his meat pie. "Where did you get this?"

"A lady around the corner sells them from her home."

He made an appreciative sound. "Monty didn't correct me when I suggested he'd hired on with the Pinkertons," Riot said. "He said he could move up there. So for whatever reason he wanted me to go on believing he was working as a Pinkerton."

"And everyone else," Isobel said. "The patrolman who discovered his body found a Pinkerton badge in his locker at The Den. It was fake."

Riot swallowed that bit of information with his next bite. Isobel told him the rest—her chat with Sims, the discovery that Liam Taft and his partner hadn't known Monty, and finally her swim in a cesspit.

That last bit troubled him. One bullet. No other cartridges in the chamber. A discarded rifle of a popular make found across America for the past three decades. It also brought a new perspective to Liam Taft's questions.

"Taft must've thought Ravenwood Agency was involved in the deception."

"I think so," Isobel said. "He's still not sharing information. Though I plan to corner him again."

"Was Taft already investigating someone impersonating an agent?"

"I'm not sure. But when I confronted him in his office, he wasn't keen on anyone else overhearing our conversation."

Riot gave a half smile. "I wish I'd been there when you found the murder weapon. I wager Geary was grinding his teeth. Excellent work, Bel."

She lifted a shoulder—the exposed one. "It was obvious. But thank you. You know I wasn't expecting Geary to release you until tomorrow. Did you see Mr. Fry's exclusive?"

"I did."

"What spooked you today?"

He told her, then sat back with a sigh, the thermos warming his hands. "Maybe I'm just paranoid."

"You and me both. Everything about your release has me worried."

"I should've walked bold as brass down the street to draw out an ambush. Then we'd know for sure."

Isobel gave him a look. "No. You should not have."

"Well, I didn't. But twenty years ago, I would have."

"Twenty years ago, you were single and sleeping in a cold bed."

Riot ran a hand through his hair, feeling the scar at his temple. "There are a surprising number of lonely widows and divorcées in the world, you know."

"And now you're saddled with a divorcée."

"Saddled isn't the word I'd use."

"What would you use?" she asked.

"I think you have me saddled."

Isobel snorted. Then, with a cocked grin, she plucked up the whiskey bottle and an apple and went over to the fire. He set down his empty thermos to follow, and they settled themselves on the hearth rug, backs against a trunk, feet stretched towards the glowing coals.

"So what was Liam Taft after when he interrogated you?" she asked.

"He asked after my time with Pinkertons. Specifically why Ravenwood and I left."

"Which was?" she asked, pouring him a shot.

"*It isn't the mountain ahead that wears you out; it's the grain of sand in your shoe,*" he said, then downed his whiskey in one gulp.

She cocked her head, trying to place the quote.

"An imaginative young fellow by the name of Robert Service I once met. They called him the Bard of the Yukon."

"That's lovely, Riot, but it doesn't answer my question."

"In this case, the grain of sand was a fellow detective by the name of Jim Hagen. I discovered he was extorting money and blackmailing folks. He was more criminal than some outlaws we were hunting. I didn't have proof. Just a hunch. Word of mouth. Rumor. He was a hard one to pin down. I wrote a report without proper evidence, which didn't go over well. So Ravenwood and I severed ties with the Pinkertons and went our own way."

She shifted at his side to look at him. "You mean Ravenwood feared you would take the law into your own hand and gun the man down."

"Did he write that in his journals?"

"You haven't read all of them yet?"

"The ones you gave me. It feels like I'm invading his privacy."

"You don't like looking at yourself through his eyes."

"Would you enjoy looking at yourself through your mother's?" he countered, despite his better sense.

"I know precisely what my mother would say," she said dryly.

"I don't have your mettle, Bel."

"But you're good at changing the subject. Just like me."

Riot held out his glass, and she poured him another shot. "I did have a mind to shoot Jim. But I didn't."

"Why would Taft suspect you of impersonating a Pinkerton, though? Aside from Monty working for you? You exposed a dirty operative."

"He also mentioned my record with the Pinkertons."

She waited for more, but nothing more came, so she arched a pointed brow. "Your record?"

"I brought back more wanted men dead than alive."

"Hmm."

A coal shifted in the fire, stirring flame to life. Riot looked down at his whiskey and found another shot gone.

"Why would Monty be posing as a fake agent?" she asked.

"The same reasons men impersonate police officers," Riot said. "Extortion. Blackmail. Power. Getting folks to open their doors. There's also a number of jobs the Pinkertons won't touch—least they're not supposed to. If word got around that there was an agent willing to take on dirty work, I could see where that might be attractive to some."

"It'd be like a policeman willing to skirt the law."

"To get things done."

"Like you," Isobel murmured.

Riot didn't deny it, but her words still stung. His mind turned to the past, which was always a dangerous thing. Could he have brought more wanted men in alive? The thought of some of those men—what they'd done—rapists, child murderers, butchers. Yes, it was true, he could have shot fewer men. But Riot doubted he could have lived with himself if the courts had let some of those men walk free.

"Hopefully Taft will decide to trust us," Isobel said.

"Can we trust him?"

"I'm not sure we have a choice."

Riot swirled his glass, which had been mysteriously refilled. Was she trying to get him drunk? "The way he steered the conversation towards the reasons I left makes me wonder what Jim Hagen's up to."

"But you didn't get Hagen fired."

"My accusations and initial report eventually did."

"Is he the type to hold a grudge?" Isobel asked.

Riot knocked back his whiskey, teeth clicking against the glass. "He's the type."

28

GARBAGE DUTY

TIM PERCHED ON THE FIRST RUNG OF A ROUND PEN, ARMS hanging over the side to keep him in place as he admired a horse being worked, its trainer turning with it as it pranced in a circle.

"That there is a fine horse," he said to his companion.

"Maiden now, but I'd bet my hat she'll be a banker," said Skunk. The fellow looked like he'd fallen on his face one too many times. Flat-faced, flat-nosed, and skin like a gnarled oak. He mumbled something fierce, too. Everyone called him 'Skunk' on account of him not being able to smell a skunk spraying him.

"Tell you what," Tim said. "I wouldn't trade one of these fancy fellows for a good bangtail. Can't get down a mountain-side on one of these."

"Amen. But I'd take one in a race any day."

"Damn straight," Tim said. "I could do without the owners, though. Constant burr in my ass back in the day."

Skunk eyed him. "You got the look of a jockey."

"Fellow my size? Sure enough. Nothing…" Tim waved his

pipe at the surrounding stables, "so fine though. Now these rich folk got their own bookies catering to them."

"No races without them rich folk. I could do without the crime going on here."

"What is it about tracks and crime?"

"Money, I suppose," Skunk mumbled. "A man doesn't bet less'n he's hungry for cash."

"Or food. What would it be, spend your last twenty-five cents on food for one meal or bet it all on a horse?"

Skunk chewed on the thought. "Guess it keeps men like me working."

"There's that, too."

A gentleman in a flat cap came walking around one building. Noise from the grandstands carried cheers and thundering hooves, but it was fairly peaceful in their corner of the grounds.

"There he is." Skunk had sense enough not to nod towards the man. Tim eyed the fellow as he climbed a wooden stairway to an office above a stable house.

"Don't look like much," Tim noted.

Skunk shrugged. "Does his job."

Tim shook his head. "Pinkertons at the racetrack. I suppose it's 'bout time." The Pinkertons did have a branch for private security.

"Stop the crime 'fore it happens."

"For those that can afford it."

Skunk chuckled, a deep rolling sound. "Ain't that the way of things?"

"Why the secret, though?" Tim asked.

Skunk shrugged. "Hard to stop lardons when everyone and their mothers know you're a lawman. Them Pinkertons keep low."

"Sure, but *you* know who they are."

Skunk tapped an ear. "My sniffer may be knocked into a cocked hat, but my wattles are just fine."

Tim knocked his own hat against his thigh and hopped off the fence. "Welp, wish me luck."

"You're gonna need it."

"I may be old, but I still got some kick in me."

"Stable hand be a better bet."

"I aim high," Tim said. He tipped his cap, and walked bold as brass towards the upper-story office. There was nowhere to hide around the building. It was set apart from the others, and the upper story was higher off the ground than usual, so that made climbing through one of the narrow windows near impossible without a ladder.

Tim eyed the door as he applied his fist to the wood. Solid core. New lock. There'd be no easy break-in here.

"Come," a voice said.

Tim stepped in and removed his hat. The man in the cap looked up in surprise, eyes narrowing. He was in his late forties, with salt and pepper hair, of average height and strong build. He wore a revolver on his hip, and his hand rested on the grip. "Who are you?"

Tim ducked his head, turning his cap in his hands. "Name's Tim, Mr. Carson. I hear you're the man to see for a job."

"I'm not hiring."

"I'm handy in a fight." Tim flashed his gold teeth as he stepped up to the desk. "Ornery as heck, and still alive. I'd be useful."

Carson's hand fell away from his gun. "Useful? I don't need someone with one foot in the grave."

"But I need work somethin' awful. I can shoot. Still got one good eye."

"Get out, old man."

"I can clean. Be an errand boy." Tim grabbed the trash bin. "I can take this out right now. Shine boots—"

Carson came around the desk and gave him a shove. Tim stumbled against the wall, clutching the bin to his chest.

"Out, before I toss you down the stairs."

"Mr. Carson, please. I'm good for a lot."

Carson jerked his head to the side. "Go."

Tim ducked an apology. "Yessir." He hurried past Carson, making for the exit.

"Wait."

Tim froze, then turned. "Had a change of heart, Mr. Carson?"

Carson wrenched the trash bin from his arms, then nudged him out none too kindly. The door slammed on his back, and Tim skipped down the stairway with a whistle on his lips.

29

SCIENTIFIC METHOD

"Dare I ask what you've been up to?"

"Oh, you know, visiting brothels, meeting with prostitutes, being threatened by my twin's madam."

"So the usual?"

Isobel flicked his ear.

"Careful. I'm fragile."

"Like hell."

"Did your meeting with Hera have something to do with the Nymphia?" Riot asked.

"Before I tell you, I'd like to test a theory. You're the only test subject who will do."

"All right…" Riot said slowly.

Her eyes flashed with excitement. "Bed or rug?"

"What's your theory?" Riot asked.

"I can't tell you. *Yet*. How much have you had to drink?"

"You tell me. You've been filling my glass."

"Would you say that you're fully in control of your senses?"

"I'm likely more relaxed than I should be considering that look in your eyes."

"Riot," she said, with a flutter of lashes. "Surely you trust your wife?"

"Will this involve anything flammable?"

"No."

"The rug is fine, then."

"The rug it is." Isobel was on her feet, bristling with energy. She pushed the trunk out of the way, placed the whiskey bottle on top, then he stood so she could lay down a blanket. "Right. Off with the underwear."

"I'm relieved you didn't ask another man to strip for you."

"I need someone with an athletic physique and strength." She gestured up and down his body. "If you'd been in lockup one more day, I might've had to start looking elsewhere."

"Remind me to thank Mr. Fry for that article." He stepped out of his drawers, planted his feet and spread his hands. "Satisfactory?"

"You'll do. Now lay down." She gestured impatiently at the floor.

Riot crossed his arms, stroking his beard in consideration. "In the middle of the blanket?"

"The bed was narrow. Maybe three feet wide."

"Am I supposed to be a side sleeper, back, or stomach?"

"However men usually lie with a lady of the line."

"I wouldn't know."

"*Really?*"

"That surprises you?"

"I just assumed…" she trailed off.

"That I was like most men?"

"No." Isobel frowned, then amended her statement. "Yes. Honestly, I try not to think about it. You did grow up in San Francisco, and were a lifelong bachelor who clearly knows his way around women."

"And with the number of brothels it's easy to imagine every man in the city frequents one."

"It does seem that way."

"I grew up in a crib, Bel. I've seen too much pain to get any pleasure out of that world."

Isobel caught his eyes, and he gave her a lopsided grin to lighten the mood. She played along. "But widows and divorcées are fair game?" she asked.

He spread his hands. "Apparently they find me charming."

Isobel's gaze drifted downwards. "That *must* be it."

Riot cleared his throat. "Back to your mysterious theory. From my second-hand experience, terms of transaction are always discussed first."

"Ah." She tapped her lips.

"Maybe it would help if you told me what you found?"

"No, I want you to be surprised. I need a reaction. Let's assume the terms were for a... erm."

Riot cocked his head, waiting, while color spread down her throat. He helped her along. "A frenchie? Tip the velvet? St. George? Haul the ashes? Beast with two backs?"

Her blush deepened. "I can't help but note the first thing that came to your mind. When do you think a man is at his most vulnerable?"

"Were there marks on his wrists?"

"No. Not of the rope variety. I checked. He put up a fight, fending someone off from the front."

"This won't involve any sharp objects, I hope? Scissors, perhaps?"

"You really think that of me, Riot?"

"I'm going to tactfully ignore that question."

She crossed her arms.

"St. George, then." Riot lay on the blanket, folding his arms behind his head.

Isobel narrowed her eyes as she straddled him. "You look entirely too smug."

"Just playing my part."

"You can't fake *this.*" Isobel gave a wiggle, and all thought fled his brain. Riot gripped her arm and drew her down, but she stopped short of kissing him.

"I'm told whores don't kiss," she whispered.

"I'm not a client."

Isobel smiled. "Humor me."

With the way she was moving on top of him, Riot was willing to do whatever she wanted. A number of pleasurable minutes passed until Riot forgot how or why they had ended up on the floor.

Then without warning, Isobel shifted her body to wrap her legs around his thighs, pinning him, then pressed his hands over his head, against the floor. "Fair warning, Riot, I'm going to try to kill you now."

Mind muddled with pleasure and whiskey, it took a moment for her words to sink in—at least until she pressed a handkerchief over his nose and mouth.

Riot narrowed his eyes. And she rolled hers in return. "Would you at least *pretend* I'm smothering you?"

It wasn't hard to pretend. He couldn't breathe. But he wasn't all that concerned, only eager to get back to what they'd been doing. Though pinned as he was, it was proving difficult.

Riot tried to raise his arms, and she bore down on him with her weight. He tried to kick up, but was pinned by her legs. Then she started stuffing the handkerchief into his mouth.

That got his blood pumping. With a surge of power, Riot broke her hold, and after a brief but fierce struggle, he came out on top, pinning her in much the same way. Riot spit the handkerchief out.

They were both panting now.

"Damn," she breathed. "That was too easy."

"My turn," Riot said.

"Are you going to try to kill me?"

"No, but I'll leave you breathless."

He did. Thoroughly. Again.

A FIST BANGED ON THE ADJOINING WALL. "PEOPLE ARE TRYING to sleep!" It was her neighbor, Mr. Crouch, a semi-retired forger.

Isobel panted against Riot's neck. She was too overwhelmed for embarrassment. "That was louder than I intended," she breathed.

"I could still arrest him."

"Don't you dare."

"Or you'll bite me again?"

She glanced at the mark she'd left on his shoulder. "It's *your* fault."

"Entirely."

When they finally broke apart, Isobel collapsed onto her back, trying to catch her breath. Riot stretched alongside her with an appreciative glint in his eye. A sheen of sweat and firelight glistened over their bodies.

Her head fell to the side to meet his eyes. "I do believe you deviated from our terms."

"You broke terms first. Trying to kill me wasn't part of our deal."

"Hmm." She snuggled closer, head on his chest, and he idly stroked her back. They lay for a time, drifting in a daze. Then the weight on his chest left, and footsteps padded towards the bathroom.

When Isobel returned, she pulled a blanket over him, but didn't stretch along his body. He could *feel* her thinking. Could practically hear the gears of her mind whirring.

"I beg your pardon?" he murmured.

"I didn't say anything."

Riot opened his eyes. Isobel was propped on an elbow, looking thoughtful. She was wearing a chemise that was near to translucent set against the firelight. His mind was muddled

—dazed, even—and she seemed a dream. Sleep beckoned, but there was something he wanted to know... the thought fought its way to his lips. "What *have* you been up to, Bel?"

She told him, and he listened, fighting against the urge to sleep. By the time she finished, he was left trying to sort through the details. Why was it proving so difficult? He felt like a dumb brick.

"Thank you for playing along. I needed to know if someone my size could smother a man like Dominic Noble. The prostitute who rented the room, if that was her locker, wore clothes of my size. Same goes for Jacob Dixon. He's taller than me, but I'd wager a hundred dollars I could best him in a fight."

"There's the laudanum to consider."

Isobel was trailing her fingers over his chest. "I may have put a small dose in your tea," she admitted.

Riot blinked. Suddenly the fog in his mind made sense.

She smiled back. "You're more relaxed now," she pointed out.

"It's fortunate the fellow wasn't poisoned."

"I would never use anything lethal. I promise."

"If I fall asleep while you're talking, it's your fault."

"I'll try to be interesting," she said. "But this scratches off two suspects, I think. I'm stronger than most women, and I didn't stand a chance against you. Even drugged, you broke free of my hold with little effort. Dominic Noble was both younger and larger than you."

"Footballer?"

She shook her head. "A rower. And I think a swimmer by the look of him. Possibly trained with weights."

"There's the back doors, fire escape, and the resident passages in the brothel to consider. Someone could've slipped into the room."

"Hell, there could've been two people. Or four."

"I don't think he'd have been able to fight as much. One would have pinned his arms while the other smothered him. I'll admit, the handkerchief is a disturbing detail. It's personal—revenge for an assault, maybe?"

"I thought of that. Perhaps Dominic nearly choked a woman to death during sex."

"Wouldn't be the first time it happened."

He felt her cringe.

"A large woman might be able to manage," he suggested. "Years ago, there was a woman by the name of Miss Marshall in the Barbary Coast. Everyone called her Big Louise on account of her size—she was over three hundred pounds and was known to fall on anyone who irritated her."

Isobel stared at him in disbelief. "You're joking."

"I'm not." He started shaking with laughter. "I won't ever be able to get the image of Tim crushed under her out of my head."

Isobel snorted. "It's a wonder he's alive."

"He's tough as leather."

"I spotted a few women of considerable mass in the Nymphia, but I can't see them managing to pin Dominic's hands."

"There are other ways to smother a man."

She cocked her head.

Riot gripped her waist, and slid her up, until he was eye level with her breasts, then he buried his face between them to demonstrate.

Isobel got the hint and wrapped her arms around his head. "But can't you pry me off?"

"Why would I want to?" came his muffled reply.

"Obviously you can still breathe." She tightened her hold. With his arms free, he tried to push her away, but she wrapped her legs around his torso in a bear hug. His legs flailed, useless, as he struggled to buck her off.

Finally, Riot tapped her back, and Isobel let go. He gasped for air.

"That could work, Riot," she said, rising to her knees. "It would explain why Dominic had blood under his fingernails. He may have been trying to claw her off, in which case, she'd have scratches down her back."

"With a heavier woman, there wouldn't be much fight at all."

"You mean a curvier one."

"A man can certainly get lost between a pair of breasts."

"Speaking from experience?"

"Purely theoretical."

"Wise answer," she said. "But if this is a case of death by cleavage, why the handkerchief and pencil?"

"He may have blacked out. The murderer thought him dead, then he came to, and they grabbed whatever was closest."

Isobel pursed her lips in thought. "He could just as easily have fallen asleep, dazed with drink and laudanum, then woke to someone smothering him."

"All possibilities," Riot agreed.

She sighed. "Then I can't discount the woman who rented the room. And it still leaves the question... what would a man like Dominic Noble be doing in the Nymphia?"

Riot's jaw cracked with a yawn. If he stayed on the floor a moment longer, he'd drift off to sleep, so he sat up to stoke the fire. "A proper brothel will have a madam overseeing every-thing—to make sure men behave. It's the women of the house who have the control, or should. Women set the rules in a respectable brothel. But the Nymphia... it sounds more like a street of cribs." He stabbed at a log with the poker. "Men go to those places when they want to be in charge."

"Lotario was fond of Dominic. Close, even. But that doesn't mean Dominic couldn't have had a darker side. So, say he gets rough with the Japanese woman in the room, she smothers him, steals his clothes because her bill wasn't settled, and leaves."

"Or she just plain robbed him."

"There's that, too." Isobel leaned against the trunk with a sigh. "Hundreds of suspects, all with fake names. Most escaped. And only a carpenter's pencil to be found. The family doesn't want their own son's murder investigated, the police won't investigate, and even my twin and his madam warned me away. I can't help but think maybe I pushed Miss Hayes into making the wrong choice."

"You were honest."

"Was it honesty, or was I looking after my own interests? I find this case intriguing. The complexity daunting in a perfectly splendid way."

Riot stared appreciatively at his wife. She was breathless with excitement—a brimming energy that was a tangible thing. She had that same intensity when they made love.

"Why are you looking at me like that?" she asked.

"Like what?"

"Fondly."

Riot had to laugh. "Arousal suits you, Bel."

"I'm not…"

"Stimulated?"

"*Mentally*, yes."

"Either way, you're entrancing."

"It's because you can't see me without your spectacles."

"I can see you blushing."

"The fire is hot," she said primly. "What if I don't like the climax?"

"I'm certain you weren't faking the last two…"

"To the *investigation*."

"Ah. Interesting word choice."

"Are you trying to distract me?"

"I'm not the one who brought up climaxing. Fair warning, I'll need some time to recover before we—"

"You're insufferable."

"And you're flustered."

"Do try to focus, Riot."

"I might be able to, if someone hadn't drugged me."

"It was a *small* dose."

Riot draped an arm over his knee. "So you say."

"It wasn't enough to impede your… vitality."

"Here I thought you married me for my wit and charm. Turns out you were after my prick."

Isobel poked him with a toe. "You're not even slurring your words. Though I'll have to remember laudanum makes you vulgar."

"Would my 'doodle' have been a less vulgar euphemism?"

Isobel's lips twitched as she fought down a laugh. "I'm sorry I drugged you without warning." Her voice only wavered a little.

He stared at her. Waiting.

"And pretended to murder you."

Riot gestured for her to keep going.

"I won't do it again. Though you are rather amusing like this. *And* relaxed. You haven't reached for your gun once."

"That's because you had it firmly in hand the whole time."

Isobel sighed. "I left myself wide open for that one, didn't I?" Riot started to reply, but she quickly pressed fingertips to his lips. "*Don't* say it."

A smile tugged at the corner of his lips, and a moment later a warm, velvety soft tongue flicked across the pad of her finger.

Isobel took her fingers away. "Are you quite done?"

Riot thought for a moment. Then looked under the blanket around his waist. "Maybe not."

She arched a brow. "Do try to be serious, Riot. What if we

don't like what we find at the end? What if the poor woman was only defending herself?"

The question sobered him. "A knock on the head is defense. Stuffing a handkerchief down someone's throat with a pencil is another beast entirely."

"Still."

"Bel, the police aren't looking for a murderer. They're not even reporting it as one. If we don't like what we find, we'll leave it be."

"And hope we haven't stirred up a mess."

"We usually stir up a mess," he pointed out. "We may uncover something more sinister."

"Like blackmail."

"That was my first thought. If Dominic was being blackmailed for his affairs with men, he might have confronted his blackmailer. Or this could be a crime of hate, and the murderer is targeting men with similar tastes."

"In which case we need to stop him—or her."

"Where to start?" he asked.

She quirked her lip. "You know precisely where to start. You're just being courteous."

"It's your investigation. You're a police consultant, after all."

"Don't sound so surprised."

"That's pride you hear, Bel."

A blush spread over her cheeks. "Discretion isn't my strong point, nor patience."

"I had noticed."

"As much as I loathe to suggest this… I think we need to divide our forces."

"I'll take the Nymphia," he said quickly.

"But I could just as easily disguise myself as a young man."

"No."

Isobel arched a brow. "Are you telling me what I can and cannot do?"

"Yes. On this."

She searched his eyes. The whimsy was gone, replaced by a haunted look. "Men don't go to brothels like the Nymphia for companionship. They go when they have a mind to be worse than animals. I'll hire on as a watchman. It'll give me freedom to poke around and make friends with the women."

"Perhaps I don't like the idea of you wandering around a hotel full of naked women."

"I won't be wandering, Bel. Besides, disappearing will keep the hired guns off my back, and give Tim more time to dig into what Monty was up to."

"About that…"

Riot frowned at her.

"What?" she asked.

"That's it?"

"What do you mean?"

"You're not indignant over being tied to a domineering husband?"

"You sound disappointed."

"I'm not. I just expected a proper tongue lashing."

Isobel rubbed her arms. "I wasn't much looking forward to a prolonged visit. That place made my skin crawl, Riot." He shifted to wrap an arm around her, and she leaned into his body, eyes on the fire. "And… you're right. I'll have more luck infiltrating the Noble household."

"That won't be without risks," he said. "But while we're planning… I think it's high time I have a chat with the people who robbed me."

"What's your plan?"

"It could be dangerous."

"Then perhaps you should wait to finalize any plans until you're sober."

30

PARANOID LAWMEN

THE MONDAY HUSTLE ON POST STREET WAS REASSURING. A man could get lost in the crowd. That's precisely what Atticus Riot wanted. He leaned against a brick wall under the shadow of an awning, watching the street traffic. Wagons, cable cars, bicycles, electric motorcars, and horses—it was an impromptu orchestra of near collisions. To say nothing of the pedestrians. And the noise. The ringing of bells, whistles, clop of hooves, engines, shouts, and clatter of cable cars could drown out a gunfight.

Riot took a sip from his thermos. He'd prepared the tea himself that morning (though Isobel had offered with a flutter of innocent lashes). He smiled to himself, then took a bite of the muffin he'd bought from a nearby wagon. A line of its customers stretched along the sidewalk, as others stood off to the side enjoying a quick breakfast. Dressed in cloth cap and rough clothes, he was just another face in the crowd on his way to work.

Across the street, Riot spotted his quarry. A graying, bow-legged man sauntered out of an office building. Liam Taft paused to settle a Stetson on his head as he eyed the crowded street, then started walking down the sidewalk.

Riot handed thermos and muffin to a little girl in a patched dress drooling at the bread wagon, then weaved his way through traffic after the agent. The Pinkerton was easy to follow—tall and distinctive, he stood out in a sea of city suits.

Riot knew the man's destination, so he took his time, letting his quarry get farther ahead. He wanted to make sure no one else was following the agent. When Riot was satisfied, he slipped from the flow of pedestrians to stick a cigarette between his lips. His position offered an excellent view of a coffeehouse across the street.

Liam Taft sat inside at a front window. Riot knew the place well, which was why he'd chosen it (and because there were three exits from the building).

He reached for his pocket watch, then sighed when he found it gone. Losing Ravenwood's watch, along with his walking stick, stung. Riot wagered Monty had taken the heirlooms out of spite.

Out of the corner of his eye, he took in the street scene. No one was loitering behind a newspaper or perusing a shop window; no hacks waited and no one was lingering where they shouldn't be.

Risking life and limb, Riot struck off across the busy street, trotting in front of a cable car. He paused halfway to let a motorcar zip past, then weaved his way between a hay wagon and a lumber cart, and finally tipped his hat to a woman riding a bicycle.

The coffeehouse was clear of its morning rush, but not empty. A few glanced his way when he entered, but no one avoided looking at him, or stared overly long. He removed his cap, and took a table in a corner, with a view out of the window and a clear path to the exits.

"Can I get you something, sir?" a waitress asked, pouring him coffee without prompt.

"Full breakfast, if you please, and..." he dipped his chin to where Liam Taft sat, "bring that fellow's order over here. Old friend of mine. Tell him I'll pay."

She smiled and went off to relay the message. With an irritated push of his chair, Liam stood and strode over, coffee in hand. He tossed his hat on the table, and took the chair opposite.

"I don't care for damn spy games. My back was itching over there."

"Do you have a bounty on your head, too?" Riot asked.

Liam turned a squinty eye on him. "Best to always assume so."

Riot gestured at their table. "Is this better?"

Liam scooted his chair to the side, so his own back was to a wall. Now Liam had a view of the window, too. They sat at opposing walls, the corner between them, elbows nearly touching.

"Two paranoid lawmen walk into a coffeehouse..." Riot said wryly. "There must be a joke somewhere in that."

Liam grunted.

Riot didn't waste time with any more pleasantries. "Are you satisfied my agency has nothing to do with that fake Pinkerton badge?"

"I don't have proof either way, but if you're involved I should retire here and now."

Riot waited for more, but Liam seemed content with silence. Unhurried, he drank his coffee, then swiped the liquid from his mustache. "Mrs. Riot is some woman. I figured she'd tell you about that badge."

Riot watched the man for any hint of threat, but the compliment seemed sincere. Still, he didn't want to bring Isobel into this anymore than she already was, so he steered the conversation in another direction. "You asked me why I left the Pinkertons. Does this business have something to do with Jim Hagen?"

Liam grunted, then nodded in thanks when the waitress set down their orders. He picked up his silverware and dug into his bacon and eggs. Riot did the same. After last night, he was starving.

"I reckon we both keep our cards close," Liam said after a time. "This could be a long breakfast."

"You've already interrogated me, Mr. Taft. It's your call. How about you just tell me what's going on."

Liam smoothed his mustache. "No guesses?" he murmured.

Riot considered the challenge over his next bite. "You don't like the city. You don't like crowds. You're not from here. Like most Pinkertons you travel extensively, but from your accent, I gather you've lived or still live in Oregon. You were transferred to look into rumors of corrupt Pinkertons, because they needed fresh blood." Riot looked at him. "Or rather, old trustworthy leather."

Liam gave a dry chuckle, then returned to his breakfast. They both ate until their plates were clean, then Liam pushed his away and leaned back in his chair, hooking thumbs under his vest. "This might have something to do with Jim. Some rumors reminded me of that pile of horseshit. 'Course you seemed the type, too."

"I know better than to use the Pinkerton name."

"Figured that out," Liam said.

"What rumors made you think of Jim?"

"Four years ago, William Pinkerton came to San Francisco to negotiate a deal with the Southern Pacific to provide railway security for their lines. He signed contracts with several other corporations, too. So the agency set up an office in the city. Our arrangement has been good for railway travel, and overall, we have a favorable reputation in California, unlike the bad blood between us and other states. But recently word wormed its way up to the Oregon division that the Pinkertons were willing to do anything for the Southern Pacific, even if it went against policy."

"How recent?"

"Rumor reached us midsummer," Liam said. "And I got left holding the short straw. My wife doesn't much care for this city, and this investigation is taking longer than she'd like. I was putting a lot of hope in you—that somehow you were involved."

"Sorry to disappoint."

"Me and Sam haven't found anything within the agency office either, so when that police officer came to us with a fake badge, I got to thinking maybe this ex-Pinkerton agent who struck off by himself—that'd be you—was using our name to drum up work or discredit the agency out of spite. That might explain why his agent had a badge."

It made sense. Riot might think the same himself. He'd be fuming if someone was discrediting Ravenwood Agency, or even using its name. A bad reputation ruined a detective—at least for any sort of lawful work.

"Usually whenever someone impersonates a Pinkerton, it's to intimidate," Liam continued. "A man will think twice about picking a fight with a national detective agency known for being relentless hunters and staffing a small army. Then there are the fellows who just like to look important. Others want a free ride on a train. Hell, I caught a fellow tossing our name around to get women. That's how I got *my* wife."

Riot liked the man's dry humor, but he showed no reaction. Only took a sip of coffee in thought. "What type of jobs are these fake Pinkertons taking?"

"Rumor says they'll take anything, which makes me think of the bounty on your head."

"The Southern Pacific doesn't much care for me."

"Why's that?"

"Because my agency exposed and humiliated Alex Kingston. He's the attorney for San Francisco's elite, with strong ties to the Southern Pacific and the Union Club set. He's a man who gets things done for his clients."

"Your wife's ex-husband, too."

"That, too. He blackmailed her into marriage."

"Sounds like a man I'd like to shoot."

"You'll have to get in line."

"I followed some of that trial." Liam gave a shake of his head. "Those were dangerous waters you got yourselves into. But I'd think bringing down an organization working against the Southern Pacific would clean the slate for you."

"I suspect Alex wants me dead, but he also has a long line to get behind."

Liam gave a raspy chuckle, as he slipped free his tobacco pouch. "I will say Inspector Geary doesn't much care for you either. But then I don't much care for him. And any man with a wife willing to climb into a cesspit for him must be all right by my book."

Isobel was also willing to drug him in the name of an investigation, but he didn't mention that part, only waited to see where Liam would take the conversation next.

"So let's say this agent of yours gets involved with these fellows—fake Pinkertons who do dirty work for the fine gentlemen of this city. Monty pays some brutes to dynamite you. It all goes wrong. Then you confront him. He doesn't kill you like he's supposed to, so they pop him one in the head for being disloyal."

"That's what I think happened," Riot said. "But have you considered the possibility that the badge isn't a fake?"

"What are you getting at?"

"A new branch of Pinkertons you don't know about."

Liam ran his tongue along the cigarette paper. "I'd know. This isn't official," he muttered. "I got my orders from The Principle."

That meant one of the Pinkerton sons.

"All right," Riot said. "So maybe this group is hiding behind the Pinkerton name. If word got out about their activities, as it has, eyes would turn to the Pinkertons. When it comes to railway barons and mining magnates, your agency already has a shady reputation. Easy to point fingers your way."

Liam struck a match, cupping his hands around the cigarette, as he nodded in agreement. "All fits," he said with a puff of smoke.

"So where is Jim Hagen?"

"We lost track of him. If the rumors are true, which I think the fake badge confirms, then we're dealing with professionals rather than some young fellow flashing a fancy badge around."

"Jim certainly knew how to cover his tracks."

"Funny how easy it is to pick up those skills in this line of work."

It was true. A detective learned all the mistakes made by criminals. Deep down they knew they could do it better, and if there was one thing Riot had learned early on, it was that politicians were the most skilled of them all.

"We have an agent working on a lead at the Oakland racetrack," Riot offered.

"Do you?" Liam asked, surprised. "Sam's been poking around there, too. Hasn't turned up much of anything yet, but he hasn't been at it long."

"This agent has a way with people."

"Have you figured out where Monty was bunking?"

"No, but I have an idea on how to find out. If you're willing…"

31

FRIENDS

"*MARGARET*," ISOBEL HISSED.

The woman jerked in surprise, nearly dropping her teacup. Tall and sturdy, Margaret was better suited to a bicycle and riding bloomers than to the prim blouse and skirt she was wearing. Her broad shoulders always stretched her blouses in the wrong places.

"Good Lord!" She glared at Isobel through a window and wiped the boiling liquid from her hand. "What on earth are you doing here?"

"Visiting you."

Margaret gave her a look. "Do you have something against front doors?"

"I do, as a matter of fact."

"Might as well come in."

"I swear your housekeeper has it in for me."

"She's like that with everyone," Margaret said. "She doesn't want anyone disturbing my father."

"Hence the unorthodox entrance." Isobel closed the door to the conservatory, and sat opposite her friend.

Margaret usually took her books into that glass-encased

patio to escape the mad rantings of her father. He was no longer in his right mind. And most days, Margaret had confided, he didn't know who she was anymore. Doctors called it 'brain congestion.' They'd urged Margaret to put him in an asylum, but she refused. Even though she employed a nurse, the strain of caring for him took its toll.

His illness disturbed Isobel—that one's own mind could betray the body so thoroughly was a terrifying thought. Worse, the moments of lucidity that Margaret's father sometimes had were filled with grief over his madness. He seemed to be mourning his own death.

Isobel picked up a book from the table. "*Carmilla*. Scandalous."

"If you ever come across a case that involves vampirism, I'm your woman."

Isobel scoffed. "I'll just bring in my mother. She keeps a ready supply of sharpened stakes under her bed."

"Really?" Margaret asked.

The two women shared a look, then fell to laughing, until Margaret pushed a teacup towards Isobel. "You weren't invited, so I'm not serving you. Why have you come?"

"Can't I visit a friend?" Isobel asked.

"When hell freezes over," Margaret quipped, then took a bite of a scone. "I haven't seen you since your wedding."

"I've been rather busy…"

"I know precisely what sort of friend you are—the splendid kind that doesn't require any work. But I do love giving you a hard time of it."

Isobel flashed a grin as she helped herself to tea and scones. Margaret was studying her, eyes alight with curiosity. "How *is* married life?"

Isobel gave a small smile. "I have no complaints."

"I saw the newspapers."

"Well, there is that," she admitted. "But Riot was released yesterday—a reporter cleared up that mess."

Margaret leaned forward. "I'm talking about your agency being attacked. A gun fight? Dynamite? One of your agents killed. And that business with the murdered girl? Most women spend the months after their wedding on a wedding trip."

"We had one," she defended.

"For a *week*," Margaret said. "Then you were nearly blown up, and your husband was beaten near to death. How is Atticus, by the way?"

"Tired."

"What's happened now?"

"I thought you read the papers."

"I'm sure there's more to it." Margaret waited, while Isobel tore her scone into little pieces, considering how much to divulge.

"You're terrible, you know," Margaret finally said. "Your life is more exciting than any book I could ever pick up."

"Oh, come now. That's not true." Isobel gestured at Carmilla. "I haven't run into a single vampire yet."

"Do you know who killed your agent?"

"The man who killed Mack is dead," Isobel said. "But he was only a paid assassin. Whoever wants us dead is probably the same person who hired our ex-agent to kill us. Only now Monty is dead too." She frowned at her scone.

Margaret's eyes widened. "What on earth?"

"It's complicated."

"Remind me not to work for you."

"Keep that to yourself, will you?"

"I've learned not to repeat a thing you say, especially in proper company." Margaret leaned forward. "If I was sure my married life would be as exciting as yours, I'd snag the first eligible man who asked."

"I could do with a little less excitement," Isobel admitted.

Margaret made a surprised sound. "You? Never."

Isobel took a sip of tea, and grimaced. "You and Riot," she muttered. "Always tea…"

"Put more sugar in it."

Isobel did so, but she doubted it would help.

Margaret studied her friend. "You have had quite a year."

"My own doing."

"You're not one to leave things alone. Just accept that."

"I only wish people would leave *me* and Riot alone."

"At the very least, you make for thrilling company."

"I'm happy to provide you with some amusement. Now I need your help."

"Oh, let me check my busy schedule." Margaret made a show of consulting her book. "I'll try my very best to fit you in."

"Do you know the Nobles?"

"Mostly I know *of* them. I've met the sisters. Violet is good friends with the eldest, Imogen, then there's Faith, and Helen, who's twelve. They came to one of the Falcon's Sunday luncheons."

The Falcons Bicycle Club hosted a number of parties in Carville that were attended by artists, authors, and political heavyweights. Margaret was one of their top riders.

"Does this have anything to do with Dominic's death?" Margaret asked over her teacup.

"What have you heard?"

"The obituary said he died in his bed from a heart condition, but there are rumors…"

Isobel waited.

"You're not going to tell me anything, are you?"

"I can't. Professional discretion."

Margaret gave a little growl. "Despite the danger, I have half a mind to hire on with your agency."

As much as Isobel would enjoy Margaret's company during

an investigation (far more enjoyable than Matthew's), she held back from urging her to hire on. Mack McCormick, lying dead on a slab from gut shot, was too fresh a memory. But danger wasn't the only risk.

There was frustation, too. The infuriating sting of injustice.

John Sheel, eleven-years-old, smirking and gloating after trying to murder his brother, knowing his parents would protect him. Ella Spencer, who never had much of a chance in life, killed by a friend. And Madge Ryan, set to be hanged soon, while the men who'd ruined her life walked free.

Isobel could never expose Margaret to those harsh realities.

"It's not all it's cracked up to be," Isobel said. The feeling in those words caught Margaret's attention, and she sobered.

"I imagine not."

The two women sat in comfortable silence as they finished their food, and when Margaret was through, she pushed aside her plate. "What do you want to know about the Nobles?"

"Did you ever meet Dominic?"

"Of course. I raced him once and beat him squarely. But he's more keen on rowing than bicycling, so it wasn't a fair race. Positively dreamy, and one of the most prized bachelors in San Francisco. From what I hear, the east coast, too. Heir to a fortune, handsome and single. Well. *Was*." Margaret frowned at this last. "I do recall he wasn't at all put out that a woman beat him in a race. Men usually cry foul and stomp away in a rage, or claim their 'calves cramped up.' It's hilarious."

"What about the mother and father?"

"The father is typical of his set, I suppose. A 'self-made' man who's intent on gathering a dragon's hoard of gold."

"Literally?"

"He struck it rich on a mine in Shasta early on, and more recently Colorado—his company, anyway."

"What's he like?"

Margaret shrugged. "I haven't met him. Now Mrs.

Noble... she's in every moral society under the sun. From what I gathered at the luncheon where I met them, their daughters live a strict life. Not much freedom. The oldest, Imogen, is engaged to a fellow with money, so her father approved. I think it was arranged."

Isobel and Margaret shared a shudder. Margaret at the thought of being forced to marry, and Isobel at the thought of her own coerced marriage to Alex, even as short-lived as it was.

"And how was Dominic treated?"

"How sons are usually treated—given free rein to sow their wild oats."

"A cad?" Isobel asked.

"The rumors say so, but I don't know... I thought him a decent sort. Of course, no one ever flirts with me," Margaret said, looking down at her hands. Rough from working with wood and stained with varnish, they were the hands of an athletic woman who liked to get them dirty.

Margaret didn't sound regretful, but rather relieved. With her father's health in decline, she was spared the pressure of finding a husband and starting a family.

"Really, if you want the juicy tidbits, you should speak with Violet. She gives old gossip-mongers a run for their money in that arena."

Isobel frowned. "But she's good friends with Imogen. I can't have her telling the eldest what I'm up to."

"What *are* you up to?"

Isobel considered what she could tell Margaret. "Someone has hired me to investigate Dominic's death, and I need to be careful. It could be dangerous."

"Was it murder?"

Silence spoke volumes.

Margaret eventually sighed in frustration. "Damn, Charlie. Not telling me is worse than telling me. I'm imagining all sorts of horrid things."

Isobel had first met Margaret during a case early that year and had introduced herself as Charlotte Bonnie. The nickname stuck.

"But the words can't come from my lips."

"Fine." Margaret sighed. "I suppose you could befriend Imogen or Faith. Violet would make a better person to introduce you."

"I'm not sure a friendship is possible. Not as myself, at any rate. Even if I assume another identity as a society woman, I risk reporters recognizing me." Not to mention Alex. From everything Katherine and Margaret had told her, Ian Noble sounded like the sort of man who would run with her ex-husband.

"What else is there? Short of having *me* spy for you."

"Do you know if the household is hiring?"

Margaret spit a mouthful of tea across the table. "You're planning on passing for a cook or lady's maid?"

"I assume a household of that size—"

Margaret started laughing herself silly.

"No one ever notices the help," Isobel tried again. "What is so amusing?"

Margaret wiped tears from her eyes. "I was imagining you as a maid. Or a cook. You can't even manage a proper egg."

"I can cook an egg."

"When you remember to eat."

"I was hoping you could write me a reference letter."

"You're serious."

"Am I ever not?"

Margaret considered her. "A letter from me wouldn't matter. You need to speak with Violet."

"I wasn't planning on telling Violet. That's why I came to you."

"Yes, but I don't know the family well enough."

Isobel frowned. "Can Violet be trusted with a secret?"

"If it's important. Yes."

"Violet it is, then."

"Up for a race to Carville?" Margaret asked with a glint in her eye. "I have a spare bicycle."

Isobel suppressed a sigh. After last night's activities, the thought of straddling a bicycle seat made her wince. She may have been a little too vigorous with Riot. Would she ever be able to keep her hands off the man? Did she want to?

There was nothing for it. Besides, if she were to keep up with Margaret, soreness would be the least of her worries. Margaret rode like the devil himself, and Isobel's calves would be as hard as bricks by the end.

———————

As Isobel feared, her calves were close to cramping, the soreness between her legs had doubled, and worst of all, Margaret won. No surprise, but defeat still stung.

Out of breath, she propped up her bicycle, and watched Margaret march into the clubhouse as if she'd only been out for a brisk walk.

Isobel paused to take in the endless ocean. The salt air, the biting wind and churning waves. The water would be frigid. Just the thing her sore body needed.

"You only lost by a *little*," Margaret called from the doorway. "Don't go throwing yourself into the ocean."

Reluctantly, Isobel followed her friend inside. The clubhouse was a retired streetcar with an interior resembling a Bedouin tent. Rugs, silks, and beaded curtains, with an array of paintings that bordered on lurid. But that tended to happen when artists frequented a clubhouse.

Violet lounged on a large pillow in a loose blouse and riding bloomers that were daringly close to harem pants. She came there whenever her husband became boorish, which Margaret claimed was nearly every other day.

Violet was pale, with hair so blonde it was nearly white, and she had wide, bored-looking eyes that made Isobel think there wasn't much going on in the woman's head. But Isobel knew better.

Without so much as a glance from her book, Violet waved a hand as the two new arrivals walked past to wash up in a basin. The water was cold and felt like bliss on the back of Isobel's neck.

"You'd have me beat in no time if you trained every day, Charlie."

"But then you'd train harder, and you'd still beat me."

Margaret flashed a grin. She was also close to six feet tall, and had the advantage of longer legs and thighs like pillars.

After washing up, the two women joined Violet in the main room, where Isobel plopped down on a plush cushion, and decided she might never get up again.

"You know…" Violet mused without looking up. "Just once I'd like to read something where the heroine isn't a mindless tit in a corset with heaving breasts."

"What *are* you reading?" Margaret asked.

"It's not for your virgin eyes," Violet said.

Margaret lunged across the room to snatch the book from Violet's hand. "Rude!"

"You're a married woman. Why would you need this?" Margaret asked, settling on a settee with the book. Her brows shot up as she read a page.

"Shows what you know," Violet said with a sigh.

Margaret's eyes widened. "Good heavens. What is this?" She turned the book over, but kept a finger inside the pages to mark her place. "It doesn't have a title."

"That's because it's scandalous." Violet curled a finger around a tendril of pale hair. "You know, I once kept my corset laced for bed and started breathing seductively for Ambrose. Do you know what he did?"

Both Margaret and Isobel waited.

"He waved smelling salts under my nose."

"Practical of him," Isobel said.

Violet cocked her head. "Would your own husband be so practical?"

"Depends," Isobel said. "If I were in shock or not."

The two women gave a laugh, even though Isobel hadn't been joking. Then Violet stretched to reach for a medicinal bottle of brandy. The clubhouse kept an entire trunk of medicine hidden under the floorboards.

"Drink?"

"Only water," Isobel said.

Violet poured her a glass with a look of sympathy.

"Charlie needs your help," Margaret blurted out. She had no tact.

"Oh?" Violet asked.

There was nothing for it. "I hear you're acquainted with the Noble family."

"I am," Violet said slowly. "I'm close with Imogen. Why do you ask?"

"She's investigating Dominic's death."

"*Margaret*," Isobel growled.

Margaret smiled. "You're welcome."

"The Noble family mustn't know," Isobel said. "It's a delicate situation."

Violet breathed a sigh of relief, and sat up. "*Finally*, I can talk with someone."

"Margaret doesn't know," Isobel said.

"You didn't tell her?"

"I was hired for my discretion as well as my mind," Isobel stated.

Violet nodded to herself, appearing to come to a decision.

"That's noteworthy, Isobel." She looked to Margaret. "I know you'll take it to the grave so… Dominic was murdered."

The announcement didn't have quite the effect Violet was hoping for. Why else would a detective be hired to investigate a sudden death?

"He was found," Violet glanced at Isobel, "in the *Nymphia*."

"The *Nymphia*?" Margaret repeated, with a wrinkling of her nose.

Violet glanced at her nails. "It's terribly tragic. A shame, really. Imogen is beside herself. Her mother flew into a hysterical rage when she discovered her son died there. Imogen's father decided to keep things quiet for the sake of the family's reputation. I don't blame him. Even Ambrose wouldn't sink that low."

"That's a horrible thing to say about your husband," Margaret said.

"Men will be men. Besides, his… diversions give me more freedom. Don't you find that true, Isobel?"

"I'd imagine so," she said lightly.

"Your husband is no different." Violet said, knowingly. "Every woman thinks hers is the exception. Might as well embrace it early on. I do hate living with wool over my eyes."

Isobel didn't contradict the woman; she needed Violet's help. "I'll brace myself for that eventuality." As if Riot had the energy for dalliances on the side. "How is Imogen taking her brother's death?"

"Not well, but she's relieved their father smothered a scandal. If whispers started… It might affect her own pending marriage."

Isobel wondered if Violet's word choice was intentional. "To the Englishman in New York?"

"Englishman?" Violet gave a little laugh. "Fredrick Starling lives in New York, but he does travel quite often and he likes to play the Englishman for the ladies. He's utterly refined, and I imagine his family wouldn't take the truth about Dominic lightly."

"This isn't England," Isobel pointed out. "Scandal doesn't ruin a family quite so much in San Francisco."

"True, but Freddie is from a well-bred Bostonian family, which might as well be British society, considering the family ties. The Starlings only gave their blessing to Freddie and Imogen's engagement because of the money involved, not the blood line."

"How was he killed?" Margaret asked.

Violet looked to Isobel, but she didn't answer. "The police said he was choked," Violet finally said.

"And Dominic's youngest sisters, do they know?" Isobel asked.

Violet shook her head. "I think Faith and Helen suspect something more. They're heartbroken, of course. Dom was their older brother, but he was more like a father to them."

"And their own father? Ian Noble?"

"No one crosses Ian Noble," Violet said. "Well... Dom did, indirectly."

Isobel arched a brow.

"He avoided his father as much as possible."

"Do you know what they argued about before Dominic died?"

"Katherine hired you, didn't she?"

"Is that significant?"

"Imogen said her mother and father decided against telling Katherine, to save her from further pain. It's a shame... I think she and Dominic would've been happy together."

"Did Katherine and Imogen get along?"

Violet narrowed her eyes. "Why are you asking so many questions about the family? Shouldn't you be searching for his murderer at the Nymphia?"

"I like to be thorough."

"I don't want to see Imogen hurt," Violet said. "And this doesn't feel right. I'm not your spy, Isobel."

"I'm not asking you to spy. I'm asking you what you already know."

"I don't gossip about friends."

Margaret cleared her throat. She was pretending to read the book on her lap.

Violet amended her statement. "About important things."

"That's loyal of you," Isobel said. "I'm only trying to find the truth. I don't want any of this to get out either, but there is a murderer on the loose. Others may be in danger, and it's important I find out why Dominic was in the Nymphia."

"Why else would he go there? He's a man."

"A rich one, who could afford much better than the Nymphia has to offer."

"Who knows with men," Violet said. "Get enough whiskey in them and they'd think a mule attractive."

"Mules *are* adorable," Margaret agreed, flipping through pages.

A silence fell over the colorful caravan as Violet grappled with her conscience. "Are you looking to be introduced to the family?"

"Not exactly," Isobel said. "Not as myself, at any rate. I'd like you to write a letter of reference for me. For a position in the household."

"You mean you want me to lie?"

Margaret grimaced.

"It's not so much a lie as a deception for the good of the family."

"You're an acquaintance, Isobel. Imogen is a friend. I won't lie to her. What if she ends up hurt by your meddling?"

"It's a possibility," Isobel admitted. "I don't know what I'll discover in the household. I may find nothing at all."

Violet glared at her. "I still haven't forgiven you for claiming to be Charlotte Bonnie."

"Well, I was—and am, after a fashion," Isobel said. "Besides, I thought I made up for that by getting rid of that horrid gentleman's club and their brick building."

"The building is still there," Violet said dryly. "Only now it's run-down, and there are no handsome men prancing about."

Margaret slapped the book closed. "Wouldn't it all be worth it just to see Isobel posing as a maid? You could even go over for dinner and snicker at her."

Violet tapped a finger to her lips. "They *did* lose another maid."

"Another?" Isobel asked.

"Faith and Helen don't get out much, so they tend to be bored. They make a game out of chasing away maids. Mrs. Noble tries to hire women in need."

"Prostitutes?"

"Heavens, no. Mrs. Noble hires them before they sink that low. She believes in giving any woman, no matter her race, a chance. By doing that, she's keeping them from turning to a life of prostitution. And…" Violet hesitated. "Given Faith and Helen's reputation, she finds it hard to staff the household with anyone save the truly desperate."

"That sounds splendid," Margaret said, with a glint in her eyes.

Violet appeared to be warming to the idea, too. "Yes, I think I shall write you a reference."

32

CHANGING OF THE GUARD

RIOT NEARLY MISSED HIS OWN AGENCY. GRANTED, IT'D MOVED from another building, then been blown to bits with dynamite, but he'd been inside when it was attacked, so he should've recognized it.

When he realized the address, he quickly knocked on the hack's ceiling. It rolled to a stop, and he turned to stare back at the brick building. Isobel could've warned him.

It was on the corner, white, on a street of red brick and wooden faux fronts. His fingers twitched for his missing walking stick.

Riot searched the street and windows, then hopped out and flipped the driver a coin. He pushed open the door and stepped into his agency.

Matthew was leaning on a counter, talking with the girl behind it. Aside from plush armchairs, the waiting room was empty.

Matthew grew pale, then straightened.

The girl smiled. "Can I help you, sir?"

Riot felt a stranger in his own agency. But then he hardly

looked like a detective in rough cap and clothes; he looked more like a sailor lost in the Barbary Coast.

"Where is Lotario?" Riot asked Matthew.

Matthew hurried to open a reinforced door, then pointed down a hallway. Riot passed a room with multiple desks, where Tim was chatting with Miss Off and a gentleman with a curling mustache, then stopped at a door with a plate that read: *Director of Operations*.

Riot didn't bother knocking; he let himself in. Lotario was leaning over a set of plans, in conference with a keg of a man who looked like he used his fists to hammer in nails.

When Riot entered, the keg-like man straightened, cracking his knuckles. Lotario glanced up from the plans, his face draining of blood.

It was a well-appointed office. Rich but stylish furniture, the kind one would find at a gentleman's club. Wooden filing cabinets lined an entire wall, and Riot was glad to see a modern lock on the inside of the door.

Lotario stood ramrod straight, his fingers carefully placed on the desk top. "Whatever you think best, Flinch. If you'll excuse me... I need to speak with this gentleman."

"He a problem, Mr. Amsel?"

"Goodness, no. My twin will kill him if he harms me."

After Flinch gathered up the plans and left, Riot shut the door.

"You're looking well, Atticus. The last time I saw you, you were lurching out of bed naked." Lotario couldn't resist a brow waggle. "As much as I enjoyed the show, I must say those trousers are well-fitte—"

"Don't. Start." Riot pointed a finger at the young man. Identical to his twin in nearly every way save gender, it was always a little dizzying to face Lotario. The same eyes, the same lips, the same bone structure and slim build. But whereas

Isobel was all arrogance and sharpness, Lotario was languid and easily bored. He didn't look bored now.

Riot pulled a chair in front of the desk and sat to regard his new business partner—a partner who now owned Ravenwood Agency.

"Would you like a drink?" Lotario asked.

"Yes."

Lotario turned to a sideboard, and poured two whiskeys. He handed one to Riot with a slight nod, downed his own, and sat down.

Riot waited.

It didn't take long for Lotario to crack. Words poured from his lips like a geyser. "You needed capital, and I had money I was looking to invest in a new business. Tim sold me his share. There's really nothing more to say."

"You're babbling," Riot said.

"What else am I supposed to do? You're just staring at me."

"Feeling guilty?"

"Now I am. Though I have no idea why I should be."

"None whatsoever?" Riot asked.

"This agency was in debt. I bought you out. That's what investors do."

"You invested in a detective agency. That's hardly good business."

"As if you'd know," Lotario said, with a roll of his eyes. "Look, it was either this or a brothel. And I really didn't want to deal with the drama of running a whorehouse."

"As good a reason as any, I suppose."

Lotario sniffed. "You're mocking me."

"I'm not mocking you, Lotario."

"You're angry."

"Do I look angry?"

Lotario's eyes sharpened. "Honestly, I have no idea. Do you know how much that vexes me?"

"Do I look like I care?"

"You don't give me much to work with. How on earth does Bel put up with you?"

"I don't have the faintest idea," Riot said.

Lotario took a calming breath. "I'll be blunt. You're a horrid businessman. There was no money to fix up the agency after it was dynamited. Tim couldn't even pay the surviving agents. This agency means a lot to you and Bel, so I stepped in. I have a mind for business and investigation. It's all been very diverting."

"Diverting," Riot drawled the word. "That's what I was waiting to hear."

"You were?"

"What happens when you tire of this? How many hats do you already have?"

Lotario sat back. "I've seen your hat collection; it far surpasses mine."

"I doubt that."

"This is business, Atticus. That's what you don't understand. This isn't my life's work. It's not my passion—it's a hobby of mine. Occasionally I purchase failing businesses, turn them around until they make a profit, and move on to something else."

"We kept the agency small for a reason. This is not small."

"And?"

"The only way the Pinkertons could stay afloat was by hiring out to the railroads and mining magnates. They became their own personal army, and I don't want to go down that road."

"For God's sake, I'm not planning on opening branches across America. And yes, I *can* turn a profit. The detective business really isn't much different from the whoring business. And I've had an excellent teacher."

"That concerns me."

"That I'm occasionally a whore?"

"No, your teacher. Hera. I don't trust her."

"You and Bel."

"That should tell you something."

"Why don't you trust her?"

"Because I know what's involved in operating a brothel in this city. It requires bribery, blackmail, and powerful connections with people willing to look the other way."

Lotario leaned forward. "Or a number of powerful men who lust after some good, hard *cock*." His eyes flashed at the last whipcrack of a word. But Riot wasn't scandalized. "You're no fun at all to shock," Lotario huffed.

"I've worked these streets longer than you've been alive."

"And I respect that, which is why I'm only planning to run the business side of things. I'm not Bel. I won't wrestle you for control of an investigation."

"You're hiring agents, Lotario. The people out there have no idea who I am. That means you're in charge now. When you bought this agency, you bought the name which means you have a host of hired guns, a network of informants, and a long history in this city."

Lotario's lips parted in surprise. Riot watched as a slow sort of realization crept into his eyes. "I don't have your experience, Atticus. I wouldn't presume to—" Lotario cut off as Riot leaned forward.

"I never wanted to run this agency," Riot confided in a low voice. "I have no interest in overseeing its day-to-day operations. Ravenwood hired me for my gun, not my mind."

"But Bel said it's your life."

"I have a family now. They're my life."

"That's what I told her," Lotario said, preening.

Riot stood. "Fair warning. I'm not known for following orders. As soon as—"

The door opened, and Isobel strode in, her eyes flickering between men. "Are you two playing nice?"

"I've just finished telling Atticus who's boss around here," Lotario said, settling his pince-nez back in place.

"I'm sure," Isobel said dryly.

"From now on you'll be taking orders from me."

Isobel snorted and looked to Riot. "How'd it go with Taft?"

"I think we can trust him. He's in. Did you get your references?"

She nodded, then stepped out to call in Matthew and Tim.

When Tim entered, he gave Riot a pat on the shoulder. "Knew you didn't shoot Monty, boy."

"Your confidence in me is heartwarming," Riot said.

Lotario glared at his twin. "We have an interoffice telephone for that. Yelling down the hallway is so—"

"Practical?" Isobel shot back.

"Uncouth," Lotario finished.

Tim yanked on his beard. "What now?"

"It means my twin is an arrogant ass."

Lotario snatched a notepad from the desk. "I'm writing you up for that."

Isobel gave her twin a rude gesture as she fell into the chair Riot had vacated for her.

"What is it, Matthew?" Riot asked, noticing the younger man's stony face.

He glanced between Riot and Lotario. "Who do I take orders from, sir?"

"Me," Isobel said, then dodged a thrown pencil. She stuck her tongue out at her twin.

Riot went over to the Mappin and Webb cabinet and lifted the lid, surveying the bottles of expensive liquor. "Lotario is now the owner of Ravenwood Agency. But that doesn't mean you have to take orders from him, Matt. Any more than you have to take them from me. On the rare occasions when I take orders, it's generally from whoever sounds the most sensible."

"So probably not Miss Off," Isobel noted.

Riot selected a decanter, and sniffed at it. Water. He spared a glance at his wife, who he'd noted had walked in with a stiff stride and sat down with care. She was also covered in a sheen of dust and looked to be melting in her chair. He poured a glass, cut a lime, then squeezed it in before setting the glass in front of her.

She looked up at him, eyes full of warmth. "Will you do the honors?"

Riot gave a quick summary of the Noble case, during which Lotario fell silent. Then Riot told them what he'd learned from Liam Taft.

"'Bout that," Tim said. His pipe wasn't lit, but he'd stuck the stem between his lips to search his pockets. "There's a fellow there, Carson, in charge of security. An old saddle tramp I've been hanging about with seems to think Carson's a Pinkerton."

"At the racetrack?" Riot asked, surprised.

Tim nodded. "Ask that fellow Taft about him."

"What is a saddle tramp?" Lotario asked.

Tim cackled. "His name's Skunk. Old cowboy, who spent most his time in the chuck line."

Lotario wrinkled his nose. "How appetizing."

"Me and Mack met him during that stolen horse case."

The room fell silent—heavy with grief, with the memory of a man, and the absence of his booming Scottish voice. Riot placed a hand on Isobel's shoulder. "Have you discovered anything more about Carson?" he asked.

Tim finally found what he was looking for. "Sure as heck. But I'm not certain this fellow Carson claims to be a Pinkerton. Skunk has an ear for rumor, but that doesn't mean it's all true. I tried to hire on with security, but I'm old and used up far as these young'uns are concerned, so that didn't end well. But…" Tim slapped a wad of crumpled papers on the desk. "Got a peek into his office and garbage can."

Tim had slapped down a wadded pile of papers stuck together with chewing gum. Lotario used a letter opener to poke at the mess.

"Carson had a bunch more of those on his desk. Stuck through a spike like an accountant's receipt holder."

"They're betting slips," Isobel said.

Lotario nudged one over with his letter opener. "Who saves betting slips? They're usually torn up and tossed on the ground after a race."

"I thought that odd, too," Tim said, then gave a shrug. "I'll keep poking around. But I thought… Well, I'd like Grimm to hire on at the track. You hiring him as a detective?"

Lotario looked up. "Absolutely. He's exceptional. But he darted out before I could tell him. I've telephoned and sent a wire, but he hasn't given an answer."

Tim grunted. "Boy spooks easily. I'll talk with him. I don't think it'll be dangerous. He'll have an easy time hiring on as a horse handler. He's got the gift. And everyone will think he's deaf and dumb."

Riot watched Lotario for a reaction. Did he understand the responsibility involved—the guilt and regret of assigning an agent to a case that proved lethal? Unfortunately, he'd learn. One day. Riot just hoped it wouldn't be Isobel.

"Yes, but only if Grimm is willing," Lotario said. "And I want you to check on him. Daily, if possible."

Tim nodded. "I'll get on it."

"Matthew," Isobel said, eyeing the man. "You look like you've done some rowing in your day."

"I have…"

"Good. I want you to join the Triton Rowing Club and the

Dolphin Club. Dominic Noble was a member of both. See what you can find out about his friends and habits."

Lotario frowned, but said nothing.

"I can't swim well," Matthew said.

"Then you'll have to improve your technique," Isobel said.

"In the middle of winter?"

She lifted a shoulder.

"Bel and I are meeting Taft and his partner tonight," Riot said. "We aim to catch the thieves who picked me and Monty clean."

"Want me to tag along?" Tim asked.

Riot shook his head. "Getting Grimm settled at the race-track is more important. And after…" He glanced at Isobel. "I'll be going undercover at the Nymphia as a watchman. At least that's my hope. So I won't be in regular contact with the agency."

Tim eyed Riot. "You sure you want to do that, boy?"

"*If wishes were horses, beggars would ride,*" he quoted.

Tim frowned, but said nothing more. Of all the people in the room, Tim knew Riot's past—the full horror of it. He'd found him as a ragged, starving boy who barely uttered a word.

"And I'll be playing maid at the Noble's house," Isobel said.

Lotario raised his brows. "Are you sure that's safe?"

"I don't know, is it?" she countered.

"I meant for *them*," he clarified.

33

TO CATCH A THIEF

A DRUNK STAGGERED DOWN THE STREET, WOBBLING, SINGING off-key, and bumping against warehouse walls. Fog blanketed the night, a silvery mist that covered the moon, and made the lone gas lamp shrink with fear. The drunk's boots thudded on planks, his breath stirring the fog with every breathy whisper.

He wasn't a vagrant. He had the look of a stevedore with a new hat—no doubt his pride and joy. The stevedore stumbled, slumped against a wall, and slid down to the filthy ground as he took one last swig from a bottle. It was empty. He spat out a curse and tossed it into the street with a shatter of glass.

The trap was set.

ISOBEL HUDDLED UNDER A DISCARDED CRATE WHILE GRIMY water dripped on her from some unknown source. She eyed the slumped-over drunk through a gap in the crate. A muscle in her leg was cramping, and her teeth chattered.

It was a frosty November night in the city, and somehow

the wind was keen on whipping through this alleyway, and into the cracks in her crate.

Whose idiot idea had this been?

Hers. At least her chosen hiding place. But no one ever won a game of hide-and-seek by being comfortable. Meanwhile Riot, clearly the wiser, had picked a shadowed doorway down the street. Away from the rank alleyway where she huddled.

When her teeth weren't knocking together, she was trying her best not to gag. Had a skunked opossum died and rotted there? It certainly smelled like it.

Isobel resisted the urge to check her pocket watch. As dark as it was, she wouldn't be able to see its little hands. It may have been five hours; it could've been fifteen minutes. Patience was an old enemy of hers; she'd never waited well.

Liam Taft had taken up a position inside a nearby warehouse, and Sam Batten was playing the drunken stevedore. She'd wanted that role, but Riot convinced her otherwise.

"I'd be liable to shoot if they got rough with you," he'd said in that calm way of his that never failed to send a chill down her spine.

So, a watcher it was. But there was no way of knowing what the thieves would do. Or how many were involved in the gang. Where would they drag their prey? So she waited and watched, shivering under a broken crate.

A shadow darted across the street. Then another moved at the other end of the alleyway where she waited. A third. Then a fourth. Hell, they hadn't accounted for four robbers.

The thieves were thin, quick, and silent. They converged on the drunk, dragging him into the mouth of the alleyway. She watched with rising anger as the four shadows started in on their victim—tugging roughly at clothing, careless of the cold, or their victim's life. They had done the same to Riot. Sam stirred, and a thief kicked him squarely in the ribs.

She bit back a curse. There were too many directions for the thieves to run. They'd hoped to corral the gang in the alleyway, but the thieves hadn't dragged Sam in there.

"I'd stay where you are," a calm voice said.

The shadows froze. The whites of their eyes rolled towards Riot, who stood on the boardwalk.

Without a sound, they scattered. Two away from Riot, down the boardwalk, and two into the alleyway. A gunshot barked, wood splintered. But it'd only been a warning shot.

Isobel focused on the shadows racing towards her concealment. She thrust out a leg, tripped one, even as the drunk came alive, and snatched at a second ankle. Sam got a kick to his face, and the thief she'd tripped recovered faster than expected.

The thief scrambled forward, and she tossed her crate aside to lunge for him. Isobel caught him around the knees. He hit the ground hard, grunting, then twisted, a glint of steel in hand.

Another bark of gunfire, and a spark pinged in the dark. The blade went flying. Riot was the only one quick enough to make that shot. The thief kicked out in panic. His foot connected with her shoulder, breaking her hold. He slipped onto his feet, then shot down the alleyway.

Sam's opponent had wiggled free too, and Riot took aim. But Sam was right on their heels, blocking the shot.

Isobel raced after the men.

The runners were quick. She focused on one, while Sam broke off after another. Streets fell away, her heartbeat pounding in her ears. The thief wove in and out of alleyways, over fences, and tried to lose her up a drainpipe.

Isobel shot up after the spry man. She saw a face at the top, pale with surprise. He kicked once at the drainpipe, trying to shake her free, but she was used to climbing masts on a choppy sea. This was easy by comparison.

After a few more kicks, the thief gave up and fled. Or so she thought. Isobel pulled herself up the last bit and was greeted with a fist to the face. She slipped off the edge, and caught herself on the lip. Before he could rush forward, Isobel pulled herself up and rolled, dropping to the flat rooftop. She hit his legs. They went down in a tumble. Feet kicked, fists flew, and the thief bashed his forehead into hers.

Isobel reeled back, dazed. The thief bolted across the roof. Tasting blood, she staggered to her feet and gave chase, leaping across a gap between two warehouses, down to a balcony, and finally ducking through a window frame. She landed inside a pitch-black warehouse. As she tried to get her breathing under control, she strained her ears, listening for footfalls.

This was bad, she realized. She'd allowed herself to be drawn away from the others. Her quarry was no opportunist. This thief knew what he was about.

Isobel wiped blood from her lips. "I just want to talk," she yelled. "I need information about a man you robbed." Her voice echoed in the vast chamber, the wood floor creaking and rotted under her boots.

"Like hell, you do," a rough voice answered. It bounced and amplified in the space.

"I know you didn't shoot that big fellow a few weeks back. You just picked his corpse clean. I only want to know what was on him. You can keep the money."

The thief snorted. "Really?"

"I'm a detective; not a lawman."

"You're not a man at all, are you?" the voice was leering. She might be dressed in male clothing, but they'd grappled— hard to conceal sex when you're rolling on the ground with a person.

Isobel slipped her knife from a pocket. "I'm no lady either."

A laugh bounced around the warehouse. With no light, her

eyes weren't adjusting. It was just dark and vast, and the thief's voice echoed, making it impossible to pinpoint his location.

A floorboard creaked, then a match flared. Light glowed dimly from a candle, illuminating the narrow face of a youth with a wispy mustache. He couldn't have been more than sixteen, but he was wiry and strong, and his eyes were far older than his youthful face.

"What's it worth to you?" he asked.

"I have two dollars on me."

"You should try whoring. Pays better than chasing the likes of me."

"Did you see who shot the man two weeks ago?" she asked.

"I seen lots of things worth more than two dollars."

Isobel inched forward, and the thief stepped backwards, boards sagging and groaning beneath their feet. Something was wrong here.

"I know you're bribing patrolmen to look the other way. All I want is information; I'll leave your operation alone."

Would Riot and the others be able to find her? Or were they occupied with the rest of the gang? If the other thieves were as nimble as this one, taking to the rooftops, she doubted Riot and the others would catch them. This might be their only chance. But Isobel was on unfamiliar ground, on the thief's turf, in total darkness. And why had he lit a candle?

"Fine," the thief said. "But let's go somewhere cozier." He took another step back, and made to turn.

His candle amplified the dark rather than illuminated, and she was drawn to its light. Isobel edged a foot forward. The boards held. She stepped cautiously towards the light, testing each board. But these weren't rotted like the others.

One moment the boards were firmly underfoot, then the floor dropped. A hatch.

Isobel twisted in midair, abandoning her knife to claw for something solid. Nothing. She fell through darkness. Too far.

Oh hell, she thought, *this would hurt.* But the impact of bones on ground never came—her legs caught on coarse rope. She reached blindly out, swaying in midair, to find rope everywhere. It was a cargo net.

Damn.

Isobel fought to free herself from the tangle, but the more she struggled, the more it turned, and the tighter the trap became.

Footsteps hurried down wooden steps. The candle neared, and the thief snickered up at her, a slow smile spreading over his lips. "I didn't expect a beauty." He set down the candle, then grabbed her ankle. She kicked against his hold, but he wasn't deterred, as he worked at the laces.

She stretched for his head as the net turned, her fingers brushing his cap. The thief tugged free her boot, then slapped her hand away. "None of that now," he warned.

After he tugged free her other boot, he stepped out of the candle's glow. A lever click, and the net dropped. She landed, hard. The wind forced from her lungs.

Isobel tried to relax to get air back into her lungs, but the thief reached under her coat, pawing at her body. She couldn't breathe, she couldn't move. It seemed an eternity. But he wasn't after flesh. Instead, he kicked her, then yanked free her billfold.

Air finally filled her lungs.

"You want to know what I seen?" he asked, rifling through her billfold. "Some white-haired fellow done the deed. Put lead right in that big fellow's head."

The shock of words hit her like a gut punch. She stopped struggling.

The thief cursed. "Two damn dollars? That's it?" He shoved the cash in his pocket, then gathered her boots to leave. Only he hesitated, eyeing her. "I don't buy it," he muttered.

His hands returned, this time to her trousers. She fought

against his intrusive frisking, growling and spitting curses, until he pulled free her chain watch with a grunt of satisfaction.

"Real pleasure," he said, giving her backside a hard squeeze. His fingers brushed between her legs. Isobel kicked out, her foot slipping through a gap in the net to catch him in the knee. He buckled, then with a growl, surged forward, flipping open a knife of his own, and driving a knee between her legs. He pressed the blade to her throat, and she stilled.

"No one teach you any manners yet?" he snarled.

She felt a familiar shape on the silty ground. Her fallen knife. That's right, she thought, meeting his eyes, come closer.

A gun cocked. "Drop it," an icy voice ordered. Riot. He stood in the candle's light, eyes glittering, revolver pressed against the back of the thief's skull.

The thief froze. An eye flickered, and in a blink of another eye, Riot uncocked the hammer, spun his revolver in one smooth, blinding motion, and pistol-whipped the thief.

It wasn't a hard blow—not enough to crack a skull, but enough to daze the youth. Riot kicked at his shoulder, then squeezed the trigger. The shot was deafening. A bullet zipped through the thief's hand. He screamed and dropped his blade.

Riot kicked the youth onto his back and cocked his revolver. "Empty your pockets."

This time the thief didn't hesitate.

"Slowly," Riot warned.

The youth did so, panting with pain, while blood leaked from an ear and the hole in his hand.

"Are you all right, Bel?"

"You told me you never twirl your gun, Riot," she said by way of answer.

"Needs must."

"I had him right where I wanted him."

The thief snickered. "Bet you did, ya kinky bit—"

Riot let his aim fall, and squeezed the trigger. A bullet

sliced through the thief's trouser leg and stuck in the dirt between his legs. The youth scooted backwards, pawing at his crotch to make sure everything was still intact.

"You're not part of this conversation," Riot said.

"She got her information!" the thief squealed. "It was a fair trade. That's all."

Isobel fought her way up to a sitting position. "The stolen goods. Where are they?" she asked.

"We take 'em to a fence. Fellow in Mission Bay by the name of Muddy Morris."

"If you're lying, I'll hunt you down," Isobel said. Though the threat felt hollow, considering she was still entangled in his trap.

"It's the truth."

"His partner said the same," Riot said.

So the others had caught at least one.

"Did they say anything else?" she asked.

Something in her voice made Riot glance back at her. "No."

Isobel spat out blood. "Let him go."

Riot hesitated. "He's a dangerous brute."

"He'll only be released," she said.

"Life was easier when I could just shoot men like him."

The thief went still.

"You did shoot him, Riot. Twice."

"Not where I wanted to."

"Well, with luck he'll die of sepsis," Isobel said, cheerfully.

Riot cocked his head. "We can hope. But before you go… strip."

The thief hesitated until Riot shifted his aim. This time the bullet wouldn't hit cloth. "I know what you had a mind to do, and I don't need another reason to pull this trigger."

The thief stripped at gunpoint, but Riot let him keep his hat and long johns. It was the gentlemanly thing to do.

"I suggest you find a different occupation. Now run." Riot shot the ground to get the thief moving, and when he'd disappeared into the night, Riot cracked open his No. 3, dumped out the fired brass, and reloaded. It was a swift, practiced maneuver that took mere seconds. He clicked the cylinder back in place and holstered his gun to help Isobel finish untangling herself.

"I'm an idiot," she muttered when free.

"I only care if you're an injured one."

"Only my pride," she assured him.

He didn't take her word for it. Riot fished out a flashlight from his pocket, and thumbed it on, running the dim light over her body.

A muscle in his jaw flexed. "You may have to wait a few days to play the maid," he said, handing over a clean handkerchief.

Isobel wiped the blood from her nose and lips, then took his offered hand. When she was on her feet, he reluctantly let go, and turned to keep watch while she put her clothes back in order.

"I would've been here sooner, but you're a difficult woman to track," he said by way of apology.

"And yet you always find me."

"One day, I may not." His voice was tight.

"Then it will mean I finally outfoxed you."

"I'll put it on your gravestone."

"Ever the romantic."

As Isobel tucked in her shirt, she steeled herself for what was to come. "Riot..." she hesitated. "That thief saw who killed Monty."

Riot turned slightly to look her in the eye. He held her gaze a moment, then gave a slow nod. "I figured it was Tim."

Isobel blinked. "How——" she cut off, grappling with the

revelation. "And you said nothing? Dammit, Riot. I found his rifle for the police," she hissed.

"I warned you he was sly."

"Did Tim tell you?" If so, it meant Riot *hadn't* told her.

To her relief, he gave a shake of his head. "I had some time to think on it."

Her rising anger deflated. "Tim stood there bold as brass while I investigated. He even offered suggestions and joked how he was glad I wasn't on his trail."

Riot raised a brow in a kind of shrug. Then squeezed her arm, and nodded towards a door, indicating they should leave. She let herself be pulled away.

Cold air slapped the fury right out of her. Isobel took a deep breath of it and was rewarded with the same sickly decay that she'd smelled in the crate. It hadn't been from her hiding place; the stink was coming on a breeze from Butchertown, where slaughterhouses let the tide deal with carcasses.

Riot searched the dark, which was fine with her, since she couldn't see a thing. He led her down a lane, then turned a corner onto another street that showed signs of life. A group of saloons and brothels blazed with light and laughter down the way.

Seeing he intended to keep going, she pulled him to a stop. "Riot, we need to talk."

"Taft and his partner are waiting for us."

"All the more reason to talk now," she whispered.

Keeping his eyes on the street, he pulled her into a recessed entrance of a shipping office. Riot put his back against the brick, and Isobel slumped in the corner between him and a door.

"Are you sure it was Tim?" she asked. "The thief said it was a white-haired old man, but that could be anyone."

"Could be," Riot agreed.

"But you already suspected him?"

"I did."

"And you're all right with this?"

Riot glanced sideways at her. "I've known Tim most my life. I know his methods. The killer was quick and efficient and left a hard trail to follow. I reckon he has an alibi, too."

"He shot Monty in cold blood," she whispered.

"Tim is from a different time. The west was wild in my day, but in his… there wasn't even a police force. He's lived his life by justice, not law. He was only protecting his own."

"Many a murderer has used that as justification," she said, for argument's sake.

"They have," Riot agreed.

"And we hunt them down and turn them over to the authorities."

"We're not lawmen; we're detectives. Truth is a messy business."

"Yes, but how do you know when you've crossed a line? How do we know Tim hasn't already?"

"I can't even answer that about myself, Bel."

She hesitated. "Did you intend to kill Monty when you confronted him?"

Riot shook his head. "I wanted to give him a chance to explain…" He trailed away, then muttered, "I should've just shot him."

"I don't think you sleep as easy as that, Riot."

"Can you? Knowing what Tim did?"

She didn't answer straightaway. "I'm not really one to pass judgment." Considering she'd killed her brother. But then Curtis *had* been trying to kill her.

True, Monty had hired men to dynamite the agency, and Mack had died in that ambush. But all they had was circumstantial evidence that wouldn't hold up in a court of law.

Where did one draw the line?

"Neither can I," Riot said. His voice was tight with pain, with memory, and a lifetime of blood on his hands.

Isobel closed her eyes, reining in her thoughts. "You suspected Tim shot Monty... but you let that fellow go."

"I didn't know he saw Tim."

"But there was a chance."

"There was a chance," he admitted. "But you told me to let him go."

"Would you have quieted that thief for good if you'd known?" she asked.

"I intended to turn him over to the police."

"But he's a witness to the murder. He *saw* Tim. That man's testimony could hang him."

Riot turned away from the street to look down at her. "*There's* the difference between murder and justice. Tim wouldn't kill that fellow to protect himself."

"Are you sure?" she whispered.

"Ask him."

Isobel swallowed, trying to imagine that conversation. Then she tried to imagine *not* having it. "What are we going to do?" she asked.

Riot squeezed her arm. "We find out who hired Monty."

34

MUDDY MORRIS

By the time Isobel and Riot found the Pinkerton agents, the night had flowed into twilight and the ocean wind had blown in a thick fog. The Pinkertons stood by a police wagon talking with officers, while two gang members sulked inside the cage.

Sam eyed Isobel's split lip. "Looks like you chased a curly wolf, too." He looked about how she felt.

"Something like that," she muttered.

"They're a slippery bunch," Liam noted.

"Anything more from these two?" Riot asked.

Liam smoothed his mustache. "They claim scavenger rights. The fellow was dead, so they scavenged him."

Isobel stepped up to the cage, but she didn't recognize any of their clothing as Riot's. Had this pair seen Tim, too? What if Riot was wrong about his old friend? Blinded to Tim as he'd been with Monty. The thought unsettled her.

Where did one draw the line between murder and justice?

Sick with her own moral confusion, she stepped away from the cage, and focused on the next step: Muddy Morris.

IT WAS AN APT NAME FOR THE GANG'S FENCE. MORE SCAVENGER than criminal, he lived on a barge moored in the salt marsh of Mission Bay, the smell of rotten eggs and spoiled meat permeating the area.

Isobel frowned at the flat-hulled barge mired in mud some fifty feet away. It brimmed with makeshift sails serving as canopies, old jackets left out to rot, and timber haphazardly stitched together to create a 'cabin.' Warped planks spanned the distance from shore to boat.

"I'm relieved it's low tide," Riot said.

"I wouldn't trust it to float," Liam agreed.

Isobel glanced at Liam. "Don't tell me you can't swim either?"

"No, ma'am. I should've done the paperwork and let Sam walk across that thing." He'd sent his partner off to file reports. 'A benefit of seniority,' Liam had said.

"I'll go aboard," Riot offered. "We don't want to spook him."

Liam eyed the barge. "I don't think Muddy Morris is going anywhere."

"Try not to slip and fall, Riot. I can't swim out to rescue you in mud."

Riot balanced across the narrow plank bridge. From a distance, the barge looked like a junk pile waiting to be set ablaze, but as he crossed the bridge, he realized there was order to madness. "Ahoy there," he called.

"Just a tic!"

Riot stopped on the gangplank, eyeing a tattered confederate flag drooping in the early morning fog. It wasn't long after that a gnarled old man limped from under the canopies, wrestling one-handed with his trouser buttons. He wore an equally tattered gray coat, the right arm sleeve pinned back.

He stopped when he saw Riot, his eyes darting around the cramped boat.

"Are you Muddy Morris?" Riot asked.

"I am…" Morris said slowly.

"I'm not here for trouble," Riot said. "Just looking for a few items some men from the warehouses might have sold you."

Morris licked his lips. "Lots of people sell me lots of things. Ain't none of it stolen, far as I know. I paid 'em fair for it."

"I'm not concerned with how you acquired the items. I'm only interested in buying them back."

The prospect of an easy resale brightened Morris's day. "And what might those items be?"

"A gentleman's walking stick. A silver pocket watch. A gentleman's suit and hat. Those would've been about a month back. And just a few weeks ago, rougher clothing that'd fit a large man."

Muddy Morris scratched his chin. "Don't recall a walking stick or pocket watch. I'd recall that. But come along, I'll show you what I got." He waved Riot aboard and limped to the back of the boat.

Morris muttered to himself as he rifled through his belongings. Eventually, he remembered where he'd put the items, and tore back a tarp to reveal a pile: boots, coat, trousers, a revolver. No hat. Not surprising considering where Monty was shot.

Riot recognized the revolver as Monty's—a Colt 'self-cocker.' He'd never cared for the weapon style. He picked up the large coat. Good wool. Not store bought. When had Monty ever worn anything but rough clothing?

Morris shifted nervously. "Fellow I got them from said it was their dear old pappy's."

Riot had a knack for people. He could read them like words on a page. It wasn't conscious thought, or any line of deductive reasoning—he just *knew*. And right now he knew Muddy Morris was lying.

"Of course," Riot soothed.

"I was waiting to cross the bay to sell 'em."

"Was there a billfold?"

"Eh…"

The man rummaged some more, then lifted a lid to a basket where a heaping pile of leather billfolds lay. He passed over one. "No tender in it."

"Calling cards, receipts?" Riot asked, opening it up. It was empty, and the man, naturally, shook his head. Riot tossed back the billfold, and turned to the trousers. He found a wad of receipts in the pocket. Monty hadn't been the type to empty his pockets.

Riot stuffed the receipts back inside. Best not to look too eager. "And the gentleman's suit?"

"'Fraid I sold that a bit ago."

A part of Riot was relieved. On one hand, the suit was bespoke from *Steed and Peel*, and the tailors didn't come cheap. On the other hand, he'd nearly died in it.

Riot searched through the hats, then picked through the basket of billfolds, but didn't find his own in the mess. It wasn't special to him, or even expensive, but it had his calling cards inside. In the end, he gathered Monty's belongings, and tossed the man a dollar.

"Hey now," Muddy Morris said. "That there is worth more than a dollar."

"The clothing was stripped from a man who was shot in the head." Riot turned over the coat where someone had tried to scrub out a bloodstain. "A dollar will do, unless you want to explain to the police how you acquired the belongings of a murdered man."

Muddy Morris grumbled, but said nothing more. Riot tipped his hat, and balanced back across the planks. He found

Liam leaning against a hitching post. The old cowboy's eyes glinted with amusement as Isobel paced back and forth in agitation. A cigarette dangled forgotten from her fingertips.

Riot knew his wife didn't actually like to smoke; she just enjoyed lighting matches. She stopped when he approached. "Pockets," he said, tossing her the trousers. She flicked the cigarette away and caught them to dig out the receipts.

"Seems he ate at the *Jumping Moose* a few times," she noted.

"I know that restaurant," Riot said. "There's a launderer's tag on the coat, too. We can check the hotels and laundries nearby."

"MY BROTHER CAN'T REMEMBER ANYTHING..." ISOBEL WAS saying. "First, he told me it was the Red Star Laundry down the street, then the White Star. But I think he got confused with the Golden Star Laundry. Montgomery Johnson. He's tall. Grumpy." She held a hand high overhead. "With a mustache."

The woman behind the counter was shaking her head.

Isobel tried a few words in broken Cantonese, but considering Jin claimed she sounded like a demented toddler, she wasn't surprised when the woman crossed her arms.

It was about this time that Riot walked in. She met his gaze and an entire conversation passed between them. He had found nothing at the other launderers. He took her silent cue to step up to the counter, and addressed the woman in fluent Cantonese.

The woman started, surprised, then her face softened as he bowed. Isobel went outside to wait, and in less than five minutes, Riot joined her.

"The Brooklyn Hotel."

"I really need to practice my Cantonese more often."

"It wasn't my mastery of language, it was my charm."

"Keep telling yourself that, Riot."

"You're the one who said it first."

"Among my many regrets," she called over her shoulder.

THE BROOKLYN HOTEL WASN'T THE SORT OF PLACE RIOT would have expected Monty to stay in. For one, it was clean. Second, expensive. It wasn't quite the Palace, but close to it. It was the sort of hotel a successful businessman might choose. For as long as Riot had known Monty, he'd only lived in run-down lodging houses, or shacked up with various women.

Considering his rough attire, Riot debated making up a story, but he was tired. So he nodded to Liam, who walked up to the hotel counter, and opened his coat, displaying the Pinkerton badge pinned to his vest. "Do you have a Montgomery Johnson staying here?"

The clerk consulted his book. "Room 12, sir."

"We'll need to see his room."

The clerk hesitated, then looked to Riot and Isobel, who was in her Mr. Morgan guise.

"Monty hasn't paid his bill, has he?" Isobel asked.

"No... he hasn't returned."

"That's because he's dead," Riot said.

The clerk sighed and retrieved a key, handing it over to Liam. It seemed a Pinkerton badge did come with benefits. Riot had forgotten the perks of having a badge. Small wonder Monty carried a fake one.

Before they left, Riot pointed to a telephone behind the desk. "Would you please notify Inspector Coleman at the Hall of Justice that Montgomery Johnson was staying at your hotel. Tell him the Pinkertons are here investigating."

The clerk picked up the receiver, and Riot followed Liam

into the elevator. Impatient as usual, Isobel had sprinted up a stairwell.

"That woman of yours is excitable," Liam noted.

"That's certainly one word."

"Is she usually this… focused?"

"When she's hunting."

Liam gave a dry chuckle as the elevator boy opened the cage doors. Liam had the key in hand, but when the two detectives arrived, they found Isobel already inside room 12, searching through a desk.

"I generally wait for the police," Liam said.

"The maid let me in," she replied, without looking up. "It's been cleaned."

Riot had to agree with her faint sigh. The bedding was laundered, items on the desk arranged, and the wastebasket emptied.

Riot opened the wardrobe, and cocked a grin at what he found. "There you are." He snatched up Ravenwood's walking stick and gave it a fond twirl.

"Your stolen pocket watch is on the dresser," Isobel called from across the room.

"What's that?" Liam asked.

"I'd like you to be a witness, Mr. Taft. That I'm not stealing this stick or the pocket watch. Monty stole them after he beat me near to death."

"How do I know it's yours?"

"There's a hollow in the stick." Riot thumbed a bit of filigree, then twisted the shaft once, and unscrewed the knob. He showed Liam the hollowed center. "It was Ravenwood's. He willed it to me."

Liam hefted the stick. "Not entirely hollow," he noted.

"No, but well-balanced."

"Riot," Isobel called.

He started towards her, but paused at the bedside table, a

book catching his eye. Not just any book, but a thick dictionary. Now that was odd.

"These betting slips were stuffed in this notebook. Several pages have been torn out. The rest is blank." Although the names and dates differed, the tickets were identical to the ones Tim had pinched from the racetrack's security office.

"What's special about those slips?" Liam asked.

"Does your office handle security at the racetrack?" Riot asked.

Liam straightened from where he'd been hunched over by the bed. "No, but Sam told me a fellow named Carson handles security. He worked as a Pinkerton once upon a time. We checked into his record. Nothing stood out."

"That could explain why Skunk thought he was a Pinkerton," Isobel said.

"Skunk?" Liam asked.

"A horse handler," Riot answered. He took up a pencil and started rubbing it over the paper beside the torn out notebook pages. "A stack of betting slips were in a receipt holder on Carson's desk. Tim got ahold of some from his wastepaper basket. We thought it odd."

Liam chuckled. "Wastepaper basket. Most just call it a trash can. Sure you're not from England, Mr. Riot?"

"I've traveled there often enough." Nothing showed up on the empty pages.

"I don't see a bank book," Isobel noted.

"That would be because he banked at a more traditional locale," Liam announced. The graying Pinkerton was on his knees by the bed, holding up a handful of cash. "Stuffed mattress."

"That's more Monty's style," Riot said dryly.

Between the three detectives, they searched every inch of the hotel room. Isobel thumbed through the dictionary, and found an array of postcards tucked into the pages—all of naked women in various poses. Their names were printed on the back.

"He may have visited some of these women," Isobel said, tossing the stack in front of the agent.

"I'll have Sam follow up. He'll enjoy that."

"I'm sure he will," Isobel said.

While Liam busied himself with counting the cash—a total of five thousand in bank notes—Isobel disappeared to search the bathroom. Riot tucked his pocket watch into his vest pocket, hooking the chain on a button. He felt a twinge of regret. Perhaps Isobel had been right—maybe Monty had felt slighted. Ravenwood had favored Riot with his belongings, not Monty.

Riot searched the clothing, turning it out and inspecting the lining for any hidden pockets. Nothing notable. Except Riot's stolen hat. He'd set it down in the boxing club before fighting Monty. Now that, Monty had taken out of spite.

Riot turned again to the dictionary. It could simply be a convenient place to hide pornographic images from the maids, but Monty hadn't been a reader, so why have a dictionary conveniently at hand at all? Riot was fairly sure he knew the answer.

35

A CLIFF

GRIMM WHITE STOOD ON THE EDGE OF A CLIFF. IT WASN'T A real one, but it felt like one. His mother didn't want him anywhere near this cliff. For over half a decade she'd kept him far away from the edge. Hidden. But he was sick of hiding. So he'd gone to Ravenwood Agency and interviewed, then lost his nerve.

Action had consequence, and sometimes the consequence could hit someone close. Grimm had discovered that the hard way.

He stared into the eyes of Sugar, and the horse stared back with understanding. It was time to make a choice. She nuzzled his ear, nostrils flaring softly against his skin. Grimm rested his head against hers. The scent of horsehair, of sweat, of hay, and earth. It calmed his mind.

Grimm could no longer live in the shadows. It was time to step off the cliff.

He found his mother in the manor's kitchen. It was her haven. Her comfort. Whether the family found themselves in a shack, by a campfire, or in a cramped room, a cooked meal was always special. It made a place feel like home—no matter where that place might be. And with as much as his family had moved around, home was important.

Grimm wiped his boots, washed up to his elbows in the utility sink, and stepped into his mother's domain. She was kneading bread. Her strong arms and sure fingers turned the dough over in a continuous rhythm. Bread had always been a luxury to their family. Baking bread took time, a dry space to work, along with an oven. That meant their family had a real kitchen, or something close to it.

He stood quietly by, watching her work. The stove threw off heat, and by the smell in the kitchen, he wagered she was making rosemary bread. She'd have fresh goat cheese to go with it.

Lily sighed without looking at her older son. "What has Tobias gone and done now? I swear that boy gets into more trouble than I know what to do with."

Tobias was like a cat. He got into trouble as much as he got out of it, and as far as Grimm could tell, his little brother had plenty of lives left.

Grimm shook his head. Silently communicating that he wasn't here about Tobias. Maybe this wasn't the right time, he thought. But if not now, then when?

Grimm weighed his words. He had learned early on that words had power—to heal, to hurt, to kill. Silence was the safest, but he'd been growing more reckless of late. That worried him.

"I interviewed with Ravenwood Agency for a detective position."

His mother started in surprise. Earlier this year, he'd finally broken his six years of silence, but his voice still caught her off guard. Shock quickly turned to a furrowing of her brow. His mother slammed the dough onto the counter, sending a cloud of flour into the air.

"Did Mr. Tim pressure you?" she asked sharply.

"No, ma'am," he said. "This is my choice."

Lily closed her eyes briefly. Then reached for a handful of flour, and sprinkled it over the dough. She started kneading again, avoiding his eyes.

"I know it's dangerous, Ma," he whispered. "But I can't keep living like this. This isn't a life."

"It's *our* life," she hissed. "And we have a good one right now."

He stayed silent.

Another slap of dough. "Why a detective?" she demanded. "It puts you near the law, Josiah." She'd used his actual name. A rare thing. They all had fake names, save for Tobias. Grimm's little brother didn't even know their real ones. It was safer that way.

"I'm already near the law."

Lily's jaw tightened. "We should've taken off as soon as Mr. Riot walked into this house. I knew he'd be trouble. And with that police raid... someone could've recognized us."

"I got out in time."

"What about next time, Josiah?" She stopped kneading to look at him. There were tears in her eyes.

"I can't keep running."

"We're *all* running."

"I'm the one they're after."

"You don't think they'd take me, too?"

Grimm fell quiet with thought. The slap and turn of dough, the anger and frustration in her hands, filled the silence. What price would he pay for his next words? Grimm said them anyway. "We don't know they're still after us, Ma."

"They are," she said with conviction.

Grimm knew better than to argue with his mother. She'd kept them alive this long, and caution was rarely a bad thing. But he was tired of it. "Do you want Maddie and Tobias to live like us?" Grimm finally asked. "Because it's not fair to them."

A tear rolled down Lily's cheek to mix with the dough. She scrubbed the next away, leaving a streak in the flour that covered her cheeks. "Why a detective?" she asked.

"You taught me to do what's right, not what's easy," he said. "That's what I want to do. I can't be a policeman because of the color of my skin, but I can be a private detective."

Lily's eyes shone with pride. "Did you get the job?" she asked.

Grimm gave a sheepish smile. "Mr. Lotario said I might be on par with his own brilliance."

"Those twins have enough arrogance between them to fill an ocean."

"I think they have larger hearts, though."

"It would horrify the pair to hear it. When do you start?"

"I haven't accepted yet. I wanted to tell you first—before I give my answer. It seemed the right thing to do."

"I'll be clear with you, Josiah. You don't have my permission. But you don't need it anymore."

"I know," Grimm said. "Your blessing matters, though."

"That I'll give. Just—" She caught herself, then changed whatever she'd been about to say. "Just take care of yourself."

Grimm shrugged. "My first assignment is caring for horses at a racetrack. I'm supposed to play dumb and deaf, and just listen. It's not much different from what I do here."

Lily looked relieved. "Still. There are bad sorts at racetracks."

"I'm no stranger to those sorts, Ma."

"No, I suppose not." She sighed faintly with regret, then rallied. "It's about time Tobias learns how to manage the stables alone."

"He has Jin and Sarah to help. I think they can manage."

"God help us all."

36

KNIGHTS OF CHASTITY

"I WON'T LIE," SARAH SAID FIRMLY.

"I would lie," Jin said.

Sarah shot her sister a glare across the carriage.

"We're not asking you to lie," Riot soothed.

"What if this girl I'm supposed to befriend asks me what I'm doing at the rally?"

"Tell the truth," Isobel said. "That you came with your parents."

Jin eyed Isobel. "I do not think you are old enough to be her mother."

"Yes, but Riot is old enough, and he and Sarah both have dark hair. They easily pass for father and daughter."

"I have dark hair, too," Jin muttered.

Isobel tapped her lips. "You could be his love child from a secret affair in Hong Kong."

Jin's eyes lit up. "With a pirate woman who was tragically beheaded."

"She might have been related to Ching Shih," Isobel added.

Ching Shih was an infamous prostitute-turned-pirate who

tormented the Qing Dynasty, the Portuguese Empire, and the Dutch East India Company. The pirate queen was always a source of inspiration. She retired to Portuguese Macau and in their later years was on good terms with Isobel's unconventional grandmother, something her mother refused to speak of.

Sarah gestured at the pair with frustration. "Do you see what I mean?" she asked Riot.

"My tragic love affairs with pirate women aside..."

Isobel arched a brow. "There was more than one?"

"...don't feel like you have to explain anything," he continued. "Let them fill in the blanks. Most people will be too polite to ask."

"My gramma always said silence is as loud as a lie."

Jin sighed with frustration. "This is an *investigation*. It is probably murder."

Isobel held up a finger. "I did not say that."

"Why else would you have Sarah make friends with another girl?" Jin shot back.

"Because Sarah is friendly."

Jin crossed her arms.

"Sarah, the Nobles are a religious sort of family. You were *just* telling me how you'd like to find a church. So tell the truth. You're there to meet people."

Sarah frowned at her adoptive parents. "I'm not sure the pair of you are a good influence on me."

"Likely not," Riot agreed.

Not for the first time, or the last, Sarah mused over the strange turn her life had taken. For a girl from a quiet town in Tennessee, the city was a big change. And her new family even more so.

Yesterday Isobel had swept into the manor like a whirlwind, told Jin and Sarah to dress in their Sunday best (it wasn't Sunday), then taken them in a carriage to Carville—to the

Falcon's clubhouse. When Sarah had walked into the converted railcar, a shouted '*Surprise!*' shocked her.

All her family and friends were there. Miss Lily, Tobias, Grimm, Maddie, Margaret, Lotario, Tim and… her father. She was so relieved to see Atticus that she rushed into his arms, uncaring that everyone saw her tears. It was the best belated thirteenth birthday present she could imagine. The easel and art kit they'd gifted her was a nice bonus, as was the pearl-handled derringer.

Sarah wasn't sure what to think of that. Atticus had taken her out into the dunes to show her how to shoot it. But Sarah had taken the little pistol out of his hand, loaded it, and shot the top off some purple dune shrub.

"You know how to shoot," he noted, sounding mildly surprised, which was close to shock for him.

"I'm from Tennessee, Atticus. I've been hunting cottontails since I was six. My gramma called these peashooters. This is pretty, but I'm not sure it'd kill a squirrel."

"You'd be surprised. In my experience, a bullet can do just about anything." He brushed a hand along the white slash of hair at his temple. "With the caliber and range I was shot at, I should be dead, and yet I've seen a peashooter kill a man hit in the right spot."

Sarah frowned up at him. "Is there something I should know?"

Riot adjusted his spectacles. "You're a young lady…" He hesitated, which made her worried. "It never hurts to have options. I'll feel better with you carrying it."

And that was that.

Mrs. Gunn, who ran a restaurant from an old railcar, catered the celebration-cum-Thanksgiving dinner. Despite the moody day, they'd eaten outside at a big table, with the ocean crashing beyond sand dunes and grasses bent under the wind. It was a perfect day.

And now here she was. Being asked to make friends with some girl who'd just lost her brother in death. "Ask questions. Poke around. See what you can discover," Isobel suggested.

It felt wrong.

"What about our names?" Sarah asked.

"Saavedra *is* my family name. On my mother's side."

"It sounds sinister," Sarah said.

"It's Portuguese. My mother's family come from some type of royalty." Isobel waved a hand. "Thanks to the newspapers, the names *Riot* and *Amsel* are too notorious."

"What if someone recognizes us?" But even as Sarah asked, she knew the answer. It was unlikely. The Saavedra name fit.

Riot had trimmed his beard to a point, curled his mustache, and slicked back his hair. He'd exchanged spectacles for a golden monocle and wore a formal homburg. With his sun-darkened skin, he looked a proper Spanish lord. Isobel was playing the part of his devout wife, wearing a high-collared dress with a proper amount of lace. She *looked* different, too. Softer, somehow. Even her eyes were more blue than gray.

Sarah had dabbled with costume makeup while in the company of Mr. Sin, who was a master at altering his appearance. She knew about shadowing, contouring, and layering, but it still amazed her.

"Then laugh it off and comment on how curious you find the resemblance," Isobel said. "We're going to a churchy event. You should feel right at home."

"I'm not quick like you, Isobel. I can't come up with clever answers like that."

Riot placed a hand over hers. "Just be yourself, Sarah."

"Only not so honest," Jin said.

Sarah closed her eyes and let her head fall back against the cushion.

"THIS IS NOTHING LIKE MY GRAMMA'S CHURCH," SARAH whispered. She and Isobel stood at the back of an auditorium brimming with angry voices. A fiery Irish priest stood at the pulpit, raising his fist and shouting with all the enthusiasm of his country. Four other men in clerical collars stood on stage, nodding along with the speech.

Riot and Jin had already split off to work their way through the crowd. Jin was wearing her usual oversized cap and boy's suit. She was so small that unless someone bent down to look under her cap, they'd never know she was Chinese.

"... our children are forced to walk by its gates daily. Respectable women pass it. Even the red-light districts of France would wonder that such a place is allowed to exist. The Nymphia degrades our fair city. It tears at our moral fiber, and it's an entrance to the very gates of hell. We must take our stand against vice, for God has made hell for such places. We are coming, at least two thousand strong, to protest its existence and close down that vile resort for the salvation of all!"

Cheers, angry shouts, fists, and signs proclaiming hell and damnation were raised in the auditorium.

"Now that's a Catholic Irishman at his finest," Isobel whispered in Sarah's ear.

Father Caraher, the most beloved and feared priest in the city, was as strong and stubborn as a mule. He had a broken nose and bruised knuckles, and his blue eyes blazed with damnation. Isobel would never admit it out loud, but she rather liked the old devil. He never backed down from a fight.

"They look set to burn down the building," Sarah said.

"They do, don't they," Isobel mused.

"Is that Avó over there?" Sarah asked. She was standing on her tippy-toes, trying to look over the crowd.

"Yes," Isobel said with a sigh. "My mother is a great admirer of Father Caraher."

"Not surprising," Sarah said.

By the time the reverends and preachers had finished speaking, Isobel thought the lot of them would march on the gates of hell themselves (or rather the gates of the Nymphia), yet after thunderous applause those assembled broke off for refreshments.

Anticlimatic, to say the least.

But that didn't mean there weren't those with more bite than bark present. Riot was searching out the more radical members.

They'd learned that Mrs. Noble was a founder of the Knights of Chastity—a constant thorn in the Nymphia's side. Had the owners somehow lured Dominic to the hotel with a mind to discredit the group?

"She's coming this way," Sarah whispered.

"Yes, I know. Stand behind me."

"Do you think she'll recognize you?"

Steely haired and wielding a cane, Catarina Saavedra Amsel was prodding her way through the crowd. Isobel didn't want to take the chance that her mother would cause a scene, so she slipped through the crowd and sidled up next to her.

"Mother," Isobel whispered. "You did not tell me you were in the city."

If Catarina was surprised to find her only living daughter at an assembly against vice, she didn't show it. "I'll start sharing my whereabouts when you share yours," Catarina bit out. "How are my granddaughters?"

Isobel hesitated, only briefly, an idea beginning to form. She could work with this recent development. She led the way back to Sarah, who was glued to a wall.

Catarina's face transformed when she caught sight of her granddaughter. The two shared a warm embrace that Isobel couldn't account for. "Are you keeping my daughter out of trouble?" Catarina asked.

Sarah smiled, wisely remaining silent.

Catarina turned a keen eye on Isobel. "I hardly recognized you."

"You *didn't* recognize me at all, Mother."

"Of course I did. I didn't hit you with my cane when you startled me."

"If you'd recognized me, you would have."

"Insufferable, girl," Catarina muttered, turning to search the crowd. "Is Jin here, too?"

"She's here with Atticus," Sarah said.

"What was that nonsense about Atticus being charged with murder? *Again.*"

"He didn't do it, Mother."

"Of course he didn't. He was released. I had to use that infernal device to speak with Mr. Farnon and get the story first-hand. I really do hate learning about your misadventures in the newspapers."

"I didn't have time to telephone you."

"You never have time." Catarina thought the world of her son-in-law. Isobel suspected she secretly harbored a hope that Riot would 'tame' her. "What are you really doing here? I've learned long ago not to hope you've turned over a new leaf."

"Do you know Mrs. Noble and her daughters?"

"The Chairwoman? Of course."

Splendid.

"Sarah is looking for friends her own age. I thought the youngest Noble daughter might do."

Catarina was not a slow woman. She was as razor sharp as her eyes, and as intelligent as her daughter. "Does this have something to do with their son's death?"

"I can't say, Mother."

"They're in mourning, Isobel."

"As if sentiment ever stopped you before. What do you know about their son's death?"

"Gossip is a road to hell."

"So is *murder*."

Catarina arched a brow. Hah! She didn't know the truth. And even though Catarina betrayed nothing, Isobel knew her mother was intrigued. Catarina glanced at Sarah. "I'll not involve my granddaughter in whatever scheme you're cooking up. However, against my better judgment, I will introduce you to Mrs. Noble. Perhaps some of her good influence will rub off on you."

"I don't want to be known at this point. It's a case that requires delicacy," Isobel whispered.

Catarina placed protective hands on Sarah's shoulders. "She'll not be involved."

"I just want her to make friends. She has none of her own age."

The two women locked gazes. And Sarah rolled her eyes and walked away through the crowd, ending the battle of wills. Sarah had never met two people more alike. She'd swear on a bible that mother and daughter enjoyed their bickering.

It didn't take long for Sarah to find a group of young ladies her own age. Girls always flocked together. Though two of the girls, with fur muffs and capes, stood off to one side. They were clearly wealthier than the others. And one of the wealthy girls wore a black band around her arm.

Sarah hadn't been given any details about the case, or even instructions. But she knew she was supposed to find out as much as she could. Whatever that might be. If this Dominic Noble had recently died, then it stood to reason it would be his sister wearing the black ribbon.

Sarah gave the two girls a tentative smile and was relieved when the girl with the mourning band motioned her over—a brown-haired girl with rosy cheeks and warm eyes.

Introductions were made, but Sarah stumbled over her name. She just *couldn't* lie. "Sarah Byrne. I'm here with my gramma." For whatever reason, Isobel seemed intent on keeping her new family name out of it. So this seemed an easy workaround.

The girls giggled at her Tennessee drawl. Then a girl standing next to Helen Noble, an Annie Simpson, got wide eyes. "Say, I've read about you in the newspapers, haven't I? Your picture was on the front page."

Sarah blushed all the way to her toes. "Yes," she admitted. Isobel would be so disappointed with her. And the next thing she knew, the girls were pressing for details about the trouble she'd found herself in earlier that year. Sarah gave them what she could, skirting dangerously close to a lie—she couldn't tell the whole truth without betraying a promise to Mr. Sin. "My uncle died, and I was fortunate to be taken in by a loving family." Never mind their eccentricities.

"Helen's brother just died…" Annie confided.

Helen's eyes dimmed with grief, and Sarah felt an instant pang of sympathy. She didn't have to pretend at all. "I'm sorry," Sarah said. "I don't know if the pain will ever go away…" It was as simple and as honest as that, and Sarah and Helen quickly bonded over their shared grief.

37

THE LINE

Talking with Tim *should* have been simple. It was only a question. Then why was Isobel dreading it? One rarely approached a friend to talk about the murder he'd committed. But was it an unlawful killing? There was the crux. Fifty years ago it would've been called justice.

Isobel found Tim in the stable house cleaning a rifle, of all things. She nearly left, but stopped herself in the doorway.

"I picked up some new locks for you to practice on," he said, without turning around.

"How did you know it was me?"

The old man started chuckling. It was a deranged sort of sound. "I hope to God you weren't trying to sneak up on me." He glanced over his shoulder. "Truth be told, I was expecting you."

"Is that why you're cleaning your rifle?"

Tim put down his instruments and started reassembling the weapon. His gnarled hands were smooth and practiced enough to do it blindfolded. "Always keep your firearms clean. Never know when you might have need of one."

Sage advice had never sounded so sinister to her ears.

"Don't you worry about the other case," Tim said, without turning. "Grimm got himself situated at the racetrack like a natural. Walked right up to a hot-blooded horse that was giving the handlers issues and calmed him right down. Got a job on the spot."

"I'm not surprised," she said.

"Me neither."

"If you need to contact me, you can always send a message—"

"We got you covered, girl." Tim turned. "I'll keep A.J. up to speed on anything we find. That twin of yours thinks there's something more to the tickets, too. But you know all that... Go on, blurt it out."

"Blurt what out?" she asked sharply. There was nothing worse than someone knowing her own mind. Small wonder others found it annoying when she did the same. Well, there was something worse—this conversation.

Tim raised bushy brows, waiting.

"A member of the thieving gang saw you, Tim." Her voice wavered. "I let him go."

"You should've turned him over to the police."

Isobel stepped closer. "He *saw* you shoot Monty."

Tim shrugged. "Did he know my name?"

"I don't know."

"What did he see?"

"A white-haired old man."

Tim scratched his beard. "Huh. Unfortunate that I'm the only one of those in the city. Guess I'm pegged."

Isobel glared. "He could identify you."

"He could identify a heap of suspects."

"Tim, this isn't a game."

"Nope," he agreed, and fished around for his pipe and pouch. "You know I'd never ask you to bear the burden of a secret you can't live with. I didn't intend for you to carry it at all." His blue eyes were bright and piercing, without a shadow of regret.

"You shot Monty in cold blood. Then left him on a street to rot. He wasn't found for *two* days. That doesn't bother you?" she whispered.

Tim stuffed a pinch of tobacco into the pipe bowl. "The dead don't bother me."

"You ever think just maybe they should?"

Tim paused, then hooked a second stool with his foot, and pulled it out. "Let me tell you a story. Then you can decide if I've gone beyond the pale. Fair enough?"

In answer, she sat and watched as Tim went about the business of lighting his pipe. "You ever keep a dog?" he asked.

"My brothers kept some around. And Lotario had one that he was fond of."

"What I figured," he said. "You don't strike me as a dog person. More of a cat lady."

She didn't argue.

"I had this dog. Piper, I called her. Found her as a puppy. Frozen little starved thing. Carried her around in my coat to keep her warm till she was strong enough to fend for herself. She followed me everywhere. Sleet, snow, rain, desert. You name it. She was my constant companion for eight good years. Then I caught her playing with a fox one day. It was real friendly, till it bit her."

"I couldn't risk it. I shot the fox, then much as it pained me, I tied her up to see if she'd go rabid. Sure enough..." His eyes misted. "Still stings when I think about her. I hoped it wouldn't take, but..." His voice cracked, and he cleared the grit from his throat. "You ever see something die of rabies?"

Isobel shook her head.

"Awful way to go. I seen this one fellow beat his head against a stone to make the pain stop." He lit a match and put it to the bowl, puffing, until the tobacco caught. He took a few savoring puffs until he was satisfied, then looked her in the eye.

"Now what do you think I did?" he asked, his voice hard. "You think I let her loose out of love? So she could cause someone else to suffer?"

"No."

"Sure as hell I didn't," he said. "You think I kicked her till her ribs broke? You think I bashed her head till she didn't know up from down, till her eyes were swollen shut, and her jaw broken? You think I tossed her in a gutter in a cold rain and left her to die alone?"

Cold fury blazed in his eyes, and his stare pinned Isobel to her seat.

"'Cause that's *exactly* what Monty did to A.J. That's the kind of man he was. What do you think *I* did?"

Isobel swallowed. "You shot her. Clean. One bullet."

Tim looked away, his hands shaking, as he rubbed at a jagged scar crossing the back of one. "Don't think I killed her lightly. Sometimes a dog has to be put down, no matter how much you love 'em. 'Specially a rabid one."

Isobel was quiet.

"So, no," he said, hoarsely. "I'm not troubled; I did what needed doing."

"There are courts for that…"

Tim puffed out a wheezing laugh. "Those same courts have more blood on their hands then I'll ever have." She couldn't deny it. Corruption poisoned the law. Alex had bought an entire jury to convict her. "*Someone* sent a rabid dog after your husband. And I admit it, I killed their rabid dog. It's the only message those sorts understand—that we bite back. But the only judge and jury I care about is you. So what's it going to be?"

Isobel considered the old man in front of her. Creased and

worn by life, his eyes bright, with laugh lines at the corners, and sadness on his lips. "You'd let me turn you in?"

Tim wheezed with amusement. "Does a dog know it's rabid?"

"I don't know," she said, honestly.

"Well, I don't know either. Maybe I'm rabid; maybe I'm not. But I *am* an old dog. And I'd prefer an honest friend to put me down rather than some lying son of a bitch."

"I don't want to turn you in, Tim," she said with a shake of her head. "I just—" Isobel couldn't bring herself to say the words. But Tim already knew. He'd been there the night she'd shot her older brother. She forced the words out. "There's not a day that goes by that I don't think of Curtis. I wish I had your peace."

Tim plucked out his pipe and pointed the stem at her. "I made a choice when I killed Piper. Same when I killed Monty. I thought long and hard before pulling the trigger. You didn't have that choice. Curtis forced you into it. And it's hell to make peace with things we can't control."

Isobel sat, stunned. It was true. It was so true it hurt. Curtis had cornered her, attacked her, and forced her hand. She hadn't had a choice.

Tim gave her shoulder a squeeze. "I didn't ask you to cover up my shit—that's for me to worry about. And I'm not here to force you into staying silent. You do what you need to. Whatever choice you make, I'll understand."

Tim left her alone. And more importantly, he left her with a choice.

38

RACHEL WALL

ISOBEL PUT THE FINISHING TOUCHES ON HER PERSONA: MISS Rachel Wall, named after the first female American pirate, who was eventually hanged. With what lay before her, Isobel felt like she was marching to the gallows.

Isobel glanced at Riot in the mirror where he perched on a trunk, watching her. "You were right," she said simply. "I spoke with Tim. He left it up to me."

"I wagered that, since you're still alive."

"Who knows, maybe he'll surprise me with a bullet. Tim does like to play the fool. By the way, upon my untimely demise, my inheritance will go to Sarah and Jin."

"That was certainly a quick change of your mother's will."

"My mother doesn't have high hopes for my life expectancy." She frowned at her dull coat, and worked at a button, until it loosened yet still hung by a thread. Her proper clothes were simple, store bought and cheap, washed to a faded hue.

"What do you think?"

Riot moved closer to get a better look. No matter what he wore, that hair of his always attracted attention. Slightly curling black hair with a white streak at the temple, to go with a salted beard. He'd let it go untrimmed for two days and wore the rough clothes of a sailor—a roguishly attractive one who was currently prowling around her.

"I hope you aren't planning to look at the master of the house like that."

Isobel put on a battered pair of spectacles, then shifted her stance. She slouched like she expected to be hit from behind, and tilted her chin down and to the side, her eyes darting around the room, looking everywhere except at him.

"Timidity doesn't suit you," Riot noted.

"I agree. Hopefully, I won't slip out of character."

Riot brought her left hand to his lips, then gently slid off her wedding ring. "Be careful."

"I should say the same to you."

"I'm headed to a brothel. Hardly dangerous."

"Yes, but you look utterly roguish."

"But I'll smell like a horse."

"Some women like that."

"Whores are looking for johns flush with cash. I'm not a prime target." Riot drew her into his arms, and she nestled her head under his chin.

"Violet was right," Isobel said with sigh.

"About?"

"All men go to brothels."

She felt Riot chuckle. "With the number of prostitutes and brothels in San Francisco, I'm afraid I can't vouch for members of my sex."

"Yes, but how many men tell their wives where they're headed?"

"Now that would be dangerous."

"Especially if you're married to a woman like Cowboy Mag," she muttered. The infamous Barbary Coast saloon owner had finally snapped Thanksgiving eve and shot her husband for cheating. After she beat up his mistress.

Riot grunted. "A shame. I'm not surprised though. Maggie always wanted to be known as a gunfighter."

"Well," she said, leaning back. "Take comfort in the fact that I wouldn't have missed the first time."

"I love you," he said.

"It's obvious."

He cocked a smile at her. "All things considered, with the bounty on my head, the Nymphia will be the last place anyone expects me to be."

"It certainly buys us some time. And if there's anything to those betting slips, I'm sure Ari will find it."

"That's my hope."

"Never tell my twin this—it will inflate his already inflated ego—but he's better at ciphers than me."

"It's fortunate you have a modest ego."

"Sarcasm doesn't become you, Riot."

"You're rubbing off on me."

"More like rubbing on you."

Riot made a sound in the back of his throat that made her want to linger another day. "It will be a long few weeks," he admitted.

"With you surrounded by a flock of beautifully naked women." She clucked her tongue. "Do try to behave, Mr. *William Kyd*. And I'll try not to let Rachel Wall be seduced by the master of the house."

"Watch yourself. I haven't heard good things about Ian Noble and there's a high turnover of maids…"

"Me and my tattered virtue shall remain intact. I'll keep my tickler in my bodice at all times."

Riot seemed disinclined to part with her, and she wasn't very motivated to move. She gave him a long, lingering kiss, and left before she lost her nerve.

39

UNDERCOVER

FAMOUS LAST WORDS. NO JOB IN THE WORLD WAS WORTH THIS.
Isobel was in danger of dying of a backache. She found herself
on her knees scrubbing a toilet for the millionth time in a week.
How many damn bathrooms did this mansion have?

Fifteen. *Fifteen* bathrooms.

Between four women, all pampered beyond imagination,
the bathtubs were the worst. And the pay dismal. They'd made
her take out a loan on her future wages to pay for a uniform.
So now she was an indentured servant. It was a wonder more
maids didn't kill their employers.

She climbed to her feet and tugged at a starched collar. Of
all the impractical attire to—

"You, girl, I want a bath poured and a large fire. It's positively frigid outside."

Isobel hadn't needed to bother with a pseudonym. She was
simply referred to as 'girl' or 'the girl'. The Noble household
had such a high turnover of maids that the family never bothered learning any of their names.

"Yes, ma'am." Isobel bobbed a curtsy, and quickly gathered
her cleaning supplies.

"Start pouring my bath *first*. *Then* gather your things." Faith Noble was a dark-haired beauty with carefully sculpted curls, bright blue eyes the size of quarters, and creamy skin. She was fifteen, smack in the middle of her two sisters, Imogen being eighteen and Helen twelve. Faith Noble thought highly of herself.

Isobel stifled a crossly arched brow, and got to work on the bath without complaint. A week into her undercover investigation and she wanted to stab someone.

As the water gushed into the porcelain tub, she cocked an ear towards the adjoining room. "I hate this dreadful black. All of it black. It's hard enough without Dom, and now we're being forced to wallow in misery. He'd want us to move on," Faith complained.

Faith was dumping clothes on the floor as she raged back and forth, venting to her lady's maid. Her maid was a quiet woman, who had the patience of a saint and made sympathetic noises at all the right places. Isobel had yet to get her alone. When Faith wasn't referring to her lady's maid as 'girl', she occasionally called her Mary.

"I want to have fun. I want to take my mind away from here…"

Isobel ground her teeth as she turned to gather her things. "Then why the hell don't you sneak out," she muttered under her breath.

"Did you say something, girl?"

"Would you like any scents in your bath, ma'am?" Isobel called back pleasantly.

"Of course, I do! I want them every time. The lavender. Are you daft?"

"No, ma'am."

"Are you contradicting me?" Faith demanded.

"I'm sorry, ma'am, I don't know what that means."

"You're utterly useless," Faith raged from the doorway.

"Let's get you in a robe, Miss," Mary said, ushering her away from the bathroom.

Isobel uncorked the vial of lavender. If she were to murder Faith, she'd use some sort of poison that was absorbed through the skin. Thallium. Ricin. Or better yet, a small poisonous jellyfish floating in the bath... *Irukandji* venom. Yes, perfect. But perhaps murder was too drastic. Maybe something simple, like smearing poison oak leaves on a towel. Or... Isobel glanced at the toilet paper hanging on a wire loop. Then began whistling at the thought as she finished her duties in the bathroom. As she swept out, whistling merrily, Faith eyed her with suspicion. "Why are you so happy, girl?"

"I enjoy my work, ma'am."

Faith glared.

Isobel took her cleaning supplies down the servant's stairwell to the supply closet. Then she headed down to the coal room to lug up another bucket for a girl who had never worked a second of her life. If Dominic Noble had been anything like his three sisters, then the only thing that surprised her was that he hadn't been murdered sooner.

———

As brothels went, this wasn't the *worst* Riot had been in, but considering the filthy dives and mining camps he'd ventured into, that wasn't saying much.

"How's your night going, Miss Small?" he asked.

"It's finally slowing down." Dollie Small sidled up to the bar beside Riot, and signaled the bartender. The women who rented rooms had to entertain any man who called, but Dollie was an exception. Men often tipped their hats as they passed by her, and they kept their hands to themselves. Though women weren't allowed clothes in the Nymphia, Dollie got away with a sheer scarf wrapped around her voluptuous body.

"You seem like you're fitting in," Dollie noted.

He shrugged. "It's work. A heap easier than wrangling cows."

"This *is* a cow-yard," Dollie said dryly.

"It's slightly tamer here."

"You know most watchmen sample the goods."

"I'm a professional man, Miss Small." Riot had his back to the bar, so he could watch the men. He was on roving duty— there to ensure civility. The women usually lingered near him when he was in the saloon. One look from Riot and men thought twice about groping them.

"I don't believe it," she murmured. She leaned in closer, her bare shoulder brushing his vest. "You're not into women, are you?"

Miss Small was in her late thirties, blonde-haired, with green eyes and a quick tongue. She sauntered around with the confidence of a woman completely at ease with herself. And despite her name, she was not small.

"There's no shame in it," she whispered. "I've seen it *all*."

"I've seen it all, too," he said truthfully. It was always dangerous lying to a prostitute. They were keener than detectives at spotting deception. "My mother was a whore. It's more like family here. And…" He gave her a bashful sort of smile. "I have a sweetheart."

"Oh?"

"Saving every penny for her."

"She's a lucky woman."

"I consider myself the lucky one, ma'am." And that was God's honest truth. Riot would be lost in some dark place without Isobel. He felt it down to his bones. She'd given him a second chance on life.

Dollie gave him a small, sad smile. "You're a good man to have around, and I don't say that about many watchmen. It makes me think I should've kept mine..." She gazed into her whiskey, then took a long swallow.

"What happened to your man?"

"Oh, you know. The usual."

The usual could mean a wide spectrum of things. Riot sensed she didn't want to talk about it, so he changed the subject. "So does that sort of thing go on here? Between men?" Riot asked.

"*Everything* goes on here, Mr. Kyd."

"What's the hotel policy about it?"

"Anything goes," she said. "Now the watchmen... They can get riled up over two men going at it, but pass them a dollar and they'll keep their mouth shut about anything."

"Even murder?" he asked lightly.

Dollie gave him a cheeky look. "So you heard about that?"

"Hard not to. Man found dead in a bed during a raid."

"No one said it was murder. Some men just give out. I've had it happen."

"What am I supposed to do if that happens?"

She shrugged. "Take him to the morgue. Dump the fellow in a gutter. I don't give a damn. Just get him out of my bed. I can't have a stiff taking up space."

"So why didn't the watchman on duty do that?"

"I suppose Earl just didn't notice."

"Earl doesn't notice much," Riot pointed out.

"Oh, he's all right. But he's in debt up to his nose. Spends all his earnings on us gals and drink."

Riot turned slightly towards her. "Are there watchmen who aren't all right?"

"Why are you fishing for information?"

"I like to know what's going on."

"You have two eyes."

Not good ones, Riot thought wryly. He kept his spectacles in a pocket and only took them out when needed. "I'm afraid

I've spent one too many hours in the sun." As William Kyd, he let himself squint. It fit the disguise.

"Still, you never know," she said, eyeing him thoughtfully. "You don't often find a decent man in a place like this."

"I never said I was decent."

His answer put her at ease. "We get all sorts sniffing around here. Those damn Knights of Chastity are always trying to get men in here to preach our sins to us."

"They come in here?" he asked, surprised.

She laughed. It was a pleasant sound, full of good humor. "Nearly every week. The last fellow who came sneaking in walked around with his eyes on the ceiling, bright as a brick, and hard as a saint's statue."

"And you think I'm some sort of spy?"

She glanced towards the crotch of his fitted Levis. "I thought you fancied men more than women. All those old studs and young cowboys need to warm themselves on the range somehow. You wouldn't be the first cowboy to develop a preference."

The edge of Riot's lip quirked. "Is there a wager going?"

"I've lost a whole dollar," she admitted.

"What do the Knights of Chastity fellows try when they come in? So I know what to watch for."

"They mainly want dirt on this place. Not like it's hard to find." She tossed back her whiskey, then tapped the bar for another shot.

"Why are you here?" Riot asked. "There are tamer brothels in town. Ones where you'd have more control."

"Then I'd have to put up with a madam." She made a disgusted noise. "Lording it over like she owns me."

"Why don't you run your own brothel?"

"Too much commitment for me, too much headache, and too much overhead. Bribing police, dealing with local gangs, and all the petty squabbles that come up between the girls. I don't get on with other women," she admitted. "This place suits me. Gets right to the point. I don't have to entertain and giggle. So here I am." She spread her arms wide and gave a wiggle that sent her breasts bouncing.

Riot was only a man. It was hard not to admire her. "And there's an impressive amount of you, Miss Small," he noted. "So it's all happiness here?"

"I wouldn't call it happiness, but then what job is? It's better than spending all day up to your elbows scrubbing laundry in a vat of lye. Then being forced to get on your knees for the overseer to keep a shitty job."

A common story, Riot knew. A good many women in the profession got there by being a laundry attendant or factory worker first. With grueling hours and low wages, an overseer could make their life a little easier in exchange for sexual favors, and just outright fire them if they didn't oblige. Many women naturally migrated into a brothel, reasoning that they might as well get paid for it.

He'd once tracked down a woman who'd shoved her overseer into a vat of boiling water. Only Riot figured she'd done the world a favor, and told her he'd be back in the morning to arrest her. She'd slipped away in the night. Imagine that.

"Miss Joe and Miss Rose sure got into it the other day," he said.

"You handled that well." She sized him up. "Now if I had a watchman like you in a brothel I owned, I'd sit back and let you do all the work." She gave him a wink. The innuendo wasn't lost on him. "It's a pecking order. We're not in a house. We're competitors here. Then there're the watchmen to deal with."

"Do they take extra off the top, or demand favors?"

"Both. Depends who. Only not you, apparently. We're all still waiting for you to climb on top of one of us. There's even a line now."

"They'll have to get past my lady first," he said. "Have you talked with the owners about the watchmen?"

"As long as they get their rent, they don't care what goes on here. It's a wonder they even pay for watchmen at all."

There were bells inside the rooms and secret locking mechanisms for safety, but there were a lot of rooms to cover. Watchmen were an expense.

"Every girl learns how to deal," she said. "As long as I slip the guards a little something, be it favors or cash, they'll come when I need them."

"And if you don't?"

"Most watchmen have selective hearing. It's what makes you so rare. It also makes you stand out."

Dollie Small didn't strike Riot as the type to call for a watchman. The way she carried herself, the way she looked him straight in the eye and didn't back down. This was the type of woman who'd push a man into a vat of boiling water before asking for help.

A man interrupted their conversation by slapping Dollie's backside. Riot tensed to shove the man back, but Dollie gave a slight shake of her head, then turned to embrace the interloper. She was all smiles and twinkling eyes.

Dollie nodded to Riot that all was well, so he moved on, away from the saloon and its cheery piano, dancing feet, and hoots of laughter.

ISOBEL FINISHED POLISHING A KNOB, THEN GLANCED UP AT AN empty corridor. The Noble sisters had gone on an outing, which only left Mrs. Noble and the rest of the servants at home.

She tried the door, and when it didn't turn, crouched to study the lock. It was a simple lever lock like most in the house.

Isobel reached under her dress hem, and pulled out two lock picking wrenches she'd stowed in the seam—one to raise the interior lever, and the other to move the deadbolt. Being one of the most basic locks, the door quickly opened.

Isobel slipped inside with her cleaning bucket. Lurking around in the dark would be suspicious, so she switched on the electric lights. Fine furniture, no frills, this had been Dominic Noble's room. His mother had been too distraught to deal with his things, so she'd ordered the door locked.

There was something personal about Dominic's murder. Something that made her think there were answers here—only she had no idea what those might be. His murder didn't strike her as a robbery, or even something the woman in the room could have managed unless he'd been drunk out of his mind. And then there was the carpenter's pencil. Who carried a thick pencil like that, aside from the obvious answer?

She went over to a desk, popped the lock and rifled through the contents. Receipts, correspondence, a day planner. Luncheons, dinner parties, rowing practices, Knights of Chastity events, and at least once a week an outing with Katherine Hayes. How romantic that Dominic wrote their walks in his daily planner lest he forget.

She turned to his account books.

Nothing leapt out at her. No regular payments to an unknown source. There were certainly large payments, but they were all accounted for with notations: jewelry, club dues, clothing.

She'd have to ask Katherine about the jewelry. There was an awful lot of it. Her mind leapt to Lotario—his jewelry collection was extensive. All had been gifts from clients. She'd check with Lotario, too.

Isobel replaced the journal, then turned to study the room. It looked lived in—cherished, even. A photograph of Katherine sat on his bedside table, while a photograph of himself with his three sisters sat on the mantel. It wasn't a proper photograph from a studio, but an informal one with the girls standing behind Dominic on a rock in a perfect line, their heads one atop the other, all silly faced.

The evil trinity looked almost human.

Isobel carefully extracted this photograph from the frame to check the back. Nothing except their names and a date. It'd been taken the previous year. Next, she slid Katherine's photograph from the frame and was rewarded with a shock —a parlor house postcard of a Venetian-style masked man wearing a bodice and garters. His face was partially covered, but she recognized the lithe build and bone structure. She saw it in the mirror every day. It was her twin, as Paris, in a provocative pose and a state of arousal. Say one thing for her twin, he looked absolutely stunning in a bodice and garters.

Isobel flipped over the card. *To finding each other. And the freedom to live.* Her twin had different writing styles for each persona, and Isobel knew them all. This wasn't one of them. Then who? Another lover?

Isobel tucked the parlor card into her bodice, and turned to the mantel, feeling under and around edges for any secret compartments. Nothing. She turned to the paintings on the wall. Bright and colorful, at first glance they appeared cheerful, but each drew her closer, holding her attention. A tilt of red lips made a woman look mournful. A shadow in the eyes of a man changed his countenance from handsome to sinister. An odd, but compelling collection.

What was she expecting to find here? A list of his enemies? Blackmailers? Plans to burn down the Hotel Nymphia to prove his loyalty to the Knights of Chastity?

A noise snapped her out of consideration. Key against lock. Isobel muttered an oath, and cast around for escape, but a maid climbing out of a second-story window was bound to attract notice in the middle of the day. And her cleaning bucket was on the floor.

Moving swiftly, she threw aside the curtains, and turned to the bed just as the door opened.

"What are you doing in here, girl?"

It was Abigail, one of the older maids, who had a tongue as sharp as the sisters and was a favorite of Mrs. Noble.

Isobel bobbed a curtsy, while she fidgeted with her feather duster. "I was airing out the room, Miss Abigail," she said with her eyes on the floor.

"Speak up!" Abigail snapped. The maid marched across the room, inspecting it with a keen eye. When she was satisfied everything was as it should be, she turned on Isobel.

"Cleaning this room is *my* job, girl."

"Sorry, ma'am. I thought I'd help."

"How d'you get in here?"

"The door was unlocked, ma'am."

Abigail's eyes narrowed. For a moment, Isobel thought the older woman would strike her, but Abigail's face softened instead. "You're a hard worker, Miss Rachel. I appreciate that. You can help me in here for today, but you're not to come in again. Is that clear?"

"Yes, ma'am." Isobel's sigh of relief wasn't feigned. She got to work, turning out bedding, dusting corners and wall paneling, and polishing surfaces that would never be touched by the room's occupant again.

"Ma'am," Isobel eventually whispered.

"Hmm?" Abigail looked up from where she was changing a vase of flowers. It was the easiest job, but Isobel didn't hold it against the woman. She'd likely give the harder tasks to a young maid too. Only a week in and her back ached.

"Did the young Mr. Noble die in this bed like they say?"

Abigail frowned. "It's none of your business."

"It's only the room feels cold. Don't it?"

"Not uncommon in houses like these. People are born and die in the same bed, and are buried in the family graveyard on the same property."

"Was Mr. Noble a nice gentleman?"

"As good as they come. Doted on his sisters, he did. And they him." Abigail frowned at a flower in her hand. "So strange." It was a faint whisper.

"What's that, ma'am?" Isobel asked.

"You get back to work and keep your mind where it should be," Abigail snapped.

And that was that. If Isobel pressed the woman for answers, it would be the end of Rachel Wall.

40

NIGHTWORK

A BELL RANG DOWN THE HALLWAY, AND RIOT SPRINTED towards the clanging noise. He pushed open a door and walked straight into a client choking the woman of the room. A large, hairy man smelling of cheap whiskey had her against a wall, choking her from behind as he went at her.

Without preamble, Riot drove his fist into the man's kidney.

It got the hairy man's attention. He abandoned the woman, spinning with a raised fist. Riot ducked under the wild swing and skipped back. The man made to charge, only he tripped on the trousers around his knees and fell flat on his face.

Riot grabbed the man by vest and collar, and hoisted him up and through the door to ram his head into a hallway wall. The hairy man went down in a heap.

Miss Sadie stepped out, spitting curses, as she threw the client's hat and coat down the hallway. Then she rifled through his billfold, taking what she pleased.

Riot pretended not to notice. "I'll get him out of here, ma'am."

For the second time that night Riot hauled a furious drunk

out of the Nymphia. He pushed the man right into the hands
of a patrolman stationed out front.

That was the kicker about this establishment. The police
knew what it was. They raided it occasionally, and even posted
guards at its gates, but officers didn't stop the tide of men
streaming into the hotel. They came by the busload from ports.

Riot paused outside to massage his knuckles and take a
breath of fresh air. The night was crisp with fog and the chill
went straight to his bones, but it cleared his head. Of smoke.
Of the smell of unwashed men and their lust, of misery and
memories.

Riot pushed off the gate and went back inside to check on
Miss Sadie. He knocked, and the door opened a crack. "I
suppose you want something in return. Come in, then."

"I came to see if you were all right, ma'am."

She eyed him suspiciously. "Are any of us?"

"Point taken. I'll leave you to it."

She seemed to deflate. "Thank you, Mr. Kyd." He started
to leave, but she thrust out a dollar. "For your help."

"I'm only doing my job."

"So let me get this straight. You don't want carnal favors
and you don't want cash. What are you, some kind of knight
protector of fallen women?"

Most prostitutes did not want rescuing. They were rescuing
themselves by working for themselves, as they saw it. They'd
get out of the business as soon as they saved enough cash. Most
of the women had a dream they were working towards—a
house with a white fence, their own saloon or a brothel, a
grocery service, or just feeding their children.

"I do want something," he admitted. "Information."

She pursed her lips, waiting.

"What do you know about the man who died on the third
floor?"

"You a bull?"

"No, ma'am."

She crossed her arms under her breasts. Angry bruises were already blossoming on her throat and chest. "I don't like owing anything, so I'll tell you what I know—I know the watchman on the third level will take money for anything."

"Earl Becker?"

She shook her head. "Earl is one watchman. Billy Blackburn is the other. A man wants to be a brute? Billy will look the other way for the right price. Two men want to go at it? Billy don't care."

"And what happens if a woman ends up dead?"

She lifted a shoulder. "Who cares for the likes of us?"

"Where is Billy Blackburn?"

"Don't know. He bought everyone drinks and took off. You got his job."

"When did he leave?"

"The night before that fellow was found dead."

———————

EARL BECKER SAT SULLENLY AT A TABLE NURSING A DRINK. THE tide of rowdy sailors had ebbed, and the hotel was relatively quiet in the wee hours of morning. Riot signaled the bartender, then took a whiskey bottle and shot glass to Earl's table.

The scruffy, disheveled man started to protest, until he laid eyes on the full bottle.

"Hard night?"

Earl grunted. "Run while you can."

"How long have you lasted?"

"Been here since it opened."

Riot used his teeth to pull out the cork, and filled the man's tumbler with whiskey, then his own. Both men knocked back an appreciative draught.

"Can't run. I need the work," Riot said with a sigh.

"Don't we all."

Riot hesitated, before leaning in close. "Say, Earl, I'm new to this... in my other line of work if we happened on a man for breakfast, we just kept riding. But what do we do if we find a body here?"

"Find a place to dump him."

"Won't we be blamed for the murder, then?"

"You'll be blamed if you're the one that finds him. Trust me. It's best to dump him, or just walk on by."

"Like you did with that dead fellow?"

Earl turned red in the face. "I did *no* such thing," he hissed. "You keep your mouth shut."

"Like I said, that's how we did it where I come from," Riot said quickly. "No shame in it. You know how lawmen are— they'll arrest any man near a body."

Earl relaxed. "Yeah. Just keep walking. That's what I do."

"It was the woman who killed him, wasn't it?"

"They say it was suicide."

Riot snorted. "Suicide, my ass." He poured Earl another drink.

Earl leaned so close that Riot was hit with a wall of whiskey-infused breath. "I don't know nothin'. That's what I told the police, and it's God's honest truth. All I know is that the oriental woman vanished, and there was a dead man in there. Billy, the other guard on my floor, took off that same night."

"So you *did* find the dead fellow?" Riot asked.

Earl glanced at the bottle and licked his lips. "I did. He was already stiff as a board, but I didn't want him to stink up the place. There was a pencil on the mattress. Odd thing. I tossed it on the floor, then just rolled him on his back so someone would find him. You know? Figured someone would start screaming when they saw him, all contorted like he was. Then

I could claim I didn't know nothin' till sum other fella found him."

"Seems a wise thing to do. Christian of you, making sure he was found."

Riot refilled the tumbler.

"Amen to that." Earl clinked glass with Riot. "And... well, I figured it'd give that woman some time to put distance between here and there. She likely had a good reason for killing him."

"I heard she was nursing, though. What about her baby?"

Earl shrugged. "Don't know nothin' about a baby. Some women keep the milk going, you know. Fellows with an itch pay extra for that, and the girls can make some money on the side selling milk."

Riot hoped that was true—that no infant was involved in this dark affair, but as the son of a crib whore, he knew that was likely too much to hope for.

"Where is your friend Billy Blackburn?"

"What?"

"Where'd he take off to?"

"How the hell do I know? He ain't no friend of mine. And why do you care?"

"One of the doves says he owes her money," he lied smoothly. "I figure if I can track him down, there might be something in it for me. And maybe you, too."

Earl snorted. "Don't count your chickens before they hatch. Billy owed lots of money. He's a drunk."

"Does he have a favorite saloon?"

"It's a blind pig, *The Laughing Mule* off Front Street. He's into cock fighting."

41

THE GUEST

"Now you take that out and place it on the sideboard. Don't spill a thing. Then wait in the corner in case someone needs you."

"Yes, ma'am."

The cook sighed. "Seems like I'm training a new maid every month."

Isobel carried the platter out as dignified as Rachel Wall could manage. She battled with the swinging door and backed out so as not to disturb the delicacies. Then kept her head down all the way to the sideboard.

"...Egypt, India, Australia, New Guinea," a voice droned in an accent that spoke of too much education and a high opinion of himself. "I've traveled the world, but there's no place like San Francisco." Frederick Starling was the picture of a gentleman. His chin had the look of elite blood and his collar was as crisp as his blond hair. He had a little mustache on his upper lip and a high brow.

"I don't believe it, Freddie," Imogen said. "I just don't. It's cold and damp here, and the people are just plain barbaric." Imogen Noble, the oldest daughter, was a slight thing, with sandy hair, a round face, and full lips. She played the doe-eyed beauty, but Isobel suspected she was more intelligent than she let on. She was, after all, friends with Violet.

"But there's so much charm here," Freddie insisted. "A wildness you won't find anywhere else."

"You can find it in Alaska. Godforsaken place. Cold as…"

"I'm sure it's cold, Finny," Mrs. Noble cut off her husband's curse. Mr. Ian Noble was not refined. His whiskers refused to be smoothed, and he vibrated like a kettle about to explode. He looked uncomfortable in his formal bow tie and dinner jacket, and seemed more suited to having a rifle in his hands and something in its sights to kill. He was missing the tips of his ears. Frostbite. Along with two fingers—on his writing hand, no less. She'd seen him using a thick pen to write with.

Isobel had no idea why his wife called him Finny.

"Now there's a place I haven't traveled," Freddie said. "I've heard the grizzly bears are particularly fierce. I should like to hunt one, to compare with the lions of Africa."

"You've been to Africa, too?" a familiar voice asked.

Isobel nearly dropped the silverware she was arranging. It was Sarah's voice. She quickly set down the utensils, and moved to a corner. Sarah sat between Helen and Faith, and was leaning forward with eagerness on her face.

Pride welled up in Isobel's breast. Her daughter had infiltrated the family with ease. But worry quickly replaced pride, and Isobel's heart gave a flutter. There was no telling what Isobel would uncover in this house—Sarah could very well be dining with a murderer.

What on earth was she doing there? Isobel had only wanted her to *talk* with Helen, not get herself invited to dinner.

"I've been all over, my dear," Freddie said with a flick of his napkin before arranging it on his lap.

"Freddy is in shipping," Imogen explained.

"My family business."

Mr. Noble grunted. "Good to find a hardworking man who's not afraid to roll up his sleeves."

"Talking business at the table is crude, dear," Mrs. Noble reminded. The woman's golden hair was tinged with grey, and she wore a mourning shroud of black, folded back to reveal a pale face. Her black satin dress shone under the lights.

Freddie began regaling the girls with an account of a tiger hunt in the jungles of China. Imogen listened with rapt attention, her eyes lingering on his face with what was obviously affection. Faith sourly moved food around her plate, while Helen and Sarah hung on his every word.

While Imogen was asking about a detail of the hunt, Faith poked Sarah to get her attention. Helen perked up. Then Faith raised a glass, signaling for a refill. Since no one else was in the room, Isobel hurried over to refill her lemonade. But as she was pouring, Faith jerked the tablecloth.

Yellow liquid spilled over the pristine tablecloth. Isobel wanted to kick the girl in the shin, but Rachel Wall gave a suitable squeak and started patting at the tablecloth.

"You dim-witted, girl," Faith said, shooting to her feet. "You've gotten it all over my dress."

Helen stifled a giggle, and Mrs. Noble rose from her chair, calling for help.

Sarah quickly grabbed a napkin to help clean Faith's dress. "It's really all right. It's nothing that won't come—" Sarah cut off when she saw the maid's face. Her eyes flew wide.

Isobel winked at her daughter, and continued her clumsy cleaning as Sarah spluttered. She hadn't told Sarah where she and Riot were headed. Only that they'd be on a case for the next few weeks.

Faith seethed. "I'll need to change now. You're so clumsy, girl."

"Get out of this dining room," Mr. Noble barked.

Isobel jumped at the order, then ducked her head and bolted for the door. As the door swung shut, she heard Frederick Starling say, "One thing you *can't* find here are satisfactory servants."

42

A LIVELY THEATER

A BROTHEL WAS A THEATER, EACH ROOM A CAREFULLY constructed stage where the audience came to participate. And sometimes, watch. Riot was interested in what was behind the curtain. That was the view he'd seen as a child. All the tears and bruises, the pain and self-loathing. The drink. And along with it, a near to unbreakable bond between women. But that bond was missing in this brothel. The women were at each other's throats.

After breaking up another catfight, Riot stepped through a door into the back hallways, and nodded to the passing women. A few even smiled back. With the night done, most were headed to whatever homes they had, while others were coming in for a shift. With haggard faces and shadowed eyes, they smoked and chatted in the back hallways.

Riot made his way to the manager's office. As he'd suspected, the manager wasn't Mrs. Honeyford. She was only a front—an older woman who was paid to take the blame for the actual manager during a raid. Mrs. Honeyford was likely still in jail.

A middle-aged man with whiskers and a lazy eye sat in her

place. He was all business as he tallied up weekly wages. "I admit, I wasn't sure about you considering your size, but I'm told you do good work, Mr. Kyd. Had no complaints from the girls. They usually nitpick every watchman to death. Lazy, complaining bitches. Will you be staying on another week?"

"If it suits you, sir."

Mr. Kane counted out Riot's earnings for the week. In coins. "Here you go."

Riot frowned. "That's not even half of what was promised."

"Well, you ate at the hotel, didn't you?"

"I was told it was on the house."

Mr. Kane gave a rumbling laugh. "Ain't nothing free here. The rest I took out for that wall you ruined."

"The wall?"

"You smashed a fellow's head clean through. Someone's got to fix that."

Riot stared long and hard at the fellow, who stared right back. A large watchman stood behind Mr. Kane. He didn't talk to any of the other watchmen, and the women only called him Claude. Claude crossed thick arms, and stared too.

"You got a problem, Mr. Kyd?" Kane asked.

"No, sir." Riot snatched up his coins, then opened the back door to leave. But a man and a woman stood in the way. The man wore a bright silk vest and a striped suit. Smooth-faced with a slick black mustache, he gripped a gold-capped walking stick. The knob was obscene—a woman bent double with all the anatomically correct bits.

Riot stepped back, and after a look from Mr. Kane, remained in the office.

The pimp pushed his whore through the door.

"Get off of me, you slime. I'm not working here," the woman was saying.

"You'll work where I tell you to work," the pimp ordered.

He slapped a fiver onto Kane's desk. "She's getting high and mighty. I'm sick and tired of dealing with her whining."

"How long you want me to keep her?" Mr. Kane asked, holding out his palm. Another five was placed in his hand.

"I'll come get her in a week."

"I won't work here," the woman said. She was in her early twenties, her eyes were sunken and darting, and she fidgeted obsessively with her sleeve.

"If I have to spend one more day with you, I'll wring your neck till you shut your mouth. Got it?"

She spat at him. And he slapped her.

"You'll do as you're told. And don't think you can slack off work. I want double your upkeep. Understood?"

The woman was rubbing her hot cheek.

Riot took a slow breath, forcing his jaw to relax.

"Come on now," Mr. Kane crooned. "It's not so bad here. You'll have your own room." He consulted his logbook. "Number twenty. Now that's a good one."

The pimp reached under his coat and brought out a flask. The little shake he gave drew the woman's eyes. "One a day. It's double the usual dose. You know I care about you, sweet."

The woman snatched the flask to take a drink. She instantly relaxed. The pimp passed her a small packet. "And a bit extra to keep you working."

The pimp left, and Riot stood by as Kane explained the hotel rules and layout. With a glassy-eyed stare, the woman stripped and went to the next room to place her clothing and belongings in a locker.

Mr. Kane leaned back in his chair to watch. "You won't earn your keep looking like that, lovely. Give us a little wiggle to get things going!"

The woman started to give him a finger, then thought better of it. Instead, she gave a wiggle before leaving with her drugs.

"I didn't know pimps dropped their cows here," Riot said.

"Odd Stick there brings his gals in when he's looking to charm another. They get jealous of his affections otherwise. I reckon that one was his latest toy. She probably still thinks he loves her. A week here will knock that idea loose."

"Are we supposed to make sure they don't run?" Riot asked. He knew the answer, but he was playing dumb.

Mr. Kane looked up. "Where they gonna run?" He jerked his head towards the lockers. "They don't got no clothes." And to demonstrate, Mr. Kane hauled himself out of his chair to lock the locker. He tucked the master key in his pocket, giving it a fond little pat.

"What happens if a girl doesn't come up with rent?"

"Same as you. If you eat more than your share or drink your earnings... I own you."

Riot glanced at Claude, who rolled his massive shoulders. Riot was really starting to loathe this place.

43

VIRTUOUS LIES

"*This* is where you've been?" Sarah whispered.

Isobel glanced to the side. They were standing in a wide corridor outside Faith's room. The girl had had Isobel pour her yet another bath, and now Isobel had the lemonade-stained dress over an arm.

"I told you I was on a case."

"Yes, but—" Sarah faltered, taking in Isobel's uniform: little white hat, white lace collar and black dress. She stifled a giggle.

"I'm on the verge of murdering all three sisters," Isobel admitted.

"Helen is sad. Faith was only trying to cheer her up," Sarah said. "They're spoiled and don't think highly of anyone below their class."

"I've noticed," Isobel said dryly. "How are they treating you?"

"Because I'm below their class?" Sarah asked, insulted.

"I didn't mean—" She caught a mischievous glint in Sarah's eyes. "We're rubbing off on you."

Sarah couldn't contain herself any longer; she pulled Isobel into a fierce hug.

Isobel patted the girl's back. "I haven't been gone *that* long. And don't ruin my cover. I'd hate to come back as a cook."

Sarah took a step back in case anyone wandered down the hallway. "Yes, but I'm glad to see you all the same. Is Atticus here, too?"

"No."

"Where is he?"

"On another assignment. You never answered me about the three devils."

"We get along perfectly. Well, aside from their game of chasing away maids."

"Why do they do it?"

"Mr. Noble is a bully. He doesn't strike them, but he hollers something fierce. So they take their frustration out on the staff. And their mother is a bible thumper."

"A what?"

"She's one of those religious types who threatens anyone she doesn't like with hell and damnation."

"Sounds like my mother," Isobel muttered.

"No… It's not that. It's…" Sarah searched for the words. "If your mother came across a hungry woman on the street with a child and tattered clothes, she'd get her fed and cleaned up, and see she found a proper job. Even if she was a… whore. Mrs. Noble would likely use the good book as a bludgeon, and then walk right on by."

Isobel started to argue, but it was true. For all her mother's strict morals, she wouldn't deny someone in need.

"But I heard Mrs. Noble hires women from charities."

"It's selective."

"So she's no Good Samaritan," Isobel said.

Sarah put a hand to her throat in mock surprise. "Next you'll be quoting verse."

"Sarah, as fond as I am of sarcasm, save it for later. I need a succinct report. We don't have much time."

Sarah looked cornered. Panic flickered across the girl's eyes as she searched for something useful. "I don't know what else to tell you. Helen is nice enough. I truly like her. She and Faith miss their brother something fierce. Imogen does too, but she's also infatuated with Mr. Starling."

"What's your opinion of him?"

"He's pleasant enough. He sketches, and always has an interesting story."

"But?"

Sarah made a face. "My gramma would say he has a bit too much mustard."

"A braggart?"

Sarah nodded. "If someone said they caught a foot long fish, Freddie would claim he caught one two feet long while battling off a bear."

"So ego issues," Isobel mused. "How did Dominic get on with his father? Have you heard anything?"

"As soon as I ask about their brother, everyone goes quiet. Helen said she's not allowed to speak of him, and Mrs. Noble took down all his photographs. What's going on?"

"It's best you don't know, but I want—" Footsteps clicked in the corridor, and Isobel quickly bobbed a curtsy. "I'll get right on it, Miss."

Sarah didn't miss a beat. "Thank you." And then they parted ways. It left Isobel feeling uneasy—she'd been about to tell Sarah to stay away from this house.

───────────

ISOBEL BOBBED A CURTSY INTO THE READING ROOM. WHEN Mrs. Noble failed to acknowledge her, she shuffled off to the side, folded her hands over her apron, and tried to melt into the papered wall. Hard to do when you were wearing black and white.

Was that why maids wore such stark colors? So their employers could keep track of them? True, black and white was traditionally formal and the style mimicked the formal suits of gentlemen, but—

"*Girl,*" a voice said. It didn't sound like it'd been the first time Mrs. Noble said her 'name'.

Isobel hurried over to the woman. "Yes, ma'am?"

Mrs. Noble was sitting at a small writing desk. A stack of correspondence, papers, and pamphlets crowded the top.

"Abigail tells me she found you in my late son's room."

"Yes, ma'am."

"How did you get in?"

Isobel pushed up her spectacles with a finger. How did Riot manage to make these things seem refined? "I, uhm… well, I walked in, ma'am."

"Don't get smart with me."

"Yes, ma'am." It took all of Isobel's self-control *not* to get smart with the woman.

Mrs. Noble waited. Isobel stood meekly. She could keep this up all day if needed. Anything that delayed cleaning more bathtubs.

"Was the door unlocked?"

"Yes, ma'am." *After* I picked the lock, Isobel added silently.

"You are not to go in there. Do you understand?"

"Yes, ma'am. Miss Abigail made that clear."

"Finny wanted you gone after your clumsiness at dinner. I convinced him not to dismiss you."

"Thank you, ma'am."

"I don't want it to happen again."

"Yes, ma'am."

Mrs. Noble raised her brows. "Nothing to say in your defense?"

"No, ma'am. It was clumsy of me."

Mrs. Noble waited. Then made a satisfactory sound, and set down her pen. "You came highly recommended, Miss Wall. And I see why. Most women in my employ would take the opportunity to point fingers at my daughters."

"Yes, ma'am."

"You haven't."

"No, ma'am. I should've been more careful."

Mrs. Noble sat back with a sigh. "I'm well aware of my daughters' games. I've spoken with them, but the more I chastise them, the more they persist in driving away the help. Don't think I approve of their antics. They can be cruel."

"Yes, ma'am."

"Abigail is pleased with your work. It takes forbearance to remain calm and endure here."

"A fruit of the Spirit, ma'am."

Mrs. Noble sat up straighter. "Yes. Indeed. You're a woman of faith, I see."

"Yes, ma'am. I was… It's only…"

"Speak your mind."

"I usually go to church on Sundays. Then spend the afternoon in reflection and prayer. I was hoping at some future date, if you're satisfied with my work, that is… Could I have a full day off on Sunday?"

Lie upon lie upon lie. It was well and good Sarah was not in the room. The girl would've fainted dead away. However, no lightning burst from the ceiling to strike Isobel down. Perhaps that would come later.

"You have my permission, but I expect you back in time to help with dinner. I'll inform Abigail."

"Thank you, ma'am."

Mrs. Noble made a dismissive gesture, and Isobel turned to leave, but when she was nearly to the door, a throat cleared. "Miss Wall."

"Yes, ma'am?"

"Virtue is also a divine trait," Mrs. Noble said. "I expect my employees to remain chaste. I do not tolerate courting, roller skating, bicycling, vaudeville shows, or any other obscene activity of the like. Is that clear?"

"Yes, ma'am."

Mrs. Noble nodded. "You may go."

As Isobel left, she had the overwhelming urge to break Faith and Helen out of this boorish prison.

44

WITCHING HOUR

"I can tell this is your first household," a voice said.

Isobel looked up in surprise. She was on her knees, scrubbing the kitchen floor. Out of respect for the cook, she climbed to her feet and stared at her toes. "Am I doing something wrong, Miss Grace?"

"No, not at all. And don't let me stop you."

"I could use an excuse to straighten my back."

Grace was a thin woman with a stooped back. She had coarse black hair, a broad nose, and a proud tilt to her chin. She eyed the scrubbed floor. It gleamed. Isobel was used to scrubbing the deck on her cutter, so this work was slightly easier than bathtubs.

"Most girls in service learn to pace themselves. I noticed you don't, so it's clear you haven't worked as a maid before."

"I want to make a good impression, ma'am," Isobel said, avoiding the question.

"You've made one. Don't slack off too much now," Grace said, shaking a chopping knife at her. "But you can rest that back of yours. I've never seen a girl attack a task with so much anger."

Isobel tried to summon up a blush, but she didn't have Lotario's skill. "It's only I heard about the other maids... how they were let go. I need this job, ma'am."

Grace turned back to her chopping. "And what have you heard?"

"Only that no maid stays long. You said it yourself the other day—that you're constantly training new maids."

"The Noble sisters enjoy their little games. Most young women can't take it."

"I've noticed, ma'am."

"You don't seem to mind."

Isobel raised a shoulder. "I had three sisters. I'm the youngest of them, and they weren't kind girls. But you learn to get on with things."

Grace gave a nod of approval.

"Do they try anything on you?"

Grace chuckled. "Goodness, no. I'm the cook." She turned slightly, brandishing her knife, then gave it a skillful spin before chopping the final carrot. "And I might've put the fear in them early on."

A laugh snuck out before Isobel could stop herself. She quickly put a hand over her lips. Grace's eyes twinkled. "That's better. The Missus knows all about her daughters. And Abigail knows it too. They're not blind to the girls' antics. Eventually the Noble girls will get bored with you. If you last that long."

"Thank you, ma'am. I will."

Grace glanced towards the door to the dining room. It wasn't yet lunch, and no one else was about. "But a word of warning..." her voice lowered. "You make sure you don't get caught alone anywhere."

Isobel gave her a puzzled look. "I don't understand, ma'am."

"You're an attractive girl, Miss Rachel. A girl like you can't be too careful with her virtue."

Isobel met Grace's eyes. The older woman wanted to say more, but couldn't. It didn't take a far stretch of imagination to know what she was warning her against.

"Don't feel you have to stay and clean if you find yourself alone with a man."

"Are you referring to Mr. Noble?" Isobel asked, trying to goad the woman into saying more.

"I didn't say no such thing. I just said to be careful."

"Yes, ma'am."

———

THE HOUSE WAS STILL. QUIET. ONE COULD EVEN SAY DEAD. Isobel was used to the witching hour. She'd spent most of her childhood looking forward to it—a chance to slip out her window and down the side of the house towards freedom. No one was ever awake at three in the morning. Even saloons closed their doors.

The hour pulled at the mind of the hardiest night worker.

Rather than share a narrow bed with another newly hired maid in the cramped servant's quarters, Isobel had opted for a thin mat on the floor. She grimaced as she sat up, and glanced at Cecilia, who was snoring softly. The servants wouldn't wake for another hour. She quickly dressed, tucking the awful hat and starched collar away in her dress, picked up her shoes, and slipped out of the room.

On stockinged feet, she padded down the pitch-black hallway by memory, passing the head housekeeper's room, as well as her keys. She didn't risk stealing those. Instead, she tied the laces of her boots together, cracked open a window, and stuck her head out to breathe in the night air. Fog and moonlight mingled, giving the night a ghostly allure. It made her giddy with excitement.

Isobel climbed out of the window to hang from the ledge,

her toes brushing the siding. She stretched towards a drainage pipe (ever convenient), and once she had hold of it, closed the window that she'd oiled the day before.

She climbed down to a balcony, then over its railing to a ledge that curbed the manor. It was a quick shuffle to another balcony. No light escaped the curtained windows and French doors.

Isobel flipped open her tickler and worked the knife between the windowsill and frame. With the tip of her knife, she carefully pushed the hook away from the eye, then slid the window up. She was inside Ian Noble's study in under thirty seconds.

Isobel hurried across the empty study, snatched a cushion from a chair, and stuffed it against the gap under the hallway door. Then she thumbed on a handheld battery light. The light was dim and unreliable, but these new flashlights had their uses.

The light flickered, and she slapped it a few times until it stayed on as she padded to the desk. Ian Noble spent a great deal of time in his study, and it reeked of cigar smoke. This was his only sanctuary in a house dominated by women.

She moved quickly, knowing the household would soon stir. First searching his desk, the papers, the logbook, taking care not to disturb anything.

The expenditures looked in order for a house so large. The family wasn't hurting for cash. Far from it. Still, one entry caught her eye—a payment of five thousand, with a notation that read 'racetrack'.

Isobel frowned. Ian Noble did not strike her as a gambling man. Perhaps he owned race horses?

She turned to a locked drawer, and slipped out her lock picks. Minutes ticked by as she held her breath, concentrating on the more complex lock. Why was this so difficult for her? Jin would've already had the lock open.

Her wrench turned, and satisfaction zipped through her body. She opened the drawer and shined the light over its contents. A lockbox with cash and valuables. Checkbooks. Bank notes. Bonds. Plans and letters. This would take more than… Isobel froze at the sight of a betting slip.

She picked it up, reading the numbers. The bet was for five dollars to win. Seven to two odds. Sixth race, on a horse named Lucky Connor, with a date that was four months old—the same date as the payment of five thousand dollars recorded in his account book.

Her gaze slipped off the betting slip to the drawer below, where a folded newspaper sat. It bore the same date as the slip and was folded back to a specific page. She narrowed her eyes at the familiar headline.

Footsteps clicked in the hallway outside. Isobel cursed under her breath, then hesitated over the newspaper. She wanted to stuff it under her blouse along with the betting slip, but surely it'd be missed from a locked drawer?

In the end, she replaced the items, closed the drawer, and hurried over to remove the cushion from the door. There'd be no time to lock the drawer. Or even to leave.

The door opened, a shadow filled the entry, and Isobel ducked behind an armchair. Electric lights flicked on, the door shut, and heavy footsteps headed towards the desk. Isobel held her breath, aware of her exposure, her precarious concealment, and the closed door.

A cloud of cologne drifted into the room. As drawers opened, Isobel peeked from behind the heavy leather armchair. Ian Noble stood behind his desk. Broad-shouldered, with a weathered face and a perpetual scowl. Even his gray whiskers seemed to bristle. He tucked a billfold under his coat, then plucked up a cigar, and tucked that away, too.

The curtains stirred, and he froze.

Damn, she'd left it open.

Ian quickly turned to the window and threw the curtains aside.

There was no time. As he bent to peer out the window, Isobel rushed towards the door, turned the knob, and tried to slip through. Only the hinges squeaked, giving her away. Heart in her throat, she knocked loudly, then made as if she were just stepping into the study.

"What the hell?" Ian rumbled, turning on her.

Isobel squeaked in shock, and paled, making like she was backing out of the door that (hopefully) it appeared she'd just walked into. "I'm sorry, sir. I'm here to clean the fireplace. I didn't know…" She bobbed a curtsy and took a step backwards.

"Get in here."

Isobel hesitated.

"Now!" he barked.

She stepped inside, but didn't close the door.

His gaze flickered down to her feet. "Why the devil are your shoes around your neck, girl?"

Isobel glanced down at her stockinged feet. "They click loudly in the morning. I didn't want to wake anyone."

Ian moved across the room, two long strides, and he was looming over her as she backed into a wall. "The window was open."

"Was it, sir?"

"Didn't I just say that?" he asked.

"I'll let Miss Abigail know straight away, sir."

He plucked at her uniform with his three-fingered hand. "Where's your collar?"

Isobel fished her collar out of a pocket. "Here, sir. Cleaning the fireplace makes it dirty, sir."

Rachel Wall would be shaking with fear. So that's what Isobel did. But it made her furious. Every bone in her body rebelled against this persona. Just as she'd loathed the woman she'd played while married to Alex.

Alone, vulnerable, with not a soul awake—if ever there was an opportunity for Ian Noble to take advantage of a maid, it was now. She gave her sleeve a shake behind her back and her knife slid into her hand.

"Close the window, lock it. Then clean and get *out*," he ordered, then left.

Isobel nearly slumped against the wall. Instead, she slid her knife back up her sleeve and went to close the window.

45

THE RACETRACK

"I SHOULD'VE COME AS A MAN," DAISY REED MURMURED.

Lotario dropped his theater binoculars to look at his companion. "I was just thinking I should've come as a woman."

"I shouldn't have come sober," Garrett said.

"Amen," Lotario said with a sigh.

"There's always time to fix that, boys," Daisy said. She was resplendent in white. Rosy cheeks and dark curls spilling from beneath a wide-brimmed hat.

Garrett toyed with an end of his curled mustache as he watched a group of men below.

"And risk him going near the betting ring? I think not," Lotario said, putting his eyes back on the binoculars. He wasn't watching the thundering horses, but a group of people in one of the grandstand's private boxes. "Do you see someone you know?"

"I've lost count," Daisy admitted.

"I wouldn't worry, my dear," Garrett said. "They won't recognize you. They'll be too busy admiring my mustache."

"It *is* splendid," Lotario said.

"Flatterer."

"You likely spend more time curling your mustache than I spend on my hair," Daisy noted.

"Do stop," Garrett said. "I may blush."

"Now, now, what do we have here," Lotario murmured.

"A private bookie," Daisy noted. "I swear I've entertained half the men in that seating area."

"And I've done the other half," Lotario said.

"A group rich enough to afford you two would have their own bookie," Garrett noted.

"Hmm," Lotario said. "But the racing has already begun. I'll wager a hundred dollars that the bookie doesn't return to the betting ring."

Garrett shook his head. "I may be a bit of a speeler, but I have standards."

"A bit?" Daisy asked.

Garrett was already moving out of their box at a leisurely pace. So Lotario offered his arm to Daisy, and they followed.

"I doubt anyone will recognize you, Daisy," Lotario whispered as they strolled down the stairs.

"There's always a possibility," she said.

"True."

"Has it ever happened to you?"

"Not outright—the masks help—but some find me familiar in a way they'd never admit in public, so they're more apt to run the other way."

"You're a man. I'm a woman. I doubt you get leered at."

"Your new start will work. I know it will."

"Then why do I feel like I've wandered into the wrong world?"

"Perhaps you simply don't like horse racing," he said.

"It's not that…" she admitted. "I'm not sure I'm cut out for any other work."

"My twin's reputation is in shambles and she doesn't let it bother her."

"Your twin looked down her nose at me, then waltzed right past."

"She does that with everyone."

"And Mr. Riot... well, he gives me chills."

"Deliciously dangerous, isn't he? When things settle down, you'll fit right in. Trust me."

"The last time I trusted you, I woke up with the worst hangover of my life."

They descended the grandstand to ground level, where arched windows lined the building, along with a pair of arched doorways.

Garrett strolled ahead, his white Panama hat easy to pick out in the crowd. He had his eyes on the bookie. As Lotario suspected, the bookie didn't head towards the betting ring or the restaurant. Instead, he walked around the grandstand, towards a two-story clubhouse with arabesque turrets, capped with blooming onion domes.

Was he meeting someone at the cafe? That might complicate things. But the bookie veered towards the stables, and right on cue Garrett trotted ahead, holding up a billfold. "Sir! Excuse me, sir. I do believe you dropped this." His voice boomed with authority.

Lotario quickened their own pace as the crowds formed a pocket around the bookie, who turned to look at the man with a billfold.

The bookie patted at his coat pocket. "Sure thing, that's mine."

It always was.

"Wait a moment!" Lotario called, patting his vest. "I do believe it's mine. I seem to have misplaced my own."

Garrett turned, surprised, and the billfold slipped through his fingertips onto the ground. Daisy floated off Lotario's arm and kept walking, while the bookie bent to retrieve the fallen billfold. Daisy collided with him as he tucked it into his vest.

"Goodness!" She tripped, but the man caught her before she tumbled to the ground. She pressed her breasts against his chest, her eyes wide and fearful, lips parted as she stared up into his eyes. "I do beg your pardon," she said breathlessly. "I didn't see you."

"Quite all right, Miss," the bookie said.

"Oh, say now… I *do* have my billfold," Lotario murmured. He tipped his hat, and slipped into the crowd.

Garrett gave a shake of his head. "Far too many dishonest men in the world."

"It appears there's a few gentlemen left," Daisy said. With a shy smile, she pulled away from the bookie. "Thank you for saving my dress, sir." She blushed and sauntered away, while Garrett disappeared into the crowd.

Lotario had positioned himself near the stable, making a show of inspecting the horses. He didn't care for horses. They weren't trustworthy. Out of the corner of his eye, he watched the bookie trot up a stairway to a second-story office over a stable.

Daisy soon joined him, and they headed to the clubhouse where Garrett was waiting. Inside there was a lovely English cafe with timber ceilings and open fireplaces. And while the grandstand resembled a Japanese pavilion, the saddling paddock was built in Mexican-style adobe. The cultural influences should've clashed. But somehow it worked.

After they were seated, Daisy passed over the billfold she'd pinched from the bookie. The man still had Garrett's billfold tucked under his coat. Men were so easy to distract.

Lotario ignored the cash in favor of the betting slips. "Quickly now, jot down these numbers. Make sure to keep each separate."

Daisy retrieved a pencil and notepad from her handbag.

"The dates aren't even for today," Garrett said.

"This one is for last year," Daisy noted. "And none of these names match the horses racing today."

"What do you think their game is?" Garrett asked.

Lotario frowned at a slip. "I'm not sure, but anything involving that set can't be good."

When the slips had been copied, Garrett tucked them back into the stolen billfold and went to find the bookie to explain there must've been a mix up.

46

GOING COURTING

RIOT HAD NEVER BEEN AN ANXIOUS YOUNG MAN WAITING FOR his sweetheart, but he felt like one today. He stood under a tree in Golden Gate Park, searching the crowds of ambling couples, families, mothers with strollers, dog walkers, bicyclists, and picnickers. The sun was out, and so was San Francisco.

Jack nuzzled his shoulder, and Riot absently rubbed his old friend's nose. They stood under a tree, its leaves offering a cool resting place after a hard run on the track. Jack never liked to finish second, which proved tiring on a circular path, but Riot had let him keep trying for first place anyway.

A woman caught his eye. It was her brisk stride rather than her appearance that snagged his attention. Frayed straw hat, battered spectacles, and a blue coat that had seen better days.

As Isobel walked along a pathway, she searched the crowds. His partner was possessed of a rare gift. She took in every detail, analyzed it, and came to a conclusion in the blink of an eye. It was not something she could switch off, and Riot had observed that crowds tended to overwhelm her senses.

As he watched her from his shaded spot, people fell away, conversation, the rustling trees, even his horse. It was a dangerous moment of distraction, but then Isobel always slipped through his defenses.

Riot forced himself to stop gawking at his wife and focused on his surroundings. The bench where they'd agreed to meet was occupied, but if she kept on her current course she'd walk right past him.

When he went to pick her out of the crowd again, she'd vanished. She must've spotted Jack—the pinto horse was hard to miss. Riot waited, and soon enough Jack snorted and raised his head in alarm. A rustle behind them caused the horse to dance to the side and turn.

"I nearly had you—" Isobel cut off as he turned to greet her. Her hand went to her lips, eyes wide. She looked on the verge of fainting.

Riot grinned, whipped off a black Stetson, and stepped forward to wrap an arm around her waist before she fell.

"Good Lord," she said faintly. "What on earth did you do to your beard?"

"Men have been known to shave them off on occasion," he said.

Her lips worked, but no words came out. She tugged off a glove to touch his naked cheek, fingers sliding like silk over his skin. "I feel like I'm cheating on my husband with a younger man," she whispered.

"Probably best not to tell him."

Riot ducked under the brim of her hat to kiss her, but their spectacles bumped together, and nearly locked. Isobel laughed as she untangled the wiring, then threw her arms around his neck. Honest, pure, and full of joy. His world brightened.

Riot carefully removed her spectacles and tried again. He'd intended it to be a chaste kiss, but Isobel melted against his body. He lost himself. It'd been a long two weeks.

"I've missed you," he murmured.

"I can feel just how much." She smiled against his lips. "You should know, Riot. You have a tell."

"It's hard to hide when you're around."

"Extremely hard."

Before things got out of hand, Jack stepped into Isobel, trying to knock her out of the way.

"*Jack*," Riot said through his teeth.

"You're quite right, Jack," Isobel said, sparing a glance at the busy park. "I'll get fired if I'm caught courting." She searched his face, lips twitching with amusement. "You have dimples."

"Only when I smile."

She touched the jagged scar on his chin. "And this?"

"I put that there so people wouldn't notice my dimples."

Isobel snorted. "So... tell the truth. Did you grow the beard to hide your dimples or to hide the scar?"

"I thought a beard would make me look older and respectable."

"You do look *awfully* young."

"Is that bad?"

Isobel slowly circled him, studying his disguise. "Not at all. But I can't say I like the idea of you walking around a brothel in that getup."

"Extra fabric chafes on a saddle."

"Hmm."

Riot shifted slightly. "These trousers *were* a bit looser last time I wore them," he admitted.

"It's all that good food I cook for you."

"That must be it."

She finished her inspection, then met his eyes. "I thought William Kyd was supposed to be a sailor?"

"Change of plans. The Nymphia caters to sailors from the Presidio, so I wagered I had a better shot hiring on as a ranch hand in from the country."

Isobel ran a gloved finger over his knuckles. "You've been fighting," she said.

One by one, Riot tugged off the fingers of her remaining glove, then took her warm skin in his own. "I'm a watchman in a brothel. That's our lot."

"I thought you said it wasn't dangerous?"

"You're the one holding yourself gingerly." There was a question there, and she answered it without prompting.

"Whatever Miss Lily pays the cleaning maids for Raven-wood Manor, we need to double it. I've scrubbed more bath-tubs and toilets than I can count. That, or I'm getting old."

Riot gave a silent chuckle as he retrieved Jack's reins. The horse was eyeballing Isobel, and she was doing the same. "I'm not going to take him away from you," she said. "I don't know why you still have a grudge against me."

The horse snorted. She reached up to pat him, but Jack avoided that with a quick snap of his teeth. "Oh, stop it. You can come for a walk, too."

Riot gave Jack a firm look as he settled his hat back in place, then slipped Isobel's arm through his. They headed towards less traveled pathways. "He's protective of me," Riot said.

"So am I."

"I think you enjoy the rivalry."

"Do you enjoy being fought over, Riot?"

"It's the pinnacle of my life. Being caught in a love triangle with a woman and a horse."

"Jack does adore you."

"We've been through some things together."

Isobel tilted her head in thought. "You've likely spent more time with Jack than me."

"I plan on changing that."

"Did you hear that, Jack? He wants to spend more time with *me*."

The horse swiveled his head into Riot's chest, knocking him back a step. He didn't let up until Riot gave him a proper rub.

"How's the Nymphia?"

Riot's hand stilled. "I've nearly blown my cover several times."

"That bad?"

Riot focused on Jack, not daring to look at his wife. "It's bad," he said simply. He didn't want to talk about that place just now—not in the sunlight with a beautiful woman at his side.

Only she knew him too well.

Isobel ran a hand down his back. "You don't have to stay there, Riot. Blow your cover all you like," she whispered.

"I plan on it. When the time is right."

"And in the meantime?"

Riot rested his forehead against Jack for a moment. "I've seen worse," he admitted, then glanced her way. "I haven't come across any underage girls yet."

"There's that at least," she said with a sigh. "My skin is crawling just thinking about the hotel."

"I feel the same," he admitted. "Before I came here, I refilled a bucket three times and scrubbed my skin raw."

"Doesn't your boarding house have a bath?"

Riot grimaced. "I'm earning a watchman's wages. I couldn't afford a suitable stable *and* a room of my own, so Jack won out. He gets a good stable, and I get to toss down a bedroll near his stall."

Riot had never slept easily with other occupants (save Isobel) in a room. At least in the stable he had Jack to watch over him.

"You're sleeping with your horse, Riot?"

He gave her a crooked grin. "You found me out."

"With those dimples of yours, I find it impossible to be angry with you."

"I'll have to grow my beard back as soon as I can."

"So you can argue with me?"

"So I can make up with you."

Isobel cleared her throat. "Must you be so charming? I'm sorely tempted to drag you into the bushes."

"There's a hayloft at my place."

"I think the novelty of you clean-shaven has just worn off."

"We'll see if you can resist these dimples after another hour," he purred.

Isobel quickened her pace. "You're impossible, Riot," she said over her shoulder.

"So that wasn't a no?" he called.

She kept walking.

When he caught up, she glanced his way. "I'm fairly sure 'no courting' includes a roll in the hay."

"A rule Miss Rachel Wall would never break."

Isobel slipped her arm back through his. "Unless it included a back rub."

"I may be able to oblige. You're looking lopsided."

"*Riot.*"

"You *are* crooked," he said flatly. "Your right shoulder is higher than your left and your back is hunched."

Isobel cursed under her breath. "Splendid. I'll have a hump by the end of this case."

"Other than your budding hump—"

"I should kick you."

"—how are you finding life as a maid?"

"It's tedious," she said. "I've contemplated all the ways I could kill the family."

Riot looked at her in alarm.

"In *theory.*"

"*All action is of the mind…*" Riot murmured.

Isobel ignored the quote. "I saw Sarah at the Noble's manor. She made friends faster than I imagined. Have you checked in at home?"

"No, but I woke up the other morning to find Jin feeding Jack an apple."

Isobel coughed in surprise. "She tracked you down by Jack, didn't she?"

Riot nodded. "She was rather pleased with herself. I think she must've pieced together we were involved with the Nymphia raid in some way, then went around to all the surrounding stables."

"That child is far too clever for her own good."

Riot smiled. "She is, isn't she? Just like her mother."

"I'm brilliant, Riot. Not clever."

"And apparently not humble."

"I never claimed to be," she said. "Back to our clever daughter—she should *know* better than to sneak up on you."

It was true. Riot had quick reflexes that were on a hair trigger. It was the only reason he was still alive, but those same reflexes couldn't be switched off at will.

"She didn't even flinch when I drew."

"Let me guess, she gave you that smug look of hers and made some smartass comment?"

"That's about it." He smiled at the memory.

"At least she didn't venture into the hotel."

Riot skirted away from that thought. "I thought it best to sate her curiosity, so I told her the particulars of the case."

"Hmm."

"She's up to something."

"Dear God."

"Tobias may be involved. He was wisely waiting outside the stable."

"At least there's that."

"Tobias does have a tempering effect on her," Riot agreed.

"What do you think they're up to?"

"I don't have the faintest idea."

Isobel sighed. They should've sent Jin and Sarah to stay with her parents. But then the pair would have missed more schooling.

There was nothing for it now, so she told him of her nocturnal break-in and her close call with Mr. Noble. "If ever there was a chance for him to take advantage of a maid, it would've been then."

"It was early in the morning, though. Doesn't mean he's not the type after a few drinks."

"Are you suggesting I wait until he's drunk to put myself in harm's way?"

"I am not," he said.

"Perhaps as a last resort..." she mused.

"Bel."

She squeezed his hand. "Yes, yes. I know. But, here's the interesting part. Along with the betting slip, there was a newspaper of the same date. It was folded back to a page featuring a small article about a union leader named Lester Capp. He was the head of a group trying to unionize a mining operation in Colorado."

"One of Ian Noble's mines?"

"Margaret mentioned he had interests in Colorado. Do you remember when I was gathering all those newspapers before the agency was attacked?"

"I do." And he was glad he did. After Monty beat him near to death, his memory had been fuzzy for weeks. "I recall you saying that it might be nothing."

"And you said when something catches my eye, it's generally *something*."

Riot raised his brows, waiting.

Isobel gave a huff. "Fine, you were right."

"Wagering on your intellect is always a sure bet." Riot

picked up her hand and brushed a kiss across her fingertips. Either his compliment or his kiss rendered her speechless for a good few seconds.

"I was looking for a pattern to several strange murders. A body was found in an orchard near Los Angeles. The body was badly burned. Another in Oregon. A few weeks later, Colorado. But I couldn't find any connection between the victims aside from the killer or killers trying to erase evidence."

"Let me guess, the Colorado victim was identified as Lester Capp?"

Isobel nodded.

Riot rubbed the scar on his chin. "I'm due to check in at the agency before my shift tomorrow. I'll have Lotario look into who has a stake in that mine, along with the murders. The Pinkertons might know something, too."

"Tell Ari to compare the dates on the betting slips with corresponding newspapers. The dictionary we found in Monty's room may have nothing to do with those slips."

"If we find anything, I'll get word to you somehow."

"You'll have to. I barely got permission to take off on Sundays. And I'm not even allowed to go to the grocers."

Riot massaged her hand, the skin raw from cleaning solutions. "Sarah could pass messages."

"I hadn't intended for her to set foot in that house," Isobel admitted. "But she seems to genuinely get on with Helen Noble."

"Do you think she's in danger there?"

"Aside from Grace's warning? No. Maids are easy prey, but a friend of Helen's... not so much. And I'm close at hand. Dominic's murder may have nothing to do with the household. It could simply be what it appears: an influential family trying to smother a scandal." She gave a tired sigh. "This could all be a waste of time. I feel like we're shooting in the dark."

"We're bound to hit something."

"Yes, well, it would be simpler if I could just interrogate the lot of them."

"And God have mercy on their souls," Riot murmured.

"I'm not *that* bad."

He wisely remained silent, and the two set aside business to simply walk and talk like every other courting couple in the park.

47

PROPER INTRODUCTIONS

With a gentle cluck of his tongue, Riot signaled Jack to a stop. Horse and rider stared at a brick building. The horse snorted.

"I know. I know," Riot said, sliding from the saddle. "May as well paint a red target on the front. It helps to know Ravenwood would've been struck with apoplexy." Riot draped the reins loosely over a post. Jack was the sort of horse that resented being tied anywhere. "I'll be back," he said, offering Jack an apple. "If anyone comes close, give 'em hell."

Riot gave the horse a pat, and headed into the office. The door knocked an overhead bell, and it gave a pleasant ring.

He stepped up to the high counter and smiled. The last time he'd been there, he hadn't paused long enough to introduce himself. No longer in rough clothes with an untrimmed beard, Riot supposed he struck quite a different image now. The girl at the counter didn't appear to recognize him, so he played the client.

With bouncy black curls, rosy cheeks, and bright blue eyes, she didn't look over sixteen. But Riot had a feeling she was older than she appeared.

The girl gave him a friendly smile. "Welcome to Raven-wood Agency, sir." She eyed the holster at his hip. "Are you here for a consultation?"

Riot removed his hat, and cocked his head slightly. "I'm here to see Mr. Ravenwood," he said, laying on an accent.

"That's just the name of the agency, sir."

"Is he the owner?"

"No, sir. Mr. Ravenwood founded the agency. Mr. Amsel is our Director of Operations."

"I see. Then I reckon I'll see that fellow."

"Your name, sir?"

"William Kyd."

While she consulted an appointment book, Riot rapped his knuckles against a wall. A dull thud returned. Brick or iron-plated, he decided.

"Was this part of the bar?"

"I beg your pardon, Mr. Kyd?"

"This used to be a saloon. I recall there was a bar here."

"Very likely," she said, and smiled again. "Mr. Amsel is currently in a meeting, but other agents are available to take your particulars."

"Are they?" Riot asked.

"Yes, sir."

He knew she was lying. Lotario wasn't with anyone. But she was good at it. Barely a flutter of a lash, and a smile that would make most men weak in the knees.

"I suppose it won't matter," he said.

"Wonderful." She pushed a piece of paper forward. "What is the nature of your concern? You can write it down if you wish."

Riot put an elbow on the counter and scratched his chin in thought. "Possible embezzlement. A proper crook stole my business right out from under my nose."

"I'm sorry to hear, sir. I'll have to ask you to surrender your firearm."

"You can certainly ask, but I'm afraid I must decline."

"I promise I'll handle it with care," she said with a flutter of lashes.

"I'm sure you will, but I'm fond of it."

She gave a helpless shrug. "I'm afraid it's policy."

"I wouldn't want it to misfire…"

"Don't worry, I know my way around a weapon."

He unbuckled his belt, winding it around the holster before handing it over. "I didn't get your name, miss."

"Daisy Reed."

"A pleasure, Miss Reed."

"Likewise, Mr. Kyd. I'll see you get this back when you leave. Someone will be with you shortly."

Riot sat down in a comfortable armchair as Daisy picked up a receiver. Somewhere in back another telephone rang.

"A client is waiting," Daisy said. "A Mr. Kyd." She must've sat down, because she disappeared from view, and lowered her voice.

Riot eyed the setup of the waiting room. A heavy oak door led to the main offices. It was reinforced and looked like it could withstand a dynamite blast. There was a gap in the ceiling above the counter. A retractable barrier of some sort? Lotario wasn't taking any chances.

"Then surely you can see him?" Riot had excellent hearing. He could hear half the conversation Daisy was having on the interoffice line. "Yes, *you*. Why not?" Silence. And the line clicked.

It wasn't long after that the door opened. A slim man in a white silk vest and a striped shirt stepped forward to offer a hand. His mustache was impressive, curled to tips, and his black hair was parted and slicked.

"Let me guess," the man flashed equally white teeth. "You

weren't expecting a negro. My father wasn't either. The name's Garrett. You've come to the right place."

Garrett carried himself with a lazy swagger as he gestured Riot towards a conference room. But Miss Off was heading down the hallway and stopped in her tracks. The woman gave a wolf whistle, then started cackling. The sound was in sharp contrast to her nearly respectable blouse and skirt (aside from the rat on her shoulder).

Garrett smiled smoothly. "Miss Off is always ready with a laugh and an encouraging word." He tried to direct Riot away from the madwoman, but she had other ideas.

She showed off her missing teeth as she circled him. "Well ain't you a looker. Never could resist a tight-assed cowboy."

"Well thank you, ma'am," Riot said.

"She can't resist a compliment either," Garrett said, giving the woman a firm look.

Miss Off reached up and gave Riot's cheek a squeeze. Then called down the hallway. "Boss is here!"

Matthew came around the corner, froze, and stood there with mouth gaping. Garrett looked from Miss Off to Riot, eyes narrowing.

"Is everyone here?" Riot asked.

Miss Off pointed up with her middle finger. "Lazing around upstairs."

"Best not to keep the *Director of Operations* waiting," Riot said, extending a hand to Garrett. "Let me guess, you weren't expecting a cowboy? The name is Atticus Riot."

Garrett chuckled and shook his hand, his fingers long and his grip solid. "Surprise keeps life interesting. Good to finally meet you."

"Likewise, and you as well, Miss Reed." He gave her a reassuring smile, and inclined his head towards his gun.

Daisy quickly pushed the belt and holster into his hands. He draped the gear over his shoulder, and headed upstairs.

As soon as he left, Daisy planted her elbows on the counter and hid her face. "I may as well pack up my things."

"Now why do you say that?" Garrett asked.

Daisy grimaced. "I wanted to prove I'm more than just a pretty face. This is the *second* time I've met Mr. Riot, but I didn't recognize him from last time. He looked like a rough sailor sort. I thought he was older," she whispered.

"Apparently not." Garrett patted her back. "Cheer up. I didn't recognize him either."

"But I'm done for. You didn't *flirt* with him," Daisy hissed. "Lord, no one told me he was so… handsome."

"At least you didn't tell him he had a tight arse."

THE UPSTAIRS HAD BEEN RENOVATED—AT LEAST THE MAIN room, which was taken up by a pool table of all things. Lotario looked up from where he bent over the table with a pool cue. A flicker of surprise, and his fingers slipped. His shot went awry. He straightened to admire Riot, as the man walked around the room poking his head into doors.

"Are you trying to win favors with your new boss? Honestly, I don't know if I prefer you with or without the beard. But I *do* prefer you in those trousers."

Riot ignored the comment. "I'm surprised there's not a faro table."

"There wasn't room."

Riot took a seat in a comfortable armchair. It seemed to be a requirement of Lotario's, and in truth, it felt good to sit in something so plush after spending his nights bedding down in a stable.

"Have you seen Bel?" Lotario asked, perching on the edge of the table.

"I have."

"Does she prefer the beard, or not?"

Riot took out his deck of cards. "Bel is doing well. I'll tell her you asked."

"She'll know you're lying." Lotario fidgeted nervously with his pool cue for a moment. "Any progress on Dominic's murder?"

"Nothing that stands out. A few leads, though. Bel is trying to find out what Dominic and his father argued about before he was killed. Ian Noble seems a disagreeable sort. Did Dominic ever speak of his father?"

"Not to me." Lotario moved into a chair next to Riot, lest his voice carry. "Our relationship was more physical than emotional. What do you think of the Nymphia?"

"It's one of the worst cow-yards I've come across. Considering what I've seen, that's saying a lot."

"Do they have donkeys?"

"I suspect the restaurant serves donkey meat masquerading as beef, but live animals aren't generally allowed on the premises."

"Well, there's that at least," Lotario said. "I do agree with you. It's unprofessional, crass, and gives prostitution a bad name." Lotario sighed. "I actually hope the Knights of Chastity and their ilk succeed in shutting it down."

"I do, too. Not all the women are there of their own free will, but closing it down won't fix that problem."

Lotario gave him a sympathetic look. "It must be hard."

"It is."

"All those naked women—"

"*Lotario*," Riot warned.

"You *are* in a bad mood."

Riot gave him a flat stare. "Bel found something of interest related to the racetrack case."

Lotario arched a brow. "Do tell."

"When is Tim due?"

"He's late," Lotario said. "I'd rather get any business out of the way that has to do with the Nobles."

"You invited the Pinkertons?"

"We discovered something, too. I thought it might be beneficial to establish a working relationship with the Pinkertons."

Riot couldn't disagree. That didn't mean he was happy with it.

A few minutes later, they heard Matthew, Garrett, and Tim stomping up the stairs. Tim was muttering about his knees. The old man paused at the top to savor his victory over the staircase, then his blue eyes sharpened on Riot. He started cackling. "I'll be damned. Just like a button. Haven't seen that look in a while, boy."

"The real shock would be if you ever shaved," Riot said. "I don't think I've ever laid eyes on your chin."

"And you won't. Shot clean off in the war."

Riot started to surrender his seat, but Lotario hopped up and returned to his perch on the pool table. "What did Bel find at the Noble manor?"

"A betting slip in Ian Noble's desk for a horse named Lucky Connor," Riot said. "Along with a newspaper folded to an article about a union overseer named Lester Capp, who was later found dead in an orchard. His body burned. The case caught her eye a few weeks ago because there were two other such cases, all in different states. There was also a large payout of five thousand to the racetrack in Ian Noble's account book."

Lotario rushed to the top of the stairs. "Miss Off!" he yelled.

"You said not to shout!" she hollered back.

"Never mind that. Bring me Bel's newspapers."

"They're all burnt."

"I don't care, bring what's left. And bring the file on my desk." Lotario turned back to the assembled agents. "I went to the racetrack with Daisy and Garrett the other day. We noticed a private bookie catering to an extremely influential set during the race. We followed the bookie, and acquired his billfold, which had several betting slips inside."

"Did you keep them?" Riot asked.

"No, but we wrote down the numbers and names before Garrett returned the billfold."

Tim grunted. "And I take it this bookie headed over to the track's head of security? To report to Carson?"

"He did," Lotario confirmed. "At least the office. I didn't lay eyes on Carson."

Tim gave a low whistle. "Well, ain't that suspicious."

"I've tried every form of code using the dictionary we found at Monty's, and nothing. But newspapers could work as cipher keys just as easily," Lotario mused.

"So that's what Mrs. Riot was so obsessed about before the attack?" Matthew asked.

"Bel sensed a pattern, but didn't have time to pin it down," Riot explained. "If there's something to this as we suspect… it will be difficult to prove."

"They're using the racetrack to hire men to kill? With betting slips?" Matthew looked like he didn't believe a word of what was coming out of his own mouth.

"That's about it," Tim said. "Reminds me of the Molly Maguires. Damn hard to trace."

Riot frowned as he squared his deck, then went on to explain for Matthew's benefit. "The Molly Maguires are an Irish organization. When mining owners started trying to break up unions in an attempt to squeeze every dime out of miners who were already struggling, the Molly Maguires fought back. But they were smart about it. A Molly never carried out a hit in his own district. It was an exchange system of assassinations—you kill this fellow for me and I'll kill that one for you."

"A deadly game of scratch my back," Garrett murmured.

"Nothing tied the murderer to the victim, so it was hard to pin anything on the group until a Pinkerton, James McPharlan, infiltrated the Mollys."

Tim grunted. "Seems these rich fellows are paying, though. What with that cash you found in Monty's mattress."

"This Carson fellow might not even be aware what's happening with the betting slips," Riot said.

"*We're* not precisely sure what's going on," Lotario reminded them. "Though it all fits nicely together. Dammit, Bel's not even on this case and she's practically solved it."

"I think you're right to get the Pinkertons involved," Riot said. "Organized crime is a multi-headed beast. Chop off one head and another will take its place. We need to strike at the body."

Lotario cocked his head. "Have you been reading epics featuring mythical beasts? You sound like Homer."

"What he means, boy," Tim grumbled. "Is that this sort of thing isn't wrapped up in a tidy bow overnight. It's a pile of shit. It takes some damn patience and a heap of evidence, which considering my great age, I don't have time for."

Riot hoped the old man wasn't planning on dynamiting anyone. "If we spook them too soon, the main players will fold and bolt. We'll be left with underlings. And even with a mountain of evidence, this city runs on graft, so it's quite possible they'd be released."

"There must be another way," Lotario said.

"Sure there is," Tim said. "Find a handy journal where the ringleader writes all his diabolical plans."

"That would certainly be convenient," Lotario said. "Barring that discovery, I'll persuade Mr. Taft to use the time and resources of the Pinkertons. That way I don't have to pay anyone for a prolonged assignment we weren't hired for."

"This isn't about money, boy," Tim said. "Someone wants A.J. dead."

"A good many want me dead, Tim."

"So this wet-behind-the-ears laze about is just gonna sit back and let the Pinkertons track this fellow down?" Tim asked.

"You're the one who sold him your share of the agency," Riot pointed out.

Tim scowled. "Don't get smart with me."

The edge of Riot's lip raised. "It could be a woman who wants me dead."

"Grow that damn beard back. I forgot how cocksure you are without it," Tim grumbled.

Lotario cleared his throat. "Mr. Tim, I'm aware of the gravity of the situation, and I assure you I haven't forgotten that a group of men nearly blew up my twin. But the Pinkertons have more resources, and any evidence they produce will carry more weight in a court of law. Considering the past year, I'd rather keep us clear of the courts."

Tim grunted in agreement. No one could argue with that logic.

"If there's something to those betting slips, I'll find it. But I need time to break the cipher. Meanwhile, keep Grimm at the racetrack. The Pinkertons don't need to know we have another agent there."

"Speaking of the Pinkertons. Before they arrive..." Riot looked to Matthew. "Have you discovered anything at the rowing club?"

"I'm not sure it's important," Matthew said, digging out his notebook.

"You never know."

"The current owners of the Triton Rowing Club are Valentine Jr. and Emil Kehrlein. They founded the Triton after they were expelled from the Dolphin Club by their father. They also started the *Twinkling Star Improvement Company*—"

"What a *dreadful* name," Lotario said in despair.

"It's a real estate development company, which…" Matthew paused for dramatic effect "…owns the Nymphia."

"Why were the brothers expelled?" Riot asked.

"I don't know. I haven't been able to find out why, but considering the atmosphere at the rowing club, I think it might have something to do with womanizing, or maybe embezzlement. They were expelled along with seven others a few decades ago."

"Weren't Valentine and Emil recently on trial and convicted for running the Nymphia?" Riot asked.

Tim grunted. "Appealed. Got sent to Judge Cook. I wager his palm was greased something fierce. He found some minor flaw in the law and changed their sentence to a two hundred and fifty dollar fine. Pennies for those two."

"Was Dominic friends with the Kehrleins?" Riot asked.

"Far as I can tell, he got along with everyone at the rowing club," Matthew said. "Freddie Starling, Imogen Noble's fiancé is a member, too. He cleaned out Dominic's locker for the family. The club members are devastated. Dominic was one of their top competitors in rowing and swimming. And they all think he was found at home.

"I also found out the *Twinkling Star Improvement Company* is trying to get permits to renovate and attach an adjacent building. The front of it would be off Stockton. There's a basement they're keen to excavate for more rooms. They want to enlarge the cow-yard so it can hold a thousand prostitutes, but the city won't grant them permits."

Riot stopped shuffling, his knuckles going white.

"There's hope for this city yet," Tim said around his pipe.

"Father Caraher and the Knights of Chastity are putting up a fight. They've rallied every priest and preacher in the city and beyond to put pressure on city officials."

Riot watched Lotario out of the corner of his eye. He had fallen silent at the mention of permits, and was looking pale.

Construction. So far that was the only thing connecting a carpenter's pencil to the scene of the crime.

"So this Dominic is the son of a family trying to shut Valentine and Emil's cash cow down. Maybe he went to the Nymphia to negotiate some sort of deal, or friends of his from the rowing club lured him there to send a message to his mother and the Knights of Chastity," Tim mused.

"Was the body moved?" Garrett asked.

"Yes. But I'm not sure how far," Riot admitted. "The blood was pooled on his back. Before he got stiff, someone turned him over to make it look like he was sleeping, then one of the watchmen, Earl, found him and turned him onto his back again, so he'd be found by someone else. The other watchman on duty, a Billy Blackburn, took off the night of the murder. I was told he haunts a blind pig by the name of the *Laughing Mule*. He's big on cockfighting, but he wasn't there when I stopped by. Of course, I've been working most nights."

"I can help with that," Garrett said. "Finding people is a specialty of mine."

"I'd appreciate your help."

"I thought you only wanted to involve yourself in respectable office work?" Lotario asked.

Garrett flashed his teeth. "It turns out sitting around on my arse answering telephones all day doesn't suit me."

"I hired you for your charming voice," Lotario said.

"Cockfights suit me better."

"I'm all too aware, Garrett."

Garrett placed a hand over his heart. "Two drinks. One bet. That's it. I swear it on my mother's grave."

"Per saloon?"

"Let's hope I find this fellow at the first."

"Are you a gambler, Mr. Garrett?" Riot asked, interrupting the pair.

"Well, now that sounds professional, Mr. Riot. I assure you I'm no professional, but I *do* enjoy the occasional thrill."

Lotario rolled his eyes away from Garrett to settle on Matthew. "Keep on the rowing club. If you get a job offer for the *Twinkling Star Improvement Company*, take it. There may be nothing there, but at the very least you could try to get them to change their dreadful name."

48

A SHOT IN THE DARK

"I HATE THIS AWFUL BLACK." HELEN PLUCKED AT THE RIBBON on her arm. "I hate this fog. I hate this cold."

"I'd say it'll pass, but it is San Francisco," Sarah said in sympathy. "I miss a real summer. And a real spring... Well, just seasons in general."

"And snow at Christmas time," Helen said dreamily.

"That, too. Here, it's just... dreary," Sarah said. "Have you been to Sausalito? It feels like a whole different continent."

"Dominic took me there last year on the ferry, then we rode the Muir Woods railway." Helen's eyes dimmed, and Sarah put a comforting arm around the girl as they walked along Stow Lake, breath misting from their lips.

The thing about San Francisco's cold was that it was wet. It was the sort of cold that cut through cloth and went straight to bone. No insulation in the world could guard against it—at least none that Sarah could find.

"I always wondered what it would be like to have a brother," Sarah said. "My uncle was the closest person I had to one, and he turned out to be a scoundrel."

"Oh, Dom was impossible," Helen said. "He teased, and

we argued, and yet… I only ever laughed when he was about. It was all good-natured. We can't do that sort of thing with father."

"Freddie seems good-natured, too," Sarah said.

"He's splendid. Though Dominic would never have let us wander off alone like this. He was always so protective."

Freddie Starling had offered to take the girls on a picnic to Golden Gate Park. Mrs. Noble had reluctantly agreed, with promises that he'd protect their virtue and not allow any obscene behavior like bicycling. He'd crossed his heart and kissed Mrs. Noble's cheek, and sworn on his future grave that he'd watch them as keen as an eagle. But the moment they arrived, Freddie had handed the girls five dollars and told them to go have some fun. Then Imogen grabbed his hand, and the couple ran off with the picnic basket and blanket.

Sarah had no idea where Faith had gone, but she wasn't worried. She and Jin wandered the city all the time—their parents weren't concerned about Golden Gate Park. Then again, they did give her a pistol to carry around in her handbag.

"Your mother is a little too protective," Sarah said dryly.

Helen made a sound of disgust and threw a piece of bread at a honking goose. "She never lets us do *anything*. If it wasn't for Freddie sneaking us out like this, I'd go mad."

"Does he always leave you?"

"He and Imogen like to be *alone*," Helen confided, with a roll of her eyes. "And he says we're too cooped up, which is the utter truth. Thank goodness for Freddie."

"What would your mother do if she found out?"

Helen's eyes widened, and she grabbed Sarah's arm. "Please don't tell her."

"I won't. My sister and I come here alone all the time."

"You do?"

"We just have to be back before dark."

"Can I come live with you?"

"My family is…" Sarah hesitated. How to explain? "A little odd."

"Mrs. Amsel, your grandmother, seems just like my mother."

"Not as strict." Before Helen started asking after Sarah's mother and father, she changed the subject. "Would Freddie get in trouble if your mother found out?"

Helen seethed. "No. Mother would blame us. Freddie bought me a bicycle a few months ago, and I got in trouble because I accepted his gift."

"That's not fair."

"Mother says a lady is morally responsible for her own virtue."

Sarah shivered against the cold, pulling her coat closer.

"Are you all right?" Helen asked.

"Yes… it's nothing."

"You look like you've seen a ghost."

Sarah hesitated. "I just remembered a bad situation I was in at my uncle's. Two men came to visit…" She didn't want to talk about those desperate minutes. The oil in the men's voices, the look in their eyes, her harried flight up the stairs and her frantic attempt to escape. "It's hard when bad things happen in your own house. I'm sorry you had to find Dominic there. It must be hard."

Helen leaned in close before whispering, "But he didn't die in our house."

"He didn't?"

"No. I overheard Imogen and mother talking. Dom died in the *Hotel Nymphia*."

"What?"

"That's the horrid place half the city is trying to shut down."

"How?"

"He was choked to death. You mustn't tell anyone."

Sarah hesitated.

"Swear it."

Sarah couldn't swear. She had to tell Isobel. "That's terrible," she said instead. "Who killed him?"

"Mother said a prostitute, but…"

Sarah waited.

"I heard him arguing with father the day before he was killed. They were furious with each other. Father's shouting shook the plaster from the walls."

"What were they arguing about?"

Helen sighed. "A maid. Faith and I chased away another one. We were cruel to her, and I think Dom was angry that father didn't punish us. Dom never liked us playing tricks on the maids." Helen hugged Sarah's arm to her. "I think it's all my fault that Dom went to that disgusting hotel."

"How could that possibly be?" Sarah asked.

"Dom probably defended us, and father drove him out. Of course he had to go to a hotel," Helen said, with tears rolling down her cheeks.

"He could've gone to a nicer one," Sarah pointed out.

"But… it forced a confrontation. You know how that goes with family. One little thing comes out, then another, and the next thing you know Faith and I are screeching on the floor trying to kick each other."

"Did your father really tell him to leave?"

Helen sniffled. "The last thing I heard father say was, 'It will be the death of you.'"

———

"DID YOU GET ON WITH THE LAST MAID?" ISOBEL ASKED AS SHE changed the bedding in Dominic's room. Despite his death,

Mrs. Noble had the room cleaned daily as if nothing had happened and her only son would return any day now.

"What was that?" Abigail asked. She was sitting in an armchair rubbing her stockinged feet while Isobel did the cleaning.

"The maid before me." Isobel gave the older woman a smile. "Did you get on with her?"

Abigail sighed. "She was a hard worker."

"It must be difficult… having a new girl so often."

"I won't deny it. Some I'm glad to see go. Others not so much."

"Any advice for staying in the Noble's employ?"

Abigail frowned. "Mrs. Noble values chastity, girl. You keep your legs closed, don't pay no mind to the sisters, and you'll be just fine."

"You mean the sisters didn't chase the last maid away?"

"The last one, sure. She didn't last longer than a few months. But the one before… she was a loose sort. But what do you expect of one of those orientals? I warned Mrs. Noble not to hire some oriental girl that can't speak English."

"Oriental?" Isobel asked sharply.

"That's right. Mrs. Noble thought someone who couldn't speak English would fare better with her girls."

Isobel pinned the woman with a stare. "Did the oriental maid get along with the sisters?"

Abigail blinked, surprised by the sudden change in the mousy maid. "Why, yes. She was a hard worker, and the girls were kinder to her… intrigued by her. Even picked up some Japanese. She lasted over a year, but then she went and got herself with child."

49

THE CLINIC

"KYD!"

Riot nearly missed the call. The Nymphia was packed—a combination of ships steaming into port and a recent boxing match. Hoots of laughter mingled with music and the din of conversation, along with impromptu hallway games and bouts of drunken singing.

He heard his name again, so he stepped up onto his watchman's stool to get a better view of the crowded hallway.

"Kyd!" He caught sight of Dollie Small, who was taller than most men, her blonde hair blazing in the electric light. She looked worried.

Riot stepped down and slipped through the tide of guests. She grabbed his arm and shouted in his ear. "There's a group in front of one of the rooms downstairs. I think the gal inside drank herself to oblivion. Happens 'bout once a month. Usually the girls and I can break up the mob and lure them away, but they're all drunk as piss, and hootin' and hollerin' somethin' fierce, with the half of 'em at full mast. There's too many for us gals to handle."

"What about the watchmen on that floor?" Riot asked as they fought their way downstairs.

"Worthless sons of bitches said they ain't heard no bell, so it's business as usual."

Riot pushed his way through the crowds to the other wing of the hotel. The watchman for the hallway had his feet up, chatting up a woman and ignoring the large group congregated in front of a door farther down. A few women stuck their heads into the hallway, eyes worried, faces grim.

Dollie spat on the floor beside the watchman. "Yellow-bellied bastard." Then pulled Riot into an open room.

"They're too riled up, Dollie," the occupant said. "Corned up to a frenzy and going at it like a coop full of roosters on a hen."

"I don't give a damn," Dollie said, shoving open the room's secret door.

Riot followed, unhooking a billy club from his belt. He'd prefer his revolver, but weapons weren't allowed on the premises. That rule included the watchmen, since they were just as prone to getting rowdy as the clients. But it didn't stop Riot from keeping a Storekeeper tucked in a holster at the small of his back.

Dollie stopped in front of the room's back door to cinch her robe. He vaguely wondered where she'd acquired the garment.

"With you here, maybe I can talk them down," Dollie said.

Riot met her eyes, but before she could charge in first, he slipped past and entered the room.

It was the woman who'd been dropped off by her pimp, Odd Stick. Face down on the bed, unconscious or dying, and covered in bodily fluids. Two young men were busy adding to those fluids, while a third was having his way with her. A crowd at the door hooted encouragement while waiting their turn.

Riot had no intention of talking. He slammed his billy club

against a man's lower back, then twirled it and caught a second under the jaw. He grabbed the third by the hair and dragged him off the woman, raising his billy club to strike. Riot nearly brought it down on the man's skull, but diverted his blow at the last. His club cracked a shoulder instead.

A few from the crowd rushed forward, and Riot spun to meet the drunken mob. A boot connected with the back of his knee. He staggered, nearly falling. Then arms latched around his neck.

The man he'd hit first hadn't gone down. They must be drunk as piss and numb to blows.

Riot bent the man's fingers back at a cracking angle, as another bum-rushed him from the front. He slammed against a wall, the man on his back colliding with a hat hook.

The man howled.

Riot drove the second man's head down as he brought up a knee. Bone crunched, and blood gushed from the man's bent nose.

In the free-for-all, he was aware of Dollie in the room, standing in front of the bed, guarding its occupant. She'd run one man's head through a wall, but another was closing in on her.

Before Riot could shout a warning, Dollie snatched up a chamber pot and used her superior height to upend it onto the advancing man's head. He recoiled, screaming and clawing at the helmet of filth.

Dollie rushed forward to shove the filth-covered man into the crowd. The fight went right out of the mob. They dispersed, some shouting, others cursing, and a good number laughing like it was all a game.

Riot beat down the last two until they collapsed in the hallway. Then Dollie slammed the door shut and locked it.

"I like your way of talking," Dollie panted.

Riot worked his jaw, grimacing as it popped. It had only just healed.

Dollie checked the girl for a pulse, then picked a bottle from the floor and sniffed at the contents. "Laudanum," she said in disgust.

"Her pimp gave her something else, too."

Dollie cursed as she used a sheet to wipe filth off the woman.

"Is there somewhere we can take her?" Riot asked.

"There is." Dollie stuck her head into the back hallway. "Someone get me a damn blanket!"

One was brought. Riot bundled up the semi-unconscious woman, scooped her up, and followed Dollie down the back hallways. Women watched them pass. Some muttered a curse, others looked on with eyes of flint, but most simply turned away. Life was harsh. Many of the women had been there; everyone expected to be one day.

To his surprise, Dollie led him to the manager's office. Kane was sitting in his chair, a woman on his lap and a cigar between his lips.

Claude lounged in the corner, reading a newspaper.

"Kane, the men ganged up on this gal. I need to take her to the boarding house clinic."

Kane pushed the woman on his lap aside so he could see what was going on. "Don't bring that filthy whore into my office, Kyd."

Claude leapt to his feet, and Riot stopped at the doorway.

"She don't look injured."

"She's unconscious," Dollie explained.

Claude came closer to lift an eyelid. "Looks drugged to me. It's Odd Stick's girl."

Kane cursed. "He wants her working. I can't waste space in the clinic on a whore that won't pay me back. Put her back upstairs, Kyd. Plant yourself outside her door, and make sure the johns pay first."

Riot shifted his stance, relaxing. A cool calm ran through his veins that put the world into sharp focus. He was aware of every twitch, flicker of lash, and shift of weight. Claude seemed to move in slow motion.

Sensing his shift, Dollie put a hand on Riot's arm. "This hotel is supposed to have standards, Kane. You want this joint to be another sick dive in the Barbary Coast with limp women covered in their own filth? Are you really gonna let the likes of Odd Stick push you around?" she challenged.

Kane chewed on his cigar, running a hand up the woman's arm in his lap. "Claude, unlock the passage."

Riot followed Claude into the locker room. The big man took out a key to unlock one locker, then reached inside and did something that caused a click. A thick door of lockers swung open.

Of course there'd be escape tunnels in the hotel. Most brothels had at least one. Dim light shone from the passage beyond. Riot carried the woman down a flight of stairs, then followed Dollie down a tunnel. The door closed behind them.

"You must be some kind of cowboy, Kyd," Dollie said, as they walked.

"Why do you say that?"

"I've seen men look at others like you did back there." She jerked her head in that direction. "The others ended up dead."

Riot didn't reply.

"You won't last long in this business if you care."

"Is that a bad thing?" he asked.

"No. No, it's not."

When they reached the end of the tunnel, they climbed a staircase, and Dollie knocked on the door. One knock. Pause. Two rapid. Then a tap.

The door opened.

A burly guard stood inside a small room with a narrow bed, a round table, and chairs.

"Hey, Dollie." The man actually blushed.

"Hey, Croaker. Got one for Mrs. K."

Croaker stepped forward to take the limp woman from Riot's arms.

"She's filthy," Riot said. "I might as well save your shirt and take her in."

Croaker grunted, waving them on. "Mrs. K will show you where to put her."

The place was run-down, with threadbare carpets, peeling wallpaper, and mold climbing the walls. A faint cloying scent of almonds drifted in the air. Opium. Somewhere a baby was crying. Two babies, Riot corrected.

A woman with a high collar and hair pulled up in a tight bun greeted them at the base of the stairs. "Second floor. Third door on the right."

Riot creaked up the stairs with his load. A young, copper-haired woman with a storm of freckles across her tawny face paced in the hallway, bouncing an infant in her arms. She frowned when she saw the unconscious woman. "Not again," she said with a sigh.

"Shannon, get someone to fetch warm water. She needs a cleaning."

"Sure, Dollie."

Riot hesitated when he saw the clean linens on the narrow bed.

"What's this?" Mrs. K said from the doorway. "Did Kane hire a man with brains?"

"He's got more than brains," Dollie said, as she peeled back the bedspread to lay a thick towel down.

"I don't know about brains, but I am housebroken."

Mrs. K laughed. "That's a rarity."

"Go ahead now." Dollie gestured for him to put the woman down.

"Do you care for these women?" he asked.

Mrs. K looked at him in surprise. "Why are you interested?"

Riot lifted his shoulders. "Surprised they're not tossed out to the gutter."

"There's always a place for women willing to work." Mrs. K jutted her chin towards the door.

"And those who aren't?" he ventured.

"Where else would they go?" Mrs. K asked.

That was an ominous question.

Dollie pulled him out of the room, and leaned in to whisper. "I owe you, Kyd. And here's some advice. Don't go poking that fine nose of yours where it shouldn't be."

"Habit of mine," he said.

She eyed him.

"What will happen to her?"

Dollie sighed. "Probably drink herself to death or overdose once we get her back on her feet. You get going now 'fore Kane docks your pay for lingering on the clock."

Riot hesitated. It was hard to walk away. It went against every bone in his body to turn his back on that woman in the bed. But what could he do? He could barely keep his own family fed.

Closing the Nymphia wouldn't even fix things for these women. Options for a fallen woman with no money were slim. If they went to the streets and tried to go about business alone, a pimp would pick them up in no time. They wouldn't be able to find respectable work either, and most were too prideful to go to a charitable organization. Starvation or this—there was a reason they were called fallen women. It was near to impossible to get back up.

His own mother had found a way out, though. At the end of a noose.

On his way out, he stopped in the hallway to smile at a sniffling baby. "How old?" he asked.

"Four months now," Shannon said. It was said with both pride and sadness. "I don't know what kind of life she'll have."

"She's got a voice on her."

Shannon laughed. "Maybe she'll be a singer."

"You never know. My mother raised me from a crib on Morton Street."

"Good Lord." She studied him with new eyes. "What kept her going?"

"She always had a dream," he said easily.

"I have those."

"What are they?"

"A little country cottage with a white picket fence and plenty of land for Fiona and me. We'll raise chickens and garden, and maybe even have a vineyard."

"Now that's a dream," he said.

"I'm saving up." She gave Fiona a bounce. "Just as soon as I'm clear of debt and have a little nest egg, we'll be gone. Did your mother ever see her dreams?"

A flash of dirty toes hanging in the air hit him. Riot swallowed down the memory. "She did," he lied.

Shannon beamed. "And you didn't turn out half bad, eh?" She gave him a wink, then sobered. "But you're still here."

The edge of Riot's lip quirked. "I'm still here," he admitted. Another baby started crying from a nearby room. "What do you do with Fiona while you're working?"

"One of the others here watches her. We all take turns. The ones who decide to keep theirs. Mrs. K is swell like that. She don't mind the crying, just as long as we pay our board. And speaking of that…"

Shannon stepped into the room, and laid down Fiona in exchange for another infant. She put the screaming baby to her breast, and it quieted right down. But her own was fussing again.

"May I?" he asked.

"Sure."

Riot gently picked up Fiona and laid her against his chest, rubbing her back. The infant quieted.

"You're a natural."

"Seems so," he said, then caught sight of the infant at Shannon's breast—a mop of black-hair, chubby pink cheeks, and large brown eyes that sparkled like gems.

"What's this little one's name?"

"Akira. We all call her Kira."

Kira's features whispered of Japanese descent. Clearly Shannon wasn't her mother. "Who's her mother?" he asked.

Shannon took a protective step back. Then her face fell when she realized he was holding Fiona.

"Does Kira belong to the woman who fled? After that man was found in her room?" he asked softly.

"You need to put my baby right back."

Riot carefully set Fiona back in her crib. Shannon relaxed, though she planted herself between Riot and her daughter.

"You're taking care of her baby, aren't you?"

Her eyes darted to the doorway, but no one was standing there.

"I'm trying to help her," he whispered.

"I doubt that."

"She lived here, didn't she?"

Shannon hesitated, then dipped her chin.

"Has she been back?"

A quick shake of her head. There was fear in Shannon's eyes. Not of Riot, but of that open door. She could get in trouble, he realized. But didn't know just how much.

"Why hasn't she come for Kira?"

Shannon shrugged. "Must be dead."

Riot glanced at the infant. "Mrs. K doesn't strike me as the sort to raise a motherless baby."

"She's not," Shannon whispered. "She's usually quick to hand them to the orphanage."

"Can you leave at anytime, Miss Shannon?"

She shook her head. "I owe Kane for the doctor and boarding. I couldn't work straight away after I gave birth, and I was already behind. I'm even farther now."

And he wagered Kira's mother was in the same situation. It was unfortunately common. The Queen's Room in Chinatown was notorious for it. Women were duped into coming to America with false promises of a better life, then made to sign their lives over and work off what they 'owed' by selling their bodies. Only it was near to impossible to do that. The handlers took a cut from their earnings, including room and board, and charged them when they couldn't work during their monthly cycles. It assured they never paid off their debts. But the women rarely considered themselves slaves. There was always something to work towards. Always a sliver of hope to dangle in front of them like a carrot.

"What's her mother's name?"

"Sakura," she whispered.

"How much does Sakura owe?"

"Five hundred dollars."

Riot's next question was met with a firm line of lips. Shannon would say no more on the matter. But if Riot had read what she'd left unsaid correctly, then the managers of this hellhole were holding Akira captive. That meant Sakura was still alive, or... someone had an interest in Akira.

50

BULLSEYE

WHILE THE NOBLE HOUSE WAS NEVER TRULY EMPTY, IT WAS close to it today.

"I'll finish up here, Cecilia," Isobel said in broken Spanish. "You can start on the next room."

Cecilia was a middle-aged woman who'd survived three months in the household. She also spoke rapid-fire Spanish. And while Portuguese and Spanish shared similarities, communicating anything of substance was slow going, involving a mash of three languages until one of them recognized a word.

She'd confided to Isobel that it didn't matter what the Noble sisters said to her or the tricks they played. As long as they paid her, she'd keep working. Day in, day out. Isobel wasn't sure which was worse: jail or life as a live-in maid.

Cecilia surveyed the big bed and its heap of pillows. "Are you sure?"

"I can manage the bedding alone. Besides, if we finish early, we might be able to relax in the garden."

Cecilia laughed softly. "When we're in a grave."

The woman had a practical sense of humor.

Isobel started changing out the bedding in Imogen's room,

but as soon as Cecilia left she went for the desk. It was festooned with scented papers, flowery stationary, keepsakes, notes from friends, and invitations to every social event in the city.

Isobel quickly sorted through the mess, then turned to a locked drawer. This one, thankfully, wasn't as complex as the one in Ian Noble's study. She had it open in under ten seconds. Chocolates, a book of poems, and letters from female friends. Nothing from Freddie or other men.

Isobel narrowed her eyes at the drawer. It wasn't as deep as it should be. She removed the items, and bent to inspect the inside. There was a gap in the corner, large enough to fit a pencil in. She used one to pop the bottom up, revealing a journal and a stack of tied letters.

Isobel dove into the journal. Father this, Mother that. Freddie makes my heart flutter. *Oh, Freddie.* I can't wait for my happy day. My one and only. The words gushed poetic. With the occasional thinly veiled euphemism that made it clear Imogen was not as chaste as her mother would like to believe.

Isobel stopped her flipping when she spotted an entry about Dominic.

Oct 28 - I'm furious. My hand shakes even now. Dom had the audacity to tell me Freddie wasn't a good match. As if he should be pointing a finger with his womanizing ways. Men will be men. I know Freddie will be devoted to me once we are married. Dom begged me to call off the engagement. He's always been terribly protective of us, and I can't recall one suitor he thought suitable for me. Sometimes he can be such a pain.

Nov 9 - Father and Dominic fought today. We could hear father raging in his office. Helen said she heard the word 'maid' a number of times. My sisters chased off another. But surely father wouldn't be enraged over such a little thing? I heard Freddie's name more than once. I worry Dom is trying to dissuade father from allowing me to marry. Damn him. I'll kill him if that happens. Whatever was said, Dom left the house without a word.

Freddie doesn't know what the argument was about, but said he'd ask father.

Isobel flipped past a few tedious entries between the argument and the next mention of her brother.

Nov 14 - He's dead. I can hardly believe it. Father wouldn't say how. Mother is tight-lipped. Furious, I think. But at whom? Dominic?

Nov 15 - Why have the newspapers claimed he died in bed? He wasn't at home. But father made us swear to tell anyone who asked that Dom died at home. Mother didn't even protest the lie.

Nov 16 - I pestered mother for details. She was worn down with grief, I think. And she finally confided in me, though the truth is so horrid, I can't bare it. I wish she hadn't told me. Dom died in that horrid hotel—the Nymphia. I can't bear it. My own brother at such a place, but mother told me even the best of men have needs—a wild, untamed need to sow their seed, that brothels and women of ill repute are a constant temptation. She said he gave in to desire and his heart gave out.

That's preposterous. Dom was as strong and hearty as they come. And why would he visit such a low brow place when he was a man of means? Father and mother have decided not to tell Katherine. I agree. It would devastate me to discover that Freddie visited such a place. Let her think him faithful, and that her love died peacefully in sleep.

Nov 16 - Father has called off the police investigation. I suspect he had to reach deep in his pockets to keep this scandal from the press. I don't blame him. He has our best interests at heart. It could ruin our reputation and any chance of my sisters finding suitable matches.

Nov 25 - The secret weighs heavy on me. Despite my promise to father, I confided in Freddie. He should know about our family's stain. I didn't dare hope, but Freddie understood. He saw no reason why my brother's actions should affect our pending marriage. He is such an honorable man.

Isobel frowned at the journal, then glanced at the stack of letters. Noting the ribbon tie, she carefully undid it, and read the most recent letter. It oozed romantic sentiments and thinly veiled references. Signed by Freddie. It was a wonder the man wasn't on fire with all the sentences containing the phrase 'burning for you.'

A sheet of paper caught her eye. It was artfully done, the entire thing in neat calligraphy. One name was written repeatedly: Imogen Noble Starling. Each name was drawn in a unique style.

Her eyes lingered over two names written with pencil. One had a wide stroke in a Gothic style. The other seemed to be written with two pencils. Or with a notched bit of lead.

A noise in the hallway brought her back. Before someone walked in on her (again), she folded the sheet, tucked it away, and continued about her cleaning.

51

FLYING CLOUD

True to his word, Garrett had tracked down Billy Blackburn, and now he and Riot stood across the street from the *Flying Cloud*—a saloon that was built from a beached clipper ship, its figurehead stretching out into the street.

"The place has a lane around back set up for fighting matches," Garrett was saying around his cigarillo. He favored the long, slim types. "Dogs, cocks, women, and anything else the fellows will bet on. Last month they tried out cats."

"How'd that go?" Riot asked.

Garrett gave a slow, rhythmic laugh. "The two toms spat at each other a bit, looked at the cheering crowd, then turned on the men. They ended up running off together over the rooftops."

"Smart cats."

"I imagine we'll have a gang of cats attacking people in the streets soon."

"It is San Francisco."

"Anything goes," Garrett agreed, then nodded to the ship's hull. "What's our game?"

"No game," Riot said. "I intend to have a word with Mr. Blackburn. Nothing more."

"So you're a civilized man like myself. I should warn you, there are some shady sorts in there. They aren't keen on coppers."

"I only asked you to find the man," Riot said. "You don't have to come inside."

"I wouldn't mind a drink."

Riot considered this new, unknown agent. "Is there anything I should know about you and saloons, Mr. Garrett?"

"You would be referring to Lotario's comment at the agency."

"I like to know when my agents have an Achilles heel."

"I have something of a hole in my pocket, and it gets larger when I've had a few drinks. Lotario is trying to turn me into a proper miser." Garrett flashed his teeth. "I'm not much use in a fistfight, can't shoot to save my life, but I know my way around a blade. What's your weak spot?"

"I have a weakness for hats," Riot said, adjusting his own. "And I'm not civilized." He started towards the *Flying Cloud*, leaving Garrett pondering that last.

Piano music and conversation assaulted Riot as he pushed open the saloon doors. The place was crowded. A line of women kicked up their heels on a stage, while others mingled and danced with men in a space that'd been cleared of tables.

"It's ladies night," Garrett said at his side, then pointed his cigarillo towards a side room that was less crowded. "When our man isn't watching the fights around back, he's usually chatting in there. Fancies himself a Peaky Blinder."

"Is he affiliated?" It was a term for an Irish street gang out of Birmingham, England.

"No idea."

A woman with a smile on her lips sauntered towards the pair. Riot touched his hat brim and deftly sidestepped her, leaving Garrett to deal with her while he threaded his way through the crowd.

The side room was quieter, filled with men and women sitting around tables enjoying more subdued conversation. Billy Blackburn was easy to spot: peaked flat cap, blue silk scarf, and starched collar with a little metal tie button. Riot guessed him to be in the middle of a hard thirties. He was swarthy and clean-shaven, with the sides of his black hair nearly shorn.

There were two men at the table with Billy, dressed in similar fashion. Their table was in the middle of the room, so there would be no putting his back to a wall. Riot pulled a chair over from a nearby table and sat down at theirs without invitation. Conversation died, and the trio glared.

"I need a word with Mr. Blackburn here," Riot said, placing his hat on the table.

They eyed his rough attire: battered Stetson, a worn rancher's coat, and a loose neck-kerchief. What they couldn't see was his shoulder holster and his No. 3 nestled inside.

"And you are?" Billy asked. A bit of Irish lilt warred with the enunciated tones of a Californian. Not a hint of Brummie.

"A man with connections in England of the type you're impersonating. They don't take kindly to that sort of thing, Mr. Blackburn. Now a word if you will." He looked to the two other men at the table, and jerked his head to the side.

Obvious confusion flashed across their eyes. One didn't meet a cowboy claiming to have connections to an Irish street gang in England every day.

Billy nodded to his friends, who vacated the table. Riot took a moment to study the framed photographs on the wall he faced—all of posing ladies of the line in various states of undress. The frames were polished and so was the glass.

"You best not be wasting my time," Billy said.

"I hope the same can be said of my own time. I'm not with the police, and I'm not working with Mr. Kane."

"Then who are you, and what do you want?"

"I'm a private detective."

Billy tensed.

"Running won't get you anywhere, Mr. Blackburn. Trust me. I want a few questions answered, then I'll leave you to the rest of your evening."

"You have some bollocks coming in here."

Riot glanced around the room. "It's a popular place."

"It's my turf."

"Then you shouldn't mind answering my questions."

"I don't have to answer anything."

"You don't have to," he agreed. "But I guarantee you'll tire of me and my agents shadowing your every move."

"You with the Pinkertons?"

"Something like that."

Billy rubbed his chin, then shrugged. "I have nothing to hide. Shoot."

Riot cocked a grin at the turn of phrase, and Billy's cheek twitched. "The dead fellow in room 136."

"I don't know nothing about a dead fellow."

"He died on your floor. On your watch. Then you took off that same night. It's looking bad for you, Mr. Blackburn."

"No, it don't, 'cause I left. I got tired of working there. Long hours, shit whiskey, and drunk cows."

"Those same drunk cows, along with your employer, might think you an easy scapegoat. Now the police haven't caught wind of your name, but I have." Riot let that sink in. "Tell me what happened and I'll keep your name quiet."

"You're full of piss and wind."

"Humor me, Mr. Blackburn, and I'll make it worth your time." Riot slid a five dollar bill onto the table, and tapped a finger on it.

Billy licked his lips, then after a moment of thought, shrugged. "What the hell," he muttered. "I didn't kill that fellow. I don't even know his name. Came in a while back asking for a Japanese whore. I pointed him to two of the ladies. He looks in the first room I show him, then asks after the second. Peeks in there and goes inside. After twenty minutes or so, he comes out. He must've liked what he got, 'cause he came again the next week."

Riot continued to tap his finger on the bill.

"That time, I heard a scuffle. The bell rang once, so I walked over and peeked through the peephole and saw two men going at it."

"What do you mean 'going at it'? Sex or fighting?"

"Hard to tell when two cocks are having a tumble."

"What did the other man look like?"

"Fancy, like the dead fellow."

"Be more specific, Mr. Blackburn."

"Those rooms are dark. I really can't say."

"Were the lights turned off?"

"Maybe. Some women turn off the lights when they want privacy. There's also bad wiring in some of those rooms. Whatever the reason, there was only a candle."

"Where was the woman?"

"I didn't see her."

Riot had a knack for reading people. He could pick up on a tell in seconds. Billy's tell was in the puffed up way he held his chest. The man was trying his hardest to be confident in the lies he was spouting through his teeth.

Riot shifted his coat, and took out his billfold. "Now why don't you tell me what really happened. That'd be ten dollars for your time, or I'll haul you to the police station. It's your choice."

Riot laid down another five dollar bill. Billy licked his lips, but his eyes weren't on the bills. It was on Riot's billfold.

"You're not with the Pinkertons."

"I never said I was."

"I think you're lying all around."

"I'm not a lawman. The less you know about me, the better, Mr. Blackburn."

A sharp, lively whistle from the crowd caught Riot's attention. He cocked his head at the reflections in the glass photographs.

"Well, whatever the hell you are, you've found yourself in a bind," Billy said.

"If you're referring to your two friends sneaking up behind me, then I suggest you order them to stop before I show you what I really am."

A floorboard creaked as the two men paused. "And what's that?" Billy asked.

"A gunfighter."

Billy snorted. "You've been reading too many dime novels. Every cowboy thinks—" Billy cut off as Riot drew his revolver, turned slightly in his chair, and fired off a shot under his arm. It happened in a blink. His bullet pegged the hand of a man holding a knife.

The saloon didn't miss a beat. The music kept right on going, even as customers nearby cleared out, hurrying past the man clutching his hand.

Riot repositioned his chair, so he could keep a better eye on the trio. "What were you saying?" he asked. "That every cowboy with a gun thinks he's fast?"

The third man, sporting a pair of brass knuckles, took a careful step back.

"Yes," Billy said. "That's what I was going to say."

Riot holstered his revolver. "Was it fast?" he asked the trio.

The men hesitated.

Riot drew again, making the men flinch. Then he spun his revolver and holstered it in a blink of an eye. "Well?" He waited for an answer.

When the two men nodded, he looked to Billy, who readily agreed.

Riot tucked his ten dollars back in a pocket. "I'm not a lawman, I'm not a knife fighter or a brawler. I'm a killer, Mr. Blackburn. And my patience has run out. Answer my questions or I'll introduce you and your friends to an undertaker."

Billy looked to his friends and jerked his head for them to get lost. Riot watched the two out of the corner of his eye as they disappeared into the crowd, leaving a trail of blood on the sawdust.

"It's like I said, honest," Billy said. "Only the two fellows were fighting."

"Did you get a good look at them?"

"One was that dead fellow. The other was maybe thirty. Seen him around the hotel before. He's a bit of a nob. Blond hair, a little mustache, fit fellow in fancy duds."

"Did he come out of the room?"

"No. I didn't see him go in either. Must've used the back ways."

"But *you* went in after."

"I did," Billy admitted. "The oriental whore was on the floor. Her head was bleeding. Must've hit her head on the alarm bell, I suppose. That other fellow was dead in the bed."

"Was he wearing clothes?"

"He was."

Riot waited for more, already guessing at what happened next.

Billy shifted. "So I... just helped myself to his belongings. He didn't need worldly possessions anymore."

"Be more specific."

"His billfold, pocket watch, silk necktie." Billy gestured at the one he was wearing. "I snatched them real quick and left."

"Did the woman wake up?"

"No."

"Did you check her pulse?"

"No."

"Was she breathing?"

"I didn't check. It wasn't my concern."

"How much cash was in the billfold?"

Billy glared.

"I don't care about the money," Riot said. "But I do care about your answer."

"Five hundred dollars and some change. I paid up my tab at the Nymphia, then washed my hands of the mess."

Riot's stare made Billy uncomfortable. The man was trying his best to find something else to look at in the prolonged silence that followed. It was hard to ignore a predator sitting at your table, though.

When Riot was satisfied Billy knew nothing more, he picked up his hat and settled it on his head. "You're a despicable man, Mr. Blackburn. But I wager you know that already." He pushed a bottle of whiskey his way.

Billy didn't reach for it.

The crowd parted for Riot as he walked towards the exit. Garrett tossed down some coins on the bar and fell in step beside him.

"Thanks for the warning," Riot said.

"I do what I can," Garrett said, as they stepped out into the street. Cool air caressed Riot's bare cheeks. The fog was heavy tonight, clinging lazily to the ground. Riot tucked back his coat, and stood for a time, taking in the street. He didn't sense any lurking danger, so he headed down a boardwalk.

"If you don't mind me asking... what the hell are you, Mr. Riot?"

"I'm still alive."

Garrett chuckled. "I get that. Did you find anything out?"

"Dominic fought with another man. I wager Sakura was shoved against the wall during the fight, and hit her head on the room's alarm bell—that or the killer knocked her out with a blow. She was left for dead. After the killer finished with Dominic, he left out the back hallways, which means he's familiar with the layout of the hotel."

"What did our friend Billy do?"

"Our friend Billy robbed Dominic. He was carrying five hundred cash and some change—the exact amount Sakura owes to the manager of the Nymphia."

Garrett gave a low whistle. "Surprised the killer didn't take it."

"I don't think the killer was short on cash."

"So who stripped our corpse naked?"

"I have an idea."

52

PROOF OF DIVINITY

LOTARIO SAT BACK IN HIS CHAIR, RUBBING AT HIS LEFT shoulder. The bullet wound ached today. It usually did in the damp cold, but he couldn't account for it today. His office was warm and dry. Perhaps he'd been hunched over too long.

He was surrounded by a wall of newspapers, one stack marked in red, others discarded. Isobel had been right. But who was orchestrating this bit of brilliance? It wasn't a common gang of thieves—not with the sort of elite clientele sitting in that private box at the racetrack. That realization led Lotario to a rare moral dilemma. He'd broken their cipher, and now he faced a choice.

He picked up the telephone. "Daisy, is Mr. Tim in the office?"

"No."

"Matthew?"

"Hold on."

Daisy hung up, and he stared at the receiver, insulted. Foot-steps approached from the hallway, then his door opened without permission.

"It's easier to talk face to face," Daisy said.

"I had the telephone put in so we wouldn't have to walk back and forth."

"You make an art out of laziness, Lotario."

He glanced at his nails, then frowned. The tips of his fingers were stained with newspaper ink. "Shameful," he muttered, springing up to wash his hands in an attached bathroom.

"Miss Off is the only other one here," Daisy said, leaning on the doorway.

"What time is it?"

"Closing in on seven."

"Why are you still here?"

"It's not like I have anywhere to go that's good for me."

"Who's to say what's good and what's not?"

"I'm here to make a new start, not to get sucked into my old ways."

"Hmm." When Lotario had dried his hands, he turned to her. "Yes, but what is right and wrong? Is it better to sacrifice a single life for a greater number, or save the one and let the others die?"

Daisy laid her head against the doorpost. "I don't think we get to choose who lives and who dies."

"But if we had to."

"We live and die regardless. Now or later... does it matter?"

Lotario frowned at her. "Yes."

"If you had to choose between me or your twin, who would you choose?"

"That's unfair."

"Life isn't fair," Daisy returned. "I wouldn't know if you chose your twin over me. I'd be dead. Death only matters to the people left behind. What's all this about?"

"I broke the cipher."

"How's it work?"

Lotario motioned her over to the desk, then pointed to a series of numbers—from a slip they'd copied at the racetrack. "It's simple once you have the correct newspaper." Lotario shuffled through his stack and slapped down a folded article. "The date on the betting slip indicates the date of a newspaper. These numbers here, represent page, column, and so forth. The name of the horse on the slip matches the initials of the target. The fee, in this case two dollars, is in thousands, I suspect. The newspaper article gives instructions for each job."

"With another code of some sort?"

"No, it's a report of a completely unrelated crime. This particular one points to an article about a robbery—the man was killed by thugs on his way home from work."

"And these numbers are another date?"

"Yes, but sometimes instead of a date the numbers point to an advert about a hotel or boarding house. That's what took me so long to work out."

"Why would they do that?"

"Perhaps the instructions are too sensitive or too compli-cated. Or maybe it's to hand over payment... I'm not positive."

Daisy frowned down at the numbers, then looked at a slip Tim had fished out of the garbage can. "These slips have to be prepared beforehand. Unless the men hiring killers are coming up with the instructions themselves?"

"I don't think so." He tapped the betting slip. "I think it's organized somewhere else, and then a paying customer takes a slip to the racetrack and hands it over to a middleman for delivery to someone like Monty, who then hires thugs of his own. The middleman may have no idea what the slips are."

"How do these rich fellows get the slips then?"

Lotario shrugged. "The numbers could be given over a telephone line for all we know. After a customer pays at the racetrack, a slip is mailed to them, or delivered by a paid messenger boy. Even slipped through a lottery booth."

"It seems complicated."

"Not really," Lotario mused. "Think of it in terms of whoring. A john meets with a madam, and indicates his desired scenario. He pays the madam. Then the madam selects a fitting whore. The john is given a time and place, and the whore carries out his wishes. Transaction completed. No names, no set locations, identities protected. Now imagine the john doesn't actually meet with the madam, but indicates his pleasure over the telephone and sends payment by messenger."

"Except the madam knows…"

"Yes…" Lotario said, tapping the desk. "There's a mind behind this. It's a brilliant system, really. If one little fish in the pond is caught in a net, there's hardly any connections. Most would slip free. Perhaps a few underlings would be arrested, such as the actual killers, but I doubt they know the source of the pond they're swimming in."

"So in the case of Mr. Riot… A man wants him dead. Instructions are given. The private bookie passes off the betting slip to the fellow at the racetrack, and it gets passed on to someone else."

"To Monty, who for some reason kept his betting slip. A momento, I think. The instructions on his slip pointed to an article about dynamite being planted by the Molly Maguires."

"So then Monty hires thugs to do it."

"Who botch up the job. Monty likely didn't know who wanted Atticus dead any more than we do."

"And as far as the men who carried out the attack know, it was Monty who wanted him dead."

"Exactly. All to protect their very wealthy clients. No one looks twice at a gentleman of means blowing thousands at the racetracks. It's a perfect 'Cleaning Service' for the elite. I suspect it's why Bel could never pin anything on her despicable ex-husband."

Daisy made a face. "I had him once. God-awful man

wanted the full fantasy of an 'unwilling virgin maid' to mount. Thought himself a stallion. Liked it real rough. I couldn't sit for—" Cold fury flashed across Lotario's eyes, and she cut off, shocked. Daisy had never seen that look on his face before; she didn't think him capable of it. "I'm sorry, Lotario…"

"*Don't*," he snapped. "I'll never forgive that man."

Daisy hesitated. "Is that why you're doing this?"

"Doing what?"

She gestured at his office. "*This*."

"I find it mentally stimulating."

Daisy wasn't buying it.

"Yes, all right, fine," he admitted. "Bel didn't come to me for help. She never does. She's always trying to protect me. Last year, she charged in and tried to take care of things herself, then ended up in over her head and trapped with a brute. I hate Alex Kingston. I hate everything he stands for. I hate bullies. Take this Ghost Organization for example…"

"Did you just make that up?"

"I did," Lotario sniffed.

"It could just be a business."

"I prefer my term."

"It's usually called a gang," she pointed out. "I rather like the name the Molly Maguires came up with."

"Oh, stop it."

"Right, so let's catch them. We set up a trap…"

"We've come back to my moral dilemma."

"I didn't think you actually had those."

"I've just discovered one." Lotario slid over a newspaper and tapped an article. "A hit is scheduled for tonight, Daisy. I have to choose between saving *one* man's life or letting him die for the greater goal of gathering evidence and finding this 'Ghost' who will undoubtedly harm more people."

She frowned. "Why can't you do both?"

"If I interfere tonight, they'll suspect we've infiltrated their organization."

"You don't know that."

"Trust me. It will spook them. They'll pack up and go underground. It's what I would do."

"I'm relieved you're not a criminal."

"Technically, I am."

She rolled her eyes. "Sodomites and whores aside... Is the fellow who's slated to meet his Maker a good person or a bad one?"

"Is anyone really good?"

Daisy lifted a shoulder. "Some are better than others."

Lotario tossed a newspaper in front of her. The article was about a militant priest.

"Father Caraher?" Daisy asked.

Lotario nodded. "The method of murder is by thugs on his way home from work. Tomorrow. I believe he has a habit of walking home after he closes up at St. Francis."

Daisy started laughing. "Doesn't that just tickle you?" she said, wiping her eyes. "The life of the famous militant priest in the hands of two whores."

Lotario appreciated the irony in that. But Daisy soon sobered. "You know I went to confession once."

"Why on earth would you do that?"

"Fit of madness, I suppose. And do you know who I got in that hideous confessional? Father Caraher."

"Hmm, I'm sure you got an earful. Was it fire and brimstone, then?"

"No..." Daisy studied her hands. "He told me a story about a whore in those bible times. Rahab. He claimed she was the only righteous woman in an entire city, and that she saved God's servants. The city failed, but she didn't. And then he told me that this city failed me long ago, but I could still make a choice to save myself." She met Lotario's eyes. "It was right after you offered me this job. I didn't tell him about your offer. So I'm thinking it's some sort of divine will... for us to save a servant of God, and all."

Lotario raised his brows. "I always knew I was divine; now I have proof."

"Oh, stop it." She slapped his shoulder. "Let's be good little whores and go save a priest. To hell with your Ghost."

53

CONNECTIONS

THERE WAS ALWAYS A DANGER OF DIVIDING FORCES DURING AN investigation, especially when it required subterfuge. Riot couldn't easily get word to Isobel about what he'd learned. And she couldn't get word to him. But what did he have? That Dominic had fought with a man and been killed. That he'd had enough in his billfold to pay off a woman's debt to the Nymphia.

The gaps in events were being filled with facts, giving him a more complete picture of what happened the night Dominic Noble was murdered. But Riot needed more; he needed to find the woman from room 136.

It was close to noon when he returned to the Nymphia for his shift. The hotel was quiet. It usually was before noon. Most women stumbled off to what passed for a home during the wee hours of the morning, others slept in the rooms they'd rented. A few clients remained, too. But the men were generally too drunk for the women to move, had paid for the privilege, or were regular customers.

He found a man sleeping in Dollie Small's bed. She wasn't in the hotel's restaurant or bar, so he struck off down the street to a row of cafes. She sat in a tearoom, golden hair pulled back in a bun, a little hat perched on her head, and in a proper lady's collar.

Riot felt like a ruffian in his rough clothes as he entered the quaint tearoom. He removed his hat, adjusted his spectacles, and smiled at the proprietress. "I have an appointment with Miss Small. I'll have some tea, if you please."

The woman blinked at the King's English he used. But Riot didn't wait for the woman to recover from her shock. He weaved through tables to stop in front of Dollie.

"Miss Small. I'm sorry to intrude, but I need to talk with you."

Dollie raised a brow at his proper accent. "I'm not working, Kyd. I don't owe you anything. You have no right to interrupt my breakfast."

"You're right. I don't. I'm here to help Sakura get her baby back."

Dollie's eyes flashed. Shock, anger, resentment. She leaned forward to yank him into a chair. "So says every man trying to play the knight in shining armor for a fallen woman," she hissed. "You ever stop to think we can do just fine by ourselves. You men got us into this hellhole. It's up to *us* to dig our way out."

Dollie drew back as a waitress brought his tea. They smiled pleasantly, and in the ensuing silence, Riot added cream and sugar to his teacup.

"You know, my mother was a crib whore," he confided as he stirred, watching the swirl of colors mingle and mix. "No one ever offered her anything but pain. She escaped, eventually. I found her dead, still hanging by the noose she fashioned out of a rope I'd scavenged a week before. I thought she could sell it, or use it as a clothesline."

The tearoom fell away, Dollie's watching eyes and all the years between then and now. Riot wasn't aware of his lapse.

But he'd fallen silent, and when he continued, his voice was rough as nails. "She killed herself before I even learned my proper name. I was left to dig my way out of that same hellhole I was born into. When help came along, I took it." Riot focused on her and let fury and frustration bleed into his voice. "Don't you dare spit on the graves of women who never got the chance to turn down an offered hand."

Dollie met his gaze, eyes hard, her body near to vibrating with anger, but slowly the tilt of her shoulders softened. "Who the hell are you?"

"Atticus Riot," he said. "I'm a detective with Ravenwood Agency, but foremost I'm the son of a whore. Those same men who push women into hell make me as sick as you."

"I doubt that," she said. "You got a scratch compared to the holes men dig in us."

"Then let me even the odds for Sakura. Give me that, at least."

"How do I know what you're really after?" she shot back. "You lied about your name. You lied about being a cowboy, and you strike me as far too charming for your own good."

"My wife accuses me of the same thing," Riot said, taking a sip of his tea. "As to the other things, I don't know my proper name and these clothes *are* my own. To be honest, Miss Small, I'm many things: gambler, gunfighter, detective, and more recently husband and father. I'd like to think I've been a gentleman as well."

Dollie pointed her spoon at him. "You're that detective fellow that brought down those nobs."

"Unfortunately, the key players escaped. It's always the little fish who get left behind for the hook."

Dollie gave a bitter laugh. "Sounds like the Nymphia. There's always some hotel resident willing to take money in exchange for being arrested. They just have to claim they're the manager, then lounge around in a cell for a while until the attorneys spring them."

"I'm afraid they won't spend a dime on Miss Sakura."

"No, they won't," Dollie said with a sigh.

He could sense her hesitation. The doubt. Decades of men lying straight to her face, promising all sorts of happy endings, then repeatedly betraying that trust. It wore a person down, eventually.

"Dollie," he said, softly. "If I was after Sakura to hand her over to the police, I would've just shadowed you, and arrested her when you led me to her hiding place. In order to help her, I need your help, too."

His reasoning nudged her over the edge. "A few weeks ago, on Tuesday night or Wednesday morning, however you reckon time, I found Sakura stumbling around the back hallways. Blood was gushing from a cut on her forehead. She was crying. So I went back to her room to see what the fuss was about because she was too addled to speak the little English she knows."

"I found this nob of a fellow dead in her bed. Some scratches on him, but no obvious wound. I figured he got rough and maybe she knocked him on the head, or maybe he got a little too excited and his heart gave out. Either way, she's a foreigner and doesn't speak hardly a lick of English. It didn't look good for her. The police would hang her without a second thought. Billy was nowhere to be found, and I didn't know what Earl would do..." She tapped her spoon against the table, hesitating over the next. With a deep breath, she confessed. "I stripped him, then helped her get dressed in his clothes. I told her to keep her head down, get out of the hotel through the front door, and go wait at my place. But she didn't want to leave without her baby. It took some doing, but I eventually convinced her I'd get Kira."

"After she left... I arranged the dead fellow to look like he was asleep, and put a blanket over him, then went back to finish my shift. Afterwards, I went to Mrs. K's to get Kira. When I have free time, I help watch the little ones for the mothers, so it wasn't all that strange. I like to walk with them in the parks. Only Mrs. K said Kira wasn't to leave on the manager's orders. Turns out Sakura owes him a hefty sum."

"Then the police came," Riot noted.

Dollie nodded. "I was already out of the hotel, so I didn't get caught in that mess."

"Where's the street entrance to the boardinghouse?"

"Grant Avenue," she said. "Looks like a quaint little board-inghouse for women. But you know the funny thing... that 'refuge for women and children' is funded by the Knights of Chastity. Do they know what goes on there? I don't know. It wouldn't surprise me if they did. All they care about is that there's a place to stuff fallen women to ease their guilty consciences, because half those damn women in the charity know their husbands go to whores."

"All these preachers preach at us, wanting to close our busi-ness, but they don't have any proper work for us to go to 'cept starvation. And those same sorts of men won't let women work in jobs 'meant' for men. If they do, they pay us pennies in comparison, then complain about women who turn to whoring to feed their children."

Riot let her vent. He couldn't change society; he couldn't take her pain away. But he could listen.

"The proper ladies come once a year to inspect it, and under threat from Kane we all smile and dote on the little ones, and say how grateful we are that they provide a roof for us."

"Is there more than one guard?"

"Yes. And men paid to track down girls who run before paying off their debts." She nodded towards him. "Same goes for the watchmen, mind you. Make no mistake, Kane is a dangerous sort, and life is dirt cheap to him."

"Was Sakura at your home?"

"She was. I promised her I'd work on getting her baby back, and that the girls and me would watch Kira in the meantime."

"Can I speak with her?" he asked.

Dollie sighed, shoulders slumping. "She took off one day while I was gone. I don't know where she is, but I'm worried sick about her."

"Are you sure she left voluntarily?"

"I'm not sure of anything."

"You can be sure she didn't kill that man," Riot said.

Dollie raised her brows in surprise. "Who did then?"

"I tracked Billy Blackburn down. He saw two men fighting inside the room. A blond man, pencil mustache, wealthy. I think he came through the back door. Sakura was likely knocked against the wall in the fight, or hit."

"Why didn't she say something about the second man?" Dollie muttered.

"Because she fears the man who left that room—the killer. The dead man in her room had enough money in his billfold to pay off her debt."

"His billfold was empty."

"Billy stole the money."

"Bastard," Dollie cursed. "So Sakura knew the dead man?"

Riot nodded. "I think she knows the killer, too. Now I'm wondering if she tried to get Kira and was picked up by Kane's men."

"That would make sense. I've been looking everywhere for her: morgues, parks, going around to pimps. I even checked with Miss Cameron at the mission."

Riot was impressed. Dollie had been thorough, going above and beyond to help a stranger. He tapped a finger against the table, his mind wandering back to something Matthew had said at the meeting. And like links in a chain, it clicked with a rush of thought: the *Twinkling Star Improvement Company* owned the Nymphia and the Triton Rowing Club, which Dominic belonged to; the womanizing atmosphere at the rowing club; the high turnover of maids at the Noble's house; the two nobs fighting.

There was the connection. And the company had tried to get city permits to renovate and attach an adjacent building to the Nymphia. And that building had a basement.

Riot stood and flipped on his hat. "I may know where she is," he said with a grimace. But after twenty years in the business, Riot dreaded what he'd find.

———

"Psst, Sarah."

Sarah about jumped out of her skin. She'd stopped in a hallway to tie her laces while Helen kept walking. Isobel pointed to Sarah and made a shooing motion towards Helen.

"Er… Helen," Sarah called. "I need to use the bathroom real quick. I'll meet y'all outside."

"All right."

As soon as Helen rounded the corner, Isobel pulled Sarah into another hallway.

"Helen said her brother died at the *Nymphia*," Sarah whispered urgently.

"Yes, I know."

"Oh."

"What else did she say?"

"That Dominic argued with his father about a maid."

"Which one?"

Sarah hesitated. "I don't know. Helen thinks Dominic left because he was angry with them for driving another maid off, but that doesn't make sense. She said her father told Dominic, "It will be the death of you.""

Isobel laid a sheet of paper on a hallway table, and smoothed it. "Do you know what this is?"

Sarah frowned at the sheet. "Someone obsessed with their name?"

"The calligraphy."

"Yes, it's calligraphy."

"Do you know who did it?"

Sarah bent to examine the handwriting. "I had a friend who was sweet on a boy. She'd fill notebooks writing her name and adding his surname. It was probably Imogen. Though she's not artistic."

"She's not?"

Sarah shook her head. "Maybe she was practicing, but this is really good calligraphy."

"How would one go about writing this one?" Isobel jabbed her finger at the wide Gothic-style writing where one line mirrored the other.

Sarah frowned at the name. "It looks difficult, but it's really not—you can just hold two pencils together. But these lines are wide…" she scratched a nail over a letter. "It's not charcoal, so it's just a thick pencil with a notch in the middle. I've done it before."

Isobel sucked in a breath at the word notch. "Does it take a special pencil?" she asked.

"There are some special ones for art, like the one in the kit you got me for my birthday. But there's a poor man's version, too. I had hand issues when I was younger. The muscles in my hands just weren't strong enough to grip a pencil." She blushed, rubbing her hand. "My teacher was constantly hitting my knuckles with a ruler because of my poor penmanship. But my gramma wouldn't hear of it, so she gave my teacher heck, then solved my problem by handing me a carpenter's pencil. It worked just fine, and later, when my hand got a little stronger, I used it for all sorts of art."

"You're brilliant, Sarah."

"It was my gramma who did it."

"Yes, well, she's brilliant too. I wish I'd known her." Isobel folded the paper back up. "I need you to give Tim a message to pass onto Riot. Tell him what you told me about the pencil and the calligraphy; that the maid here was Japanese and with child, and was fired some months ago; and that I intend to find proof, which may be dangerous."

Sarah's eyes widened. "Can I write all that down?"

"No."

"What are you planning?"

"It doesn't matter," Isobel said. "I want you to leave. At once. Is that clear?"

"But we're going for a walk in Golden Gate Park. Everyone is waiting for me in the carriage."

Isobel gripped her shoulder. "I don't care, Sarah. I want you out of here. Now. Dominic was murdered by someone in this house. Do you understand?"

"Yes…" Sarah said faintly. "What will I say to Helen?"

"Tell her you're feeling sick and need to head home. *Do not* go near Mr. Noble or Freddie."

"What about you?"

Isobel squeezed Sarah's shoulder. "Don't worry. Whenever the teacher hit me, I ripped the ruler from his hand and hit him back."

In the end, Sarah left with a promise that she wouldn't go back to the Noble's house. That settled, Isobel turned to the task at hand.

54

PLAYING GOD

DAISY CRANED HER NECK AT THE GOTHIC TOWERS AS SHE walked through the heavy doors of St. Francis. Its dark gray stone and curving arches reminded her of a castle, at least the ones she'd read about. As she stepped through the dark doorway, she sketched a hasty cross, and hurried down the aisle between pews, her heels clicking on stone.

St. Francis was beautiful—with its vast ceilings, flickering candles, and stained glass windows, but she felt so small staring up at the saintly figurines and divine murals. Some found comfort in the serene faces, but she thought they all looked sad.

A priest came to greet her with a smile on his face. She knew men; she knew that look in their eyes. This one tried to hide it, but he enjoyed seeing her just a little too much.

"I need to confess, Father."

There, the flash in his eyes. Hunger. Enough men had used her as a confessional for her to know that feeling. They dumped their trash on her, then left her bed feeling renewed.

Some whores relished dirty little secrets, but they left her feeling like filth. Were priests the same? Now there was a sacrilegious thought to share with Lotario: the similarities between priests and whores.

"Of course, child. Come this way." He extended an arm towards the confessional booth—dark ornate wood with two doors and heavy scrolling.

Daisy stood her ground. "I confessed to Father Caraher last time."

"All ears are God's ears," he intoned.

She summoned tears, then a pain-filled sob escaped her throat—an act she'd perfected after years of being a resident virgin. Her distress echoed in the domed chamber, and several petitioners turned in surprise.

"You don't understand," she choked between tears. "He's my guiding light. It must be him."

The priest tried to calm her with placating words, then finally gave up as her sobbing increased. Eventually she was shown to the confessional with promises he would find the priest.

Daisy settled onto the bench to wait. Some minutes later, the door opened to the other booth, and a balding man seated himself on the bench behind the wooden screen.

"I hear there's a hysterical girl I'm guiding," Father Caraher said by way of greeting. His gruff voice had a lilt to it that softened the severity of his words.

Daisy skipped the 'Bless me, Father' spiel, and got right to the point. "You took my confession some weeks ago, Father. I'm Rahab. Do you remember?"

A pause. "Why, yes. Of course. How are you, child?" It was a sincere question.

"I made my choice. And that's why I'm here. I left my life behind and hired on with a detective agency."

"A step in the right direction, but hardly... wholesome. It puts you in the path of unsavory sorts."

"Like the two spies in that story about Rahab. Or like being a priest," she said cheerfully.

Father Caraher gave a grunt, scratching the stubble on his chin. He'd likely been there since the crack of dawn. "So it is," he admitted. "What can I do for you? You hardly sound as if you need my guidance."

"I'm here to save your life. You're in danger, Father."

To her surprise, he barked a laugh. Then caught himself with a quick clearing of his throat. "My life is always in danger, child."

"This is a more pressing threat, I should think," she said. "Tonight, in fact. A group of men posing as common thugs are set to kill you on your walk home. My agency discovered the plot."

"Every brothel owner, corrupt city official, graft-ridden judge, saloon keep, and gambling den wants me dead. I'm waging war on organized vice, and the people who profit don't care for my tactics."

"But this isn't ordinary, Father."

"I entrust my life to God's hands. If it's His will, then so be it." Father Caraher cracked his knuckles. "But I won't go down without a fight."

"You told me that story about Rahab and those two spies for a reason. And now here I am, a whore, offering you help. I think this might be God's will. It would be rude not to accept my help."

There was a long moment of silence as he considered her reasoning. Put like that, a man of the cloth could hardly refuse.

"What do you propose?"

"I need your clothes."

"DON'T YOU FEEL JUST A LITTLE COWARDLY?" DAISY ASKED.

Lotario had his elbow on an armrest with his chin in his hand as he gazed out of the carriage window. Fog swirled in the night, pools of electric light flickering and fading, then rallying and blazing, trying to push back the dense mist.

It didn't have much more luck than gaslight.

"I'm the *Director of Operations*. A director doesn't act, Daisy. He watches."

"Or she."

Lotario waved a languid hand. "I considered wearing a dress, but Matthew has such delicate sensibilities."

"I think it's cute."

"He's also available and kindhearted."

Daisy sighed. "That's the problem, isn't it? He's a nice fellow who deserves more than a soiled dove."

Lotario clucked his tongue. "So judgy."

"That is not a word."

"It is now," he drawled, rubbing his shoulder. "God, it's cold."

"Don't you ever stop whining?"

"I don't want to get out of practice."

Daisy sat up straighter. "The show's on, I think."

"It looks that way." He drummed his fingers on his cheek. "Shit. There's four of them. I hadn't accounted for that."

Daisy frowned into the murky night. 'Father Caraher' walked under one lamppost to another with a purposeful gait, his hat pulled low and his collar turned up against the cold.

It was a night for murder. Quiet, concealing, with the kind of silence broken only by a death rattle. Daisy chewed on her fingernails. What if they shot the decoy? Wouldn't that be the easiest way to murder him?

Everything happened at once—smooth and practiced, the four men moved as one, coming at the priest from the four points of a compass. Four shadows converged. Two stepped out of a lane, another peeled away from a lamppost, while the fourth approached the priest from the front.

The thugs didn't waste time with words. They rushed forward. The priest jumped back as the man in front slashed a blade, but he leapt right into the blade of the assassin at his back. Gunfire shattered the stillness. A police whistle blew. And the priest elbowed the man behind him, then slid a billy club from his sleeve and bashed the man in front.

The man in the rear dropped from a bullet, and a man emerged from a doorway to tackle the third thug. The priest finished bashing two thugs into submission, and all went quiet. Four men lay dying or wounded at his feet.

'Father Caraher' ripped off his hat and coat, and kicked the closest. But it wasn't Terence Caraher. He was safe in his parish. It was Sgt. Price, who matched the priest in height.

Matthew was busy latching irons onto the thug he'd rammed, and Inspector Coleman stepped out of a doorway, holstering his revolver. He'd shot the knifer. Three more officers stepped out from various hiding places.

"Are you all right, Sgt. Price?" Matthew asked.

Price slapped a fist against his chest. "Chain mail. Old hatchet man trick. Works like a charm, but my back will be black with bruises."

The booming voice carried in the quiet, and Daisy breathed with relief from the carriage.

"Well, that is that," Lotario bumped his stick against the ceiling, and the carriage rolled forward.

"Aren't you going to question the thugs?"

"I know what they'll say," Lotario said. "And I think I prefer to be an invisible director."

Daisy frowned at him. "Should I start calling you 'The Ghost'?"

"Too dramatic." He thought a moment as their carriage drifted through the fog. "EL."

"What?"

"Like the letter 'L'."

Daisy shook her head. "I thought you weren't going to make up any more identities, Lotario."

"This one is all-encompassing."

"You're full of it. That's what you are."

"Of course I am." Lotario smiled, charmingly. "But tell me... how did it feel?"

Daisy felt her cheeks warm. A true blush. Not a made-up one like from her previous profession. "I think I enjoy saving people."

Lotario snorted. "I meant, how did it feel to play God?"

She kicked him in the shin.

55

A DANGEROUS TURN

THE TIME FOR SUBTERFUGE WAS ENDING. ALL ISOBEL HAD WERE theories; she needed proof.

Mrs. Noble was resting. Mr. Noble was in his study, and the sisters, along with Freddie, were headed to Golden Gate Park. Sarah would be safely on her way home.

With cleaning bucket in hand, Isobel walked to the far wing where the guest rooms were located. Freddie's room wasn't locked. There wasn't even much in the way of possessions. She suspected he kept rooms at the Palace.

She set down her supplies, opened the drapes to air out the room, and took her feather duster to the desk. A thorough search turned up nothing of interest.

Where were his art supplies? He'd likely taken them to draw at Golden Gate Park.

She checked the bedside table: sleeping pills, a vial of laudanum, headache tablets and stomach seltzer. All likely cures for hangovers.

Isobel knelt beside a travel trunk, and slipped out her lock picks. The lock gave. Most everything had been hung up in the wardrobe or put into drawers, but there were a few odds and ends: neckties, a pair of shoes, socks, a baseball, and a swimsuit.

Isobel set those aside, then felt around the lining. It was filled with stuffing for cushioning, except for one panel that was uneven. When she inspected it she discovered a tear at the base of the lining. Isobel pulled free the uneven bulge, but it wasn't padding; it was a shirt.

Isobel shook out the garment. Dark stains on the collar. Rips in the sleeves and the back encrusted with blood. Freddie's blood.

Footsteps clicked in the hallway. Isobel stuffed the shirt back inside, closed the trunk, and darted to the mantel to start dusting.

The door opened. But it wasn't Abigail, or Cecilia. Or even Mrs. Noble. It was Sarah, standing stricken with a gun to her head.

56

ALL ACTION

THE NYMPHIA WAS A LARGE U-SHAPED BUILDING THAT TOOK UP an entire block, its wings stretching back from Pacific Avenue along Stockton Street and Grant Avenue. A narrow lane ran between the hotel and a derelict building of red brick, three stories high and with a fire escape attached to the front. It looked like an old block of apartments. It wouldn't take much to attach the two buildings.

Riot clenched his jaw as he examined the boarded-up windows. A thousand women crammed into cell-like rooms—the thought made him sick.

The street was clogged with traffic from Chinatown and with children walking home from school. It was home to grocers, restaurants, and residences. Small wonder preachers were fighting the expansion. It would put an entrance to the hotel on a main thoroughfare frequented by families.

Riot stepped into a recessed doorway where a sign welcomed him: Trespassers will be Shot.

"How do we get in?" Dollie asked. "Doesn't look like anyone's home."

"It's ungentlemanly of me to ask, but I could use some concealment," Riot murmured as he slipped out his lock picks.

It took Dollie a split second to realize what he was asking. Then she chuckled to herself and planted her girth in front of the alcove, shielding him from prying eyes.

The lock gave, and Riot slipped inside, gun in hand. He stood for a moment, letting his eyes adjust. It was dark. And silent. He thumbed on his flashlight and felt Dollie step in beside him.

"You don't have to come," he murmured.

"I'm in here, aren't I?" she whispered, closing the door.

His light illuminated dingy carpet, peeling wallpaper, and shattered lamps. Glass crunched underfoot as he moved forward, the floorboards creaking with each step.

The hallway smelled of urine. Rats, judging from the pellets on the carpet. A mark on the floor caught his eye—two thin lines trailed through leftover rubbish.

There were other signs of life too, of the human variety. Footprints on the dusty carpet, brush marks from a broom. The rooms themselves were empty of furniture and garbage, as if the *Twinkling Star Improvement Company* had cleared it out to prepare for renovations.

Riot hesitated at a stairway leading up. Should he head to the next floor, or search for a basement? Basements were always a favored hiding place for a body, so he moved farther back into the building. He stopped when he spotted a door with candles on a small table next to it. It looked like a door to a basement, and it was close to the back door of the building.

Dollie picked up a candle, and fished around her handbag for a matchbook. Warm light flooded into the hallway. Riot exchanged his flickering flashlight for a candle, as she lit a second.

"Good Lord," Dollie whispered. "There's a lock." She was

right. A padlock hung from a latch on a basement door. Hope edged into his heart. Could Sakura be alive?

Riot holstered his gun, handed over his candle, and had the lock open in seconds. With Dollie behind him holding the candles, he moved down a rickety staircase with gun in hand.

A thin form curled on a dingy mat in a corner. A chain linked her ankle with a rung in the wall. Dollie made a strangled noise and rushed past him, kneeling beside the woman.

The sound of boots stomping up the back steps alerted Riot. He rushed back up the stairs, and burst through the basement door as the back door opened. A hulking man filled the doorway, holding a tray in hand. Claude.

Riot leveled his gun at the guard. "We can do this the easy way, or the hard way."

Claude tensed. Riot saw intent in his eyes—the muscles of Claude's arms, the flexing of his thighs, the way he shifted onto the balls of his feet. *All action is of the mind and the mirror of the mind is the face, its index the eyes.* It was all there, plain as the words on a page. Riot squeezed the trigger as Claude flung the tray at him.

The tray hit Riot in the face. Food and water splattered, pottery broke, and Claude dropped to the floor. Dead.

Riot wiped food from his face, then bent to drag Claude farther into the building. Blood blossomed over the carpet as he closed the door.

"Kyd?" Dollie called from below.

Riot moved to the basement doorway. Dollie stood in a pool of light, with a little derringer in hand. "Is she alive?" he called down.

"Barely," Dollie said. "What was that about?"

"Claude."

"Is he dead?"

"Yes."

"Good riddance."

"We need to get her somewhere safe."

"There's a chain around her ankle. We'll need those lock picks of yours."

Riot glanced at the back door, hesitating. The gunfire could draw attention, and he didn't like the idea of being cornered in a basement. While no one generally paid much mind to gunshots in San Francisco, Kane would eventually notice when his guard didn't return.

"Come up here," Riot said.

Dollie didn't ask why. When she emerged, he drew the more powerful Storekeeper from his back holster, and handed it over to Dollie. "Shoot anyone who comes through that door."

He moved downstairs to kneel beside the woman. Sakura was battered, one eye swollen shut, and angry bruises covered her face. She shivered with cold, staring at nothing. When he touched the chain, she jerked.

"We'll get you to a doctor," he said, softly. "And I'll bring Akira."

At the sound of her daughter's name, her gaze came into focus, looking at him for the first time. Careful not to touch her, he popped the lock off her ankle, and removed his coat, placing it over her shoulders. Although weak, she shrank back from his offer of help.

"Sakura," he said. "I'm Atticus Riot." He didn't know how much English she spoke, but hoped his voice sounded reassuring. "Who did this to you?"

She shook her head.

"Was it Kane? Ian Noble? Freddie Starling?"

Sakura hesitated at the last. Answer enough. He held out his hand, and she searched his face. Whatever she saw put some light back into her eyes. He helped her up the stairs, and when she saw the bleeding corpse of Claude, she kicked the man with her bare foot.

It seemed to bolster her. "Starling," Sakura said with a nod.

Riot's heart skipped. Freddie Starling. Based on Billy's description, he'd suspected Freddie, but the confirmation made him sick. Isobel was in that household. And Sarah. He had to warn them, but he needed to ensure Akira's safety first.

Kane was capable of anything.

"You said the clinic opened up onto Grant Avenue?" he asked Dollie.

"Yes, but it's guarded. And they won't let just anyone in for the 'safety of the residents.'"

Riot pondered his options as he locked the back door, then propelled Dollie and Sakura out the front. He searched the street for a likely candidate and settled on an old man with a handcart.

"Honored father," he addressed him in fluent Cantonese. "This woman is injured. I need you to take her to Dr. Wise."

The old man looked to the woman leaning heavily against Dollie's arm, hesitated, then sketched a bow, gesturing to his cart. As soon as Dollie helped Sakura into the cart, the old man tossed a tarp over her, and trotted off at remarkable speed.

Dollie had to run after him.

That taken care of, Riot had another matter to deal with. He wished he could count on the police, but Kane had likely bribed the patrolman in the area. So he set his sights on a group of men lounging in the mouth of an alleyway. They had the look of laborers. Maybe even a few low-ranking hatchet men in the mix.

The group watched him warily as he approached. "You fellows look bored," he said in Cantonese.

A twitch of surprise rippled through the group. One young man with a cigarette dangling from his lips jutted his chin towards the street. "Get lost."

Riot touched the brim of his hat. "I suppose you're not interested in cash." He made to leave.

"Wait," another man said. "He doesn't speak for us. What do you need?"

Riot took out his billfold. "Nothing too illegal. And I guarantee it'll be entertaining. I just want you to make some noise."

57

TIGRESS

Isobel tried to speak, but only a choked sound emerged as Freddie stepped into the room, holding Sarah in front of him as a shield. He closed the door with his foot.

"I debated what to do about that shirt," he said easily. "I couldn't leave it at the hotel. It has my launderer's tag on it and it'd look awfully suspicious for me to be walking out with no shirt under my coat. I thought of burning it... but that could also draw attention. So I just tucked it away."

Sarah was trembling, clutching her handbag, and making a whimpering sound that tore at Isobel's heart. Freddie leaned down to whisper in her ear. "Your mommy is nosy."

He knew Isobel's identity. How the hell did he know? Isobel tried to think, to scheme, to come up with some brilliant plan, but her heart was in her throat and her mind consumed with an instinct to charge the man.

"Oh, yes. I figured it out. I'm not as careless as I appear. Helen told me Sarah was famous, then Ian told me he caught you snooping, and naturally dear Imogen told me you never worked for Violet."

"Leave Sarah out of this," she finally croaked.

"You brought her into it."

"She's friends with Helen. That's all."

"No, it isn't 'all'. Sarah claimed a sudden illness, refused my offer of a carriage, and tried to take off. I know who you are, *Mrs. Riot.*"

"My agency knows I'm here, Freddie," Isobel said. She took mental stock of the room, but all she had in hand was a feather duster, and Freddie, she reminded herself, was a hunter.

For all his flippancy and charm, he was a crack shot and enjoyed the act of killing. He had the instincts of a hunter, and it showed—he was being cautious, keeping his distance from her, using Sarah as a proper shield and giving Isobel no opportunity to attack. Cunning man.

"Ravenwood Agency is aware of my suspicions of you. If you kill me, they'll know who pulled the trigger."

"It's a pickle," he admitted, tapping the barrel of his gun against Sarah's head. Each tap made Isobel jerk. Her knees quaked. She was furious, quivering with restraint against an overwhelming urge to attack the man holding her daughter hostage.

"I could shoot you, then Sarah, and claim I caught you thieving. Tragically, Sarah got in the way," Freddie mused. "Or better yet... *you* shot her."

"No one will believe that," Isobel said with a snort, her mind rebelling against the absurdity of his plan. "The angle of the shot won't match the blood pattern—no matter how you arrange our corpses. You're a hunter, Freddie. You know that as well as I do."

"The police aren't very observant."

"My agency *is*." Isobel shifted her stance, moving away from the mantel. "You forgot about my agency again, didn't you? Or that a certain San Francisco Police Inspector *assigned* me to investigate Dominic's murder. I'm not just nosy, I'm a consulting detective, Freddie."

"You're bluffing."

"The inspector called me in as a consultant to Dominic's murder. I saw the scene. The handkerchief you used to stuff down his throat. I was the one who found your carpenter's pencil."

His cheek twitched.

Isobel dropped her feather duster and removed her spectacles, tossing them onto the bed. She met his eyes, staring daggers at the man. Even ten feet away, that stare would unnerve anyone. Freddie was no exception.

"Don't move!" he ordered, pointing the gun at her.

"Let me see if I have this right, Freddie," she purred. "You assaulted the Japanese maid while she worked here. Probably multiple times over the course of months. She barely spoke English. What could a woman in her position say, after all? She needed the work, and she knew Mrs. Noble would blame her for your sexual urges. When she started showing, Mrs. Noble had a fit and kicked her out onto the street. Then you came along like a knight in shining armor promising to care for her. Instead, you dumped her at the Nymphia with your child in her belly."

"I do enjoy exotic women, and I must say Sakura was an amusing little diversion."

"Until Dominic discovered what happened," Isobel continued. "From the rowing club, I should think. You likely couldn't resist the urge to boast about your conquest." A twitch in his eye confirmed her theory. "So Dominic, ever protective of his sisters, warned Imogen about you, even as he was searching for the maid... Sakura. But Imogen wouldn't hear of it, so he went to his father, who saw nothing wrong with your actions."

"Dominic wouldn't drop it," Freddie snarled. "The self-righteous bastard took his surname to heart. And when Ian told him to drop the matter, Dominic threatened him."

"He threatened to expose the business at the racetrack," Isobel said.

Her deduction was confirmed when Freddie faltered, his smug smile deflating. He tightened his grip on the revolver, taking careful aim at Isobel's heart.

"You could just let us go!" Sarah whimpered.

No, no, *no*, Isobel thought. Don't draw attention to yourself.

Freddie slid his arm around Sarah's neck, pulling her firmly against his body. She gasped for air.

"Take me," Isobel said, quickly. "Leave Sarah locked in the wardrobe. You can kill me somewhere else and still get away."

"She'll snitch on me."

"No, she won't. She'll be too scared of you."

Sarah choked down a cry, tears leaking from her eyes, dripping onto Freddie's arm.

"I think I'll take both of you." He jerked his head towards the bedside table. "Do you see that vial on the table? Yes. There. Drink it."

Isobel could see the label from where she stood. It was his laudanum tincture.

"*All of it.*"

She hesitated, and Freddie tightened his hold on Sarah, the girl's nostrils flaring in panic.

"It won't kill you," Freddie purred.

"If I drink that, you'll kill us both."

"No. I won't. I'll drop Sarah off somewhere far away. Alive. I swear. And you, too. Better yet, I'll put you both on a steamer to China. How's that for a deal?"

Isobel didn't believe a word of it.

"*Or*, I can kill you and take Sarah with me for company."

The way he said Sarah's name made Isobel's skin crawl. Now that, she believed. But at least it would give Sarah a chance at surviving. A horrible option that would buy Sarah time. Time for Riot to hunt down the scoundrel.

Isobel edged over to the table. She picked up the vial, and read the label. He was right, she'd probably survive drinking the full dose. There was a risk, but Isobel didn't expect to live long enough to discover whether the laudanum would kill her.

Isobel considered diving behind the bed, but Sarah was there. What could she do? She could throw the glass... No. Her knife. She could slip it free into her hand, charge, risk a bullet, and hope it hit nothing vital. But what good would that do? He'd simply drag Sarah from the room. Or worse, shoot Sarah.

"*Now!*" he barked.

Isobel put a hand over the cork. She needed to buy them time. Time for Riot to track this bastard down and shoot—

"*Or* I could just shoot you."

Sarah.

Time slowed and sped all at once as Sarah pulled out a derringer from her handbag. Without pause, she pulled the trigger. A gunshot barked, the bullet catching Freddie under the chin, even as he squeezed his own trigger, pain jerking his aim to the side.

A wave seemed to crash into Isobel as she threw herself at Freddie Starling. It hit her full on, its shock rippling through her body, but she tore through it with the ferocity of a tiger.

Freddie reeled from shock, and Sarah threw herself at his arm, dragging down the hand that held his gun. Freddie fired off another shot as Isobel crashed into him. It felt like slamming into a brick wall. The man was all muscle and bone, an athlete in the prime of life. But he was also bleeding from his mouth.

The force of her charge knocked Sarah to the floor and slammed Freddie against the door. Freddie ignored the jagged hole in his cheek, and grabbed her hair, twisting and bringing up his knee. They went down in a painful tumble.

The flesh at the bottom of his chin was ragged and bleeding. There was another hole in his cheek, where the bullet had punched an exit wound, showing broken teeth. Blood slicked their hands and bodies as they grappled. Even wounded, he was strong—fit enough to overpower a grown man like Dominic.

Freddie pinned Isobel onto her back, his hands at her throat. She felt weak, blackness creeping at the edges of her vision. She couldn't fight against his strength. Something caught her eye on the floor. The vial. Isobel released the hands locked around her neck and jabbed fingers into the bullet wound under his chin.

Freddie screamed in agony. His grip loosened, and she was on him in a flash. But rather than attempt to pin him, she snatched up the vial, bit off the cork, and stuffed the mouth of the vial into his own.

Freddie spluttered, coughing, trying to push her away. Isobel drove her knee between his legs, and he gulped the liquid, eyes bulging. Then gradually his strength faded, until he finally went limp.

"Isobel…" Sarah slid onto the floor next to her.

"Are you hurt?" Isobel demanded, pawing at Sarah with bloody hands.

"No."

Isobel shuddered with relief.

Sarah's eyes were wide. "But you are."

Isobel barely heard the last. She was slipping away into darkness. The room was spinning and tilting, and she was falling.

58

A SLY ONE

RIOT RUSHED INTO KANE'S OFFICE, WAVING HIS HAT. "POLICE raid! They got Claude," he hollered.

Kane was talking with a man in a neat suit. They broke off the conversation to look at the frantic cowboy. "What?" Kane asked.

"Clear out now," Riot urged.

"There's no raid scheduled today," Kane said.

Of course someone in the station would be in Kane's pocket to warn of impending raids.

"Well, there *is* one now." Riot said, and like clockwork the first popping bangs burst from the front of the Nymphia. Whistles blew, mimicking a police raid. It was Riot's hired gang of bored laborers and hatchet men. They'd rushed the Nymphia armed with firecrackers, smoke bombs, and screaming whistlers. As long as Kane remained in his office, he'd never know it was a ruse.

Kane's eyes flashed. Without prompting, the man in the suit fled out the back door. Kane pulled open his desk drawer, grabbed a logbook, and shot to the locker room. "Kitty!" he shouted. "You're the manager today."

Kitty stood in front of the lockers. She was half-dressed, her own locker door open. "What?"

"You're taking the fall."

Kane unlocked a cubby, thrust his arm inside, and twisted a catch in the back. The secret door swung inward. Before Kane could close it, Riot rushed past him. "I'll guard you!"

Kane sneered, but didn't object. He followed close on Riot's heels. The man at his back made Riot's fingers twitch, but the feared blade never came. Riot waited at the clinic door as Kane climbed the short staircase. He squashed himself against the wall, as the man gave a different series of knocks than last week.

Croaker wrenched open the door, but before Kane could charge through, Riot drove his fist into the manager's larynx, then shoved him down the stairs.

Croaker stood stunned. Only for a blink. The guard recovered, throwing his weight and fist forward. Riot ducked under the clumsy blow, grabbed Croaker by the belt, and used the guard's own momentum to propel him down the steps. Croaker landed on his boss.

A gunshot cracked, wood splintered, and Riot threw himself into the clinic. He kicked the door shut, then surged up to throw the heavy bar into place. With luck, Kane and his lackey would be too afraid to head out the secret entrance with a supposed police raid swarming the hotel. Riot just needed to get word to Inspector Coleman in time.

He moved up to the ground floor. The gunshot had drawn a second guard's attention, but the man thought it'd come from upstairs, not the secret tunnel. Riot caught the guard peering up the stairwell.

"Drop it," Riot said.

The guard froze, eyeing him sideways.

"Is your pay worth your life?"

The guard dropped his revolver, then raised his hands. Riot

jerked his gun towards a coat closet. The man moved obediently into it, and Riot shut the door, then dragged over a chair and wedged it under the handle.

The guards in the clinic were there to control the women, not to confront a hardened detective with a hair-trigger finger. Riot rushed up the stairway. Then froze. He hadn't counted on a third guard, but he'd miscalculated. Mrs. K was standing at the top with a shotgun leveled at him. "Not a step farther," she warned.

Riot raised his hands, holding his revolver loosely. "I'm Atticus Riot, a detective. I was hired to rescue Sakura's baby."

"I don't give a damn."

In a split second, Riot considered his options. A shotgun blast would do him in. He might be able to get a shot off first, but she had her finger poised on that trigger, and there was intent in her eyes. To kill. She'd claim she mistook him for an intruder trying to harm the women.

Riot dropped to the stairs, hitting his chin, and thrust his gun up the stairway, just as a form moved behind Mrs. K. Glass smashed, and Mrs. K crumpled to the ground. The shotgun fell to the floor. It went off with a flash, propelling itself backwards as the shot blasted over his head, splintering the wall. The sound woke up the entire house, including the infants. They started screaming in chorus.

Shannon stood at the top of the stairway, a broken gin bottle in hand. "That was close," she said.

He flashed a grin, then rushed up the stairs. "Are there any more guards?"

"No, but what about the tunnel?" she asked faintly.

"Barred, with Kane trapped inside."

Shannon wobbled.

Riot bent to check Mrs. K's pulse. She was alive, but blood was gushing from a head wound. Other women stuck their heads into the hallway to look at the commotion.

"Kane will kill us," Shannon said.

"Probably just you." He straightened to address the other occupants. "If you want out, now's the time to leave."

"They ain't just gonna let us go," one woman said.

"We got nowhere to go," said another.

It was true, he couldn't fix the world, but he could give them the option to take a chance. "I can't guarantee anything, but I'll do my best to assure this boardinghouse treats you right. If you're willing, tie Mrs. K up, and put some pressure on her wound. The police will be here shortly."

Riot didn't wait for their answers. Dread was growing by the second. He wanted to abandon everything, storm the Noble's manor and drag Freddie Starling down Nob Hill and into a jail cell.

Instead, Riot walked into Shannon's room, took a calming breath, and stepped over to the cradle. He smiled down at the squalling infants as he holstered his gun. "Sorry for the noise. But…" He plucked Akira out of her cradle and wrapped her in a blanket. "I think you'll want to see your mother."

"You found Sakura?" Shannon asked, trying to quiet her own baby.

"I did," he said. "And I know a place where you and Fiona will be safe."

59

DEATH AND DELUSION

THERE WAS BLOOD. BLOOD EVERYWHERE.

"Isobel!" she shouted, shaking her. Sarah's heart was trying to claw its way out of her throat. She couldn't breathe. Couldn't think.

Isobel lay on her back. Blood seeping onto the carpet.

"Help!" Sarah screamed.

Isobel's entire right side was wet with blood. Sarah darted to the bathroom, snatching clean towels and everything else in sight, then rushed back to press a towel against the gunshot wound. Keep pressure on it. Stay calm.

Isobel's eyes snapped open. "You all right?" she wheezed, her breath ragged, eyes out of focus. Isobel was trying to rise, but her body wasn't cooperating and Sarah could see the confusion in her eyes.

"Yes, I told you. I'm fine."

"Stop… shouting."

"I'm not shouting. You've been shot."

"A scratch."

Right, Sarah thought with rising panic. Then her gramma's patient voice came to her: Stay calm, dear. Don't let her see your fear.

Sarah took a breath to steady herself. "I told Atticus that gun was a peashooter."

Isobel coughed out a laugh. But pain sent her eyes rolling.

The door opened, and relief shook her body. Finally, an adult. Someone who'd call an ambulance.

"What on earth is…" Mrs. Noble stopped in the doorway. The pale woman took one look at Freddie lying on the ground with a bloody hole in his cheek, and started screaming.

"Mrs. Noble, call the police!" Sarah hollered. "Freddie shot her."

But the woman just stood there screaming. Useless. Then her husband arrived. Mr. Noble walked into the room and glowered down at the scene.

"Isobel needs help, Mr. Noble. She's a detective. Please call an ambulance. Freddie *killed* Dominic."

Mrs. Noble choked on her screams, then her eyes blazed. "*Lies!*" she hissed. "You lie!"

"I'm not lying," Sarah argued. "Freddie got your maid with child—"

Isobel tried to shake her head in warning. Tried to tell Sarah to stop. To be quiet. But her body was numb. And so very far away.

Mr. Noble placed a hand on his wife's shoulder. "I'll have someone clean up this mess, darling." He grabbed Freddie's gun from the floor, then dragged Freddie out by the collar. The door slammed, and the lock turned.

Sarah stared, stunned. She was trapped in a room with her dying mother.

60

TIME TO FOLD

GRIMM WHITE BRUSHED A HORSE WITH CALMING STROKES. IT was skittish and quick, and no one else wanted to deal with the racehorse. High-strung, they said. But Grimm knew he was just eager to run. Gale loved running. It's all the horse wanted to do. But when Grimm brushed him, he calmed right down.

Gale also enjoyed being pampered.

This wasn't what Grimm had expected when he interviewed to be a detective. He was only doing what he loved, while he watched and listened to folk—he didn't even have to talk.

He watched rough fellows coming and going from the security office at all hours. They didn't have the look of guards. Others were sharply dressed. And once daily, he saw Mr. Tim.

Part of his duties were cleaning, so after he finished with Gale, he went to sweep offices and empty garbage cans. Keeping his head low, he stepped into Carson's office to sweep. Despite his height, no one paid Grimm any mind. He didn't talk, so people assumed he couldn't hear, and that made him near to invisible to most folks.

That was what Grimm had been doing for most of his life

—ever since he made one tragic mistake. The office telephone rang, but he didn't react. He went about his sweeping.

Carson glanced his way. "Boy, get out."

Grimm didn't respond. He was playing deaf after all, and his back was to the man. He'd done that on purpose.

"Boy!"

Sweep, sweep, sweep.

Carson cursed under his breath and picked up the line. He said nothing, only listened to the man on the other end.

"I need a cleaner now," a demanding voice thundered through the line

"That's not how this works," Carson murmured.

"I don't care how it works. Send a man now. That little problem I hired you to take care of has blown up."

"What do you mean?"

"There's a dying female detective in my house, and a girl is accusing my son-in-law of murder. I need them gone."

Grimm breathed in through his nose and out, keeping his breath even and his movements steady. But after hearing that, it was hard. He forced his hands to relax, despite a thundering heart.

"Did you burn everything as instructed?"

A pause.

"Yes."

Carson hung up the line. Grimm emptied the pan into the garbage can, then picked it up. He didn't linger, or do anything other than what he usually did. Grimm carried the can out, and another man rushed past him, disappearing inside. The door slammed.

Grimm lingered outside to listen.

"Men were waiting last night. The target is still alive."

So cryptic. But whatever it meant caused Carson to pick up the telephone again. "Get me the Principle." If the person on the other line said anything, Grimm couldn't make it out. But he could hear Carson's muffled voice through the door. "I think we've been compromised, sir."

A pause.

"Yessir."

The telephone clicked.

"Time to fold," Carson said. "Burn it all."

Footsteps approached from the other side of the door, and Grimm shot down the stairs. He ducked under the wooden stairs, clutching the garbage can to his chest and pressing himself into shadow.

Carson hurried down the stairway. The man walked off in a hurry to sounds of furniture being toppled above.

Grimm frowned. Were they actually going to burn the stable house? There were horses under the office.

There's a dying female detective in my house... The words chilled his blood. He needed to find Mr. Tim. He needed to save the horses. But there was only one of him. Grimm didn't have time to consider his actions. He had to act. *Now.*

Carson was halfway around the training pen when Grimm caught sight of another man—wiry with longish brown hair. He stood at the fence smoking.

Grimm froze. The stranger was looking right at him. He stared far too long, before peeling off to follow Carson.

Grimm wanted to run, but he was frozen with fear. *Sarah.* She was in danger. Grimm dropped his garbage can and ran into the stable to save the horses first.

61

THE ART OF CUSSING

EVEN DYING ISOBEL WASN'T THE TYPE TO GO QUIETLY. SHE pawed at Sarah's hand, then shoved it aside, and pressed her own against the towel.

"The window," Isobel croaked.

"I'm not leaving you."

"You have to."

"*I'm not leaving you*," Sarah insisted.

"Get me help."

Sarah faltered. It was hard to argue with that logic. Isobel rolled onto her side and struggled to her knees, swaying with pain.

"You need to lie down."

Isobel clenched her jaw and tried to stand, still pressing the bloody towel to her side. A jerking lunge sent her careening into the bed. Sarah rushed over to put an arm under her uninjured side.

Isobel growled against the pain, even as her knees buckled, then started cussing up a storm. It gave her strength. Sarah helped Isobel stagger over to the window, where she collapsed on a nearby armchair.

"They'll... kill you," Isobel wheezed.

Sarah wiped her hands on her dress. She didn't dare look at them. She knew by the smell and slickness what she'd find, so she focused on the window.

Sarah unlatched it, pushed open both windowpanes, and looked over the ledge. The ground seemed to pull her down-ward—her head grew heavy and the world spun as if calling to her. Just a shift of her weight forward, a loosening of her hands, a push of her legs, and...

She jerked backwards. "I can't," she said, frantic. "We're on the third floor."

"Have to."

"I can't even climb a tree."

Isobel swallowed, seemed to gather strength, then pushed herself up and staggered over to the windowsill. She didn't so much as lean on it as fall. Sarah grabbed her as she slumped, but Isobel caught herself on the sill with one bloody hand planted on the outside of the house.

"You can't climb out!" Sarah said.

"I can fall," she breathed.

Sarah looked at her. "I can't tell if you're joking."

"I'm not."

"Fine! I'll climb down and get help." Sarah started shed-ding her coat, as Isobel's head drooped. Sweat beaded on her bloodless face, and she shuddered with every breath.

Sarah stepped up to the window, but Isobel shook her head. "Rapunzel."

"My hair isn't long enough," Sarah said.

Isobel nodded to the bed. "Sheets."

"Right."

Sarah ran over to the bed and yanked off the sheets to begin tying every piece of bedding, linen, and drape she could find with a good sailor's knot the way Isobel had taught her. Then she tied one end to the four-poster bed and tossed the bundle out of the window. It unfurled, ending just shy of the ground. But it would do. Sarah had fallen out of enough trees to know she could drop at least five feet.

Panic fluttered like a bird in her rib cage. She'd only wanted to go to the park today. Why couldn't she have a normal life? She put one leg over the sill and felt the pull of the earth. She grabbed onto the linen rope and squeezed her eyes shut, trembling from head to toe.

"Sarah," Isobel wheezed.

Sarah cracked open an eye.

"Move?"

Sarah tried to move. But Isobel was right. She wasn't moving. She just sat there on the sill with a death grip on the rope.

Isobel slid back inside, slumping to a stop on the floor. "It's all right," she whispered. "My fault."

"No, it's not!"

"Tell Riot…" Isobel never finished. She just sort of faded.

"*Hell* no," Sarah growled, dropping back onto the bedroom floor.

Working quickly, she ripped apart the buttons on Isobel's dress and stuffed the towel against her bleeding side. Then she tore a strip of cloth from Isobel's chemise and used it to cinch the towel tight and keep steady pressure on the wound.

Keep them warm. Keep them calm. Keep their feet up, her gramma whispered from memory.

Sarah straightened Isobel out on the floor, put pillows under her feet, then snatched a blanket that'd been too heavy to use for the rope. She bundled her mother up, then turned back to the window.

"Shit, shit, *shit*…" Sarah kept up a litany of curses as she slid over the windowsill and down the rope. And damn it. Cursing *did* help.

IAN NOBLE STARED AT THE TELEPHONE WITH RISING ANGER. That fool on the other end had hung up on him. *Him.* Ian Noble. Fury rose in his breast, heating his flesh. He tore the telephone stand from the desk, and threw it across the room.

How to fix this? Who was the woman upstairs? Ian stormed over to his locked desk drawer and knelt to examine the lock. Scratches.

She'd definitely been snooping in his office. What had the girl called her? "Isobel…" Where had he heard that name?

It clicked, and the blood turned cold in his veins. His fingers twitched, even the ones he'd lost to frostbite. The cold had tried to kill him once, but he wasn't one to go down easy. Ian Noble always did what needed doing.

He glanced at the fireplace, then quickly unlocked his desk drawer and gathered up the betting slip, the newspaper, and anything else that might damn him. He dumped it all into the hearth. He struck a match, savoring the warmth of flame, and lit the edges of paper.

The door opened to reveal his wife. Her eyes were red from crying, her cheeks wet, her face drained of blood. She looked like a ghost. And her eyes… her eyes were so vacant.

"Finny, we need to call…" she cut off, focusing on the ruined telephone. "Have you called an ambulance for Freddie? I think that horrid little girl is working with the maid. Freddie must've caught them stealing. I should never have trusted a reference from one of Imogen's friends…"

Yes, that was it. Stealing. Ian hadn't fired a shot. He'd only locked a pair of thieves inside a room. He turned from the hearth and went to his wife, taking her by the arms. "I'll fix this, my darling. I'll take care of it all," he said softly. "Don't I always?"

She rested her head against his chest. "You do. You always

do. But…" she sniffed and craned her neck to look at him. "That horrid girl and her accusations. We can't have those sorts of rumors floating about."

He rubbed a hand along her back. "Yes, I know. They won't leave the house."

"Swear it?"

"I swear it, darling."

She gazed off into the distance. "I warned Dominic. Sin ruins a heart. His gave out, and now this… *thieves* in our own home. Freddie dying. He's such a heroic young man."

Ian looked down at his wife. Somewhere along the way she'd started believing her own lies. It was easier that way. And he knew better than to shatter her illusions—her health was fragile, and he loved her so very much.

"Why don't you go to bed, darling. Rest. I'll take care of everything."

"You're such a good man, Finny."

He bent to kiss her lips, then watched her drift down the hallway like a ghost. Ian Noble would take care of business. His way. For his wife's sanity.

62

DARK PLACES

GRIMM THREW OPEN THE STALL DOORS AND DROVE THE HORSES out with an urgent smack. They were racehorses; it took little urging to get them moving. He opened Gale's door, and as the horse danced out he swung onto his back, urging him towards the open barn doors.

There was a sound like wind. A *whoosh* of it sucking inwards, then bursting outwards. The blast hit Grimm, nearly knocking him off Gale's back. Shards of flaming debris rained down on them and he hunched over the horse's neck, trying to shield him from the worst of it.

Gale took off like a bullet, charging towards men who were running towards the stable. They dived out of the way as Gale thundered past.

Grimm's ears rang. The world moved with frantic silence. He saw alarm in men's eyes; smelled acrid smoke and gunpowder; felt Gale's frantic breathing. The horse was out of control, and Grimm was on top of him.

Gripping the wild horse with his thighs, he held on tight to the mane and hunched down like a jockey, stretching his arm out along Gale's neck. "Whoa there, boy. It's all right. Slow it down," he soothed, patting the horse's neck.

A quick volley of gunfire sounded over the chaos. Gale screamed, and reared. Grimm slipped off his back and rolled out of the way, as the horse stomped back to earth. Then Gale bolted with a spray of dirt.

Grimm staggered to his feet. His back felt like it was on fire. He glanced over his shoulder and saw that he *was* on fire. Cursing, he rolled onto the ground to smother the flames, then scrambled over to a building and put his back to the wall, trying to make sense of what was happening.

Black smoke billowed from the building. Men rushed towards it, shouting as they lugged water buckets. The horses had scattered, screaming in panic, and handlers and jockeys were chasing after them.

Another gunshot. Grimm didn't think. He bolted. Straight towards a volley of gunfire. He rounded a corner, and came skidding to a stop when he saw Carson behind a hay cart with a gun in his hand.

Grimm threw himself back around the corner as a bullet zipped through the air. "Give it up, Carson!" a voice shouted. It was Mr. Tim.

Grimm risked a peek around his corner. He spotted a flash of white beard in a darkened stable doorway.

"Detectives are all over your operation."

"I don't know what you're talking about!" Carson yelled. He popped up and fired. But his gun wasn't aimed at Tim, it was aimed in a different direction. Wood splintered somewhere across the yard.

Keeping low to the ground, Grimm risked another peek to see who Carson was aiming for. It was the stranger he'd seen outside the stable house. The Stranger was hunkered down behind a water trough. He and Tim had Carson pinned in a sort of triangle pattern. With a gun Grimm would have had a clear shot at Carson, but he was no killer.

"Then lay your gun down and we'll have a civil chat," Tim said. He sounded so friendly, so conversational and calm, like he was just sitting down to eat with the family.

Grimm wished he felt so calm. Sweat rolled into his eyes as he quaked with fear. He didn't like violence. There was no time to think. No time to consider. Grimm wanted this nightmare to stop. It was taking him back to dark places.

He squeezed his eyes shut against memory.

"Look here, we know you're not pulling the strings. We could strike a bargain," Tim offered.

Carson tensed, then sprang up and fired off a shot at the Stranger, before bolting towards Grimm's corner.

Carson ran for his life as gunshots barked, and bullets zipped past to splinter wood. A bullet pegged the man, and he staggered but kept running. Grimm thrust out his foot as Carson rounded the corner. The man tripped and fell, his gun tumbling to the ground.

Grimm didn't stop to think. He dove for the gun and reached it first. Carson tackled him, trying to pry it from his hand. Grimm drove his elbow back into Carson's throat, then scrambled away. He cocked the gun and aimed it at Carson's face.

The man froze.

"I don't want to shoot you, mister," Grimm murmured. "But I will."

Surprise flickered across Carson's face, then came the realization that Tim was telling the truth—he *was* surrounded by detectives.

Carson raised his hands, and Grimm slowly scooted back. With the gun still aimed, he climbed onto his knees. His hand wasn't shaking now; the finger he had poised on the trigger felt right.

A gunshot shattered everything.

A hole appeared on Carson's forehead—perfectly round, blood spilled from the wound. Grimm blinked. He'd fired. How?

No.

Carson fell forward. Dead.

Grimm stared in shock at the revolver in his hand. But no… something wasn't right. It was still cocked. He hadn't fired the gun. What the hell?

Mr. Tim's face bobbed around the corner for a peek. When he saw Carson, he stepped out into the open.

"He was gonna kill the boy," a voice said at Grimm's back.

Tim's eyes narrowed to slits of ice. Grimm spun around to find the Stranger standing there, a smoking gun in his hand. He holstered it with a smooth motion.

"You all right, Grimm?" Tim asked.

Grimm hesitated. Carson *hadn't* even flinched. It was on the tip of his tongue to say so, but he caught a dangerous glint in the Stranger's eye.

Tim stepped forward and carefully reached for the gun in Grimm's hand. He uncocked it before prying Grimm's fingers off the grip. Tim held his eyes for a tick, then glanced towards the Stranger.

"That's some fine work, Sam," Tim said.

Grimm didn't have time to worry about the man—this Sam. Maybe Carson *had* been reaching for a hidden weapon. It didn't matter. He cleared confusion from his throat. "I think Isobel and Sarah are in trouble, Mr. Tim. I heard Carson on the telephone. Whoever was on the other end said there was a dying female detective in his house and a girl was accusing his son-in-law of murder. And that he needed them gone."

"Jesus H. Christ," Tim swore. "Pray there's someone at the agency. I'll find a telephone."

As the old man took off with surprising speed, Grimm blew out a breath, a weight of worry leaving his shoulders. He climbed to his feet.

"Thank you, sir," he said with a nod.

Sam touched his hat brim. "No problem, *Josiah*."

Grimm turned ashen. He went cold inside, as the man hooked a thumb over his belt, directly beside his holstered gun. Grimm didn't dare move. There was a dead man at their feet with a hole in his head, blood still seeping into the dirt. This man had just shot him, and the more Grimm thought about it, the more he realized Carson hadn't so much as flinched.

"Who's Josiah?" Grimm croaked.

Sam plucked a cigarette from behind his ear. "I thought I recognized your mother during the police raid," he said, striking a match. Keeping one eye on Grimm, he bent to light the end of his cigarette. "Little Josiah Shaw all grown up, and with an unclaimed bounty on his head."

Grimm's mouth went dry. He felt like he was falling into darkness.

Sam flicked the match on the ground. "Does your friend Mr. Tim know who you are?"

Grimm pressed his lips together, shaking his head.

"'Course not. I'll tell you what, Josiah. You've done me a favor here," Sam said, nodding to Carson's corpse. "So I'll return it and we'll call it even. I'll give you a head start before I tell the authorities where to find a wanted man. Deal?"

Grimm jerked his head.

Sam waited, smoke curling from the end of his cigarette. Then he made a shooing gesture. "I'm not inclined to wait long."

Grimm took a careful step back.

"*Git*, boy! You'd best run quick."

Grimm backed around the corner, nearly tripping over the

dead body. As soon as he was out of the man's sight, he bolted like a racehorse, expecting the bite of a bullet in his back.

Josiah Shaw ran for his life.

63

HOLD ON

IAN NOBLE STEPPED INTO THE GUEST ROOM WHERE HE'D dragged his future son-in-law. Abigail and another maid were attending to him. The Mexican, his wife called her. He hadn't bothered to learn her name. The damn servants never stayed long enough.

"I've tried to make him as comfortable as possible, sir," Abigail said. The women had Freddie on the bed. They were holding bandages to his chin and cheek. "I cleaned it as best I could."

"Let me see."

Abigail peeled back bandages and nodded for the other woman to do the same. A fresh well of blood leaked from the jagged hole. It wasn't a lethal shot. The tiny bullet had passed under his chin, shattered teeth, and punched out a hole in his cheek. Freddie would lose some teeth and have two nasty scars, but he'd live.

"I don't know why he's unconscious."

Ian sniffed at his breath. Sweet and strong, under the scent of blood. He lifted an eyelid. His pupils were pinpoints, and his breathing was shallow. Laudanum. Perfect.

Ian nodded. "Well done, Miss Abigail."

"Is an ambulance on the way, sir?"

"Yes, it is," he said. "Mrs. Noble needs attending to at once. I'll sit with Freddie."

"Of course, sir," Abigail hesitated. "And the new maid?"

"Locked in the room. Freddie caught her stealing along with an accomplice."

Abigail put a hand to her lips. "I'm sorry, sir. I should have spotted it sooner."

"She was a cunning thief."

Abigail shooed the other maid out and closed the door, leaving Ian alone with Freddie Starling.

Was the girl telling the truth? Had Freddie killed Dominic? Ian sighed as he picked up a spare pillow. He couldn't take the chance. There was no way to tell what that female detective was after.

Freddie Starling had powerful connections, ones Ian needed. And Ian had used them. He truly liked Freddie, unlike his spineless layabout of a son who'd thought a little too much of his surname. Freddie had backbone. But he'd become a liability.

Ian Noble pressed the pillow against Freddie's face. Imogen would move on. He was sure of it. When Freddie's chest stopped moving, Ian checked his pulse. One couldn't ask for a more peaceful death.

Ian stood, replaced the pillow, and walked from the room. As much as he disliked the thought, the girl and the detective would have to be silenced. One couldn't have rumors floating about.

———————

ATTICUS RIOT WRENCHED OPEN JACK'S STALL, AND SLIPPED THE bridle over his head. "We need to fly, old friend."

Jack stomped impatiently as Riot flung a blanket and saddle onto his back, and cinched the straps. He took the reins in one hand and swung himself into the saddle.

Riot didn't need to dig in his heels. Jack sensed his urgency and danced out of the stable before tearing off down the street.

————————

SARAH HAD ALWAYS HAD WEAK HANDS. HER GRIP GAVE OUT TEN feet from the ground. She screamed, hit a bush, and fell through its leaves. Branches snapped and tugged, then she hit the ground, pain shooting up her foot.

She rolled free of the bush, a myriad of scratches burning along her face and hands. Her dress was caught on a branch, and she gave it a tug. It tore. Sarah gritted her teeth, clutching at her throbbing ankle. *Isobel.* She had to keep moving. She looked up, following the path of the sheet rope to the window so far above.

Sarah had done it. She'd *climbed* down. But Isobel was still dying. At that panicked thought, she rolled onto her knees and tried to stand, but staggered and would have collapsed except for the arms that caught her.

Sarah yelped in fear and tried to break free, but the hands on her arms tightened.

"*Sarah.*"

Sarah blinked in shock. It was Jin. "How…" It didn't matter. Jin was *here.* Sarah threw her arms around her little sister and squeezed.

"Stop it! What is going on?"

"How did you…"

Jin stepped back with a glare. "Tobias and I have been watching the manor with my spyglass to make sure Isobel is safe."

"She's not safe, Jin."

"Yes, I figured that out when I heard gunshots, then saw you climbing down the side of the house. I sent Tobias to fetch the police."

"Isobel is *dying*."

Jin's eyes blazed. "No."

"We need an ambulance," Sarah whispered frantically. "Freddie shot her. He tried to kill me. Mr. and Mrs. Noble locked us in a room even though Isobel is bleeding all over."

"Go," Jin ordered, pushing her away.

Sarah hopped on one leg, nearly falling with pain.

"Make sure you bring someone back. *Anyone* willing to help."

Sarah didn't have to ask what Jin was going to do. The girl was already climbing a drainpipe, then skirted a bit of decoration. She paused a moment, leapt for the sheet rope and caught it, then scrambled upwards like a monkey.

Sarah didn't linger to see if Jin made it through the window. She already knew the answer. She limped through the gardens, biting her lip and dragging her foot. Then she stumbled and fell through a hedge right into the path of a horse.

It leapt over her without pause, landed, and spun around, dancing impatiently. Sarah gaped. She'd found someone all right.

SAO JIN CLIMBED OVER THE WINDOWSILL AND SLIPPED INTO THE room. She didn't look overly long at Isobel—she didn't let herself. Not yet. But it was difficult to ignore her adoptive mother bundled in a blanket, as still as death and just as pale.

Jin focused on the room. Blood trails, the splatter, broken furniture. Sarah's discarded handbag. And finally, the door.

Jin knew what walked through doors. She'd learned the hard way.

She snatched a chair and jammed it under the handle, so the door wouldn't budge. Her knife was tucked snuggly up her sleeve, but she'd feel better if she had something else to protect her mother with.

Jin's gaze bounced from Sarah's handbag, to the wreckage and blood path, to Sarah's little pearl-handled derringer. Jin snatched it from the floor, pressed on a small latch, swung open the barrel, and pushed on the extractor. One spent casing, the other still live.

Keeping it open, she shook out Sarah's handbag. Pencils, notepads, charcoals, a pocket watch, and all manner of useless things tumbled onto the floor. Along with two spare cartridges. Jin pushed a new round into the empty chamber, half-cocked the derringer, and flipped the barrel closed. Only then did she let herself check on Isobel.

Jin crouched to put her cheek over Isobel's lips. Faint breath stirred against her scarred skin. She shuddered in relief. Then set the derringer down and shifted the blankets. Blood saturated the fabric. So much blood.

Jin wanted to peel back the towel and look at the wound, but she didn't dare. Instead, she leveled a glare at Isobel. "You will not die, *Faan tung*," she said with all the conviction she could muster. "I will never forgive you if you do."

Isobel did not move. But the door handle did, stopped short by the chair.

Sao Jin planted herself in front of Isobel and raised the derringer as the door shuddered. Jin had watched helplessly as men butchered her birth mother. But not this time. She would *never* let that happen again.

RIOT SLID FROM JACK AND GRABBED SARAH'S SHOULDERS. Scratches marred her face, and there was blood on her collar, on her sleeves, and her dress was torn. She looked on the verge of fainting.

"Isobel…" Sarah thrust a shaking finger back at the manor. "She's dying. Freddie shot her."

Riot said nothing. He crashed through the bushes and raced for the front door. Jack bolted after him, tossing his head in triumph when he took the lead. Riot hit the front steps, paused long enough to shoot the lock, then kicked open the door. "Where is my wife!" he demanded.

A butler froze at the end of the entryway. The man's lips trembled as a dusty cowboy marched into the house with a revolver in hand. A horse trotted in after.

Riot pointed his gun at the man. "Isobel. Where is she?"

"I… I…" the butler stuttered. Then raised his hands, dropping the silver tray with a clatter of utensils.

"The new maid," Riot said cooly.

The butler pointed up the stairs.

Riot kept a gun trained on the man as he moved to the steps. "Hitch up a carriage, or I'll shoot you when I come back down."

Riot didn't wait to see if the man obeyed. He left Jack to explore the manor (the horse loved houses), and raced up the stairs, past screaming maids and a well-dressed woman who fainted at his approach. He paused at an intersection of hallways. Then came a crash of splintering wood.

Riot raced towards the sound to find a lordly man throwing his shoulder against a door. He raised his gun. "Step away from the door!"

Ian Noble froze, poised for another blow.

"Hands up. Step away," Riot ordered.

Ian had lived long enough to know that look in a man's eyes. And he knew not to argue with it. Ian took a single, calculated step back. "Who the devil are you?" he demanded.

"Is there a wounded woman in there?"

Ian's cheek twitched—a moment's hesitation—but enough for Riot to spot the man's bluff.

"You mean the *thief*?" Ian rumbled.

"I mean my partner."

"We thought she was a thief."

"Looks bad for you. I'm with the police." It was a bald-faced lie, but Riot was a convincing sort. "Open your coat. Turn out your pockets."

Ian gnawed on the inside of his cheek, but did as ordered. He didn't have a weapon. "We didn't know. I locked her inside to wait for the police. Now the door won't open."

Hope swelled in Riot's heart—a dying woman couldn't jam a door shut.

THE DOOR STOPPED SHUDDERING. VOICES CAME THROUGH THE wood, and Jin stood poised to fire at the first person who came through the door.

"Bel, it's me! Open the door."

Jin's eyes narrowed. Ever suspicious, she called back. "Who are you?"

"*Jin?*"

"Who are you?" she shouted.

"*Bahba.*"

Jin's knees went weak, but she'd never admit it. She kicked aside the chair, and the door flew open, nearly hitting her in the face.

Riot glanced at her as he hurried past. But when a man behind him tried to enter, Jin raised her derringer. "*Get back*," she growled in warning.

"You're the one trespassing. I have every right to go in there."

"Try it," she said.

RIOT'S WORLD NARROWED TO THE WOMAN ON THE FLOOR. HIS hands shook as he pressed fingers against her neck. "Bel," he whispered. "*Hold on*. Stay with me. I'll get you help."

He shifted blankets, dreading what he'd find. The smell of her blood made him sick with terror; the sight of it a nightmare. Riot choked out her name, forcing down the rising bile in his throat.

She was so pale. So lifeless.

His gaze snapped to where Jin was holding Ian Noble at gunpoint.

"I'm a vengeful man, Mr. Noble. You'd best hope there's a carriage or ambulance waiting for us." Moving with extreme care, he lifted her into his arms and hurried out the door. Jin followed on his heels, keeping the derringer trained on anyone who got too close.

64

FRANTIC

THE NEXT HOURS PASSED IN A BLUR. A FRANTIC CARRIAGE RIDE, every bump jerking Isobel's limp body. Riot couldn't think. The receiving hospital. Doctors. White coats. Nurses urging him back. He felt helpless. No amount of shooting would fix this. He could race back to the Noble Manor and put a bullet in Freddie Starling's skull, but it wouldn't help.

Isobel was dying.

Slowly the terror rushing through his veins subsided. His heart slowed to an agonizing rhythm, and the world came back into harsh focus. He noticed a hand in his own.

Riot looked down to find Jin clutching his hand. The little girl was stone-faced and pale. Sarah was at his other side, quietly weeping, each breath a shudder.

Riot took a deep breath, like a man emerging from a frigid river. He tore his gaze from the surgery door and squeezed Jin's hand. Then put an arm around Sarah, steering her towards a nurse.

The nurse got Sarah settled on a cot, and they sat nearby as a doctor saw to her ankle.

Jin's hand snuck back into his. "Isobel will be fine," she said.

Riot didn't reply.

"She is too stubborn to die." This was said with more conviction.

"I think I'm supposed to be comforting you," he murmured.

"Yes," she said, resting her head against his arm. "But I will forgive you. Only this one time." He looked down, and she looked up, giving him a small smile. "We are a very exciting family."

"Maybe a little too exciting," he admitted.

Jin snorted, so like her mother. "You forget where you found us, *bahba*. We were all trouble to begin with."

OUT TO SEA

Isobel drifted in an ocean. She'd lost her boat somewhere along the way. But this ocean was warm and soothing. It was the kind of stillness that came after a storm, with water rippling like silk and sparkling under the sun. So she drifted, relishing the peace. Far, far out to sea.

A HASTY MESSAGE

Tobias White gripped a saddle horn. He wasn't sure what he was supposed to do. The horse underneath him was scary. Grimm had only let him ride Sugar, and that was just around the yard.

When Tobias had run back to Noble Manor from the police call box (he'd finally gotten to use one!), he found Mr. Riot loading a dead-looking Isobel into a carriage, and his mouth had fallen open.

Jin and Sarah had climbed in, and Tobias went to follow, but Riot stopped him. "Get word to Tim and the agency." Then he pointed to Jack, who was eyeing the carriage horses with derision. "Take Tobias home."

The carriage rolled away, leaving Tobias with the pinto horse. It wasn't fair. But he'd been given a job to do, and apparently the horse too.

Jack had snorted at him, but then stepped up and bowed his head to nibble on Tobias's laces. What kind of man talked to a horse like it was a dog?

When Tobias tried to pull on the horse's reins to lead him away, Jack had reared and snapped at him. Then police wagons started to roll up to the manor, so Tobias had scrambled on top of Jack, who took off in a hurry.

Smart horse.

It turned out Jack knew how to get home—in a roundabout way. The horse preferred a more scenic route that passed several grocers with barrels of apples outside. It was all Tobias could do to hold on, so he let the horse do his thing.

Eventually, horse and rider trotted up the lane to Ravenwood Manor. It was dark by that time. Tobias slid off the saddle, dropping to the ground. The horse seemed to be waiting for something, so Tobias gave him a pat. "Thanks."

He tried to walk towards the house, but Jack moved in front of him, and started sidestepping him back towards the stable house.

"I'm going to get Grimm. He'll take care of you." Tobias ducked under the horse and made for the house.

Jack tossed his head, danced in front of Tobias and pushed him back towards the stable.

"Fine." To keep the horse happy, Tobias picked up the reins and marched to the stable. It was dark inside, but Mrs. May was hitched to the hack. That was strange.

A hand grabbed Tobias's shoulder, and he yelped, falling backwards. He scrambled away to hit his head on a post.

"*Toby*," a voice hissed.

Tobias squinted up at his brother. He was crouched over him, with Jack standing over them both, nibbling at Grimm's ear. He should have known it was Grimm when Jack hadn't gotten all riled up.

"Toby, go inside and get your things. Ma and Maddie are waiting for you."

"Why are you whispering?"

Grimm hushed him. "Do it."

"I liked it better when you didn't talk," Tobias said, dusting himself off.

Grimm hung his head. "I got us in trouble again," he whispered. "We got to go."

"But Miss Isobel is dying. We can't just leave."

"We'll all end up dead if we don't."

Tobias curled his fists. "*No*," he said with a stomp of his foot. "I'm sick and tired of moving around. This is our family."

"They're not our family. Ma works for them."

"That's not true, and you know it. Mr. A.J. can help us. Whatever it is…" That was the thing, Tobias didn't know what *it* was. No one told him anything. Something about him not being able to keep secrets.

Grimm made a grab for him, but Tobias ducked under his brother's hand and fled the stable house. He skidded to a stop in the middle of the yard. Was Grimm serious? Someone would kill them if they stayed? They'd moved around for as long as Tobias could remember. He was only now realizing it wasn't because they liked to travel.

Grimm headed straight for him, so he ran to the only place he could think of—his fort. Tobias ducked inside the rickety fort and slammed the door, then curled a little wire he'd fashioned around a hook to lock it.

"Toby!" Grimm hissed.

"Not coming!" Tobias yelled.

"Shh."

Tobias heard a door open, and put his eye to a peephole. He watched his Ma hurry down the steps with a suitcase in hand. Maddie was on her heels, carrying another suitcase.

Tobias's nostrils flared. He didn't want to leave. His telescope wouldn't even fit in a suitcase. Frantically, he snatched a folding knife from his pocket, and began carving a message on the wall.

"Tobias White, if you don't come out of there right this instant, I'll—" His mother cut off. What would she do? Take away his dessert. His telescope? Give him more chores?

Tobias kept carving.

"Toby," she continued in a softer voice. "There'll be men after us soon. After Grimm and me. You can stay here if you like, but we have to leave."

Tobias stared at the door in horror. His ma sounded defeated. Either leave his family or leave Ravenwood Manor? It wasn't right to make him choose.

Footsteps faded, and he cast around for something more. Some hint to leave... But what? He didn't know where they were headed. He never knew.

Tobias clenched his jaw as he carved out one more message. *There*. That would do it. He stabbed his knife into the wall with all the force he could muster, then scrambled out to catch his family.

67

THE TEMPEST

ISOBEL STIRRED IN THE WATER AND LIFTED HER HEAD TO GET her bearings. No land. Where was the land? A seal popped up to stare at her with large dark eyes. It looked afraid. Of her?

The seal disappeared, and she let the current take her. Then she started to sink. And that was pleasant, too. Salt water caressed her lips as the ocean embraced her, its calming scent a drug she ached to inhale.

It was so very peaceful.

She frowned, squinting at the blue skies with their lazy clouds and drifting birds. Where was the howling wind and thunder of waves?

Where was the *tempest*?

This wasn't right.

Soon, the sun beat down on her. Her lips were parched, her tongue swollen. She needed to find her boat. At that thought, Isobel jerked in the water, but her arms didn't obey, and although her legs kicked, she sank.

Something pulled at her from the darkness—a tentacle from the ocean deep, tugging her downwards. Isobel fought, clawing her way to the surface until she broke the water, gasping in air. The sun. So relentless.

She started swimming and kept at it long into the night. The water turned icy, her limbs filled with lead. Then it grew hot until she was dizzy with thirst. And still she swam, through another day and night. A light appeared on the horizon. Wind howled, waves surged, slapping her face, and in the fury of a storm she heard a call.

Bel.

What an odd name. But it gave her strength; it gave her purpose. The waves parted, the wind died for a second, and she glimpsed a snatch of red sails. Her boat.

Isobel swam for her life, only now realizing the danger she was in. How had she let herself drift so far away? She struggled and fought and swam into another long night.

Then her hand slapped wood.

As waves pounded her against the hull, she clawed at the boat, but the wood was slick with algae. She hadn't the strength to climb aboard. There was nothing left. She started to sink, her fingers gouging the hull.

A hand grabbed hers. It was real. She focused on that touch, palm against palm, and used it to pull herself out of the sea.

———

ISOBEL OPENED HER EYES. HER LIPS WERE CRACKED, HER tongue swollen. And the pain... God, the pain. Every breath was agony.

White all around. Murmuring voices. The sting of disinfectant. A hospital.

The hand was real, still clutching her own. She looked down her body—covered by white blankets—and saw a head of black hair with a wing of white at the temple.

Riot had his forehead pressed to their clasped hands.

"*Sarah*?" she tried to ask, but her lips barely moved. Instead she squeezed his hand.

Riot lifted his head, mist shadowing his sunken eyes. "Bel?" he whispered.

She certainly hoped so.

"Sarah?" Her question emerged as a rasp this time.

A light chased the shadows from Riot's eyes. "She's fine, Bel. Sarah is fine. Her ankle is on the mend."

Isobel closed her eyes. It must have been some time later when she opened them again, because the room was dark. A light flickered somewhere in a corner.

Riot looked better too. He sat in a chair, holding her hand, and when she looked at him, he smiled.

"Your beard," she said. She tried to reach for his face, but the pain nearly sent her spiraling into the dark. He bent down to rub a cheek against the back of her hand. It was rough like sandpaper.

"It was gone… wasn't it?"

"It's been a week," he said.

Her mind was sluggish, and it took a worrying amount of time to make sense of his words. She tried to swallow.

Riot used a cloth to drip water onto her lips. She wanted more, but couldn't very well grab the pitcher from him. "I was drifting," she whispered. Riot bent closer to hear. "On a sea with no boat. There was a seal."

"Don't drift away again, my love."

She stared into his eyes. Rich like chocolate, full of warmth, and something more that made her eyes water. "I'm on my boat now."

"Good."

THE NEXT TIME SHE AWOKE, SHE WAS MORE AWARE. OF PAIN.

"God, I should have followed that damn seal," she croaked, trying to find a better position. But when she moved, her rib cage made a grinding noise.

Riot put a hand on her arm. "A moment." He left, then returned with a doctor, who injected her with something that made her float again. Not as far as she wished, but it helped.

"A seal?" Riot asked, settling back in a chair.

"It kept popping up to stare at me."

"Was it dancing with fairy wings?"

Isobel frowned. "I don't remember. Maybe?" She fought past a wave of pain to peek under her blanket. A thick padding of bandages circled her torso. "What happened?"

"What do you remember?"

"That's an unfair question, Riot."

"At least you recall my name."

"Smart ass, wasn't it?"

The edge of his lip twitched upwards. Then he told her everything that happened after she lost consciousness.

"Sarah's shot skewed his aim. His bullet hit at an angle, punched through a steel stay in your corset, and got cozy with your ribs..." He took a steadying breath. "Surgeons had a time digging out the bullet. They removed some sharp bits of bone, too. It was the fever that nearly did you in."

Isobel barely heard the last part. She was busy trying to make sense of his case summary. "Jin was watching the house this entire time?"

"I told you she and Tobias were up to something."

"I thought the seal looked familiar," she murmured.

Riot was looking down at her, one side of his lip raised, as he tucked the hair away from her face.

"You've been here this entire time, haven't you?"

"Much to everyone's dismay," he admitted.

"If you changed my bedpan, I will divorce you."

Despite himself, Riot laughed, then started shaking with it. "I left the bathing and bedpans to the nurses," he assured.

"That's fortunate." Isobel fell quiet as he ran his fingers through her hair, tracing the contours of her scalp. His touch nearly lulled her back to sleep, but she latched onto a sudden thought. "The maid," she whispered.

"Safe."

"You knew?"

"From what Sarah told me, it seems we took two different roads to the same destination."

"How silly of us."

"I agree."

She listened as he filled in the gaps of the investigation. Sakura was recovering, her baby was safe. Freddie was dead. Not by Sarah's bullet, thank God, but from an overdose of laudanum, according to the coroner's report.

"How's Sarah?" She wasn't asking after her physical health.

"She's far too practical to worry over shooting a man, but she's sick with guilt that you got shot."

"She saved my life. He would've killed me and taken—" Isobel couldn't finish the thought.

"I know."

But guilt rarely gave way to logic.

"Mr. and Mrs. Noble stuck to their story that they thought you were a thief, with Sarah being your accomplice. They said they would have called the police but discovered the telephone had been destroyed, which they also blamed on you."

Isobel snorted, then regretted it when her ribs shifted.

"I aimed Father Caraher and your mother at the so-called house of charity that the Knights of Chastity fund. Dollie is now the caretaker, and... I think the Nymphia will finally be closed for good."

"You sound like that's a bad thing," she noted.

He sighed. "The women there still have to make a living. If

a brothel won't take them in, they'll be picked up by a pimp on the street or find themselves in a mining camp."

"You can't save them all, Riot."

"I can't seem to stop trying."

"That's what I love about you."

68

A TIDY BOW

IT WAS A RARE DAY THAT RIOT SLIPPED AWAY TO REST; IT had taken her mother to convince him to leave her bedside. Isobel worried about him. He was looking gaunt of late.

Time had lost meaning under the electric lights. She didn't much care about day or night, or the date in general. She supposed it was a new year. And her time in the hospital was becoming tedious.

Riot had brought in a chess set, and she stared at the little figurines without seeing them. Instead, the frantic minutes of her standoff with Freddie kept spinning in her mind. Of Sarah. And the gun held to her head.

So it was a welcome interruption when Lotario poked his head into the room. He arched a brow. "Aren't *you* the picture of feminine fragility."

"I'll kill you."

He grinned. "I've brought a visitor. I thought you'd like to tie up loose ends."

Isobel frowned in puzzlement. Then Lotario stepped aside, and Katherine Hayes glided into the room with her 'butler' who was dressed in immaculate silk robes. He had his hands tucked into wide sleeves.

Katherine lifted a black veil, revealing her face. She was quite beautiful, and made Isobel feel like an unwashed heathen. Maybe Riot had left because he couldn't stand to look at her sickly self anymore.

"I'd get up, Miss Hayes, but…"

"Please don't, Mrs. Riot," the woman said, taking a seat. Lotario moved to the other side of the bed, and Mr. Chang stepped behind Katherine.

"When I asked you to investigate, I had no way of knowing how dangerous it would prove."

"It's part of the business," Isobel said.

Katherine leaned forward. "Tell me… did Freddie really murder Dominic?"

"Yes."

"But *why*?"

"Because Dominic Noble lived up to his name. Your fiancé died trying to protect his sister, his family, and a maid of no consequence."

Katherine sat back. "I knew he'd never——" She cut off. It never had to be spoken of again.

"Everything you said about Dominic is true, Miss Hayes. Your faith in him. Your… love. He was the best of men. I'm sorry I wasn't able to know him before his death."

Lotario sat down on the edge of her bed. She didn't look at her twin, but she could *feel* his emotion. He was struggling. She knew if she touched him, he'd crack. So she gave Katherine a succinct report of everything that happened.

"Oh, Dominic…" Katherine whispered when Isobel finished. Mr. Chang placed a hand on Katherine's shoulder. "The woman. Sakura. Where is she?"

"Under the care of a Dr. Wise, on the edge of Chinatown."

Katherine looked up at the man behind her. They shared a

silent conversation that Isobel knew well. She and Lotario communicated in such a way. Her own parents did it. She and Riot did as well.

Mr. Chang inclined his head, ever so slightly.

Katherine turned back. "I should like to meet this woman. There will be a place for her in my household, if she wishes."

"That is generous of you," Lotario said. "I'll arrange it."

Katherine removed an envelope from her handbag, and stood. "Your payment."

Isobel accepted it. With tears brimming in her eyes, Katherine lowered her veil and left, and Mr. Chang paused to offer a deep bow before following.

Isobel heard a sniff at her side and found her twin dabbing at his eyes. "I'm sorry, Ari."

"And here I asked you not to investigate at all."

"It was fortunate I did."

He cocked his head.

"Is my bodice still here?"

"Yes, what's left of it…" He rummaged through a trunk. "Atticus had them bag everything for evidence in case Mr. Noble pressed charges."

"Good. Look in the lining of my bodice."

He searched through her bloody clothing while she tore open the envelope. They gasped as one. Isobel at the check and Lotario at the postcard of himself.

"Where did you find this?" he asked.

"Dominic's room. It was tucked behind a photograph."

He was staring at the message on the back, and she motioned him closer lest their voices traveled. "It's from Katherine."

He blinked. "Are you sure?"

Isobel showed him the check so he could compare the handwriting. Lotario was too stricken to bat a lash over the sum she'd paid them. "She knew about Dominic..." he trailed off, sitting back on the bed.

Isobel placed a hand over his.

"I don't understand," Lotario murmured. "Katherine knew he preferred men, but still agreed to marry him—even encouraged him to see me."

"Yes," Isobel said, waiting for her twin to make the connection.

"Do you suppose Katherine is sapphic?"

"Good God, Ari, have you gone daft?"

"It appears so."

"She's in love with Mr. Chang."

"Are you sure?"

"Yes. I took the girls along when I interviewed her. While I was speaking with Katherine, Jin sneaked into the study and saw that the desk was being used. There was tea there. Mr. Hayes, her father, was away on business. Jin noted that Mr. Chang acted as an equal, not a servant. I thought little of it at the time, but when I found that postcard... by the way you look extraordinary."

"I know," he said, fanning himself with the naked postcard of himself.

"Any road, I put two and two together. Dominic needed to marry, or he'd lose his inheritance. And I suspect Katherine wanted to avoid society gossip about her and Mr. Chang. A union in this state, between Chinese and whites, is illegal. Dr. Wise and his own wife were married in New York where it's legal, but here they're living in sin and could be charged on a whim."

"A marriage of convenience," Lotario mused. "The amount of trust that takes... Well, it's frightening."

"Dominic and Katherine must have loved each other a great deal, as friends." Sadness crept into her words, and she felt suddenly crushed by it all. "It's tragic for anyone needing to hide their feelings."

"Well," Lotario mused, tapping his lips. "I knew a man who was enamored with his sheep…"

"Ari. Don't. I don't want to know."

"Yes, we must draw the line somewhere."

"*Somewhere*," she muttered in agreement.

Lotario plucked the check out of her hand. "I believe this is mine."

"What?"

"Don't worry," he said, giving it a straightening tug. "You'll be paid hourly wages, and I'll toss in a hazard bonus."

"I hate you."

Lotario smiled. "This nearly makes up for you almost dying."

She leaned over to look at the figure again. "It does, doesn't it?"

"*Never* do that again!" he snapped.

"Rescue Sarah?"

"No." He gestured sharply. "I mean, yes. But don't get shot. God, you didn't even get shot *properly*."

"What on earth, Ari?" She gestured at her wounded side. "I'll be lucky if I can ever raise a mainsail again."

"You're lucky to be alive, Bel." Then he pulled her into a hug that hurt, but she savored the pain. It was easier than feeling his.

He pulled away to blow his nose, which she was thankful for, because it was that or her hospital gown.

"You got shot in the *wrong* place. We have mismatched scars now."

Isobel stared at him. "Really?"

"Do you know the trouble I'll have replicating the horrid amount of scarring on your side? Do you realize how much longer it will take us to swap places?"

"The scarring is under my breast, Ari. You can't show off *my* breasts when you impersonate me."

"Yes, but *I'll* know."

———

LOTARIO SPOTTED A FAMILIAR FIGURE AT THE NURSE'S DESK ON his way out.

"Mr. Taft."

"Mr. Amsel." The old cowboy looked embarrassed without his hat. His gray hair was plastered to his head.

"I hope this lawman is treating you well, Miss Dawson." Lotario favored the nurse with a smile, her pale cheeks blossoming with color.

"He was just asking after your sister."

"Oh?"

"I came to pay my respects," Liam said. "How is Mrs. Riot?"

"Sleeping," Lotario said, turning to Miss Dawson. "I don't think she should be disturbed anymore today." He gave the nurse a pointed look.

"Of course not."

"Hard to find rest after a gunshot like that," Liam noted.

Miss Dawson pretended to check her logbook.

"Ah, the power of a badge." Lotario gestured at the one pinned to Liam's vest. "I imagine they loosen tongues."

Liam grunted.

"Walk with me, Mr. Taft?"

Liam's eyes crinkled to slits. He was a man of few words. But he followed when Lotario headed for an exit.

Isobel wasn't really sleeping, only resting in a fitful daze. Pain made sure of that. But Lotario was uneasy with the idea of a Pinkerton visiting her. Especially after Tim described what had happened at the racetrack.

"Perhaps I should design an official Ravenwood Agency badge."

"Are you planning on expanding the agency?" Liam asked.

"Time will tell."

Lotario stepped outside and took a deep breath of fresh air. The fog washed away the smell of disinfectant and blood, and the feel of sheets that were too crisp. Hospitals brought back too many memories of his own recent shooting and tiresome rehabilitation. Pain. So much of it. But that pain was nothing compared to watching his twin suffer.

Lotario slipped on his fedora, then straightened his cuffs without looking at the Pinkerton. "Why did you want to speak with Bel?" he asked.

"Just came to pay my respects."

Lotario smiled. "That's kind of you."

The Pinkerton had his hat back on, the brim pulled low over his already hooded eyes.

"I've been there."

"Shot?"

"Several times."

"I always find it curious—who lives and who dies. A slip off a stepladder and one fellow's dead. Another is gut shot, and lives to get shot again."

Liam took out his tobacco pouch to roll a cigarette. "It's not their time yet."

"Fate?"

"Whatever you want to call it," Liam said, his voice like gravel. "We each have an appointment with our Maker. Some sooner than others."

Lotario watched the man's calloused hands move through the delicate process of rolling the paper. When he was finished, Liam stuck the cigarette between his lips and struck a match on his Levi's. Fire flared, smoke joined fog, and Liam looked down at Lotario. He was a good foot taller, but Lotario was comfortable with his height.

"Was there anything left of the stable house?" Lotario asked.

Liam shook his head.

"It's a shame your partner shot Carson. We might have caught his clients."

Liam grunted. "Sam said the fellow reached for a weapon. You should have told me you had another agent at the track."

"Hmm, it slipped my mind."

"That boy has a bounty on his head."

"Does he?" Lotario asked in surprise. "How much?"

Liam didn't answer. Instead he said, "I read your police report. Not sure I could have cracked those ciphers."

"I do love puzzles."

The edges of Liam's mustache twitched. "My wife does, too."

"I imagine Mrs. Taft is looking forward to returning home to Oregon?"

Liam dipped his head. "My investigation seems to be wrapped up."

"In a neat little bow."

"Did Mrs. Riot learn anything from the Nobles?"

"Only how to clean a bathtub. Why do you ask?"

"Sam said he saw Mr. Noble in the private box at the race-track you mentioned in your report."

"She was working an entirely different case. Coincidence, I suppose."

Liam squinted down at him. He looked long and hard at Lotario, then extended a hand. Lotario shook it. The man's skin felt like leather, with a grip like a vice. "Been a pleasure, Mr. Amsel. I wish your sister the best."

69

THE PLEA

GETTING SHOT WAS TEDIOUS. SO WHEN ISOBEL WAS FINALLY cleared to go home (she suspected her mother's daily visits and her little talks with the staff may have expedited her release), she jumped on the chance even though she wasn't fully recovered.

Well, not so much jumped as shuffled.

"I could carry you," Riot offered, as they stood at the base of a long stairway. It felt good to be home, but as she gazed up at the daunting number of steps, she wished her room were on the first floor.

"Don't you dare." She'd just take one step at a time.

Riot was close beside her, an arm wrapped around her waist in case she buckled. Sarah was on her other side, and Jin was standing on top of the first landing with arms crossed, looking displeased.

Isobel climbed one step, then another. Her legs shook, sweat beading on her brow.

"Oh, this is ridiculous, Isobel," her mother snapped. "Let your husband carry you."

"I'm not a child, mother," she shot back.

Catarina threw up her arms. "Then why are you still so stubborn?"

Anger flashed through her veins, and she used it to conquer a few more steps. Then stopped to catch her breath. "Because I take after you. Why the hell do I have an audience?"

"Because you are slow," Jin said from above.

"That's my *neta*," Catarina said with pride. "Atticus, just pick her up."

"I would not dare pick you up without permission," Marcus Amsel said.

"You would," Catarina accused.

"The last time I—"

Catarina shushed him with a sharp gesture. "I'll have Mr. Hop do it then."

That comment nudged Isobel up another step.

"You could not pay me enough, Mrs. Amsel," Hop said. "I think this is an excellent lesson for Wu Lei Ching."

"My daughter being shot and nearly dying is not to become one of your proverbial stories..." As Catarina and Mr. Hop continued their bickering, Isobel stood panting one step away from the first landing.

"Would you like to get away from your parents?" Riot whispered in her ear.

"*Please* rescue me."

Riot shifted his hold, and she sank against his chest with relief as he lifted her easily in his arms. She'd been on the verge of collapse. He carried her up to their room, and set her down by the bed, where she fell, more than sat.

There'd been an attempt to restore order to their room after the police trashed it. The books were stuffed haphazardly onto shelves; the mattress had been repaired (and was now lumpy); and their clothes had been picked up off the floor and draped over various pieces of furniture.

Before she could protest, Jin knelt to tug off her shoes, and Sarah opened the curtains to let in light.

Isobel felt like a doll, too weak to remove her own shoes, and decided fighting over letting others unbutton her clothing was too much effort just now.

"We'll bring up a tray," Sarah said, when they'd settled her under the covers. Jin followed, but not before tucking a blanket under Isobel's chin.

"Good Lord, getting shot is humiliating," she said.

"Or humbling," Riot offered, tugging off his collar.

"Aren't they the same thing?" Morphine tended to muddle her mind. She thought she could hear a baby crying in the house.

"Probably," he admitted. "though I've always thought humiliating was from something done to me, while humbling was more a self-realization."

"That is far too complicated right now."

An hour later Sarah carried in a tray. "Jin is cooking some sort of noodle soup," she whispered, handing the tray over to Riot. "It will be awhile yet."

"Why is Jin cooking?" Isobel asked from the bed.

"It's a new hobby of hers," he said, settling the tray over her lap.

Their room was quiet save for a crackling fire. It was warm and familiar. It was home. After weeks of hospital food, Isobel was looking forward to Miss Lily's culinary talents. She took a sip of broth, then coughed, spitting it back into the bowl.

"This tastes horrid."

"About that…" Riot began.

Isobel gaped. "Does morphine affect the sense of taste?"

"No."

Isobel grappled with the idea that anything in this house could taste so bad. "Is Miss Lily angry with us for hiring Grimm? I told Lotario—"

"She's gone."

"On holiday?"

"I'm afraid not, Bel."

The world swayed. Everything felt surreal. She'd been in the hospital close to a month; why hadn't Riot told her?

"What happened?" she asked.

"The White family is gone. They left the night you were shot, only taking what they could carry. A stable contacted Tim to let him know Mrs. May and our hack were in a carriage house. They'd paid for the boarding."

The bowl in her lap blurred. "Why?"

"I don't know," he admitted. "I've asked before. I've offered my help, but Miss Lily wouldn't take it. She warned me they might be gone one day. All she would say was the less I knew, the better. And if I didn't let it rest, I might not like what I stirred up."

Isobel stared numbly at her soup, trying to imagine life without the White family—their wit and banter, their warmth and friendship. And Tobias's boundless curiosity and courage.

Her heart lurched.

"I hired a cook, in exchange for room and board. A Miss Shannon. She has a baby named Fiona."

Isobel looked up at him. "The woman who saved your life?"

He nodded. "She's not much of a cook, though. And I'm afraid the new Mrs. Löfgren has taken it upon herself to mentor Shannon in the culinary arts."

Isobel poked at the soup with her spoon. "Is the, uhm… salty fish taste Shannon's fault or her mentor's?"

"Mrs. Löfgren *is* Swedish."

Isobel laid down her spoon. "That is no excuse for *this*."

"Don't tell her it tastes bad. Mr. Hop made that mistake, and she burst into tears. Mr. Löfgren said his wife was so mortified she wanted to leave."

"And we can't afford to lose a lodger." But the look in Riot's eyes told her that had already happened. "How many left after the police raid?"

Riot sat on the bed beside her. "Bel, I'll handle things. Focus on getting your strength back. *Heal.* That's all. I'll deal with the rest of it until you're better."

"You've been dealing with all of this for weeks. Along with my injury, it must've been… tiresome."

"*Tiresome?*"

"I'm trying to not be overly dramatic."

Words couldn't express what he felt, so he took her hand and held on tight. "You're alive." His voice was raw.

"You can't get rid of me that easily," she said lightly. But the look in her eyes said something entirely different.

Isobel untangled her hand from his to run fingers through the wing of white at his temple. He closed his eyes, savoring her touch. She could feel him trembling. Tiresome was definitely not the right word.

Riot cleared his throat. "On a positive note, the lodgers are eating less food, so our grocery bills have dramatically reduced."

She smiled. "Are you handling the finances, too?"

"Sarah wouldn't let me near the account books—on strict orders left by Miss Lily. It seems Miss Lily was mentoring her on managing a household."

Isobel sighed. "Why is our life such a mess?"

"According to Mr. Hop, it's karma for what you put him through as a child."

"Yes, but you shouldn't be involved."

"I may have cleaned Hop and your father out during an impromptu poker game at the hospital."

Isobel arched a brow.

"Your father gathered a group of players. He insisted I play."

"Did you cheat?"

"I never cheat, Bel."

Isobel wasn't so sure about that, but she was too tired to argue.

Riot squeezed her hand. "One thing is certain, whenever we split forces things go badly."

"Agreed."

"And I've been thinking it over…"

"Good God," she muttered.

"I don't think this is any kind of life for our family."

Isobel ignored that comment. "Do you know, I had no idea maids lived such a dangerous life. I freely admit I'm not cut out for that type of work."

He gave her a look. "I was referring to detective work."

"Oh Lord, Riot. I could slip in the bathtub tomorrow. Your creaky old middle-aged knees could give out on the stairs and you could break your neck. We saved a woman and her child's *life*. It wouldn't matter if you were a plumber. It goes against every bone in your body to turn your back on someone in distress. Besides, I would get bored."

"A plumber? Really, Bel?"

"It's the morphine talking. It makes me delusional."

"And apparently overly dramatic, too."

"*You* cornered me into that," she accused. "Just remember I got shot working as a maid, not a detective."

"And you developed a hump."

She glared.

A knock on the door rescued Riot. He hopped up to open it and found Jin standing outside with a new tray. With a furtive glance out the door, he ushered her inside.

"I told the salty fish lady I had to cook this soup for a sacred Chinese tradition. I do not know if she will believe me the next time."

"Good thinking."

Jin's soup was far, far better. While Isobel was noisily slurping noodles, Jin pulled Riot to the side. "I need to show you something, bahba."

"Now?"

"Yes."

They left Isobel to her slurping, and Riot followed Jin downstairs, noting that she used the front door to walk around back so they wouldn't have to risk the kitchen.

Riot had assumed Jin was leading him to the stable house. Instead, she led him to Tobias's fort.

"There is a message on the wall. It was not there before Tobias left."

Jin kept her emotions buried deep. It'd been vital for her survival. And she'd been doing it for so long that emotion rarely crept out. But it did now. Her voice had cracked when she said her friend's name.

Riot crawled into the fort, then sat back against a wall to study the carvings. The words tugged at his heart as he reached out to trace the letters. The message was hasty. Frantic. His eyes fell on Tobias's knife stuck deep into the wood. The handle practically quivered with anger and frustration.

Jin poked her head into the door. "What will we do?"

"I don't know, Jin. Miss Lily didn't want my help."

"Do you know what happened?"

"I do not."

Sitting on her haunches, she considered this, while Riot considered the message Tobias had left: *Help us. Please. Men after Ma.*

How could he ignore that plea?

AN ENDING
To be continued…

CONNECT WITH AUTHOR

If you enjoyed *Beyond the Pale*, and would like to see more of Bel and Riot, please consider leaving a review. Reviews help authors keep writing.

Keep up to date with the latest news, releases, and giveaways. It's quick and easy and spam free.
Sign up at www.sabrinaflynn.com/news

AFTERWORD

I wish I could tell you the Hotel Nymphia is a horrible figment of my imagination. It is not.

The *Twinkling Star Improvement Company* opened it in 1899. They intended to call it the *Nymphomania*, claiming it was a hotel for women suffering from that affliction, but city officials refused to issue them permits, so they changed the name to the more acceptable Nymphia.

There's little detail about life inside, though one can fill in the gaps with known facts: the female 'residents' had to be naked at all times. Women were not allowed to turn away a man who called. The dime peepholes were really a thing and the women were subjected to constant voyeurism. The peepholes were later done away with when the men started using slugs in place of dimes.

The San Francisco Call wrote this about the Nymphia in 1909:

"One of the most notorious of the unspeakable dens of vice on the Barbary coast was known as the "Nymphia." It was the worst of almost inconceivably low kennels of infamy, and it aspired to become the worst in the world. The plan was to enlarge the brothel until it should house 1,000

fallen women. This place was run by one Emil Kerlein and a partner named Valentine.

They were tried before Judge Graham and sentenced to six months' imprisonment each. On a technicality they appealed, and their appeal was tried by three superior judges sitting en banc. One of these was Carroll Cook, who was later to became Father Caraher's arch enemy. Through a flaw in the law found by Cook the men were permitted to go free on payment of $250 fine each."

The brothers would later be involved with a political crime boss, who managed to get a puppet mayor elected in San Francisco.

One visiting 'Chief of the Detective Department of a certain Eastern city' commented on the Nymphia: "*Is it possible that San Francisco can tolerate and stand for such a place?"*

From the small number of details I've gleaned about the lowest dives of the Barbary Coast, I tried to paint a picture of life inside the hotel for the residents, or inmates as they were often called. But out of concern for my readers' sensibilities, I've kept some truly horrible details out of my narrative. Life for the lowest Barbary Coast prostitute was horrendous, and it paints a rather vivid picture of the type of men who frequented the brothels.

In 1917 a newspaper editor by the name of Fremont Older (an early defender of prostitutes), published a story in the San Francisco Bulletin: A Voice from the Underworld by Alice Smith, a Barbary Coast prostitute. In it she writes: "*We were the men's big show; put there by men; kept there for the use of men, to be used as they chose and talked to as they chose, meant forever to be the satisfaction and the victims of their worst hours. Our trade was not our own; it wasn't even invented by us; it was created by the men when they had a mind to be lower than animals. And they were animals. I don't know whether animals have speech; but if they have, they don't use it as men do. And animals don't have prostitution. It took men to achieve that."*

I also wish this were a thing of the past. It is not.

But where there is darkness, there is often light, no matter how small. Father Terence Caraher was known by San Francisco as the 'militant priest.' He served at St. Francis from 1896 to his death in 1914, where he waged unrelenting war on organized vice in San Francisco. His life was threatened numerous times, but he never backed down from his fight.

As one Call article put it: *He has met and conquered municipal bossism and graft, corrupt men on the bench and of the bar, all welded by the common cause of greed.*

After being mired in legal battles, shut down and reopened numerous times, the Nymphia was eventually closed for good in 1903. It was sold, and the massive U-shaped building on Pacific Street still appears to be standing today, as a block of apartments.

Father Caraher was also instrumental in halting the blasting and quarrying that threatened the destruction of Telegraph Hill in the early 1900s. So we have him to thank for the half-quarried iconic landmark of San Francisco.

For anyone wondering if I came up with the method of murder using a handkerchief and a carpenter's pencil all on my own... I didn't. I found two such incidences in newspaper archives. The victims were women, and the man was eventually caught.

During my research into the Pinkerton's Detective Agency and the famous detective James McPharlan along with the Molly Maguires, I came across a number of interesting facts. The entire infiltration of the Molly Maguires by the Pinkerton's came about as a result of a wealthy mining magnate, Franklin Gowen, who wasn't satisfied with what he had. He wanted it all. So he skillfully maneuvered and manipulated the railroads, mines, and workers to dominate the anthracite (also known as hard coal) market, in what was one of the first recorded cases of industry-wide price fixing in the U.S.

Gowen squeezed every last penny out of already over-worked and starving miners so he could grab more wealth to add to his already significant holdings. But it eventually back-fired on him when J.P. Morgan ousted him as president of the Reading Railroad. He later died by a gunshot wound to the head. There is some controversy on whether it was self-inflicted or payback by the Molly Maguires.

I also came across numerous references to "various people impersonating Pinkerton's agents" in my research. I found an image of an old six-pointed bronze star on an antique site with the label "fake Pinkerton badge." The site claimed there was an agency, circa 1900, that used the Pinkerton's famous name to drum up business, and that the fake agency was eventually sued by the real Pinkerton Agency.

Further digging turned up a burglary gang who were in possession of a fake badge. The Call article said that "Superin-tendent W.H. Fields of the Pinkerton agency saw the badge and said it was issued by a man named Pinkerton in Chicago and Milwaukee, who advertises for detectives and gives appli-cants a fake Pinkerton badge for a small sum."

Although I don't know if these two references are related, they do provide plenty of fodder for a mystery writer's overac-tive imagination. What with all the subterfuge and manipula-tion of America's wealthy elite, the Anti-Pinkerton Act, and the Pinkertons laying the foundation for the CIA—it certainly makes one wonder.

ACKNOWLEDGMENTS

A huge thanks to you, dear reader. I definitely wouldn't still be writing without your support. And I'm continually awed that people want to read what I write.

And to the usual suspects…

To Merrily Taylor for taking out the time to read a messy first draft in the middle of a move. She's been along for every word of the journey, and hasn't kicked me to the side of the road yet.

To Alice Wright for her eagle eyes and prodigious memory. I can always count on her to find a forgotten detail about a character that's hidden somewhere in eight books. For this book she found me Bill Cody. How could I forget that dirty little kid's name?

To Lyn Brinkley-Adams for her kindness and support. (I don't think you realize how much it means to me!)

Thanks to Erin Bright and Rich Lovin, who keep reading the rough drafts I write. And finally to my line editor Tom Welch, who is a joy to work with and polishes every manuscript to a shiny gleam.

ABOUT THE AUTHOR

Sabrina Flynn is the author of the ***Ravenwood Mysteries*** set in Victorian San Francisco. When she's not exploring the seedy alleyways of the Barbary Coast, she dabbles in fantasy and steampunk, and has a habit of throwing herself into wild oceans and gator-infested lakes.

Although she's currently lost in South Carolina, she's lived most of her life in perpetual fog and sunshine with a rock troll and two crazy imps. She spent her youth trailing after insanity, jumping off bridges, climbing towers, and riding down waterfalls in barrels. After spending fifteen years wrestling giant hounds and battling pint-sized tigers, she now travels everywhere via watery portals leading to anywhere.

You can connect with her at any of the social media platforms below or at www.sabrinaflynn.com

GLOSSARY

A man for breakfast - a murdered body found in the streets at dawn.

Avó - grandma in Portuguese

Bai! - a Cantonese expression for when something bad happens (close to the English expression, 'shit')

Bahba - Dad

Banker - a horse racing bet where the bettor believes their selection is certain to win

Between Hay and Grass - teenager

Blind Pig - an illegal drinking establishment

Bong 幫 - help

Boo how doy - Hatchet Man - a hired tong soldier or assassin

Bull - an officer of the law

Capper - a person who is on the lookout for possible clients for attorneys

Chi Gum Shing 紫禁城 - Forbidden Palace

Chinese Six Companies - benevolent organizations formed to help the Chinese travel to and from China, to take care of the sick and the starving, and to return corpses to China for burial.

Chun Hung - a poster that puts a price on someone's head

Dang dang - Wait!

Digging into your Levis - searching for cash

Din Gau 癲狗 - Rabid Dog

Dressed for death - dressed in one's best

Faan tung 飯桶 - rice bucket or worthless

Fahn Quai - White Devil

Kwei - Foreign Devil

Fence - a person who knowingly buys stolen goods to sell at profit.

Graft - practices, especially bribery, used to secure illicit gains in politics or business; corruption.

Hei Lok Lau - House of Joy - traditional name for brothels at that time

Hei san la nei, chap chung! 起身呀你個雜種！- Wake up, you bastard!

Highbinders - general term for criminals

Kedging - to warp or pull (a ship) along by hauling on the cable of an anchor that has been carried out a ways from the ship and dropped.

King chak - the police

Lardon - a thief

Lo Mo - foster mother

Mien tzu - a severe loss of face

Mui Tsai - little Chinese girls who were sold into domestic households. They were often burdened with heavy labor and endured severe physical punishments.

Nei tai - you, look

Neta - Portuguese for granddaughter

Ngor bon nei - I help you

No sabe - Spanish for 'doesn't know' or 'I don't understand'. I came across a historical reference to a Chinese man using this phrase in a newspaper article. I don't know if it was common, but it is a simple, easy to say phrase that English speakers understood.

Pak Siu Lui - White Little Bud

Sau pan po - 'Long-life Boards' - coffin Shop

Si Fu - the Master

Siu wai daan 小壞蛋 - Little Rotten Eggs - an insult that implies one was hatched rather than born, and therefore has no mother. The inclusion of 'little' in the insult softens it slightly.

Speeler - a gambler

Slungshot - a maritime tool consisting of a weight or "shot" affixed to the end of a long cord, often by being wound into the center of a knot called a "monkey's fist." It is used to cast a line from one location to another, often a mooring line. This was also a popular makeshift (and deadly) weapon in the Barbary Coast.

Sock Nika Tow - Chop Your Head Off - a very bad insult

Wai Daan 壞蛋 - Rotten Egg

Wai Yan 壞男人 - Bad Men

Wattles - ears

Wu Lei Ching 狐狸精 - Fox Spirit

Wun Dan - Cracked Egg

Wun... ah Mei - Find Mei

Yiu! 妖! - a *slightly* less offensive version of the English 'F-word'.

CPSIA information can be obtained
at www.ICGtesting.com
Printed in the USA
LVHW041925230421
685383LV00007B/1270